CHARLOTTE AND EMILY

ALSO BY JUDE MORGAN

Passion
Indiscretion
Symphony
An Accomplished Woman

JUDE MORGAN

CHARLOTTE AND EMILY

A Novel of the Brontës

St. Martin's Press New York

Printed in the United States of America. For information, address St. Martin's Press, 175 Fifth Avenue, New York, N.Y. 10010.

www.stmartins.com

Library of Congress Cataloging-in-Publication Data

Morgan, Jude, 1962–
Charlotte and Emily : a novel of the Brontës / Jude Morgan.—1st U. S. ed.
p. cm.
"First published as The Taste of Sorrow in Great Britain by Headline Review, an imprint of Headline Publishing Group."
ISBN 978-0-312-64273-0
1. Brontë, Charlotte, 1816–1855—Fiction. 2. Brontë, Emily, 1818–1848—Fiction. 3. Brontë family—Fiction. 4. Women authors—Fiction. 5. England—Social life and customs—19th century—Fiction. I. Title.
PR6113.O743C47 2010
823'.92—dc22

2010003586

First published as *The Taste of Sorrow* in Great Britain by Headline Review, an imprint of Headline Publishing Group
First U.S. Edition: May 2010

10 9 8 7 6 5 4 3 2 1

For Ann, with thanks

PART ONE

1

Salvage

'Oh, my children. Oh, God, my poor children.'

The woman in the upstairs room cries out often in the madness of pain and extremity. Broken words, regrets, even – and her kneeling, praying husband shudders to hear them – violent curses. But this is the recurring cry that rises to a scream, just as the dry, loutish wind idles and grumbles about the house and then will assault it suddenly with a gust and a shriek.

'Oh, my children. What will become of *my children . . .*?'

And this is his fight, his greatest fight – this austerely handsome man, lean and spare in clerical black, who has become who he is by a long exercise in will and conquest. Now he must fight the devil. Because nothing else, not even the delirium of mortal sickness, could make his gentle forbearing wife say the things she is saying. The devil is seizing his moment, when the fate of the soul is in the balance, and entering her.

(Entering her . . . He must put aside the dark surge that is like jealousy at that thought. The possession of her soul, that is what is at stake.)

Sometimes the pain is such that it thrusts her into terrible acrobatics, her chin digging between her breasts, her clawing feet scaling the wall behind her bed. Then he grips and holds her, speaking soothingly, entreating her to be calm, to offer the pain to the Lord. But tonight – the last night, it must surely be – as he holds her down on the pillow and inhales her so-familiar breath, her rolling eyes meet his and lock. And she begins to laugh. Madly, devilishly.

'Oh, Patrick, do you seek the freedom of my bed *now* – even *now*?'

He jolts away from her, his fingers loosening their grasp on her wasted shoulders. But he remembers the devil, and grips her again; and tries to ignore what the candlelight is doing with their shadows on the wall, making that familiar humped union.

'Oh, my dear, you must pray. Pray with me now,' he urges. 'Oh, great God in heaven, the old adversary is with us, here in this room. I know his voice – I hear him speak through your poor suffering lips . . .'

'But what if—' She stops, and he sees that she is hoisted on a great spike of pain; but she rides the obscene impalement, gasps and gags, speaks on. 'What if it is *me* speaking? What then?'

'Dearest, hush. Fight it, fight it. I fear for your soul—'

'I don't care about my soul!'

She spits it at him in her croaking voice, a blasphemy of consonants. And he is so baffled – no, tired, it must be tiredness, these endless sickbed nights – that he can only stagger back to the chair and bury his head in his hands.

At last he says: 'Remember, my dear. Remember how you were. You always walked with God.'

She turns from him, grinding her head against her pillow. 'You know nothing of the matter.'

He tries to leap across the terrible distances opening up. 'My dear, I understand – you are thinking of the things of this world. But the time has come to let go of them. You cannot go to your Maker still clinging to the things of this world, you must—'

'*They* are not *things*.'

Oh, she is fighting him hard: or, rather, the devil is. But he has his answer, even though he doubts she is equal to it: yes, they are. Certainly he loves them, as one must, but these little lives, like all lives, are only loaned to us. We must be prepared to give them back, at any time. Why won't she see that?

See . . . She keeps mentioning the sea – her sea, the place she came from, far from this northern moor. When they were courting, and when they were first married, she used to tell him stories of her youth in Penzance, the lively little port on the soft under-tip of Cornwall. The great glittering bay, the coming of the pilchard shoals with their miraculous millions of fishes, her father's warehouse smelling of tea and pepper. Hard to recall now when she stopped mentioning it. (He is a busy man, with a large scattered parish to see to, and he must ration his attention.) Perhaps indeed it was when they came here . . . His old parish of Thornton, where the children were born, had been a gentler and kindlier place altogether – but this was a better living and a bigger parsonage-house. He was pleased with it from the beginning. Cool sturdiness, stone stairs – no flammable timber, thank heaven, for he had a horror of fire – and a roomy study. He has always spent a good deal of time there, separating himself from the messy contingencies of six young children. It is necessary to him; and he is sure his wife has always understood. She is nothing if not dutiful.

He knows there are things that perturbed her about this place: the dun barricade of moorland, the crowded churchyard with its flotsam of tombs jostling to the very windows. But of course you stopped noticing these things. One of the important lessons he has taught her, he thinks, is that one place is much like another. Learn self-sufficiency, and you can pick it up like a tent and move it anywhere.

He is comfortable with severance. When they were courting he didn't mind telling her his own story: the rustic Irish cabin where he had been born, his father and mother devotedly toiling to raise ten children on a little acreage; their pride in his book-learning as he outstripped everyone at the village school and at last set up his own; the clergyman who took him as tutor to his own family, applauded his energy and ambition, and pointed him in the amazing direction of Cambridge. Yes, that is the story; and it is a thing finished and put behind him.

But her dying mind seems to be dwelling on the sea of her youth, and it is another disturbing hint that she is not properly preparing to leave this world. And then the matter of the children . . . The baffling thing is that now her time approaches she will not see them.

Yesterday morning, when she had seemed a little calmer, when her sister – staunch Miss Branwell, come all the way from Penzance to nurse her – was brushing her hair and quietly setting aside the great soft lumps that came away, he had tried again. 'Perhaps you might see them today, my dear?'

'No, I . . . Perhaps.' She lay flat. 'Perhaps just one at a time. All together I think would be – too much for me.'

Just then came the sound of them, the high fluting voices, the competitive torrent of footsteps down the stairs.

The tears, he saw, did not flow. They simply, perfectly covered her eyes, like watch-glasses.

'No – no. Perhaps tomorrow . . .'

Now tomorrow is almost here, its light melting through the shutters, and she dozes again and mumbles of the sea and then, opening her eyes and speaking clearly, says: 'Something must come of this. There must be a purpose. There must – somehow there must be redemption.'

His heart leaps. 'Oh, my dearest, yes – lay hold on that. Our redemption in Christ – there, there you will find the strength to support you, to take you triumphant and joying into the next world—'

'Not for *me*. My children.'

'My dear, I beg you not to keep thinking on that. I've told you—'

'They will have no mother!'

He pauses, struggling with his disappointment. 'They will have a father.'

Her laughter at that is horrible – throaty, long, almost sensual. But what comes next is worse. She cocks her head, eyes roaming the room. 'You said the devil is here, didn't you? Very well, then. I want to make a bargain.'

'Stop – your pain is making you mad—'

'Yes, I know. Hush a moment.' Her eyes roam again, her face all bone and sockets. Something like a smile forms. At last she sighs, and says, as if in contented answer: 'Very well.'

The surgeon has made his morning call, and gone away, and it is as he suspected. His wife will not live another night.

Her sister is with her now, and the children are with their nurse, and he can claim the sanctity of the study for a while. He tries to pray, but fear and memory between them squeeze prayer out.

What she said about the bed – the marital bed . . . Yes, he is a man of strong desires, he cannot deny it. And so the children came swiftly. Woman's lot. But she found the children so beautiful and adored them so – did not that atone for everything that happened in the darkness? From the strong, sweetness.

It is so terrifying to find her fighting him like this. Always she trusted him to be her guide in everything. He remembers during their courtship walking with her beside the River Aire, and a sudden fog coming down. She panicked. Where was the road? Where were they? They might blunder into the river—

'Here – this way.' Though he is short-sighted, he has always had a perfect sense of direction. 'See? Here is the road.'

'Oh! Yes, I see.' She laughed, and held more tightly to him. 'I was all at sea for a moment.'

Not a long courtship: they were so very well suited. She was twenty-nine, he thirty-five; she had a little income, he had recently gained a perpetual curacy in the district. They would not be rich, but neither of them cared about that. She was, he found, blessedly serious. That was what had brought her to Yorkshire: her parents had died, and she had found living with her sisters as maiden ladies on fifty pounds a year rather aimless. She had an uncle and aunt who ran a school in the West Riding, and she had travelled there to help them and be useful; and he knew the uncle, and came to the school to examine the boys in classics. And they had met.

For them to have been brought together from such far-flung places was, it seemed, the work of Providence. He was sure of it, and he thought she was sure of it too, then.

'Just think,' she said excitedly, as they planned the wedding, 'I shall have your name. I was always a little disappointed that mine was not one of the real Cornish ones – a Pol or a Pen or a Tre. I shall be glad to have such an unusual name. It is distinctive.'

'Well, it was spelt differently in Ireland – where it was spelt at all. People were baffled by it when I came to England, so I thought it best to familiarise it. To avoid confusion.' Severance. It was Pat Prunty who arrived at Cambridge to grind through his studies on a starveling pittance, but it was not Pat Prunty who left it with a degree and holy orders.

He tries, seriously, to consider whether she grew unhappy with him later. Of course marriage is a process of revelation, and he knows he has his singularities. The fear of fire that makes him insist on no curtains or rugs – but in Ireland he saw what fire could do. A wooden cabin, gone in minutes. The people inside just shapes – shapes of themselves in soot. So terrible it was almost thrilling. And he knows she never felt easy about his pistol. But he began the habit of carrying it in the days when the Luddites threatened the district, and it came to seem sensible to have it by him at night, because you never know. And he makes sure it does not lie about the house loaded during the daylight hours by firing it from the window first thing every morning. He likes to do that. Somehow it breaks open the day.

From upstairs the wail comes again: 'Oh, my children. Oh, my poor children . . .'

Almost maddening. He starts out of his chair, grips the back of it, for several seconds has a clear, compelling vision of himself picking it up and smashing it against the wall. He sinks down again. The fact is, he is very proud of his son and very fond of all the children in his way – not a demonstrative way, perhaps, but he must keep the citadel of self intact. And the children, young as they are, seem to know that. They understand there must be separation.

Suddenly his own sob takes him by surprise, and he hides his face in his hands. The sorrow is for her defying him. The rest he can bear.

Unheard, the children tiptoe past the study, like ghosts.

The surgeon, Mr Andrew, descends the steep village street pensively. Hardworking thirtyish provincial sawbones, he is neither grand nor jaded enough to view with equanimity the inefficacy of medical science; and the failure hits harder where there is friendship. In the parsonage study he had come out with it. 'I am afraid, sir, you must prepare yourself.'

The husband of the dying woman paced back and forth between the twin windows. Keen, strong-boned profile, with a kind of flourish in its moulding suggestive of the carving on a ship's prow. 'I am prepared, Mr Andrew,' he said at last, and his glance was dark. 'I can only pray that she is.'

The religious mind. Well, friendship leaves a margin around such things: witness Mr Andrew's medical mind, which has long concluded, *Too many children, too quickly*. Cancer is the last inhabitant of that overworked womb.

A heavily loaded wagon is struggling up the street. Mr Andrew steps over the little tea-coloured river of human and animal excrement, slops, suds and rot that gurgles on its merry way down to the village wells, steps up on to the sliver of raised pavement, and finds himself beside young Hartley, the butcher's son. An idle, gawking fellow, and fat. He makes no room. 'Parson's wife is dying hard, they say,' he remarks, brightly, with a nod to the top of the hill.

Mr Andrew does not answer this. The wagon lurches up a few yards, then stops again, the old sunken-necked horse in the shafts struggling for purchase on the flagstones. The driver swears, slashing and slashing with his whip. Mr Andrew meets the horse's rolling eye.

'Not as we ever saw much on her, mind.' Young Hartley watches the agonising progress of the horse with dispassionate interest – but, no, not dispassionate. Something blackly gamesome, as if it were a race or a ratting-match. 'Short-winded, look. Not far off foundering, I'd say. He'll be the one tekking the ride next.'

And now Mr Andrew sees that the wagon belongs to the knacker and fellmonger from Oxenhope, and another desperate lurch brings the load into view. A stiff tangle and dangle of hoofs, wagging.

'This is a miserably hard sort of place,' Mr Andrew finds himself saying.

The butcher's son looks blankly. 'What dost mean?'

Oh: the world, I suppose, thinks Mr Andrew, shouldering past him. And he thinks of those children, up at the parsonage; and wonders what in God's name will become of them.

Sarah Garrs, the nurse, has gathered the children in the parlour, cloaked and booted for their afternoon walk, but is unsure what to do. Something brewing – surely the inevitable – in the room above: the master, white as his cravat, has shut himself in his study, and she hesitates to disturb him, even more than usual. The children are restless. They must know, poor creatures, yet like Sarah they edge round the mention of their mother, afraid to fall in.

'Tell us a story, Sarah.'

'Yes, tell us a story.'

'I don't know any stories,' she says. Well, only grim anecdotes of boggarts and fairishes, stealing live children and leaving corpses in their place. The silence of the house, the ceiling overhead with its light freight of death, seem to bear down and crush her. Desperately she begins: 'Once there were three sisters, and they lived – they lived in a beautiful palace all made of glass—'

'Not a sister story. Not sisters, brothers.' A fractious protest, from the one boy of the six. It twists into tears. 'I don't like it today, it's not right. I want to go out . . .'

Sound of the study door opening, footsteps. And though they do not start or turn, suddenly you can see something in them all, like the faint twitch of a dog's ears as it lies sleeping on the floor: ready to move in an instant. The ripple of Papa.

He is here, looking in, if not seeing.

'Oh, sir, I was wondering – I wasn't sure whether . . .'

'Yes, Sarah?' The master does not pick up hints: he lets them lie, so you have to stoop and scrabble to retrieve them.

'I was just wondering whether the children should go on their walk, sir.'

'By all means.' He consults his watch. 'Not too long, though, if you please.'

Soon they are out of the parsonage, and climbing the path behind it to the high moors. This is the way the children like to go, and Sarah partly understands it – space for roaming, and so on. Yet if they went down the street instead they might peer in at windows, see a horse shod, watch bales of wool go swinging up on a great hoist. Out here there's nothing to look at, scarcely even a tree. Oh, they push and shove, skip and dawdle like other children, but sometimes Sarah, following them, quails to find them so purposeful. As if, without her to call them back, they would go on for ever into that wide nothing.

And thinking of the house, and what it will be like when her mistress is gone, she almost feels it would be better if they did.

Mr Andrew's prognosis is correct. As the September day dwindles, Miss Branwell comes down to fetch her brother-in-law, announcing with characteristic precision, 'I fear the crisis approaches.' And so at last – there is no choice in the matter now – the children are ushered into the room, and range around their mother's bed.

Except that, being children, they do not range. The solemnity impresses them, but death is not tidily punctual like family prayers: there is boredom in the room, as well as fear, sadness, bewilderment. The smallest girl toddles and gazes, purely investigative, pulling at the counterpane: even gives a chuckle when the ravaged face turns on the pillow: peek-a-boo. Sarah Garrs, urging her back, sees the master's frown. Not angry, just perplexed, as if he does not comprehend that they are children at all. The boy stays at Papa's side, as he feels he ought to, but cannot help looking restlessly over: what are the others doing? The two eldest girls, sensible, are united in their resolve to be still and quiet. Not so the middle two, one wriggling up on the bedside chair, the other trying to copy her. Miss Branwell clucks her tongue. They scratch their spindly stockinged legs. Their dying mother opens her eyes.

Her husband bends to her. 'They are here, my dear. Do you see . . . ?'

Muscle performs a last task, and she slowly nods, then turns her head away, as if she has done everything she can, now. Snip the thread.

The transmutation of flesh, the transmutation of names. Patrick Prunty, who crossed the sea to become the Reverend Patrick Brontë and to marry Miss Maria Branwell of Penzance, clutches his dead wife's hand and suppresses a howl (as he must, for howls must be suppressed, there is no knowing what rents and passages they may make) and prays for her soul, and tells the children to pray too; and falls on his knees, appalled at the future that had to come and that is here now. Somewhere in his mind is the thought – no bigger than the pea under the princess's bed – that he must, if it be at all possible, marry again: six children, and his work, and above all his need to be himself . . . Dear God, what can come of this?

Miss Branwell – Aunt, as she is aptly and everlastingly called now – closes her sister's eyes and mouth with a needlewoman's neatness.

The two eldest girls shed tears of knowledge: Maria and Elizabeth. The next in age, Charlotte, wriggles off the chair, and nudges her younger sister Emily to do likewise. The boy, between them in age, bearing a name that was brought all the way from the sea, the name his mother surrendered, Branwell, looks desperately from face to face to see what he should do. And the infant, Anne, smiles about, quite at ease with death: after all, she has lately arrived from oblivion herself.

The children obediently fold their hands in prayer – they all know how to do that. Still they do not range themselves. Rather they draw together in a peculiarly precise huddle, as if they stand on a rock, just big enough for them, above an encircling sea.

2

Belongings

Being in the middle, Charlotte thought she was protected.

The first shade of doubt was cast on this by Branwell. But he did it in his clever, crowing way and so it seemed, for now, a question without threat.

'But if there are six of us, you can't properly be the middle one,' he said, 'because— Oh, well, look here.' He wrote their names across a sheet of paper, in order of age. Maria. Elizabeth. Charlotte. Branwell. Emily. Anne. To his own name he added a little flourish. 'There. See? There are two older ones on one side of you and three younger ones on the other side. With six you don't have a middle because . . .' he frowned, doodling '. . . because it's arithmetic.'

Charlotte peered dubiously. 'But I *feel* in the middle.'

'Oh, well, to be sure,' Branwell conceded. Among the six of them, feeling was always accepted.

Being in the middle you could look both ways. Behind, you saw the younger ones treading a path you had already trodden – losing that tooth, suffering that temper fit. There was a safe feeling in that. And ahead of you, Maria and Elizabeth led the way, scanning the land, clearing the obstacles – oh, that was safety.

They were not grown-up, but to Charlotte they had a splendid capability that was just as impressive. When they said they would do a thing, they did it. Once she made a cobble of her sewing and Aunt, in severe mood, scolded; inattention, she said, was the devil's gateway. Maria, discovering Charlotte in tears, said she would unpick it and set it right for tomorrow. Going to bed, Charlotte could not help confiding to Sarah Garrs: 'Maria might not come to bed yet. She's going to mend my sewing.'

'Aye, well, now, I'm sure she would if she'd the time, but don't go counting on it.'

What Sarah feared (it was always easy for Charlotte to tell what people were thinking) was that she would be disappointed. But Charlotte knew better. And in the morning there was the sewing, healed, just as Maria had promised. Such vindication.

Not that she wanted to crow about it. That moment was simply one of contentment: this was how things should be. Some years ago – before she could understand years – here had been a cataclysm. It was called Mama's Death, and it had changed everything. It was that time, she guessed, that had let loose the darkness: the darkness that was lurking and waiting for you all around the edges of life. But Maria and Elizabeth were bearers of light, and could always keep it at bay.

There were some places where you couldn't sense the darkness at all. In the kitchen on a winter morning when Nancy Garrs, Sarah's sister, was baking, and you could sniff the floury, yeasty smell that was also somehow the smell of Nancy herself. Or in the little upstairs room they called their study, especially when Maria took up the newspaper and read to them, and her cool, careful voice only added to the grandeur of it: Mr Peel, and the Duke of Wellington, and the House breathless. And especially when Papa bought a new book, and Branwell was permitted to cut the pages: the book lying beautiful on the table, waiting for the knife to set it free.

But sometimes even in good places the darkness might steal up and take you by surprise. Even on the moors during the purple flush of summer, when Emily went too near the beck, hopping, even deliberately wobbling; or crept up to the old ram and looked into his devil's face, and dared Charlotte to do it too. And you knew that she was, if only a little bit, laughing at you.

Or at the tea-table when Papa, who generally took his meals alone and undisturbed in his study because of his digestion, decided to join them. And in between his long, pouting sucks of tea – as if it were soup – he would say, half winking in memory, 'Now this reminds me,' or 'Now that was a curious occurrence,' and tell them tales of the strange country called Ireland. And you were honoured and impressed and yet at any moment you knew the tale might take a black and terrifying turn, and you would feel his eye on you, impassively studying you, examining your fear.

Fear: that the darkness might reach out and get you. Thank God she was protected, she was in the middle. She looked again at Branwell's piece of paper, the sum of enchanted names. No, it still worked out. She was comforted.

Of course, this family arithmetic did not include Aunt and Papa. They stood above and beyond, in their separate and solitary spheres: Aunt with her Bible, her genteel shivers, her reminiscences of her youth in Penzance when ladies still wore hair-powder and she was the belle of the assembly ball. And Papa with his sorrows.

The sorrows of Patrick are real. They are made no less real by the fact that within three months of his wife's death he had asked another woman, a family friend, to marry him.

Haste, perhaps; but consider, the children – what was he to do with six children? The question whirled him about until he was dizzy and frantic.

The lady's refusal was indignant. So he thought hard before writing to an old flame from his very first curacy in Essex, years ago, with whom there had once been something approaching an engagement, though at the time it had seemed best to disentangle himself . . . Was she, he courteously enquired, after fully describing his circumstances, by any chance married?

A letter of superb crushing contempt came back. And forced him to accept his ineligibility. But acceptance is not natural to Patrick. Sometimes still, turning over in bed, he reaches out and expects; and sometimes it really is, for a few seconds, as if his wife is there – the imprint of her warm, breathing shape, like spots seen after looking at the sun. And sometimes, realising, he punches the empty half of the bed with great swinging overarm blows. The real punches, not the boxer's dabbing, that men use in real fights: as a boy he used to see them at it outside the shebeen-houses in Drumballyroney, and marvel, disgusted, half longing.

Acceptance is weak and passive. Better to embrace. The true martyr calls lustily for more boiling oil and arrows. Patrick must learn again the sharp, complex pleasures of self-denial. I cannot have it: I may not have it: I shall not have it. Remember his cold rooms at wintry Cambridge, ice on the windows, pennies in his pocket. Then the news that he had won a college exhibition and was suddenly richer by five pounds a year: surely the moment to buy a bucket of coals. Now I can have a fire. But Patrick did not. Once more he tucked his hands under his armpits and pored over Tacitus through the mist of his own breath. I shall not have it. A victory.

So he embraces his own deprivation. But there are other sorrows that cannot be transmuted. Six motherless children to be educated and provided for; five of them girls, with no money to entice husbands. A dark lake of future, and sailing we cannot see the banks. There is, thank heaven, the one boy: the son. Ah, he has it in his power to change everything. But Patrick, who is far from crude, would not say this to anyone, and even prevents himself dwelling on it when he coaches Branwell in his study. Those loose small shoulders hunched over the book: the weight they must bear. Though if someone had said to Patrick when he was a boy, packed with nine siblings in the smoky Irish cabin, 'It all depends on you', he would have said: 'Yes, yes, please.' With fire. He would have embraced it. And, thinking of that, he almost envies his son, for the riches of struggle.

Curiously he cannot bring to mind the faces of his brothers and sisters, though he can clearly see his father – at the plough, digging and stacking turves, sharpening his scythe on the whetstone: always doing something. Choosing a sucking-pebble before beginning to cut his way into the hayfield. The sucking-pebble stopped your mouth going dry. That is the taste of sorrows: the hard, necessary pebble in your mouth. And Patrick goes busily out into his own field, his large, scattered parish: work keeps you going. There is plenty of it. Sick visits, marriages, christenings, funerals – funerals above all. Again and again he stands by the cakey hole where pallid roots protrude and exposed worms flail, again he speaks the words, the pebble of sorrows in his mouth. Again the cut grass topples and falls.

Ask Mr Andrew, the surgeon, about the frequency of those funerals. After the first touch of defensiveness – for he is peculiarly fond of the place and has done good work here – scientific honesty will compel him to admit that the mortality rate of Haworth is comparable with that of the worst London slums. Press the point, and he may concede that in many respects Haworth *is* a slum. But the squalor is not that of decay: rather it is the raw and ruthless confusion of a place on its way up.

All across the West Riding you can see tight, perching, sweating little towns like this, where time is money and money is wool. Mr Andrew still has to resist fainting when he enters the dark swelter of a woolcomber's cellar, where the woolcomber and his family crowd and live and work and breathe mould while the stove blazes unventilated. But the combing process needs the heat and the manufacturers are hungry for the combed wool. Haworth is thriving – in a way that involves a lot of sickness and dying. Mr Andrew has had such frequent occasion to write 'typhus' in his journal that now he abbreviates it to 'T'. The trouble with the water supply, he will tell you, is that it has remained suitable to a medieval village, not an industrial population. There are just two public wells, so the women begin queuing with their pails long before dawn – which at least has this advantage: that they cannot see the colour of the water. The busy citizens of Haworth empty their privies on to the midden heaps, which totter and ooze; at the top of the hill the crammed churchyard adds its stock to the soup of the gutters.

But, then, we are making a new world here. Modernity always feels harsh. Time may cure many of these ills, soften sharp edges, bring ripeness. But even Mr Andrew will admit that Haworth is not a place you can ever imagine feeling romantic about.

'It is better to be good than to be clever,' Aunt told Emily, who had been trying to copy Branwell's Latin lesson, and had given up with a wail that she wasn't clever enough. 'That is the most valuable lesson you will ever learn.'

Anne, who slept in Aunt's room, and spent a lot of time in her shadow looking trustfully up, went around repeating it in her faintly annoying lisp. 'It is better to be good than to be clever.' And sometimes getting it mixed up: 'It is better to be clever than to be good.' Which was wrong; and knowing it to be wrong, Charlotte heard it with a secret excitement. It was like the time she shared the two-seater privy in the yard with Sarah Garrs, and Sarah made a rude noise and said, 'Eh, the wind's in the south,' and began laughing. Charlotte dared not laugh: this was wrong, But it was exciting to know that the wrong existed. Always it was there, alongside prayers and washing and obedience.

But surely you could be good *and* clever – like Maria. Once Aunt was embarked on a well-worn reminiscence of a Cornish gentleman whom she might have married: '. . . a high degree of regard. There was that difference between our attitudes to devotion, which my conscience could not accommodate, but still, a high degree of regard. He lost his fortune in the funds when Bonaparte escaped from Elba, and went into a swift decline. It remains one of my regrets at leaving Penzance, out of duty to my sister's children, that I cannot visit that good gentleman's grave now and then, and lay flowers.'

'But, Aunt,' said Maria, looking up from her sewing, 'you told us that that gentleman died at sea.'

For several seconds Aunt was caught in a narrow-lipped silence. 'He was brought home. His body . . . Maria, that hem is a shambles. You might attend to your work instead of showing disrespect to your elders.'

Later, on their walk up to the moors, Maria was subdued and silent.

Elizabeth said: 'Well, she does keep changing that story.'

'It was wrong, I shouldn't have spoken like that.'

'It was only the truth.'

Charlotte was walking between them, in the middle, gazing up at their fascinating faces: Maria dark-browed and sharp-featured, like a lady; Elizabeth softer, her delicate long-lashed eyes always looking out for the good side. Charlotte was flanked by strength and tenderness.

'Well, yes. That's why I said it – I mean, why I couldn't stop myself. But a reason is not the same as an excuse. Aunt gave up her home and her friends to come here and look after us. I was disrespectful, and that is the same as being ungrateful for her kindness.'

'Never mind.' Elizabeth put a hand on Maria's shoulder, ruffling Charlotte's hair on the way. 'She will soon forget about it.'

As Maria, both clever and good, would not. When she was sorry, she really meant it; whereas when Charlotte was sorry, it was the smooth reverse side of prickly resentment, like an inside-out garment. Of course one should be respectful and grateful to Aunt – but still Charlotte could not help noticing the way she showed her little pebble-grey teeth when she talked of the devil and damnation, or the face Nancy Garrs made behind her back when Aunt unlocked the cellar to ration out the servants' single mugs of beer. Charlotte had to hold a book up close to her face to read it, but she saw things; and she suspected that this seeing was a failing in her. That night of the tremendous thunderstorm, when Branwell came running into the girls' bedroom to yell his excitement: 'Did you hear it? That was the loudest . . . !' and then, looking down at himself in perplexity: 'Oh, Lord, it's happened again. It does that sometimes when I'm in bed.' Charlotte saw: something, some part of him, was sticking out under his nightshirt like a nail. But Maria did not see – or by some effortful virtue, which Charlotte could not match, she was able not to see. She simply took command, hushing everyone, reassuring Emily, who was bolt upright and trembling, urging Branwell back to his own room. 'Don't be frightened, Emily,' he cried, turning back at the door. 'It's only thunder.' With his crackle of red hair and jittering white legs he seemed himself like some wild electric splinter of the storm. 'That's what our name means, you know – Papa told me, it's Greek.

That's us. Brontë means thunder.' The thing under his nightshirt, Charlotte saw, had gone.

She also saw, in another sense, that you could not ask about it. Elizabeth might not know, but out of kindness would find out for you; Maria, who could hold a detailed discussion with Papa about Catholic Emancipation, would surely know, and out of her regard for truth might tell you. But to ask them would be to presume, and Charlotte had no wish to do so: she reposed in their wisdom; they were demigods, linked to the mythical past. They could remember Mama.

Charlotte had a few sketchy images, but she could not be sure whether they came from memory of Mama or what she had been told about her. Branwell, who was a year her junior, was bold in assertion: 'I can remember Mama – I can remember everything about her.' But the memories did not survive scrutiny. This was just Branwell leaping up to be king of the castle again. Once Anne tore her petticoat, and cried long and desperately about it, until Sarah Garrs helplessly sighed: 'Dear Lord above, there never was such crying!' And Branwell, hearing, closed his book on his place-marking finger and rose to the challenge. 'Oh, I cried more than that once. Much more. It was when I picked up the fire-tongs, and I burned myself so badly I nearly fainted, in fact I did faint, and I fell down in the grate, and afterwards . . .'

Then the tale began, but you didn't mind it, because it was not so much a lie as a decoration of time. And, besides, as he told it he kept a kind of grin in reserve – and besides again, that was Branwell: he fitted in, they all fitted in. Charlotte in bed, adventuring her warmed feet into earth-cold sheets, would picture them all about the house, Branwell with his collection of talismanic objects – a watch-glass, string, buttons, the horrible mouse's skull – on the night-stand, Papa awesomely alone (and not fully imaginable), Anne in her little bed at the foot of Aunt's; and it was as satisfying as a sewing-box or – most beautiful and desirable of all – that drawer in Papa's desk, with the compartments for ink and wax and penknife and silver-sand. And often the wind made muscular groans and mutterings under the eaves, as if it would lift the roof off and look in at Charlotte and her family in their compartments; perhaps disorder, rummage, destroy. But, no, the lid of the box was tight, and that could not happen.

* * *

'I have been considering, Miss Branwell, the matter of the girls' education,' says Patrick, 'and I should be glad to have the benefit of your views upon the subject.'

'By all means, Mr Brontë, though you know I cannot pretend to any expertise upon the question.'

He has invited her to drink tea in his study, and with the same ceremoniousness do they address each other. With his sister-in-law, whom he much respects, Patrick's peculiarly eighteenth-century style comes to the fore: every *on* is an *upon*; he bows her to her seat like a Bath beau. They get on very well. Even his spittoon and her snuff-box make a kind of pair. Just occasionally, when he looks at her, Patrick is swept with hatred, because she is alive and her sister is dead, and there is just enough resemblance beneath the maiden-lady angularity to make the mockery poisonous.

'I am, as you are surely aware, a great friend to learning in general, and for its own sake. The cultivated mind can never lack for resources. But it is the lack of more tangible resources that gives the question, for this family, its urgent particularity. I am not a rich man, nor can I ever expect to be.'

'But you will provide for your children, Mr Brontë, with a legacy beyond worldly wealth – sound religious principles, firm morality, a due submission before God. These are riches that can never tarnish.'

The response is as neatly formal as an exchange of bows before a minuet. Miss Branwell pours the tea, which is rather strong. That Garrs girl will not learn that leaves can very well be used twice.

'You are very good. I hope, indeed, that in the matter of religious instruction and spiritual guidance, nothing is to be found wanting from the precepts they have absorbed at home. In conduct and the womanly arts, of course, Miss Branwell, they have always at hand an excellent tutoress.' Another exchange of bows, first graceful point of the toe. 'And in fact their own studies, among my small store of books, and with such direction as my limited time allows me to give them, have set them pretty far forward in all respects. They are mighty precocious readers; and Maria, especially, shows, I think, intellectual gifts of a high order.' Patrick's voice takes on the self-justifying pitch of a parent speaking of the inadmissible – a favourite child.

'They read, and learn, a great deal,' says Miss Branwell. 'My fear, Mr Brontë, is that they learn a great deal too much.'

'Too much?' Patrick loops his spectacles more firmly over his ears, bending his sharp, birdlike attention on her. They are always ready, these two, for a good-tempered debate. 'Come, I have always supposed you well disposed to the improvement of the mind in both sexes – as your dear late sister was.'

'My poor sister loved learning. But she loved her duty above all.'

'Oh, the girls will never, I hope, be unmindful of their duty. But I cannot suppose that books could ever detract from it. There are snares and dangers aplenty in this world, heaven knows, but they are not to be found in books.'

'It depends on the books.' Miss Branwell tucks in her lace-bound chin. She is never seen without these noose-like caps – the idea is as unthinkable as nudity. 'But of course it is not my place to remark upon the bringing up of my sister's children . . .'

'No, no, my dear madam, it is absolutely your place – you who have sacrificed so much to remain here and assist me with my sad responsibilities. Indeed, part of my reason for broaching this topic is my awareness that you may wish to return to Cornwall at some time in the near future. Please, go on.'

'Very well. I found Maria reading Byron. Reading out loud, if you please, to the younger ones.'

'The poems of Lord Byron are certainly to be found in my bookcase,' Patrick says, in his most painstaking way, as if he were translating at sight, 'and I have made it clear that the bookcase is open to all my children. There may be, indeed I believe there is, much to deplore in Lord Byron's character . . .' The lips purse, but is that a wistful glint behind the spectacles? '. . . and it is to be regretted that literary genius should be so compromised by moral dubiety. But I hold to my conviction that there cannot be harm in books.'

Miss Branwell gives him a shrewd look; deep, deep below it, like a ripple in a well, there may be contempt. 'Very well, Mr Brontë, I would not presume to meet you on this ground. But I must ask, do you suppose it will content them? Will it make them happy – indulging in these dreams of corsairs and castles, grand romance and whatnot? Or will it plant in them desires that can never be satisfied? Because they certainly cannot – and they should know it.'

'You speak, ma'am, as if the aim of life were to be happy,' says Patrick, slightly smiling, and for a wintry moment there is antagonism in their understanding. 'But, certainly, we must be realistic about their prospects in life. Husbands will be far to seek for five dowerless girls without connections. I fear they had better be equipped to earn their bread in a genteel manner.'

'Governessing.' Unconscionably strong tea. Wasteful, and over-stimulating. A quarter mixture of blackberry leaves never does any harm.

'Just so. Maria in particular, with her gifts of mind, must promise well as an imparter of knowledge. Elizabeth I fancy as more suited to the domestic sphere . . . But a formal education will be a valuable resource for them all. Of course, the time will come when Branwell may be in a position to do something for them.'

Miss Branwell nods. She approves of the boy, though he is more thrustful and noisy than the quiet, biddable girls. She is even, in her stiff-backed way, motherly to him, like a gaunt sheep adopting some unruly cub. 'You will continue to supervise Branwell's education yourself? Well, that's a saving. It still leaves five.'

'Precisely my difficulty. The school recommended by Miss Firth, for example, is altogether too expensive.' Patrick sighs, but the sigh is not for the expense. Miss Firth is a friend from the old Thornton days – the days, indeed, when they had friends – and godmother to Anne. More troublingly, she represents his first attempt at remarriage; and it is only now, two years after the disastrous proposal, that she is consenting to speak to him again. He still holds to the view that, premature as his approach had been, it made eminent practical sense: Miss Firth was genteel, had money of her own, and was fond of the children. If ever the rage to possess was part of the equation, if ever he had put together in his mind candlelight, and the apricot-like nape of Miss Firth's neck, and the remembered feel of bare legs under his hands (that swelling sweep from knee up, up), then he has forgotten it. Or he has quarantined the memory, just hearing, occasionally, the noises from behind the high fence.

'I should not have thought, in any case, that a school of that sort would be wholly apt for the girls' future lot in life,' Miss Branwell says. 'The acquisition of mere elegances can hardly benefit them: by encouraging vanity and frivolity, quite the reverse. A sound, economical schooling, without fripperies, if it is to be had, would better equip them for a world in which duty must be paramount.'

Patrick nods. 'Your counsel, ma'am, is every bit as thoughtful and sensible as I have come to expect.'

'I am thinking of their welfare, of course. For the worst thing, you'll agree, Mr Brontë, the very worst thing, would be for those girls to grow up thinking themselves in any way exceptional.'

* * *

'Lord Byron is dead.'

In the children's study Maria slowly lowers the newspaper and pronounces the words with chilling plainness. A recent attack of measles has left her thin and pale, which makes the effect even more dramatic.

'Did he die in battle?' cries Branwell. 'Against the wicked Turks?'

'He died of fever, at the camp where he was making ready to fight the Turks,' Maria says. 'It was a noble and heroic death, given for the cause of Greek freedom.'

'Noble and heroic!' echoes Branwell, loving the words.

'As the newspaper says, there were grave sins and errors in Lord Byron's life, but still –' Maria's voice trembles '– we mourn the death of a great man.'

They all gaze at each other. Noble and heroic. It seems to Charlotte that their own small, wide-eyed silence has something of that quality, linking this cramped damp-smelling room with the deadly glamour of that far-off Greek strand. But she is also filled with unaccountable fear.

'Would it be right to pray for Lord Byron's soul?' Elizabeth says.

Maria hesitates. 'We had better ask Aunt.'

Over the afternoon sewing, Elizabeth asks. Aunt gives a strange chuckle; then her narrow face seems to grow narrower, as it does when she sits staring into the fire of an evening, shadows eating away at her; when she stirs, slightly shakes her head, seems to reject her thoughts like frayed pieces of thread.

'Pray for Lord Byron's soul?' Again the stony chuckle. 'Well, I dare say you could try.'

Later on the moors Branwell, with a stick broken from a stunted thorn, is a rampaging swordsman. 'I shall be like Lord Byron when I grow up. I shall kill all the Turks and teach them not to be heathens.' He slashes at the heathen heather. 'Then I shall come back in disguise so nobody knows me – ow. I hurt my hand – Charlotte, look, look at it.'

Branwell's wounds must always be displayed and given a tribute of wonder.

'It's not bleeding. Well, yes, it nearly is. Branwell, I don't think you should want to be like Lord Byron.'

'Why not?'

'I'm afraid – I think he has gone to hell.'

Branwell's redhead skin flares. He throws down his sword and stamps on it. 'I think he has *not*.' Charlotte knows that anger: the fear in it, the little gnarled wick in the heart of the flame. 'Lord Byron was a great poet and he was noble and heroic and—'

'But Aunt said it was no use praying for his soul. And sometimes he wrote wicked things and did wicked things. Even the newspaper said so.'

He turns away to hide the tremor of his lip. 'You're a pig, Charlotte. You're a pig for saying that.'

'But I don't *like* it, Banny. That's why I'm afraid. If you're like Lord Byron, you'll end up in hell where he is—'

'We know nothing about that.' Maria steps between them. 'That's for God to decide. And we can't make guesses about what God intends. We must simply trust.' She places a hand on each of their shoulders, leaning a little heavily – still weak from her illness – so that Charlotte feels as well as hears her words, right through her veins: 'There is only one thing we can be sure of, and that is that God is merciful.'

Forty-five miles away, a man who believes none of these things is contemplating the school he has built.

Like Patrick, he is a clergyman, and on the Evangelical wing of the Church; otherwise they could hardly be more different. There, the transplanted Irishman subsisting in obscurity on his curate's stipend: here, the substantial figure of the Reverend William Carus Wilson, Vicar of Tunstall, landlord of Casterton Hall, and philanthropic founder of the newly opened Clergy Daughters' School at Cowan Bridge.

Substantial in all ways. The springs groan as he steps down from his carriage, heavy-limbed, big-bodied, tight and sleek and buttoned-up in clerical black; his broad feet make cow-like indentations in the soft turf as he approaches the porch. No gravel carriage-sweep here, as there is at Casterton Hall: this is not a place for carriage-folk; not a place for exhibitions of worldly vanity. The Reverend Carus Wilson carries himself, as it were, to the door: such is his peculiar stiff gait that it suggests a thin actor wearing stuffing. The comparison would not please the Reverend Carus Wilson, who does not approve of the theatre, and in whom there is nothing Falstaffian, except perhaps the ability to believe his own lies.

The lady superintendent of the school is at the door to greet him, a little flustered. Mr Wilson's visits are frequent but not always announced. Natural, perhaps, as he lives close by, but more than that, he simply cannot leave it alone. The Clergy Daughters' School is his child, and the Reverend Carus Wilson has a great feeling for children.

The school has been open only for a couple of months, and there are the inevitable teething troubles, which the superintendent nervously relays to him while he condescends to take tea in her lodging. He is very attentive; still, there is this stuffed quality about him as he listens, his great eyes, like half-peeled boiled eggs, unblinking and lightless, so that even the superintendent, who respects him, has a curious fancy as she finishes speaking that instead of replying he will fall sideways like a Guy, or burst like a balloon.

But Mr Wilson rises, assures her in his church-filling voice that all these matters will be looked into, and proceeds to make a tour of the school. It has been planned, built and opened with great speed – even haste, perhaps; but the Reverend Carus Wilson is that most desperate of characters, a man with a vision. His vision seized on the row of stone cottages and the old bobbin mill that he often saw from the turnpike road on his way to preachings and Bible Society meetings in Leeds, and now here is the transformation. Whether it occurs to him that the choice was not ideal – so remote, exposed, difficult to heat – it is hard to say. His mind is not an easy terrain to map.

It begins with this, perhaps: the terrible conviction that nearly everything about the world is wrong; that everyone is blithely walking about on thin ice, chattering, heedless of the sharp sound of cracks. Mr Wilson heard the sound when very young. That was in the days before the course of the French Revolution had started to alert people, made them look down at what lay beneath their feet. In those days society had a sprawling, juicy, wry tone: dreadful because beguiling. An old acquaintance of his father came to visit, on his way to Scotland for the hunting and shooting. Over the port he spoke of solemn things – and left them like the splintered walnut-shells that littered the table. 'For my part I think it very ill-bred to meddle with a man's religion. Or even to talk overmuch about it. There can be nothing more tedious than hearing a lot of twittering about the state of someone's soul: it's as bad as having 'em tell you all about their ailments and the trouble with their bowels.'

This man was a clergyman. A highly respectable clergyman, with a wealthy living in Gloucestershire. And this was what his parishioners must absorb from him: this the example he set the lower orders. The young Carus Wilson, filled with shock – stuffed with it, in fact – saw the path he must follow. Thankfully he found he was not alone. The cracks from the ice grew louder, the carriages began to turn away from the gambling-dens and back to the churches as the Antichrist of atheistic revolution rose, and from Cambridge emanated the Evangelical word. Set your house in order: you have been dallying with the devil. Sometimes, for Mr Wilson, the message was not pressed home hard enough.

There was that trouble with his ordination, when the Bishop of Chester withheld the laying on of hands, because the young fellow seemed half a Calvinist – but, oh, don't you see? Assign that label to me if you wish – it isn't important. What is important is the matter of sin, and the reality, the absolute reality of hell. Carus Wilson was and is perfectly placed to warn people of this, because he is not going there: his conviction has always told him so. But he knows what it is like, he is as intimate with damnation as one of his parishioners pointing out that there is a farrier in the next village. Just down there, hard left. Just down there, everlasting fire. This is how his mind works or, rather, how it moves: *working* is not quite the right image for the way Carus Wilson thinks. It is too unimpassioned, too liable to error and fatigue.

Compare this: the third wing he has had built on to the school, a long covered walkway where the girls can take their exercise when the weather is inclement. With his heavy glide Mr Wilson moves along this walkway towards the schoolroom. One is sheltered, one might almost be indoors. But step out from under the veranda and it is not so: you are under the merciless skies, the abode of hail and lightning. Your safety is no safety. The Reverend Carus Wilson, so bovine in appearance, has always at his heart the flutter of peril.

As for that space in the middle – idle, empty, wasteful, perilous space – he intends that it shall be turned into garden-plots for the girls to cultivate. Girls in a garden. He pictures them toiling decorously, not prettily: in prettiness is peril. The picture is vivid. Mr Wilson deplores the imagination, but his own is powerful – again, he knows whereof he speaks. His singular mind and body move on, to the schoolroom.

Often here he likes to step in, to address and catechise, but today he makes a gesture to the schoolmistress to continue; instead he paces about, half hearing the comforting hum of scripture. At least, it comforts him in the sense that it mildly agitates him, reminds him of the ever-present duty of warning, of the thin, cracking ice. He studies the bent heads of the girls, who might at first sight be taken for boys in pinafores, for their hair, at his insistence, is cropped close. But only at first sight: alas for them, they still look like girls. He scrutinises their clothing for deviation from the uniform of plain short-sleeved nankeen dresses, for the devil can so easily tempt them into a frill or a lace edging. He notes with approval a copy on the schoolmistress's desk of his own monthly publication, *The Children's Friend* – approval, not pride: he simply cannot entrust anyone else with the perilous task of providing reading matter for these vulnerable minds. He investigates the store cupboard, and is gratified to see that his instruction regarding the slate-chalks has been carried out and that the smallest remnants, instead of being thrown away, are laid by in a box. For though the pupils are few as yet, and all older girls, with God's help he hopes eventually to fill all sixty places, and some may be quite infants for whose little fingers the chalk-ends will be perfectly suited. To everything there is a season.

The register gives him pause. Sixteen enrolments, but only fifteen girls present. Mary Chester, the schoolmistress tells him, is ill, and the superintendent has given permission for her to stay in bed. Behind Mr Wilson's torpid nod there is a sharp tumult. ill – how ill? If the girl is very ill there must be spiritual preparation at once. If she is not very ill, there is perhaps even greater danger. His formidable imagination pictures her lounging in bed, her thoughts unfenced, her limbs restless. Better to be up and hard at her studies, sickness notwithstanding, than be exposed to such temptation. Better, all in all, to be sick unto death, and beyond the reach of sin. Another thing to speak to the superintendent about before he leaves.

So many things, for the Clergy Daughters' School is no small undertaking. It was Mr Wilson who planned, costed, and solicited subscriptions, and the list of patrons is a distinguished one: it includes the liberator of the slaves, William Wilberforce, whose philanthropy, twenty years ago, extended to subsidising with ten pounds a year the university education of a poor young Irishman named Patrick Brontë. A lesser man than Mr Wilson might have considered his aims achieved – the establishment of a school at which daughters of clergymen of the poorer sort could receive an economical education to fit them for their station in life. But no resting on laurels for the Reverend Carus Wilson: indeed, there is peril in the very idea. Thus he hovers about the cradle of his baby, anxious that it should grow in the right way.

For when he became aware of the roiling hell beyond the veranda, he took on his mission: children, and especially girls. So much mortal sin to be avoided; and children, especially girls, can hardly step out into the world without it covering them like mud. Saving them is a hard task, for all their natural – that is, diabolical – inclinations are towards rebellion. Yes, he knows they chafe at the shorn hair and the plain stuff dresses. But his visionary imagination has shown him the alternative. The Reverend Carus Wilson can picture hell most precisely, and there the girls have long, long hair, and wear no clothes at all.

3

Flesh and Grass

It wasn't the distance that appalled her.

'Forty-five miles – in truth I believe nearer to forty-eight – sounds, I know, a good distance off,' Papa said. 'But it is not so very far – and the fact is I can see no school so very suitable and affordable nearer to Haworth.'

Forty-five miles, or a thousand: what mattered was that she would be going away from home. Meaning this house, this world captured by four walls.

Even Haworth was of no account. Charlotte felt nothing for the village beyond a mild aversion to its noises and smells. When she had to walk through it, say on a trip to the circulating-library at Keighley, she would sometimes glimpse inside other people's homes. The steep streets and narrow pavements meant you were often pressed right up against a window. Inches away, an ineffably strange chair, a kitchen range with the hot-plate on the wrong side, a lifted face. After a dizzy moment she would stare away. An imposture. There was only one home.

Aunt said: 'Of course you have learned a good deal here with your father, but school requires you to be more disciplined. This means neatness, thoroughness. But you needn't fear: you are quick at your studies, and better prepared than most girls your age.'

As if the learning had anything to do with it! Charlotte loved learning. What seemed odd, in fact, was the idea that you went somewhere to have it administered to you, like the smallpox vaccination, and then had done with it. She wanted to go on learning for ever.

But only here, here.

'You're lucky. It's an adventure,' Branwell told her. 'I wish *I* was going away to school.'

'I wish you were too,' Charlotte said. 'Then you'd know.'

'Emily won't pout if she has to go later – will you, Emily? You won't be a chicken-heart?'

Often when you asked Emily a question she would cock her head, like this, as if listening to quite another question whispered in her ear. She said: 'Why are you being so nasty to Charlotte?'

'So she'll get angry. And when you get angry you don't feel sad any more.' Branwell did one of his conjuror's flourishes. 'I know that.'

But it wasn't sadness, like finding that dead lamb on the moor with the mother ewe standing, just standing, at a little distance. It was more like anticipated sadness, or – oh, it was miserable terror. As big as the world, as hot as the sun.

Only once, on the moors, had she ever done what Emily loved to do – run down a steep hillside, a *too* steep hillside, so that the point comes when you can't stop and suddenly your body, your life is out of control. She hated it: told herself, heart drumming in her ears, *I shall never do this again*.

And now you have to. The slope has taken choice away from you, and the top of the hill might never have been.

Every day she was carefully, discreetly sick. She managed to choose times and places so that Papa would not know. The little evidences of illness put him out. Besides, she did not want to burden him with her distress. He was acting with her best interests at heart: it had all been explained to her.

Emily said: 'If you really don't like it, couldn't you just run away?'

'Oh, Emily, don't be so childish.' Well, if she were to have the responsibility of being a big girl, she might as well enjoy the benefits too. 'You don't understand these things.'

But Emily simply laughed, and that was that. You couldn't counter her laugh: it was like a book you were reading abruptly shut before your face. Charlotte took more of her trouble out on Anne. There was just something about her being the baby of the family – well, actually she was four, but that made it worse, able to think and take part and enjoy things and *still* be the baby. It was contemptible, meaning it was enviable. Several times, with snapped little remarks and retorts, she made Anne cry. Not uncontrollably, though: Anne cried humbly, as if waiting to be told to stop.

Emily always comforted her. And in bed one night she said to Charlotte: 'You know, Anne will surely have to go away to school too when she's older.'

It was enough. Charlotte let out the first sob. Emily held her hand.

'When I've finished school,' Charlotte said at last, 'when it's all finished, and we're grown-up, I want us all to live together in a house by the sea. With a garden that you can see the sea from, and we'll each have a chair in the garden, our own chair.'

Emily made a contented noise. 'Oh, yes.'

The next day Charlotte resumed work on the little book she had been making to give to Anne before the news that she was to go away to school had paralysed her. She begged a stub of candle from Nancy Garrs and stayed up late to sew the pages together. That being miserable could make you hateful was a new piece of learning, though she didn't know what to do with it.

Anne crowed over her little book, repeatedly showing it to everyone – even thrusting it on Papa, to Charlotte's alarm. Papa's attention was not lightly to be demanded. It wasn't exactly that you feared a rebuff: you simply knew better, as you knew that writing-paper was expensive and mustn't be wasted. But though he murmured how kind Charlotte was to take so much trouble for her sister, his short sight could make nothing of the tiny writing and drawing. Charlotte felt relieved, then disappointed.

All such feelings, however, were like the brief settling of a fly beside that one steadfast changeless dread that she woke and lived and slept with. Sewing lessons with Aunt were taken up now by preparation: the school required you to bring so many day-shifts and night-shifts, upper petticoats and flannel petticoats. Charlotte's dread went into every stitch.

'Am I in *every* story?' Anne asked, peeping hopefully into books.

No, you can only ever be in one, no matter how it turns out. Charlotte could hardly bear the thought of the coming day – in fact, simply would not have been able to bear it if it were not for the one saving thing. The thing that had never failed her.

Maria and Elizabeth. They had gone on ahead of her. Papa had taken them in the Leeds coach last month, and they were at the school now. Maria and Elizabeth – who had not made the least fuss about leaving home, who at the door had smiled and kissed and watched quietly as their bags were heaved, slithering, up into the hired gig – would be there to greet her.

So: I cannot be as good as them, but I can be grateful for them, and at least try to be like them; and we will be together, and they will make everything all right. Get back, darkness.

* * *

Miss Branwell says: 'Yes, she is ready, Mr Brontë. That is, her things are ready. Though you must know, she does not want to go – not at all.'

'Yes: yes, quite natural, quite natural,' says Patrick, filling in time, while he edges his mind round the gunpowdery idea. For he has discussed the matter thoroughly with Charlotte, explained what it is expected of her, and received her assurance that she is willing to go. What more . . . ? He smothers a wish that Charlotte were more like Maria: that sensible, rational mind, leading her forward like an unflickering light. Her mother's mind, in fact. Charlotte is very young, of course, but it is alarming to think that there might be dark mutinous places within her. He knows those places. Alarming; and distracting, for he has so many things to think of, so many duties calling him across his scattered parish.

'Going away from home is a great step,' he says at last, 'a considerable disjunction indeed, and Charlotte perhaps lacks the strength of mind of her elder sisters. But they will be with her; there is her anchor. Maria will inspire her, and Elizabeth will comfort her. Yes.' And that is the emotion put back, like a full glass moved away from the edge of the table. There, it won't spill now.

Patrick's duties: today there is a meeting with Mr Brown, the sexton, about the forthcoming visit of the Archbishop of York, no less, to Haworth. His grace's presence is required to consecrate a new piece of land for the churchyard. Burials, as Mr Brown grumbles, have become a nightmarish business. 'I'm afraid to put a spade in. At the bottom, where it's wet, is the worst. You never know what you'll find. I try my best to keep the cut tidy before the funeral but, ten to one, when the coffin arrives, something's sticking out or seeping.'

'I'm sure the new plot will be sufficient,' Patrick says. He has met Mr Brown at his stonemason's yard, and he gives a start as Mr Brown's son suddenly emerges from the darkness of the barn that serves as workshop, hammer in hand, and covered from head to foot in white stone dust: like a spirit of the dead, looking perhaps for his tombstone.

'Aye, sufficient for now, I dare say,' Mr Brown goes on. 'But for how long? We can't stop people dying, Mr Brontë.'

'Sufficient for our day, Mr Brown.' The Archbishop will want tea, of course, perhaps even luncheon; and then there will be members of his chapter. How many? Did the letter specify? Must make sure the children are out of the way. Patrick's myopic eyes light on a half-finished memorial tablet propped against the wall. At first it makes no sense. HERE LIE THE REMA. And for a moment it dances round Patrick's head like the jigs his brother William used to play on the fiddle. Here lie the rema, here lie the rema . . . But, of course, it is simply the unfinished word 'remains.' Latin root, *remanare*, to stay. The blessing of knowledge.

He sets out on his next call, a hill-farm below Brow Moor. Here lie the rema. A terrible thing to be mad, and find the mind helplessly suggestible: like that poor young fellow at his Wellington parish, the tinsmith's son, who would hear a bell ring, or a baby cry, and go on imitating it, with dreadful accuracy, until he was hoarse and exhausted. The rational powers usurped by the wild forces of the fancy. Brother William, going to fight for the United Irishmen in the rebellion of 'ninety-eight. They were handing out guns from a captured militia post at Lisnacreevy. Patrick, home from tutoring the Rector of Drumgooland's children, begged him not to go. 'You've made your choice, Pat,' William said, with a glance down at Patrick's sober suit. 'This is mine.'

Choice – could there truly be any choice between chaos and order? That was man's true constant struggle, without and within. Patrick marches with a conqueror's stride up the rough farm track, past a field of sparse oats, the only crop that will grow in this tight-fisted soil. It supports a similarly pale, stunted family, but they are numerous, and a new addition is yelling inside the house – the reason for his visit.

The youngest daughter of the house – seventeen, she says, but Patrick has checked the parish registers, and knows her to be fifteen – has given birth to an illegitimate baby. The usual business: father unknown, though he has his suspicions of a smirking straw-whiskered cousin who hangs about the place; the girl's mother presenting the baby as a late child of her own. Patrick deplores the moral lapse, but his chief concern is for the spiritual welfare of the child. He has not come, he cheerfully tells the girl, to read a lecture, only to urge her to have the baby baptised at once. She listens, glumly, silently, but she listens; while her mother rocks the screaming infant soul that is at issue, and a great bony hound, obscenely ballocked, slummocks in and out of the smoke-painted kitchen. Patrick comes away confident of success. A vital task almost completed. The child seems healthy, but that means nothing: he has spoken the words of committal over many a coffin no bigger than a writing-case, and he dreads sending those souls off unshriven.

Some of his fellow clergymen would be much sterner about the illegitimacy. But Patrick does not believe that the sins of the fathers, or mothers, should be visited upon the children.

Tireless walker, at forty-seven as vigorous as a colt and hardy as a donkey, Patrick makes the steep descent from Brow Moor – poor curate who keeps no carriage, or gig or even a saddle-horse. But he has his little luxuries: little tendings and fussings of himself. Despite the summer warmth, his cravat is as high and tight-wound as ever, because he must take care of his vulnerable throat; and once home, he looks forward to eating his dinner alone in his study, listening solicitously to the complaints of his digestion. Harmless indulgences, like a man tenderly keeping white mice. A habit of mild melancholy too: as he approaches the parsonage he finds himself sharply missing his wife, missing his favourite daughter Maria also. But this feeling comes as a kind of pinch, like Miss Branwell dipping into her snuffbox: it does not last, indeed it would be uncomfortable if it lasted. Possibly Patrick is beginning to find himself at home on Crusoe's island of loneliness, where you can do as you like.

There is no key to Patrick – too many padlocks, bolts, bars, and nailings-up for that – but a peep through the cracks perhaps shows us this: the widower is consoling himself by turning into an old, childless bachelor.

In other circumstances the coach journey from Keighley might have been an exciting novelty; Charlotte had never travelled so far, or spent so long alone in Papa's company. But all novelties were direful now, harbingers of the cataclysmic novelty of school. And she was much occupied with wondering when and how she could be sick. At Skipton a fat old gentleman joined the coach, offered Charlotte a comfit from a twist of paper, looked offended when she refused, then engaged Papa in a conversation about the Poor Laws. She felt strongly conscious of being a child, in a new way – as if it were an illness or disfigurement. At the coach window valleys plunged into incredible splashy greenness, cloud-shadow peeled away from sky-climbing fells. It was beautiful, and thus sinister.

'Cowan Bridge lies on the turnpike road, but there is no coach-stop there,' Papa informed her, 'so we shall have to hire a gig at Ingleton.' All this trouble for her. It was late, and she was in a daze of tiredness, when they finally arrived. *Had* they arrived? She saw roofs, cows ambling down from grass, a stone leap of bridge, heard the cold talking of a stream; then suddenly the gig had turned off the high road and they were set down before a door in a wall. She looked up and saw the red evening impaled on spikes.

At some point she stopped noticing things: it was all too much, she ran out of responses. That smell: as if laundry and and mutton-bones were boiling together in a great copper. The curly wrought-iron of the banister with which she hauled herself up the endless dark stairs to the superintendent's lodging, where a lady in a wallpapered parlour shook her hand, and she was confusingly neither old nor young: keys at her waist, like Aunt, but so many she seemed to wear them like clanking fetters. Miss Evans. Warm, bony hand. 'How do you do, Charlotte? You would be glad to see your sisters, I dare say.' And then the timid knock at the door. And though she knew they would be in that drab uniform – her own was waiting in its trunk – still, the shock of seeing them in it, as if they were engaged in some grim game of dressing-up.

Maria and Elizabeth – it was them, but not quite them. They did not run to her but came sedately and bestowed subtly altered kisses. Miss Evans said they must be sure and help their sister settle in. Yes, Miss Evans. A maid with a hairy face brought in a tray, laid a cloth: Papa was to have supper here and stay overnight before travelling home first thing tomorrow. As a treat, Maria and Elizabeth would share it. Thank you, Miss Evans. All this bobbing and chorusing . . . Charlotte's eyes were heavy: she felt she could lie on the floor like a dog and sleep. At table Papa gave them news of Aunt and Branwell and Emily and Anne – they did not ask. And their studies?

'Both Maria and Elizabeth are applying themselves pretty well, Mr Brontë,' said Miss Evans. Sometimes her look was kind, but somehow you felt you couldn't rely on it: it was like a penny found on the floor. 'There are some matters of tidiness and punctuality in which we would like to see improvement.'

'I am sure you will, ma'am,' Papa said, 'especially as they will wish to set an example to Charlotte.' Home was a million miles away: a dream. Maria and Elizabeth cast strange looks at the plain supper of toasted cheese and muffins. Was this a warning not to eat it? Yet when Miss Evans invited them, they tucked in eagerly. Perhaps it was to do with this word 'obedience' she kept hearing. She swallowed a few crumbs, obediently. Elizabeth's foot gently pressed hers under the table.

She had succeeded in not being sick and now, against the pressing weight of the world, she managed not to cry.

But the effort left her emptied and incapable. She could only blink, voiceless, as Miss Evans asked her little nipping questions about herself. 'I think,' Papa said, from far away, 'my daughter is rather tired from the journey.'

Maria and Elizabeth were to show her to the dormitory. For a precious few minutes she was in the middle once more: along a stone passage, her sisters either side of her, and suddenly themselves again, embracing her, reassuring her, urgently asking after the others. Something tight and pent-up in their voices, but that might have been the echoing stone.

The dormitory: horrible as it sounded. Here the boiled smell thickened to something fusty, furry, indescribable. Bare walls, bare boards, rows of narrow beds. A few girls putting on night-shifts, turning tousled, moon-faced, to stare. 'The older girls have study till eight,' Elizabeth said. 'It's best to be ready for bed before they come up.' Before Charlotte could ask why, her sisters faded again. Another Miss swept over them, reducing them to bobbers and yessers. This one was brisk, berry-eyed, with a high, complaining voice, making Charlotte think of a bee. Yes, Miss Andrews. She had Charlotte's trunk sent up and went buzzing and fuming through its contents. '*Three* pairs black worsted stockings, *three* pairs, it is clearly stated in the prospectus.' Yes, Miss Andrews. She droned through the rules of the school while Charlotte blinked and swayed. Yes, Miss Evans. '*Andrews*.' The little buzzing face came down close to hers. 'You will learn my name. Now undress and into bed.' She was gone.

Momentary reappearance of Maria and Elizabeth, helping her to lay out her clothes. 'You must do it neatly. Otherwise she scolds.' Then a noise – the big girls coming: Maria and Elizabeth darted down the room to their beds. Charlotte pulled the wiry blanket over her head. She was trying to picture Sarah Garrs's face: it kept melting. Clattering and shouting. The blanket put back.

'Who's this?'

'She stinks.'

'Yes, she stinks.'

Charlotte closed her eyes against the great blotted forms.

'Do you think she's a piss-a-bed?'

'She looks like one.'

'Piss-a-bed.'

Maria's voice: 'That's Charlotte, she's our sister.'

A girl echoed her, mockingly. 'She's oir *suster.*' Realisation: that was Papa's accent and Maria, though Charlotte had never noticed it, must have it too. Do I have it? Moment of shameful betrayal, cowering under that blanket: if I have, I must get rid of it.

'Why is she so small?'

'She's only eight.' Elizabeth's voice.

'She still ought to be bigger. Did your papa starve her? Did he *stunt* her so she wouldn't eat much?'

'She won't get any bigger *here,* that's for sure.' A long gibbering of giggles, cut off by a whisper: 'Andrews!'

And then Miss Andrews was there, laying about her. Charlotte heard, but did not see it: instinct kept her head down. Some time later, when the candles were out and the snuffles subsiding, she felt her hand taken. Maria.

'We'll be together tomorrow. We mustn't talk now. Good night.'

'What's wrong with *talking*?' A protest: her first.

'Hush. When the bell rings in the morning, make sure you're up at once.' And Maria turned into the darkness.

They stood in sunlight by the gig. Flies tormented the old horse, settling, circling, settling. Papa received their kisses in turn.

'Charlotte, my dear. I leave you in good hands.' He had not shaved: she felt the rasp of his bristle and, as he straightened, saw that it was grey.

As the gig drew away he turned and waved his hat – an odd, holidayish gesture. Charlotte tried to raise a hand. It wouldn't move. But Papa wouldn't be able to see them from that distance anyway.

Miss Evans, keys jingling, led them back inside. Elizabeth hung back to whisper to Maria: 'You didn't tell him.'

Maria shook her head. She was pale and raw-looking; the cropped hair emphasised the bones of her face. At home (blow to the stomach at that thought) there was a book with a picture of Joan of Arc, looking like that. 'No,' she said. 'How could I? Papa has troubles enough.'

So: it is not so much that your life has changed; rather, it has fallen from a great height, and smashed, and now you must move about among the jagged fragments.

There are discoveries to be made. Charlotte discovers that she is stupid. The teachers shake their heads. She knows a lot about William the Conqueror, even things that she should not know, but not his dates. Though she has ideas, too many ideas, about France and Switzerland, she cannot put the map of Europe together. No system.

And she discovers that they – the pupils of the Clergy Daughters' School, Cowan Bridge – are objects of charity, just as the penitential dresses suggest. That is why the fees are so low, Maria explains: because rich people give money to support the school. And that is why the rich people are remembered in their prayers.

The prayers at Cowan Bridge go on and on. Prayers before breakfast, before dinner, after tea, before bed. It is as if God must be nagged. Then there are scripture lessons, catechism, hymns, sermons, Bible texts to be learned by heart. The Reverend Carus Wilson, their patron, lays great emphasis on religious instruction. Mr Wilson: long before she sees him, that name is familiar to Charlotte. It shivers round the school. It is invoked. One or two of the teachers seem to throb breathlessly when it is pronounced: on Miss Evans's face, by contrast, it occasions a hard inward look. It is printed on the cover of a paper called *The Children's Friend*, which they are given to read in their leisure hour, or half-hour.

Charlotte soon puts down the paper, but her horrified mind continues to roll on the deathly sea of Mr Wilson's prose. A little girl is prone to temper fits, until at last she falls down dead of them and goes to hell. Two sisters watch their mother dying: one weeps, but the other, wiser, reproves her because they should be rejoicing that Mama is leaving the world of sin. Children are gored by bulls, bitten by mad dogs, struck by lightning; they lie flattened under cartwheels, giving speeches about hell-flames. Some few children are good, and look serene in their little coffins, but most are naughty: girls especially. Naughty, naughty girls. Sometimes it seems just to be a girl is enough.

'I don't believe those things are true, Charlotte,' says Maria, firmly.

'But Mr Wilson is a clergyman, isn't he?'

'Well, so is Papa, but he doesn't believe those things.'

'He did send us here, though,' Elizabeth observes mildly.

And this is when Charlotte speaks out loud the question that possesses her. 'How can you bear it here? How can you bear it?'

They are in the garden for exercise period – really the only time they can speak freely together, though in the dormitory they manage a kind of whispered shorthand. Elizabeth loops her arms round

Charlotte's shoulders, inclining her gently against her chest – a way she has: even standing, Elizabeth can make you feel you are lying in a comfortable embrace. 'Oh, it's not so very bad,' she says. 'You'll soon get used to it.'

'Papa wants us to have a good schooling,' Maria says, 'and this is the best way. We'll be glad of it when we're older.'

And Charlotte studies her fine-boned absent face and thinks: You must be only saying that. To help me, to make me feel better. It isn't a thing that can be *believed*.

How can you bear it? She doesn't just mean the obvious things, though they are bad enough: the long, exhausting hours, the harrying and chivvying, the deadly stiffness of rote-learning and repeating; the stone hut with the hideous single privy for the whole school, and the volcano of flies that erupts when you open the door. This, of course, made worse by the food, which leaves everyone loose, constipated or sick.

Food: a thing you never thought much about before. At home you had a sufficiency of it, and that, as Aunt often reminded them, was something to be thankful for. Papa needed it dressed very plain, and ate it separately, because of his digestion; and Branwell said that turnips tasted like soap; and all in all it was merely part of life. But here you cannot help thinking about it. It is like having the whooping-cough: when you wake in the morning, you know that cough will shape your day; you will not be able to feel anything independently of it.

Some of the bigger girls make a joke of the food – the boisterous ones with large white hairy mole-covered arms and loud breath: they say, 'Here comes the pigswill again,' and get it down somehow, making faces. Though noisy, they are really the sheeplike ones who, once they have got what they want ('Say you didn't say I'm a beast. Say it. Say it'), subside on their thumping bottoms and blink at the world. But most, like Charlotte, are made both anxious and subdued by the food. You ride a see-saw of hunger and nausea. There is always the hope that the food may be estable, countered by the dread that, if it is, there won't be enough of it. Porridge burned so black that you pick leafy fragments of pan off your tongue – ah, but perhaps that means, in the scheme of things, that today the milk in the rice-pudding will not be cheesy, or the nameless meat in the hot-pot high. Solely reliable are the half-slice of bread at tea and the oat-cake for supper – which the crowding hairy-arms grab and steal.

Maria and Elizabeth try to stop this filching from Charlotte – but it is hard enough to look out for themselves. Maria is not yet eleven, Elizabeth not yet ten. The biggest girls are mighty-thighed and possess breasts, which they whisper about in the dormitory, comparing them triumphantly with those of the teachers. (Distant thought, like harsh sun stabbing over hills – will that happen to me? No, please God.) But this is what Charlotte really means when she asks: *how can you bear it?* How can this happen to Maria and Elizabeth, who stood so high and are brought so low?

Here is the real shock of Cowan Bridge. Her own homesickness, hunger and misery are intense but somehow unsurprising: in a way Charlotte never expected anything better of herself. But to see Maria and Elizabeth elbowed aside, licking up crumbs, bowing their heads before the nonsensical scolding of the teachers, silenced, diminished – it overturns everything. It cannot be *right*. Yet much of her feeling for right and wrong comes from Maria and Elizabeth, and they do not complain.

Elizabeth seems to rely on her famous patience. (At home, when Sarah Garrs issues the frequent command 'You mun wait a minute,' Elizabeth does so happily, while Branwell almost explodes at the very idea.) She is at ease with time: this time is not good, but there will come a time that is better. As for Maria, both her consolations and her lot are sterner. Maria has an enemy.

Everyone is wary of Miss Andrews. Her fierce temper is her known quantity, just as inquisitiveness is that of Miss Lord, the sewing-mistress, whom you can always keep sweet as long as you can make up interesting tales about your family. Everyone expects a scolding from Miss Andrews at some time: Maria gets it every day. Something about her rouses the little bee-woman to shrill, stinging fury.

'Maria Brontë, you are not paying attention . . . Maria Brontë, set your feet *properly* on the floor . . . Maria Brontë, you are deliberately trying my patience.'

Charlotte understands it in a way. With Miss Andrews everything is appearance. Listening to her lesson is no good: you must grimly, rigidly maintain the appearance of listening. But Maria often looks distant, and when she is bored or distracted she is not adept at disguising it. If she were simply stupid, perhaps, it might be easier. Her brains are a further affront.

'That wasn't fair, that was never fair,' Charlotte cries. Evening recreation: dry bread, warm coffee taken in the schoolroom, a space of limb-stretching racket before more prayers and scripture. The three Brontë sisters sit apart. Charlotte holds her breath as Elizabeth carefully inches down Maria's collar at the nape of her neck, revealing the red weals where Miss Andrews thrashed her.

'Oh, poor thing,' Elizabeth murmurs. 'Skin isn't broken. Best sleep on your front tonight. I'll sew a button in the back of your shift to remind you.'

Maria pulls her collar up. 'Where will you get the needle and thread?' Everything is constantly counted, inventoried.

'Already got them. Miss Lord didn't see. I was telling her about Penzance, and Cousin Nobbs who fell down a tin mine.'

'It's a risk.' Maria breaks into one of her rare giggles. 'Honestly. Cousin Nobbs.'

Charlotte's chest burns, her head boils. 'It wasn't *fair*.' What happened: Miss Andrews reproved Maria for inattention during history. 'Perhaps,' she buzzed, 'that view from the window, Maria Brontë, will supply you with the answer as to the meaning of Royal Supremacy.'

And Maria, turning her dreaming eyes, said: 'Oh, that was Henry VIII, and the break from Rome. It made the monarch the head of the English Church. Well, of course Mary Tudor repealed it, being Catholic and believing in papal supremacy, but then it was brought back under Elizabeth. Though she was seen as governor rather than head of the church, being only a woman.'

Miss Andrews quivered. 'Perhaps, then, as you are so well informed, you will inform us also of the year and month and day of Queen Elizabeth's death.'

And Maria didn't know. That wasn't this week's lesson, or any week's lesson. But Maria was punished for not knowing the answer, for inattention, laziness. Everyone watched Miss Andrews's springy little arm whisking up, down. Unfair, Charlotte rages, unfair.

'Perhaps it is,' says Maria: Charlotte's look seems to pain her more than the weals. 'But a lot of things seem unfair, my love – worse things than this. Think of poor Mama, when she was so ill. That probably didn't seem fair to her, at first.'

'Well, and it *wasn't* fair,' snaps Charlotte: indignation drives her to the edge of daring. 'And nothing could make it fair. Not even God.'

'Hush, you don't mean that. And you can't know that either. This is the real lesson I'm learning – how much I don't know.'

'I'm afraid you know more than Miss Andrews,' says Elizabeth, tenderly, 'and oh, dear, she hates you for it.'

Perhaps that's another lesson: don't be clever. Or if you are, hide it. Lie, in other words.

Here Charlotte is conscious of her own bleak luck. She does not shine. Smallest and lowliest, she plods head down. Only reflected light can draw attention to her – as when she is first noticed by the Reverend Carus Wilson.

Even before he appears in the schoolroom that day, it is known that he is at Cowan Bridge: the sound of a carriage, a certain agitation among the teachers – even a reported sighting of him rooting about in the closet where the boots and shoes are cleaned. (Can this be true? Oh, yes, it is firmly believed; and it is a measure of his untouchable grandeur that no one laughs at what would otherwise be absurd.) Charlotte and the other juniors are at the sewing-bench when the schoolroom door opens, and Miss Evans, more worn and blanched than ever, ushers in a large man who looks to Charlotte as if he is wearing a barrel under his clothes. Forms scrape and screech back, voices die; frantically Miss Lord gestures Charlotte to her feet.

'Girls, here is Mr Wilson, come to observe how you go on,' Miss Evans announces; but the large man, with ghostly speed, is already among them; he is at the sewing-bench; his face, big as a horse's, is bending over Charlotte's work. Smell of shaving-soap; noisy breathing of the kind that is almost a tuneless hum.

'Miss Evans.' He has taken up Charlotte's needle like a live thing. 'Is this from the batch that was ordered from Leeds? I do not remember them so fine. Unnecessarily fine, surely, for such work as basting.' The large eyes travel over Charlotte's face. 'A new girl.'

'Charlotte Brontë, sir. Lately come to join her sisters.'

'To be sure.' He lays the needle down. 'Remind me, Miss Evans, to look up those haberdasher's receipts.'

He moves on, trailing Miss Lord's gaze of worship. Charlotte doesn't know what to think. She has become quickly used to conning faces for information – the tic under Miss Andrews's eye that signals fury, the pretty flush of an older girl about to say something filthy – but she gets nothing so definite from the face of the Reverend Carus Wilson. Only curious images of chalk, of the moon, of white stillness.

Now Miss Andrews is curtsying low, and Mr Wilson is asking to hear her form recite their lesson. Maria alone is word perfect. Charlotte glows. But: 'What is this I see?' He has spotted the misconduct badge on Maria's arm. 'The name of this girl, Miss Andrews.'

'Maria Brontë, sir.'

'Ah, here is another Brontë. Well, Maria Brontë, which badge is it you wear, and what for?'

'The untidiness badge, sir. I made a great blot on my copybook.'

'That is a great pity. Untidiness is too often the mark of a distracted mind, a mind pleased with its own inventions. But then perhaps, after all, it does not greatly matter.' Mr Wilson produces something terrible: a smile, or exhibition of tombstone teeth in a face otherwise devoid of humour. 'Hey? Isn't that what you are secretly thinking? After all, you got your lesson very well: you are, I dare say, rather clever. So, you think, what can a little untidiness signify, a little carelessness? Ah, dear me: I once knew a girl very like that.' Now his voice is at pulpit pitch and, taking a stand before the fireplace, he addresses the whole school. 'She knew all sorts of things, and was very proud of her book-learning; but she did not take *care*, no matter how much she was urged to it by her parents and her governess. I am sorry to say she was a slattern; and there is nothing more displeasing in the Lord's sight than a slatternly girl. Now this slatternly girl had a baby sister, of whom she was passionately fond. It was her greatest delight, at all hours, to creep to the crib and look in at her. And this is where her untidy ways brought her to grief. For she went in to see her baby sister one evening, taking a candle; but she neglected to take the candle away with her, and she left the crib-curtain hanging loose; and so her baby sister was burned to death.' He turns the teeth on Maria. 'Now, Maria Brontë, when that girl followed the tiny coffin to its resting-place, how do you suppose her sorrow was to be described?'

'It must have been very great,' Maria answers faintly.

'It *was* very great. So great it almost made her question God's purposes. But luckily there was a true friend by, a pious friend, to convince her of the good ends of Providence, which had preserved her baby sister from the sins of this world, and had served her a lesson which might in time be the saving of her own soul.' Mr Wilson suddenly stretches out an arm: Charlotte finds that the great white finger is pointing straight at her. 'You have a young sister here, I believe, Maria Brontë. Think of her. Think of the example you set her. What do you suppose she feels, seeing you wear the untidiness badge?'

Now Charlotte wants to speak up, to give him an answer and not one he will like. But even the wanting is a puny fancy, like a wish that you could jump out of the window and fly. She is only a child – only a girl. It is Maria who answers, properly and very clearly: 'I hope, sir, that she will learn not to do as I have done.'

The Reverend Carus Wilson gives a slight, even absent nod before moving cumbrously on. His story seems to have both refreshed and exhausted him, like a heavy luncheon.

As for Charlotte, she knows that the burning crib will now illustrate her nightmares, along with the lightning-strokes and mad-dog bites and boys pinned under cartwheels. But Maria, lifting her humbled head, manages to send her a reassuring smile – before Miss Andrews darts in buzzing and cuffing and vowing to cure her of these sly looks.

Just what *was* the Reverend Carus Wilson doing in the shoe-closet? Well: taking care. There is a cobbler in the village who performs the necessary repairs, and with thirty pupils now enrolled, each with the regulation two pairs of shoes and one pair of pattens, this is no trifling task. What concerns Mr Wilson is the system. Is the man paid per shoe, or paid for his time? Bad economy to call him in one day to do a single repair, and then two days later to do another, and so on; better to appoint, say, a fortnightly visit at which all the repairs are made. And any shoes requiring attention to be set aside in a specific place. This shelf, now, should be sufficient; if not, have the manservant nail up another next to it.

Yes, a better system. Still Mr Wilson's mind broods – full-cropped, dusty-feathered Great Auk of a mind – over the matter of the shoes, even as he descends to inspect the source of the greasy smell that enwraps the whole school: the kitchen. Here, in a kind of steamy dungeon, the girls' dinner is being prepared: a species of meat-and-potato pie, with rice-pudding, as Mr Wilson observes from a glance or two into the blackened tins. He exchanges a few ponderous genialities with the cook – his own appointee for the post. Her family have long been in the service of the Wilsons of Casterton Hall, and he knows her to be a sober, thrifty and devout woman. Whether she can cook is a different matter – a matter outside his scope. Because now look here: you must see what is being done at Cowan Bridge, the whole of it. These girls, you see, are being prepared for the world: we must *armour* them against it. Food, yes, the mortal flesh must, alas, be fed, and this, the meat-and-potato pie, or whatever it is, will do. Beyond that lies the titillation and gratification of appetite – and then the perilous gates are flung open.

Now the obvious question is, would the Reverend Carus Wilson eat this food himself? Do not he and Mrs Wilson and the young Wilsons dine choicely at Casterton Hall, where rancid meat and burned rice never appear at the great mahogany table, and would be sent indignantly down again if they did? But perhaps this is the wrong question. If he were simply a hypocrite, he would not be so strange and alarming. The hypocrite is essentially a fibber, and knows it. But the singular capacity of the Reverend Carus Wilson (and his like – he is not, never will be, alone) is the ability to believe two contradictory things at once. He believes suffering is good for the soul, for all souls; but he does not believe it is good for his soul, and he makes sure never to have any. Just look at those cheeks and lips, those thighs and buttocks: like a butcher's diagram.

Still, he is not a man at ease. The constant necessity of taking care prevents that. As he leaves the kitchen (the cook eagerly curtsying him away, his grateful admirer but still relieved that now she can really *scratch* again) his thoughts revert to the repairing of the shoes. No. Engaging the cobbler fortnightly is a wasteful system.

'Monthly?' says Miss Evans. 'But, sir, I am afraid that way – not so much now, but once the winter weather comes – some girls may find both pairs out of repair, and a long time to wait until—'

'I do not think that is likely. But if it does transpire, I hope, Miss Evans, you will not countenance their making a fuss about it. They must simply have patience. The hardship in this is really very little, such as the true Christian will scarcely notice, and the system much more economical. Well, man, well, is my carriage ready or not?'

Charlotte's dreams: once enjoyed, now feared, but still as vivid as ever. The burning crib, as expected, makes its debut soon after sleep, the sound of it even worse than the sight. But in the black centre of the night these specific images always dissolve, and instead vast shapes of menace and dread and loss move across the landscape of Charlotte's dreaming mind. The nameless threat never concerns Maria and Elizabeth, perhaps because they are quietly breathing a few yards from her. Instead she cries without voice to Branwell, Emily and Anne, who are far off, but not so far that she cannot see, looming, obliteration: like a wave at the crest, about to fall.

They were up on the moors, the place Emily liked best for their walk, they had been shut in the house for a long time while it rained and rained, but now it was hot with just a few fat drips of rain here and there, when all at once they heard the big noise, it made a clap in her ears like hands but right in her head. Anne cried. Banny jumped round and round, his eyes stared, he said What was that was it a storm I don't think so. Sarah Garrs got hold of them by the hands and pulled them in close, you could smell the cloth of her skirts and what else was it, sweat. Hush Miss Anne hush now it's nowt. The ground Banny yelled feel the ground. There was a shake all through it like when you sat on the floor where it was just boards and feet walked past. Is it the end of the world Banny said. Oh hush hush but Sarah looked as if she would cry too, and Emily yes she felt the tears in that place near your throat where they grow (seed tears) and yet she felt too as if she could laugh or shout for joy or fall down in a faint. And then a man did shout but not for joy, he came down the track with a mule, he cried out to them go back, go back home, the bog's burst up at Crow Hill and there's a great flood of muck on its way that won't stop for nowt. He hit and hit the mule to make it go fast down the track. Sarah said run so they ran, in the way that most of the time they were told not to in case they fell, then it was wrong but now it was right, full pelt straight down the moor side. She could see the church and the roof of their house, they danced up and down in her sight as she ran. Now the rain fell in quick slaps, it felt like wet leaves. The church and the house were a long way off. Emily got Anne's hand and made a game, she said come on Anne let's see who can be first to reach the beck down there, for if it was the end of the world she thought Anne should not know, she was too small. Emily looked back once and at the top of Crow Hill it was all changed round, the land moved as if it were clouds, the way she loved to watch clouds when she lay on her back on the rough grass and the sky showed you how it lived. But this was the land, she saw it turn and glide like a huge snake on the top of the hill, and it was grand and fine though it made you gasp and cry, it would strike you down and make you die and you did not want that though a part of you said I want to stay and stand and look and let it get me. And when they got to a safe place that was an old barn and Sarah pulled them in and set their backs to a thick stone wall and thanked God then Emily sobbed and sobbed, and clutched at Banny and Anne and kissed them and thought home that's all I want my home and the ones I love all safe, and then Papa was there, he had come out to look for them, and said thank God thank God, and she shut out the small voice in her head that said I wish it had been the end of the world for then you could see, oh you could see what came next.

Passing through the Stanbury turnpike on his way back to Haworth, Mr Andrew, the surgeon, sees an unmistakable black figure striding the road ahead: hat crammed low, cravat up to his ears, like a bottle of unstable mixture corked up tight.

'Mr Brontë. Will you step up and ride, sir?'

Having set up his gig, Mr Andrew is a little self-conscious about it. So useful, with all the distance he has to travel to see his patients . . . yet look at Mr Brontë, older than him, and going everywhere on foot. One up for science, perhaps: reason goes on wheels, faith on legs.

'Thank you, Mr Andrew. My, a smart turn-out. You heard, of course, about yesterday's cataclysm?'

'The bog-burst, to be sure. A great piece of luck that no one was swept away.'

'My own children were out on the moors when it happened. A truly providential escape.' Mr Brontë's deep-set eyes glitter: he is excited. 'I have just been up to Crow Hill myself to study the site of the eruption. I found I was not alone. A great many carriage-folk there, come to gape and gaze. All to the good: one only hopes they may take in the moral as well as the spectacle.'

'Yes, it was an unhappy accident for the district. I saw Mr Townend this morning, and he fears the muddying of the water will stop his mill working for a week. Others too – and then there is the oat-crop—'

'These are small matters,' Mr Brontë pronounces. 'Trifling, when one weighs them in the balance. Do you know, Mr Andrew, when my children first heard the explosion and felt the tremor, they thought it was the end of the world?' He laughs, but not mockingly: no, with exultation and delight. 'Often the infant mind hits upon a truth that we miss.'

'Dear me.' Mr Andrew takes a firmer grip of the reins. 'You alarm me, Mr Brontë. Is this event to be shortly expected?'

Mr Brontë laughs again. 'Oh, as to that, sir, we can never know: that is why, as Christians, we must always be prepared. But you take my meaning, I am sure. When the Almighty speaks to us, whether it be the whisper of conscience or the rumble of the earthquake, we do well to listen.'

'Ah, I had not supposed the bog-burst exactly an earthquake, but—'

'No? How then would you characterise it?'

'From what I have heard and seen, a simple landslide, caused by heavy rain saturating the peat.'

'Oh, no, my dear sir, no, no, I feel there is a good deal more to it than that. The strange atmospheric conditions prevailing at the time – the livid electrical sky – from all that I have read, these are invariably associated with earthquakes. And then the fact that we were at once shown this awful power, and spared its worst effects – really the divine message could hardly have been clearer. The earthquake was a warning and reminder of the great day to come. I shall preach on it next Sunday. My text shall be from Psalm Ninety-seven: "The hills melted like wax at the presence of the Lord."'

Mr Andrew doesn't know what to say. Cool when sawing off a limb, he is squeamish with apocalypse. 'Indeed, apt, very apt. Well, thank heaven, certainly, that your children were safe, Mr Brontë. Tell me, how are the older girls faring at school?'

'Hm? Oh, very well: Cowan Bridge has been quite a boon. I mean to send Emily to join them shortly. Then, when Anne follows in due course of time, I fancy Miss Branwell will be glad to go home to Cornwall, and there will only be my son and I at the parsonage, which will allow a good deal of household economy, and enable me to concentrate on his education.' He shakes his head, faintly smiling. 'Mr Andrew, this is a shocking confession from a man of the cloth, but after Mrs Brontë died, you know, I actually questioned the ways of Providence when I looked at the path that lay before me. And yet now here is that path growing smoother.' He laughs again; there is in his high spirits something of the skittish horse, even down to the flashing roll of the eye. 'And when I stood before that scene of sublime destruction this morning, I seemed to hear these words spoken in terrible and yet kindly, yes, kindly, accents: "Where wast thou when I laid the foundations of the earth?" A lesson, Mr Andrew, a great lesson. I think I shall write to the *Leeds Mercury* on the subject.'

The surgeon winces a little at the thought of his friend making an exhibition of himself in print with his earthquakes and citations from Job. But he says nothing, for Patrick Brontë is not a man to be turned from his course; the very idea of opposing or challenging him gives Mr Andrew a certain pause, as if one should try to face down a large strange dog. And for the same reason he does not voice his thoughts about Cowan Bridge, about which he has heard things – discouraging things – from a fellow member of the medical profession. There is, he tells himself, only so much good he can do in this world.

'Another Brontë girl coming soon, I understand,' says Miss Lord to Miss Andrews, as they watch over the morning exercise in the garden. Call it exercise, anyway. Apart from a few beefy hoydens, the girls merely drift and droop in pairs and threes, like pinafored spirits in limbo. Miss Lord, her eyes on Miss Andrews's tight-jawed profile, is inserting a pin of mischief. 'They really are a clever family altogether – Miss Evans was saying so.'

'No doubt they are.'

'And I shouldn't wonder if Maria Brontë is the cleverest. Miss Evans found her helping one of the seniors with her French. Exceptional gifts, Miss Evans says.'

'Miss Evans does not have to endure the girl's carelessness and insolence from morning till night,' snaps Miss Andrews. 'The fact remains that Maria Brontë is one of those *dreamy* girls. They use their dreaminess as an excuse, and so they get away with things. But it won't wash with me.'

Miss Lord wishes she were brave enough to push in the pin that little bit harder and ask: Were *you* never dreamy, then? Did you never imagine a future different from this – working long dull hours for a pittance in the middle of nowhere? Looking at Miss Andrews, Miss Lord fancies the slamming down of lids: hears kittens drowned in a bucket. But then she partly understands – for there is something about the girls, and the dreamy ones especially, that makes you irritable. Perhaps it's the fact that they are doomed to the same lot as you, but it doesn't show: they go about with covert smiles and lit eyes, as if there were some possibility of escape they know of that you never found.

Queenie had six litters, thinks Miss Lord, and I was never allowed to keep one kitten. She reaches out to slap the ear of one of the juniors, who is giving her a look she simply cannot abide.

Tomorrow, Papa: bringing Emily.

'Miss Evans didn't say as much, but I'm sure he'll stay the night again, and so we shall probably be asked down to sup with him.' Thus

Maria, as the Brontë girls bundled. November now, and in the fireless dormitory it was easier to talk, simply because everyone bundled – huddled together in twos and threes in the beds – to get warm before candles out and separation. Still Maria, Elizabeth and Charlotte, wrapping and tangling arms and marbled legs, communicated in an urgent whisper. You never knew when one of the big girls, truffling for secrets, might push in; or, worst of all, whether Jane Moorhead might appear, flushed and giggling, thrusting her middle finger out from her hitched nightdress and grunting, 'Look at my wiggler, look at my wiggler. Feel it, go on, feel my wiggler . . .' That was her brother, she said; and she would carry on until she was crying with laughter, or at any rate crying.

'It will be wonderful to see Emily again,' said Elizabeth, adding – she had developed the gaolbird's humour – 'even here. Emily, my darling, come to me – or, better still, run for your life.'

Maria shook her head, her smile pained. 'I know, I know, but – we mustn't think like that, even joking. Emily will get a sense of it, and then she'll be upset. And there's Papa.' Charlotte shifted restlessly, kicking. Maria's face sought hers. 'Charlotte, you know why, I've explained why we can't tell him those things. Yes, sometimes it's hard, but this is what we have to do to help Papa, who has not much money, and so many important things to think of . . .'

What made Charlotte say it? This helpless sensation of them being one by one pulled over the edge, like the teacups when toddling Anne fell and dragged the tablecloth with her. And, perhaps, knowing that Maria was right; and perhaps her own smarting inferiority, knowing herself weak, selfish, protesting. It came out in a rush: 'That's easy for you to say, you *like* being scolded and made miserable, because then you can show off how you bear it and that makes you better than everyone else.'

The moment's shocked silence hung, then fell on Charlotte like a girder. She burst into tears. Did she really believe that about Maria? If not, where had it come from? Surely the devil.

Maria held her. 'Well. I don't know about liking to be miserable, but it's true, I do quite like to show off how I can take a whacking. But when you're good at something you do, don't you? And I'm good at getting whacked. Charlotte, dear, shush now. And you know – you agree – when we see Papa tomorrow, we're not going to mention these things, and worry him. Are we?'

Charlotte, face lodged in Maria's neck, shook her head. It was heathen to say goddess, but Maria appeared little less to her just then: attacked and traduced, she simply forgave. All you could do with such a being was hand over to her all your love and trust. Certainly you could never, ever be like her.

Papa, the next day: 'They are a credit to you and the school, Miss Evans. Upon my word, they seem quite older girls already.'

It ought to have made it better, Emily being there. It made it that much more like home, after all. It was one more person she loved, here, no longer missed. It put Charlotte back in the middle (sort of, nearly – she pictured Branwell's mathematical exasperation). It meant she was no longer the smallest and lowliest of the school. This was all good. But to Charlotte it didn't feel any better.

She told herself: That's because I'm sad for Emily, having to come to this dismal place as well, poor Emily should have been left at home . . . But she found that the human heart, or at any rate hers, didn't work like that; instead it muttered, ingloriously, *If I have to suffer, why not you?* No, it wasn't that. If anything she was jealous.

Emily, the baby of the school, looked it. Eyebrows crinkled and voices keened at the sight of her, as they never had with Charlotte. It was the right combination of prettiness and smallness – whereas *dear me, quite the little goblin* was what Charlotte had overheard on her own first day in the schoolroom. So Emily settled in, fussed over and petted. Of course she did her share of weeping in the first days (quite the sound of Cowan Bridge, this: as other buildings have their characteristic noises, a wind-note in the chimney, a knuckle-crack of floorboards, so Cowan Bridge leaked little sobs and moans from mortise and joist). But when the tears dried she was ready again, wide-eyed, for experience; ready for one of the big girls to take her on her knee and do Banbury Cross.

And then, Charlotte thought, Emily surely had no true picture of time – the weeks and months they would have to spend here. For her it was all today and tomorrow. Not yet nine years old, Charlotte envied her sister her innocence.

Still, you could never tell with Emily. She could be humming a tune or playing with her hair and suddenly she would come out with something. Like this: 'Oh, they're silly.'

'Who?'

'The big girls. The way they pet me.'

'You don't seem to mind it,' said Charlotte, jealousy like metal on her tongue.

Emily gave her sidelong listening look. 'Yes, that's what I am. Just a doll. They won't like me when I'm bigger.'

'They might,' Charlotte said, biting down.

Emily shook her head, smiling. 'Oh, no, they won't. I know that for sure.'

Very soon Emily saw for herself the persecution of Maria. Hard to tell what she was thinking, as the birch twigs swished and struck. She had a way, when faced with the unpleasant, of taking it in and then visibly fixing on something quite separate – an object, even a spot on the bare wall – and looking at it until her brow cleared. Sometimes she would even smile, the pure pleased smile of a baby shown its reflection.

For herself, Emily was uncomplaining. The grey cuisine dismayed her, but she had always been a tiny eater. As for the cold, she bore it better than all of them. With the onset of winter, that cold took lordly precedence at the school: the food, Miss Andrews's temper, the boredom of scripture-recital, all could only lag behind it. Cowan Bridge, isolated amid those brutal fells, drew winter to it: it garnered winds and sucked in snow. You were cold all the time, but Sunday was the freezing festival, the name-day of numbness.

For on Sundays, of course, the girls attended church, and that meant Tunstall, two miles away across the fields – the Reverend Carus Wilson's own church. Not that you could be sure it would be him officiating; often it was his curate, especially when the weather was bad. So, on Sunday mornings, you walked – trudged – splashed – slithered – crunched: you tilted your face into the wind, and learned to keep turning it so as to spread the pain, give that stinging ear a little respite, expose the least paralysed cheek. And once arrived, that was your day – church: morning and afternoon service, and too far to walk back in between, and so you stayed through, eating the bread and cheese you brought with you in a little mouldy room above the porch, like an inverted crypt. And you felt the stiff, soaked, cracked leather of your shoes contend with the stiff, soaked, cracked skin of your feet, until you could hardly tell which was which.

Back at Cowan Bridge, there was a stampede to the school-room fire. The younger ones were shut out, even petted baby Emily. Eventually a big girl might take pity and haul you into the crowding circle to cough and sniff, wafting damp, and feel the wonderful, almost terrible heat on your face, as if you were melting like wax.

Everyone, of course, coughed and sniffed more or less all the time. 'We're all sharing a rheum,' as Elizabeth put it one night in the dormitory; and that made Maria go off in one of her rare, long, helpless laughs. It ended in a paroxysm of coughing: deep, manlike coughing that Charlotte suddenly realized had been waking her lately in the night. Elizabeth watched, then took Maria's hand. 'And now tomorrow,' she said, 'I *am* going to tell Miss Evans.'

'Beef broth.'

The Reverend Carus Wilson, who has been scrutinising the registers, suddenly lifts his head and directs the words at Miss Evans.

'Sir?'

'When I consulted the kitchen records earlier, madam, I observed a dispensation of beef broth. I think this is no part of the girls' daily diet. A very extravagant one, if it is.'

'No, sir, that was the doctor's prescription for Maria Brontë. She has been very low, you may recall, with a sore throat and a persistent cough. Dr Pascoe suggested a strengthening treatment.'

'Ah . . .' Mr Wilson's face becomes sculpturally still. The doctor who attends sick pupils at Cowan Bridge is, naturally enough, another connection of Mr Wilson's – his brother-in-law, in fact – which is reflected in his fees. All the same Miss Evans suspects some strain in their relation. Dr Pascoe is inclined to scowl at the domestic arrangements of the school, even to mutter under his breath: 'No wonder, no wonder . . .' The graven image stirs. 'And was there an improvement?'

'No, sir. Indeed I wanted to—'

'Ah! I am not surprised. Altogether too rich.'

'Mr Wilson, I wanted to consult you about this very question. Maria Brontë. She continues rather poorly. The doctor saw her again yesterday—'

'He did not recommend more beef broth, I hope.' A kind of unhinging of the bottom half of his great face convinces Miss Evans that he is being jocular.

'He is going to try a blister treatment. He is concerned lest there is a consumptive condition. That is why I feel it may be best to write to Maria's father, and let him know about her state of health.'

'Hm. Is this Dr Pascoe's diagnosis, or only his suspicion? Come, you take my meaning. We are *in loco parentis* for the girls while they are here. If this girl is ill, then very well, let the doctor see her again, and let her be well cared for, just as if she were at home. But we cannot have parents and guardians summoned every time there is a sniffle. Remember, these girls are to be trained for a life of duty. We do a great harm to the daughters of poor clergy, if we let them think they are princesses.'

'Very well, Mr Wilson.' Miss Evans does not exactly stifle a sigh: they have all been stifled at source, and she would hardly know, now, how to let one out. She needs no telling about the life of duty. That is precisely the world she came from. There was a Mr Smith, who worked for an attorney, had an honest homely face, would have married her: for various reasons it did not do. And now she thinks, with a faint quake of the mind, that she would marry Mr Smith, or Mr Jones, or anyone who would ask her, tomorrow.

'Whereabouts is it?' Elizabeth asked, as they gathered round Maria's bed before candles out. Earlier the doctor had applied a blister to her side, to draw the feverish humours to the surface. 'Ooh. Does it hurt?'

'No, my dear, it's exquisite – what do you think? Actually it isn't as bad as it looks. I do feel as if it's taken the fever down a little.'

Elizabeth put a hand to Maria's forehead. 'Yes, a little. You're still pale.'

'That would be the bleeding,' Charlotte put in. 'Remember when you had the whooping-cough and Mr Andrew bled you, and Banny said you looked like a cream cheese?'

This was how they kept things going, and had done since Maria had begun to be ill. You did not ignore it: you were even quite chatty about it. What you strove to avoid was moments like the one yesterday, when Emily had grabbed Maria's wrist to show her something in the garden and then, staring at her own encircling fingers, had said wonderingly: 'Look, you've gone littler than me.'

'Did the doctor say anything about writing home?' Elizabeth said.

'No, no. He never talks about anything like that. Just "Show me your tongue, cough." It isn't his business.' Maria manoeuvred herself back against the pillow, wincing.

It wasn't his business, and the sisters could not make it theirs, because they were only allowed one letter home per term, a privilege long used up. It was up to Miss Evans, but over her, everyone knew, hung the shadow of Mr Wilson.

'Well, I shall pester her about it again, as soon as I see a fair opportunity,' Elizabeth said.

Maria shook her head. 'It will only worry Papa.'

'Well,' Elizabeth kissed her, smiling, 'just sometimes, you know, it may be right to worry Papa.'

When the servant lit the rushlights and clanged the waking bell the next morning, Charlotte, dressing, saw that Maria was feverish again. She was slow to disentangle herself from sleep and dream; wagging her sweat-capped head, she kept crying, 'Mama – Mama.'

Emily, half asleep herself, plodded across the cold floor and, propping herself on Maria's pillow, murmured: 'But you are Mama.'

Elizabeth urged her away, then helped Maria to sit up. 'A bad night?'

'Not good. Perhaps it's just the fever coming out, and once it does . . . I don't know.' Maria pushed back the blanket, reached for her stockings. Her thin legs lolled nerveless and stark. She looked at them. 'I don't feel as if I can get up. What shall I do?'

One of the big girls drifting by, brushing a heavy electrical cloud of hair, stopped and stared. 'Dear God, she should stay in bed. Tell Miss Evans. Or I'll tell her when we go down, if you like. They can't expect . . .'

And that was when Miss Andrews, whose bedroom was just off the dormitory, burst in scolding them to hurry, be quiet, look sharp, and so on. In fact – Charlotte could almost swear to it – she actually entered in mid-scold; and this taken with her smooth-haired bee-brisk neatness of appearance suggested that she had not been to bed at all, just gone into her room last night and seized up like the mechanical figure on a clock.

Now she was alive again and bristling; and everyone in the dormitory was out of bed except Maria. Charlotte saw what happened next as she had seen a cat take a bird: suddenly out of quietness this erupted, the horrid flurry too fast, at first, for anything but fascination, until you realised, saw the sad spread feathered fan held in jaws.

'Get up. Get up, you are a lazy – dirty – *slut* of a girl.' The language, from Miss Andrews, was familiar enough; but she punctuated it by seizing Maria's arm and pulling her bodily out of bed so that she went flying in a half-circle and landed slap, nightdress up, with a bony tumble in the middle of the floor. 'Now get dressed.'

There was a mutter – even a little more: Maria was clutching her side where the blister-scar must have torn; girls were standing and protesting. Miss Andrews, normally ready for confrontation, slipped away. Charlotte, rushing to Maria, felt herself propelled as if a chair were being pushed against the back of her legs. The chair was indignation, rage. Elizabeth was already there.

'I think I'd better get up after all,' Maria was saying. 'No, come on, don't make a fuss, it's done now. Look, I can stand, I can walk, I'll do very well. Charlotte, hush.'

'But what are we going to *do*?' Charlotte cried.

Maria and Elizabeth (she was in the middle) looked sadly at her.

'There isn't anything to do,' Maria said, her hand on Charlotte's shoulder. It was not gentle: it felt like a clothes-peg. 'It's as well to remember that, Charlotte. Now go on, hurry, you'll be late for prayers.'

Charlotte was not, but Maria, after her slow, painful dressing and washing, inevitably was. Miss Andrews, her eyes fixed just above Maria's head, held out the lateness badge.

And it was one of Mr Wilson's days. He materialised during the grammar lesson. Jane Moorhead was wearing a punishment badge too, for stealing a slice of bread, and so Charlotte hoped Maria might go unnoticed.

Ah, no.

'Maria Brontë. You wear a badge again. And you are the one with the little sister, are you not? Dear, dear. Point her out.' The Reverend Carus Wilson solemnly transported himself down the room to Charlotte's form. She gazed up as he stationed himself before her, windy breath humming and grumbling. His bulk blotted out the wintry window-light, cut her off from the sight of Maria. 'Well, what do you say to your sister, failing to set you an example not once, but twice? Is it not a sad thing to see her wearing the badge in front of you again? It is almost as if she doesn't care – as if she doesn't love you as a sister should!'

And for the second time Charlotte could not answer him. She could not articulate any of the flailing feelings inside her, could not even assert their existence by word or look. She could only quail in his shadow, as helplessly as if he had decided to walk straight over her with his huge flat feet.

But he could not, she found, stop her thinking. And she thought: I will answer you one day. She had no notion of how or when. It simply seemed that if she could not, then life was all wrong. And much of life was beginning to appear wrong now. Out of the corner of her eye she kept seeing the darkness, new, strong.

* * *

At last Miss Evans came to the dormitory to tell them.

'Maria, I have written to your father, and have his reply. He is coming to fetch you tomorrow. The doctor agrees – we all agree – that home is the best place for you, for now. I'm sure your sisters will help with your packing.'

It was unusual to see Maria cry. It made Charlotte want to cry too, though she knew she should be glad that Maria was going home. But the hard little voice of self would have its say, even if internally: *Only Maria?*

'I feel as if I'm deserting you,' Maria said the next morning.

'Nonsense,' Elizabeth said. 'Off you go and leave us to enjoy the delights of Cowan Bridge. We'll think of you. Every time we find gristle in the porridge, we'll think of you.' And tenderly she helped Maria put on her shoes.

Papa had put up at Kirkby Lonsdale overnight, and was at the school soon after breakfast. Charlotte watched his face carefully when he first set eyes on Maria. It gave little away. But his speech became ever more airy and elaborate, as it did when he was ill at ease.

'My dear, these are rather perturbing reports I hear of your health – and your aunt Branwell, you will readily conceive, is quite as concerned as myself; and she is in full agreement that the necessary recuperation of your energies may best be achieved at home, under our care. This, you will understand, Miss Evans, is no reflection on the attention she has received here, which I know will have been scrupulous. And I am glad to see, my dears, that you are thriving. I hope you have been a comfort to your sister while she has been poorly; and if you would continue to do so, you cannot do better than be dutiful and diligent scholars, which Maria will be very glad to think of while she rests at home . . .'

So to the outer gate, and the waiting gig. Maria had been silent, and at the last she could only offer them each a sketchy kiss, and say: 'Well, I shall see you soon,' which she grimaced at as if she were disappointed by her own stupidity. For a moment she looked as severe on herself as Miss Andrews. Then Papa lifted her up into the gig. And it was like this: when you go to pick up a jug or a kettle thinking it's full, and instead it's empty, and your arm goes swooping up with the unexpected lightness. That was Maria as Papa lifted her, swooping up and printing a brief stick-limbed pattern on the bare acid February sky. Maria and Papa's eyes met in astonishment; and then they laughed a little, in the way of adults, passing something quickly off.

Charlotte said: 'I hope Miss Andrews won't take it out on you now. Now that Maria's not here.'

It was exercise, and they were skulking up and down under the veranda, shivering and wrapping their hands in their pinafores.

'I doubt it,' Elizabeth said. 'I'm not clever like her. No, no, I'm not. That's why I'm not doing the accomplishments – drawing and music and all that. You need those to be a governess.'

'Am I doing the – accomplishments?' Emily said. She made a sort of rich splash of the word.

'Yes, Em, you are. I shall probably look after Papa and the house when I'm older.'

'Oh, when will that be – and will I be there too?' Emily cried: sudden homesickness pulsed in every word.

'I don't know – well, yes, if you like. It will be a few years from now.'

'How long is that? Where is it?'

'It's not a where, Emily, it's a when,' Charlotte said.

'Show me the when. Show me a picture,' Emily snapped.

Elizabeth gathered them both closer. 'Well, think of when we walk to church on Sundays. You know there's a stile you climb, and just then it slopes down and that's when you can see the church tower? Well, that's where the when is. A fair way – but not that far.'

They are only a very little way – a few steps – down that time-road when the news comes.

Spring at Cowan Bridge: it has so many of the archetypal properties that any passing poet (on his way, say, up the Kendal road to the dependable inspiration of the Lakes) could do worse than pause here and get up some material. Lambs side-stepping on the flowered hillsides, the beck all noisy crystal, a green dream of valley below: roll out the pentameter. Omit, perhaps, that quadrangular building just past the bridge – or devote just a line to its rugged walls, 'gainst stormy blasts secure.

For spring at Cowan Bridge manifests itself less decorously inside the school: place of damp warmth and brimming chamber-pots, and a pernicious low fever. In vain does Miss Andrews buzz and dart and chide, as the girls prop their heavy heads on their hands, and smack their flaky lips, trying to remember the kingdoms of the Anglo-Saxon Heptarchy, or indeed their own names. The Reverend Carus Wilson has visited, beheld, and gone away again in perplexity. He cannot help thinking there must be a moral dimension to this: his mind hovers over biblical plagues, and he longs to give the girls a spiritual cross-examination. But he must consider the young Wilsons, and beware infection. Though it goes hard with him, he must also consider the advice of his brother-in-law, the doctor, who has roundly declared that the food at the school is not fit for pigs, that an epidemic of typhus is brewing under its roof, and that just now there must be more concern for the girls' bodies than their souls.

The Brontë girls have been lucky. Charlotte and Emily have escaped the infection altogether: Elizabeth has been rather low and sickly, but this is perhaps the remnant of the chesty cold she caught not long after Maria went home. They are able to take advantage of the new dispensation – Dr Pascoe insists on lots of fresh air for those girls who can stand up – and go walking daily in the river-meadows, even though Elizabeth tires much more quickly than her younger sisters. They are returning from one of these outings when Miss Evans, with a letter in her hand, watches them from her sitting-room window, sighs; rings the bell for the maid.

With great patience and fortitude – the phrases from the letter Miss Evans read out to them kept appearing in Charlotte's mind – *with the serenest faith in the mercy of her Maker . . . peacefully and quietly departed this life . . . the light of heaven on her face . . . all who saw her . . .*

But something kept obliterating them: images from the words and works of the Reverend Carus Wilson, pasted across them like hasty garish posters. *A bad girl . . . God struck her dead . . . she left this world in the midst of her sin.* Frantically she ripped them down. *Look at that bad child . . . she is afraid to die, for she knows she may go to hell . . . How sad it is to think of!*

'Papa wouldn't lie, would he?' Charlotte cried. 'Not even to make us feel better.' Miss Evans, in deference to the occasion, had had their dinner brought to her sitting-room and, after praying with them, had left the sisters alone. 'It must be true what Papa wrote. About Maria—'

'It's true that she's dead,' said Elizabeth. 'I should have thought that was enough to think of.' She crumbled bread in her fingers, scattering it on the floor; then lifted heavy, blank eyes. 'Sorry, Charlotte. I can't make it better.'

In bed that night Emily kept starting up from a recurring nightmare and clutching and tugging at Charlotte. 'Don't go near the edge,' she moaned, 'come away from the edge, you'll fall off.'

At last one of the big girls snarled through the dark: 'Tell that silly little bitch to be quiet. I want to sleep. I'm sick.'

Another: 'Shush, didn't you hear? Her sister died of a consumption.'

A pause, and then a groan. 'She's lucky.'

Maria was buried in the vault at Haworth church on the twelfth of May. At Cowan Bridge, Elizabeth and Charlotte and Emily stood holding hands by the gate where they had last seen her: it was all they could think of. Charlotte stared at the sky, remembering the swooping silhouette. When she moved her eyelids they felt like rusty gratings. It was true what Elizabeth said: she couldn't make it better. Elizabeth had started to mutter a prayer, then given it up. Prayers at Cowan Bridge were ten a penny: cheapened goods.

Suddenly Emily's face shone. 'I know – let's go and pick flowers.'

'What for?' said Charlotte.

'For Maria, of course.'

She doesn't really understand after all, Charlotte thought. But Elizabeth shook off her listlessness for a moment, even trying a smile, and said: 'I think that's a very good idea.'

Emily seized her hand. 'Come on, then.'

'No, no. You two go.' Elizabeth slipped from her grip. 'I think I'll rest a while.'

For the next fortnight Elizabeth did a lot of resting; but she never seemed to get any less tired.

She was, at least, not lonely in the dormitory. A good half of the girls went down with the fever. When Dr Pascoe came at the end of May he strode about harshly cheerful: well, well, this will never do. But later someone said there were raised voices in Miss Evans's lodging. And he was there the next morning, arms folded, when Miss Evans made a special announcement to the whole school before prayers.

'Girls, because there is so much fever at the school we have decided – in consultation with Mr Wilson – that those of you who are well enough should be moved to a more salubrious air. Mr Wilson owns a house on the coast at Morecambe Bay, and has most generously agreed that you may be accommodated there until the infection is in abeyance. The doctor will examine you, and decide who is to go and who is to stay. I shall have your trunks sent up before dinner. We must waste no time.'

The sea! Disloyal excitement came fluttering through the shades of Charlotte's grief for Maria and anxiety for Elizabeth, and would not be batted away. Oh, if she could only go to the sea . . . Dr Pascoe passed swiftly among them, feeling brows, peeling back eyelids, peering into throats. 'You go . . .' Emily. 'You go . . .' Charlotte. She let the excitement in. This might be the good thing they needed – good things, after all, must happen. Sea air might be the very thing to set Elizabeth up, especially as they would be away from all the memories that haunted the school. Surely Elizabeth could go: she was not as feverish as some of the girls, she was just a little low and chesty . . .

Dr Pascoe spent longer with Elizabeth than anyone else.

'Well,' she said, when Charlotte and Emily pressed round her, 'yes, I'm going, but not to the seaside. I'm going home –' and her voice broke, just for a moment, like a thread dropped but at once picked up and held taut and firm '– I'm going home straight away, like Maria. The doctor says it's best. So I'd better get ready.'

No summoning of Papa: no time, Charlotte supposed, with half the school preparing to vacate. (Or just no time?) The cobbler's wife was to accompany Elizabeth on the coach to Keighley. We must waste no time. Again the sisters stood at the gate. The breeze blew Elizabeth's hair, unshorn through her illness, across her nose and lips: it seemed to cling like a clammy web, but she did not move to brush it away. Going home like Maria. Charlotte did not know what to say. If she did try to speak, she thought, only wails, garglings, jungle noises would come out. Elizabeth did not kiss her, or Emily. Yes, I'm going, but not to the seaside. The cobbler's wife, sadly kind, motherly, told them to buck up. Again the gig wheels grumbled, paused, went away. Emily was staring with devouring concentration at a clump of moss on the gatepost. Charlotte took her hand, urged her inside. Packing to be done. She had a sensation of sockets and cavities, of cold air seeping where there should be none.

And after all she did not see the sea. The coach brought the first clutch of girls, including Charlotte and Emily, to Morecambe Bay when it was late and dark. A few were energetic enough to romp around the bedrooms when they reached Mr Wilson's summer house, to fling open the windows, say they could smell it, could see the waves coming up the beach. Charlotte busied herself getting out her own and Emily's nightgowns. Yes, I'm going, but not to the seaside. You go. You go. The sea. I'll see you soon. Doctor says it's best. I can't make it better. Look at that bad child. Charlotte wanted only to hide her head in sleep. In sleep you could dream, and in dreams you could see Maria again – so vividly that this time, perhaps, she would be real, touchable. The sea was nothing but an idea.

As for the next day, it was devoted to unpacking and settling in, with the vague promise that later there might be a walk down to the sea once their tasks were done . . . Then it was all cut off for ever by a loud, hard knocking at the front door.

'Papa.'

Emily recognised his voice first, and ran down to the hall. At Cowan Bridge you would never dare do such a thing, but perhaps they already knew that Cowan Bridge was over, for them. Charlotte ran after her.

In the hall she found Papa on his knees, embracing Emily. For a moment Charlotte froze in shock. She had never seen him kneel before: it was like a final confirmation of a world turned irredeemably upside down. Then he opened his arms again, calling her to him. Awed, she stumbled forward. His face, a white wedge against Emily's brown curls, transfixed her. He looked exhausted, harried, desperate – and also somehow furious. But not with anyone or anything: to them he spoke gently, to Miss Evans, hovering close by, with his usual courtesy. It was somewhere inside.

'The doctor's decision was to send Elizabeth home at once,' Miss Evans was saying, 'and so there was no possibility of sending word. How does she do, Mr Brontë? I fear the journey will have sadly tired her . . .'

'She is poorly, ma'am. But home, certainly, is the best place for her, and I think for all my girls, things being as they are. The seaside retreat is an excellent notion, but . . .' he rose stiffly to his feet '. . . please be good enough to have Charlotte and Emily's things packed at once, for we are going home.'

Some more children's stories.

Maria Brontë left the Clergy Daughters' School, Cowan Bridge, in ill health on 14 February 1825, and died at home on 6 May.

* * *

Waking up on her first morning back at Haworth Parsonage, Charlotte blinked at Emily sleeping ferociously beside her, listened to the big booming coughs coming from nearby, and thought: I'm at Cowan Bridge, and that's Maria coughing. When realisation of the truth came, it was such a harlequin mixture of good and bad that she could only hide under the blankets from the dreadful dazzle. Though this did not muffle the coughs.

Mary Eleanor Lowther left the Clergy Daughters' School, Cowan Bridge, in ill health on 27 January 1825, and did not return to the school.

'No, no,' Papa said absently, 'you will not be returning to Cowan Bridge.'

Charlotte squeezed Emily's hand. 'Thank you, Papa.'

He looked over at Aunt. She was in mourning: though curiously you hardly noticed it. It was her natural plumage. 'The enterprise was not successful, Miss Branwell. I shall not hazard any more on it. We shall find some other way of proceeding. In the meantime I am concerned only to – to preserve what I have.'

Aunt nodded. 'Well, Mr Brontë, you are owed a refund of fees, at any rate. Don't let them forget it.'

Mary Chester left the Clergy Daughters' School, Cowan Bridge, in ill health on 18 February 1825, and died at home on 26 April.

Branwell slept in Papa's bedroom while his was used as the sickroom for Elizabeth. He didn't mind; but he didn't want to go in there to see her – which was the only way, as within three days of arriving home she was too weak to get out of bed.

'You ought to,' Charlotte told him, with a kind of righteous prickle; they even had a tussle on the landing over it. She did it, and it was horrible. Elizabeth looked strange, lying there – like a queen, you might have said in different circumstances – and you didn't know what to say to her.

'I saw Maria,' Branwell retorted savagely. 'I watched Maria. I don't want to see any more of that.'

'It's not the same. Elizabeth isn't . . .'

'What?' He was implacable. 'What isn't she?'

'She can't die too. It just doesn't . . .' She struggled: she needed some such image as Branwell had shown her when he had demonstrated mathematically that she couldn't be in the middle. 'It doesn't work out.'

Branwell merely shook his head over that. 'She looks the same,' he said, and hugged the newel-post, digging his cheek against it until a red welt flourished on his fair skin. 'Just the same.'

Elizabeth Robinson left the Clergy Daughters' School, Cowan Bridge, in a decline on 1 March 1825, and died at home on 29 April.

Mr Andrew said: 'Her decline is very rapid, Mr Brontë. May I ask if there is a history of consumption in your family?'

Patrick looked vaguely surprised, then put an unsteady hand to his column of cravat. 'Not perhaps a history – but I myself have always been a little vulnerable about the respiratory organs.'

'This is more than vulnerability . . . Well, she is very patient, sir. As her poor sister was. I should tell you that I do not think she will have to be long patient.'

Isabella Whaley left the Clergy Daughters' School, Cowan Bridge, on 2 April 1825, and died at home of typhus fever on 23 April.

Branwell asked: 'What was it like there? Maria would never really say.'

It was a beautiful day to be on the moors. A skylark invited location somewhere above, a glinting needle of song in a haystack of blue. The turf yielded fragrantly; bees rode the warm air. But Charlotte only had to think a moment, and cold doors clanged around her. Branwell watched her face.

'You couldn't get near the fire,' she said at last. 'The big girls shut you out so. You hung about, hoping . . . But mostly you had to imagine yourself warm. You had to have the fire inside.'

Charlotte Banks left the Clergy Daughters' School, Cowan Bridge, with a spinal illness on 19 May 1825, and did not return to the school.

Anne, not usually one to pester or cling, kept putting her arms round Charlotte's neck. At last, a timid, longing whisper: 'You won't go funny like Elizabeth, will you?'

★ ★ ★

Jane Allanson left the Clergy Daughters' School, Cowan Bridge, in ill health on 30 May 1825, and did not return to the school.

They were not encouraged to come far into the sickroom now. From where she stood Charlotte could see Elizabeth lying on her side: just a bony hollow of cheek, an incredibly long eyelash. And she couldn't be sure that Elizabeth was talking to her, or to anyone, when she breathed out, 'I'm sorry.'

Elizabeth Brontë left the Clergy Daughters' School, Cowan Bridge, in ill health on 31 May 1825, and died at home on 15 June.

Church and churchyard could hardly have been closer, and they already wore mourning, so preparing for the funeral hardly felt exceptional at all, any more than getting ready for their daily walk – except for the smallish coffin resting on a trestle in the hall. And except for the fact that they would not, could not, move.

The door was open. Aunt took Papa's arm. The bearers coughed, shuffled, then shouldered. Charlotte, Branwell, Emily and Anne clustered at the foot of the stairs: clustered, then stuck.

'I'm not going.' Emily, white-lipped, gripping Anne's hand, staring at nothing. 'We're not going.'

'You've got to go. It doesn't make it not real if you don't go,' hissed Charlotte. It was all compressed in sharp, rapid whispers, the thoughts too.

'Elizabeth wouldn't mind, Maria wouldn't mind – they always understood everything.'

'You've got to go, it isn't fair, I had to go with Maria,' Branwell said. 'So did Anne. Why are you different?'

'I don't know. It's just too awful.'

'We're all going. We must all be together.' Charlotte squeezed it out through a narrow sob. They were all more or less crying, though from different places. 'That's what Maria and Elizabeth would say.'

'Go on then.' Emily sniffed.

'No – Banny, you should go first.'

'Why?'

'You're the boy, you should follow Papa.'

Branwell shook his head violently. 'No, you go. You're the eldest. I can't . . . You go first, Charlotte.'

So she had to. She went first; after the coffin (so light, swooping up), after Aunt and Papa, she led the way, and stepped out into the gentle sunlight with such a feeling of stinging, merciless exposure that she wanted to throw up her arms in protection against a world besetting her; a world where there was no longer any middle to inhabit, only edge, brunt, naked extremity.

PART TWO

So hopeless is the world without;
The world within I doubly prize.

Emily Brontë, 'To Imagination'

1

The Walls of Freedom

'What's out there?' Charlotte cries, sitting up in bed, unable to restrain herself, unable *not* to say it though she knows the answer: the wind. Even in summer it is a noisy neighbour; now, with winter setting in, it becomes an occupying force, unchecked and potent.

Emily sits up beside her, rubbing her eyes. 'That banging,' she says. 'That's the outhouse door again.'

Charlotte listens: gropes for the homely shape in that raving puzzle of noise. 'Oh, yes.' She lies back, stiffly. 'Yes, of course it is.' Inside she turns irritably on herself. This is not good; I'm the eldest; I should be doing what Maria and Elizabeth used to do, taking charge, reassuring. Instead—

'There is something out there,' she cries, jerking up: yes, the wind, but surely mere air can't produce these shriekings, these physical poundings . . .'

Emily, yawning, gets out of bed and tiptoes to the window.

'What are you doing?'

'Opening the shutter to look. I just thought – it might be Maria and Elizabeth.'

'Stop it.'

It's too dark to see Emily's expression, but her voice sounds startled, even a little hurt. 'Well, it might be. That's not frightening, is it? I was never frightened of Maria and Elizabeth.'

'They're in *heaven*.' For a moment the moon face of the Reverend Carus Wilson rears up. *Look at that bad child.*

'Oh, I know that.' Emily is shaken by a sudden great yawn, shivers, darts back to bed. 'I just thought they might have come to see us.' Within seconds she is asleep, as if she has wrapped this idea luxuriously around her; leaving Charlotte with nowhere to go but her dreams.

* * *

Inanimate objects: things that do not have life. It may be questioned, really, whether there are any such things. Like the ever-present wind around Haworth that haunted Mrs Brontë as she lay dying – the wind that never dies. There is nothing to break it, of course. This is, after all, an artificial landscape, just as much as a drained fen or a Dutch polder. Many generations ago, those high moors were forested hills. Then the first farmers cleared and burned and grew crops, and exhausted the soil; soon it was barren, good for nothing but heather. Even the few trees that subsist here are of such twisted and tortured shape that they seem rather to have agonisingly clawed themselves up from the horizontal than to have grown shootwise. So the wind has the wasted land to itself. It is not alive, but it is very lively.

Or take the long-case clock that stands on the half-landing, seven steps up the stone staircase of the parsonage. Inanimate; impassive, certainly. It ticks away unaffected by the drastic change in the house, the subtraction of two young lives from the vital sum. To be itself it only needs winding, and this Patrick punctiliously performs on the way up to his early bed. But look at the two of them together: the way Patrick lifts his face to the clock-face as he finishes winding, as if to say, *Is that all right?* and then peers at his pocket-watch, and then proceeds up the stairs, his footsteps as grave and methodical as the rhythm of the pendulum. Is there not, perhaps, a little of the clock in Patrick – a little of Patrick in the clock?

Or take this pair of pattens, leather and wood on an iron ring, airing by the kitchen fire. Neat and dainty and clean – peculiarly clean, in fact, for overshoes. But, then, these pattens are not used for going out. Aunt Branwell never goes anywhere, except to the church on Sunday. She wears the pattens indoors, with the fastidious aim of never allowing her feet to touch that cold northern stone. So when she clip-clops about the parsonage in these, she is, as it were, not setting foot in Yorkshire: she is still walking in Cornwall. Inanimate objects, but surely not lifeless.

Or take this book. Given, as it says on the flyleaf, to dear Maria by her loving father. Now it is certainly not put away – as in a sense its owner has been put away; in this household, books are to be read. And so it is, and the readers pause at that flyleaf, reflect, see. This book lives.

Now a short fancy-flight over the moors to the town of Leeds – slip by the mill chimneys and gaunt new terraces, through the soot-haze of modernity, alight at the old shopping street of Briggate: bow windows, glovers and hatters, servants carrying parcels. Into this well-appointed toyshop. Everything here from coral teething-rings and pewter feeding-bottles to dolls and ninepins and Noah's arks to stick-horses with manes of real hair and silk reins. Toy soldiers aplenty – lead, tin, wood, elaborate or rudimentary. The ones we're interested in are not on display yet: a box of twelve wooden ones, not long arrived from Birmingham, still on a shelf in a back room smelling of sawdust.

Peep under the lid. Not crudely made, quite well finished: little painted epaulettes, an attempt at faces. Still, these really are inanimate objects. You can't say they're alive.

No: not yet.

'No, not yet. I have no thoughts of sending them to any sort of school again just now. The very subject is an unhappy one to them, which I quite comprehend. The experiment in cheap schooling was – well, Miss Branwell, you will agree that it was expensive.' It is noticeable that Patrick will never mention Cowan Bridge by name. This necessitates some circumlocution, but he is adept at that. 'Let the memories of the former establishment fade. In the meantime I shall direct them on the road to learning myself, as far as my limited time allows.'

Patrick's time, strangely, seems even more limited since the deaths of his two eldest children. Parish business fetches him away, or occupies him in the study, for longer periods, and his early hour of retiring becomes earlier. It's as if he is, literally, making himself scarce.

'Boh! Madam Mope!'

Branwell bursts upon Charlotte as she sits curled in the window-seat. If only Papa would allow curtains, she could be hidden and private.

'What are you doing?' he demands, squeezing up beside her.

'Reading.'

'No, you're not, the book's closed. Are you thinking again?'

'No.' She presses her cheek against the glass. 'I'm remembering.'

'Well, that's a sort of thinking too.' He scrambles round on to his knees, stares out at the churchyard with its log-jam of tombstones. 'Does it still hurt?'

Charlotte can only nod.

'I tried this.' He gives himself a couple of smart blows on his carroty head, beaming at her all the while. 'When the thinking got too sad. It didn't work.'

'I should imagine it made you sadder,' she says, reluctantly thawing.

Branwell laughs, flattens his nose grotesquely against the glass, then huffs to mist it, draws a cat with his forefinger, halfway through alters it to a man in a hat, rubs it away. All this in moments. Often it is as if Branwell changes his mind between blinks, and being with him is like holding a bird: that pitter-pattering, almost excessive life.

'I like thinking,' he says decisively, 'and it's a shame when you can't think without it making you sad. Don't you agree?'

Part of her still wants to hide: to reject this mental chessboard he is turning towards her. But she bends, makes the move. 'Well, what's the answer? To be stupid and not think at all?'

'I suppose then you wouldn't feel sad, but you wouldn't really feel anything, so that's no good . . . Charlotte, do you ever think about things that aren't real?'

'No,' she says faintly, unable to meet his glowing eyes, and effectively saying *Yes* in the loudest accent. His grin recognises it.

'When you think about them, you really *see* them – don't you? I do. Oh, I don't mean ghosts or anything like that. Or remembering things either. I mean things you make up in your head.' He swings abruptly round, setting his back to the window and the graveyard, and dangles his skinny legs beside hers. His expression is seraphic. 'And they don't hurt. They're the best things of all. Oh, I like 'em.'

His words are sweetmeats over which Charlotte hovers, fascinated and tempted. Yes, yes, absolutely: but isn't it wrong? And *wrong* is powerful to Charlotte, the deepest magic. Is it wrong? Even now her mind makes a momentary turning – oh, Maria will know – and then staggers back again from that wall of everlasting silence.

What's out there?

Ask Mrs Tabitha Aykroyd, or Tabby as she is soon known at the parsonage, and she will tell you: lots of things. Fairishes, haunts, boggarts, giant black dogs with eyes like saucers. No stick or stone without its story: the ruined house where a man accused of witchcraft hanged himself, the devil's clawmarks on the barn wall, the crossroads where the white woman stands on midsummer evenings . . . What's out there? Things like that.

Yet curiously, when Tabby tells of them, they do not terrify – or they terrify in a good way. To understand this, you have to meet Tabby; as at first Charlotte did with mistrust, for Tabby was a sort of consequence of Cowan Bridge.

While Charlotte and her sisters were at the school, Nancy and Sarah Garrs both left the parsonage to marry. In their place, a single servant was engaged – all that was needed, it seemed, with four of the girls away practically the whole year round (Cowan Bridge being as frugal with vacations as with nourishment). So, when Charlotte returned home bereft and lost, it seemed to her only right – meaning appropriately, predictably wrong – that this stranger should be presiding over the misshapen household. Charlotte was ready to hate her.

Except that, right from the beginning, there was nothing of the stranger about Tabitha Aykroyd. It wasn't just that she had lived all her fifty years in Haworth, and could describe their mother's face and the way she trimmed her bonnet and could remember the first time Anne had appeared in church and the way she had squeaked in wonder at seeing her father up in the pulpit. Somehow there was no distance to be got over. The very first time Tabby raked Charlotte's hair with a hard brush her touch, even in its ungentleness, was familiar.

'And you'll be sick as a dog, Master Branwell, if you keep spinning round like that. Then we shall all have to hark at you greeting and feeling sorry for yoursen while bedtime.' That was Branwell exactly. Tabby knew them, it seemed, before she knew them. And now it is as if she has always been here: leather-faced, organ-voiced, snowy-aproned Tabby who, though not an overlarge woman, gives a robust impression of hips and shoulders and needing plenty of leeway.

What's out there? When nightmares shake Charlotte out of bed with these words on her lips, Tabby responds with her own peculiar practicality.

'If you want to get shut of bad dreams, you mun set your shoes right when you go to bed. Not with the toes pointing same way – set them t'other ways, coming and going. Then you'll rest easy all night.'

It works – or, at least, it seems to help. Branwell scoffs at such things. 'Superstition.' He has just learned the word, and is liberal with it. 'Aunt says it's all superstition, and heathen.' Superstition is the faces Tabby sees in the kitchen fire, where the children gather after tea; it is the sea-urchin shell she calls a fairy-loaf and keeps for luck in her apron pocket. But, then, Tabby knows her scripture, too. She can defend herself in good, godly terms. When she bakes bread, she always makes a cross on the dough. 'Crossing the witches out,' she calls it. 'Now whether there are real witches about or not, I can't say, Master Branwell, but there's one in the Bible, the Witch of Endor, and that's good enough for me.'

But Branwell is fascinated by her in any case: the way she is never at a loss. If, as she says, there are fairishes in the valley-bottom, why has he never seen them? Oh, they are few nowadays compared to when Tabby was a girl. Why? Because of the building of the mills: the mills drove them away, for they don't care for machines. There is always a *because*; and in the long narrative of reminiscence that is Tabby's life, one thing always leads to another. There was the grim death of her father: protracted and painful, and ominously foreshadowed in diverse ways. 'He had three cousins who took sick of the same, and all died on it inside a year. Mind, I'd seen what was coming from the bed-linen. I went to put on a clean sheet one day, and there in the middle were the coffin-shape in the folds, clear as noon. And the next day they brought him home on a board, as weak as a kitten. Mortal hard dying he had of it.'

How horrible . . . yet you don't stay there, contemplating the horror, because you must move on with the story, another sheet unfolds, life reveals another shape. 'He had one last cousin, who lived over Keighley-ways, and he came over to see him before he died, and that were a shock, for they'd fallen out and for years they wouldn't speak if they met in the street. And now it came out why, and it were all on account of what Mr Aykroyd's father had done to his sister, his cousin's mother, years ago, swindling her out of a legacy as should have been hers . . .'

So the flow never ends, no conditions can ever dry it up or freeze it solid: there is always another story. Even death cannot stop stories. And Charlotte finds her nightmares diminishing (not disappearing) and finds, with the coming of Tabby, that good is not only a thing that is relentlessly subtracted from human life but can be added too. Though it is Emily who seems most drawn to Tabby – or, rather, *impressed* by her, as she is by black storm-clouds, by Branwell's grandest and most brazen farts, by a word. (*Reverie*. That is a favourite, found in Byron. They use it in bed, when they re-invent life through talk. Are you asleep? No, I have fallen into a reverie. Is it a deep one? Yes, it goes all the way through the earth to China.)

What's out there? The world – and nothing inanimate about that. Rather, it's like a host, a multitudinous enemy camped just beyond the fires and sentries. Lately it made that brutal raid, dragged two of our number away, whisked them into the night before they could cry out. So we must be ever more vigilantly on our guard: we must stick closely, closely together.

* * *

'Charlotte, haven't you finished with it yet? It's my turn.'

'No, Banny, you had it till five o'clock. I counted,' says Emily. 'You can read it with me, if you like.'

'Let's see – no, I've read that page. Oh, did you see the poem just before that? It's astounding, mag-nificent.'

'It's pretty, but it's too long. And what does "lambent" mean?'

'Gentle. No, strong. I'm not sure. I'll ask Papa later. But it *sounds* good.'

Emily: 'Read the poem out, Charlotte.'

'It's rather sad. It might upset Anne.'

'Oh, please read it, I won't cry, I promise. I'm giving up crying. It's too contemptible.'

The little room above the hall – the children's study, as they call it – is the place: the publication is the latest number of *Blackwood's Magazine*, a literary review. The room is cold, without carpet or fire, the periodical superficially unattractive – paper-covered, thick as a ledger, with dense unrelieved columns of print. But something is sparking here.

'Contemptible?' laughs Branwell. 'Where did you get that from?'

'The *Arabian Nights* book.'

'You can't read that, can you?'

'Of course she can, we've been reading it together,' says Emily. 'Go on, Charlotte – the poem.'

No fire, but something is burning here. Outside the wind raves and mutters to itself, a forgotten lunatic. What's out there? Only the world. Nothing we need concern ourselves with.

When church business took Patrick to Leeds he usually performed shopping commissions for Aunt Branwell also. Huckaback towelling, Mr Brontë, if you will be so good, and sugar-soap; and my snuff, Gordon's mixture if it is to be had, but do not on any account go out of your way . . . Patrick, a painstaking and thrifty shopper, got it all at the lowest price, then crossed Commercial Street to his barber's. Haircut, simple and severe: he remembered how, even after his marriage, he used to like it brushed forward and over the ears in the style *à la* Titus. More an antique Roman than a Dane. Quite the coxcomb I was, he thought, and saw with dismay the pepper-and-salt colour of the chopped locks falling to the floor. Not pepper-and-salt, though: greying hair has no colour. Is it true that grief whitens hair? Tabby told tales of people going grey overnight from shock.

Patrick did not discount them. It was always his belief that anything was possible. (A terrifying belief to come true.) In a discreet alcove hung lustrous wigs: a furtive purchase now. When he was a lad in Ireland, you weren't decently dressed without a good, solid horsehair wig, standing up off your head with sausage curls at the side. The barber talked of wool prices and hard times. All times are hard, thought Patrick, as he watched his shorn head slowly waltz in the barber's mirror, nodded it in approval: last year I buried my favourite child, this year she is still dead. Before leaving he bought a small bottle of perfume to sprinkle on his handkerchief; it was summer, the typhus season, and he would have many sick visits. When he stepped out into the sun the barber's boy was sweeping the floor, and Patrick's hair was mingling with other hair, irretrievably; and he thought of the vault in Haworth church.

His gaze was down as he picked his way through the refuse of the street: she was there, almost touching him, before he saw her.

'Now, sir, I know you'll forgive me being forward, but it's your face, I can't resist your face . . .' He breathed the peculiar staleness of drink on an empty stomach. A beggar: poor young creature, he could afford a few pennies but she must know that liquor would only aggravate her miseries . . . To his shock he found his hand seized: she was nudging him into a doorway, covertly pressing his hand to her warm side. He peered at the painted face. Not so young. Not begging. Dear Lord in heaven, she must be far gone in desperate degradation – broad daylight, and a man of the cloth . . .

'My child, stop, think of what you are doing.' With difficulty he disengaged his hand. 'I know the liquor clouds your mind, your conscience too. Only think for a moment. Don't you know who I am?'

Readily she said: 'No, sir, I don't, and that's the honest truth, and so don't let that stand in your way. As far as I'm concerned—'

'For pity's sake, you are addressing a minister of God, does that mean nothing to you?'

'Well, now, I know that ministers can get lonely too, just like everyone else . . .' her hand, unthinkably, was invading him . . . 'yes, I know that from experience, like, and I say there's nowt wrong with it. There now, why shouldn't you have a little pleasure? You're flesh and blood, why shouldn't you?'

'Stop it.' She did not: her pretty draggled face hovered close. There was nothing else for it: he pushed. Drunk, weak, she reeled, hit the door, nearly fell. Across the street a head turned. Patrick tried to speak, to take command, but she forestalled him, blurrily smiling.

'Oh, is that how you like it, sir? Pardon me, but I think I see you do. Well, that's quite in order likewise, sir – you only had to say the word . . .'

He ran from her. He ran blind with something – anger, fury, some emotion he could not identify, hideously resembling shame. He remained sufficiently himself to avoid knocking anyone over, to keep up a muttered litany of *by your leave*s and *pardon me*s even though he was blind and mad. He thought he heard laughter behind him: who?

At last he stopped, hands on knees, panting. He was in a side-street he did not recognise. Above the roofs a church steeple wavered in smoke and soot: that meant nothing to him either. He began to walk stiffly forward, but only because his body would not permit stillness. For the first time, it seemed to him, since he had boarded the boat from Ireland, Patrick did not know where to go. This feeling – it needed to be discharged, he wished he could pack it into his pistol and blast it away. Pray: pray for that poor wretched creature, for the unspeakable state of her soul. So he told himself; but his self seemed coolly, blankly to hear rather than listen, as sometimes happened with his congregation, staring up at the pulpit unmoved and even – his myopia fancied – smirking. Prayer would not come. A new thought kept intruding: that a man could simply carry on walking in the same direction, not stopping – not stopping for his life – and nothing would happen to him. It was allowed. Freedom was all around, like air, and like air you couldn't see it.

Duty. Faith. God. Family. Position. He tried murmuring them out loud, but they merely processed through his mind: words with no images attached, like the roll-call from his school at Drumballyroney. He could remember every name. Keogh. Meehan. Patterson. Collins. McNeill. No faces. A pity. Pity that poor girl, for pity's sake – or else *erase* her from your mind. No face. No body.

He had emerged into a broad paved street: leaded bow windows on each side, high-perch carriages clipping by. Suddenly he knew where he was: fashionable Briggate. He had brought his wife some ribbons from here once. Where were the ribbons now? Given to the Garrs girls, perhaps; or just rotting away somewhere. These were the things the mind must contain and reconcile – *his* mind: he had prided himself on it. Perhaps this, this collision with madness, was the necessary fall that followed pride.

Yes, that was possible. It made sense. He wiped, without shame or even consciousness, at the tears on his cheeks. Purpose began to creep back into the world, like dawn or thaw. Purpose, sense, value. They had to exist, simply from the fact that the mind sought them; otherwise all was chaos, the bog rumbled and burst and the stinking mud swept over you.

Patrick put away his handkerchief. The feeling of having escaped something dreadful lifted him to bright receptiveness. He peered in at the nearest bow-window, and saw ninepins, a dolls' tea-set, tin soldiers; and remembered Branwell carefully mentioning that his stock of toy soldiers was getting very low. Purpose: now, without planning it, here he was. And, oh, yes, my son, my only son: purpose. Ducking his head, Patrick opened the jangling door and went into the toyshop, where the twelve wooden soldiers lay in their box, waiting for him.

'Look!' cried Branwell, flinging open the bedroom door. 'No, don't look, *behold*!'

While Charlotte blinked, dreams still pinning her Gulliver-like to the bed, Emily the cat-light sleeper leaped up. 'What is it? Charlotte, Branwell's got a box. Looking and beholding are the same, aren't they?'

'Pooh, only if – only if a *puddle* is the same as the *sea*.' Branwell laid the box ceremoniously on the end of their bed and lifted the lid. 'Papa must have got home late. He left this by my bed, I woke up and – it's funny, I had a dream about toy soldiers, and then there they were. Here they are. Aren't they superfluous?'

'Oh, absolutely superfluous,' Emily said admiringly. 'Banny, you must take care of these. Don't burn them with coals and smash their heads. I'm going to fetch Anne.'

'Soldiers do have to go into battle,' Branwell said, lofty. 'Anyway, that was when I was young. These are handsome, though, aren't they, Charlotte?'

Out of bed now, Charlotte approached the box. The soldiers, breeched and buskined, red-cheeked, varnish-shiny, gazed up at her. One in particular caught her eye. She picked him up. 'This,' she said, 'must be the Duke of Wellington. He is so perfect.'

'Well, and here is Bonaparte, your arch-enemy. See his clever look.'

Emily came back with Anne. 'Are you choosing favourites? Let me see. Oh, I like this one. Look how grave he is, as if he's thinking of great things. Anne, you pick one.'

Anne hesitated, all eyes. 'But they're Branwell's soldiers.'

Branwell was lordly. 'To be sure, they are mine – but if you choose one you can think of him as yours. Then you must protect him and be in charge of him. Like the foundling in that story in *Blackwood's*.'

Now Anne did not hesitate. 'This one.'

'What a queer one he is. Why him?'

'Because he's the smallest. I like smallest best.'

Branwell hooted. 'How funny! I like things *grand*.'

'This,' said Emily, holding her soldier up to the light, 'is Gravey. What is yours called, Anne?'

It seemed quite natural that she should ask in that way, as if the soldier already had a name instead of being given one. And Anne was prompt. 'Waiting Boy,' she said.

Then they were all laughing. Sometimes when that happened they simply could not stop: the laugh went round and round.

Tabby appeared at the door with the hot water, long face witchlike through the steam. 'Eh, don't start that. Worse than a set of cackling geese, y'are. See if you feel like laughing when you come to get bunions like mine on your feet.'

Charlotte cried: 'Look, Tabby, this is the Duke of Wellington.'

'And this is Bonaparte.'

'Is it now? Well, they'd know all about orders, and your orders are to leave off bibble-babbling and wash your mucky selves.'

Oh, dullness: then prayers, breakfast, chores – when could they play with them? It would have to be later – that word of sharpest frustration. But Charlotte put down her soldier and took up the soap, for she was the eldest and must set an example. And in the meantime, as Branwell whispered, *We can play in our heads*.

Since going to work at the Parsonage, Tabby finds herself much sought after whenever she goes down into the village to visit her nephew. People materialise from alleyways and poke up out of cellars, wanting to know: what goes on?

'Only you do wonder, y'knaw. What with them keeping theirselves to theirselves so much. When you do see parson he doesn't seem quite with you, like. And then Miss Branwell, she's reckoned to be a bit of a Tartar, isn't that right? And then the childer – when you do see 'em, like as not they're marching down to Keighley to get books from the circulating-library. Folk reckon they get too much learning, one way or t'other; like a lot of little mushrooms, stuck in there—'

'Folk say a lot they know nowt about,' says Tabby, who tries not to be drawn, but sometimes cannot help responding out of loyalty. 'Those childer are always walking up on moor – a sight further than *I* can go, with my feet.'

'Ah? Still, they don't really mix, do they? But then I dare say parson wants to keep 'em home quiet-like, after what happened at that school. And what parson says goes, so I hear. He mun have his own way in everything, they reckon, and best not cross him. It just makes you wonder – what goes on.'

Well, Tabby keeps her own counsel. She has no learning herself, and no opinions about how much of it her children (so, quite unsentimentally, she thinks of them) should have. They are clever, she knows that. They get their lessons quickly, and the master hears them when he comes in; but besides that, they are forever play-acting and reciting, or else scribbling. Even at the kitchen table, when they – the girls, that is, not Branwell – should be helping with the chores. Stories, pretending: all children do it. Hers just never stop. 'Oh, Tabby, we can't go to bed *now*, we're just founding a new city.' Tabby doesn't understand what it's all about – and yet, at another level, she understands perfectly. You have to have something apart from the world. The other night, when she sat mending by the kitchen fire, and saw the huddle of young heads in whispered mysterious conference, she remembered her grandfather and the piebald horse. He had dealt in horses, and Tabby as a little girl thought this was the prettiest ever – but how he cursed it! It wouldn't be led past lighted windows: the stripe of light falling on the ground made the horse shy as if it were water, or a hole. 'Bloody, bloody daft thing,' her grandfather snarled. But Tabby thought it was clever and special to have such a fancy, and for a time she took to jumping over those light-puddles herself. Because otherwise what was there? Just the grey cobblestones for ever.

It makes you wonder: what goes on.

The toy soldiers. Sometimes they accompany Branwell to the moors, where they bivouac on rocks, ford the stream, join battle in the heather – do things that toys do. But they have another life. They have books, specially made to scale for them – books two inches square, written and illustrated and bound by the children who are both their controlling deities and their alter egos, planning and acting out their destinies. And they are in the books: the books are about them, their lives, their adventures, and as these multiply so do the books – and presently, unsurprisingly in such a rich atmosphere of authorship, the soldiers themselves contribute to the books, and in the stamp-sized pages of, say, *Branwell's Blackwood's Magazine* relate in their own words their spacious narratives of daring and conquest. Not bad for inanimate objects. It makes you wonder.

What goes on: no one knows. Papa moves on the fringes, glimpsing a little here and there; occasionally, when some great issue in the world of the Twelves (one of their names for the soldiers) cannot be resolved, he is brought in as referee.

'Certainly, it was the strength of Wellington's squares that broke the enemy at Waterloo. Not that Bonaparte was one to squander his troops . . . but this battle is not, I take it, of that campaign?'

'No, Papa, this is in Africa,' Charlotte informs him. These are new battles in a different world. And Papa cannot even begin to decipher the tiny script in which its doings are chronicled: he is quite shut out. Which is curiously exciting.

What goes on. 'No one knows,' says Branwell, great cataloguer, cartographer, census-taker of this different world, 'the actual extent of the forest to the north-east of the Great Glasstown, on the border of Sneakysland. An expedition must be made to explore it.'

'Then Arthur Wellesley is the very man to lead it,' says Charlotte. They are, physically, squatting on the floor in the children's study, amid a litter of papers and pencil-stubs. 'He has all the qualities needed: the courage above all. I only hope he is not too impetuous.' Yes, that is his failing, but she loves him for it.

'No one knows better than I,' says Patrick to Miss Branwell, over their ritual tea, 'the potentially stifling effect of an upbringing in a remote and primitive spot. And it is certainly, as Charlotte's godmother remarked lately, something of a pity there is no company for the children here. The girls especially. Branwell can always run about and cut sticks with the village boys – there is a sort of rough equality among young males, at least for a time; but really there is no one suitable hereabouts for the girls. I'm afraid they must forgo society, unless we venture them to school again . . .' He is terribly still for some moments; then shudders, brightens. 'Thankfully they have each other.'

'Yes,' says Miss Branwell, taking her tea as if it were vinegar, 'so they do. But then I would not go so far as to say, Mr Brontë, that there is anything wrong with a limited prospect for young people. Morally, far from it. The broader the view, the more chance that the vital things – duty, humility, the proper fear of God – will be lost to sight.'

'Ah, the bay – the bay, you know, is several miles across – so it can be seen from the palace. Because you remember the old palace burned down, and the new one was built high on the cliff. So when the fleet arrived, surely—'

'It arrived by night,' Charlotte says, cutting Branwell off.

'The moon—'

'There was no moon. We looked in the almanac,' cries Emily.

'Ah, but you're forgetting the stars, they burn much brighter there, because of the latitude,' says Branwell, triumphantly. 'So if this landing was made, there must have been—'

'Treachery,' says Charlotte, meeting Emily's solemn eyes. 'Yes, but who?'

They stare into the giant dazzle of the bay.

'I need room on that table, Miss Charlotte, so you mun shift all your scratting bits, else they'll end up lining pie-dish.'

'I'll take them up,' says Branwell, scooping up the scratting bits – new and important writings, including the latest *Young Men's Magazine* and *Tales of the Islanders* – out of Tabby's way and bearing them off to the study.

Charlotte throws down her pen. 'Pooh, Tabby, I was just in the middle of a duel.'

'Well, now get in the middle o' peeling the potatoes,' Tabby grunts, holding out a paring-knife. 'Here, tek it. Take it,' says Wellesley, holding out the fallen sword to his blood-streaked combatant. 'Take it, wretched man, and fight on. The stain on my honour is not yet avenged . . .'

What goes on: the imaginary world goes on, at such a pace there is hardly enough time in the day to record it all. (Or imagine it all? No, there is always enough time for that, somehow.) As for the little books, they would fill shelf upon shelf if they were real – or, rather, of real dimensions. For everything else is authentic: the minuscule stitches of the binding, the special, painstaking handwriting that is meant to look like print. But real books are for everyone, whereas these, well, they are private. They create, constitute, and delimit a world that is self-sufficient. For anyone else to try to enter it would seem invasive – perhaps destructive; unless the attempt is made with a sort of humility, as guest not explorer; and in the same half-dreaming state that created it. Hover above the four bent heads, then over Charlotte's scribble-tense shoulder. See the lines of fly-speck script; squeeze through them; fall gently out of the world and into the world within.

'Welcome, thrice welcome to Great Glasstown!'

A magnificent figure of a man stands before you – tenders you a bow of surpassing elegance – never was such narrowness of waist and breadth of chest! And as for that fine eagle face . . . Do you have the honour of addressing the Duke of Wellington?

'An understandable confusion,' says the figure, with a twitch of cool humour at the corner of the sensual, faintly sardonic lips. 'I used to be the Duke, at an earlier stage of my existence. Now I am, generally, his imaginary son: Arthur Wellesley, at your service. It gives me more scope, you see.'

He bows again; and as he straightens, you see beneath the handsome face – flickering into brief view under the skin, as it were – the round blank face of a toy soldier. Wellesley observes your alarm, and speaks soothingly. 'Ah, yes, that too is part of my ancestry. Never fear: it is diminishing all the time. In me, at least. I cannot speak for the others.' He leads you along a colonnaded passage towards the foot of a vast staircase seemingly cut into living marble and ascending into blue oblivion. You see that his heroic soldier's gait has about it also, somehow, the lurching clump of a wooden creature. You ask: The others? Are they here?

'Not at present. We may see them. It all depends.' On what? 'Oh, on many things. The course of the Ashanti wars, for instance.'

A shift of perspective turns the staircase into a walled terrace, palm-fringed, overlooking the sea; and you breathe a sudden waft of cloying tropic air. Then, you ask, we are in Africa?

'The western coast. Though the topography and climate are more varied than you might suppose. It depends also on the outcome of the late rebellion –' from the corner of your eye you see a palace fall and melt away and then rebuild itself, and when you return your attention to Wellesley he is wearing an even grander uniform, and there are deep lines of shrewdness, even calculation about his grey eyes – 'and restoration. But above all it depends on the Genii.'

Who, you ask, are they?

A thrill seems to pass through the ground beneath your feet – now a vast ceremonial square surrounded by monumental buildings – and through the literally faceless crowds passing by, and through Wellesley, who grows an inch taller as he replies: 'The Genii – they are the ones who preside over all.'

Like gods?

'Like *gods, but there are important differences. Though they are far off, they are wonderfully close also. We feel them with us, in our hearts. Indeed sometimes we feel – and here I think I speak for the other three – that the Genii* are *us. The Four – the four founders of these kingdoms: Wellingtonsland, Sneakysland, Parrysland and Rossesland. Each of us has carved out our kingdom, with a Glasstown for a capital, and now we are a Confederacy, and here you see its capital: Great Glasstown.'*

For some time a grand presence chamber has been taking shape around you, its pure white marble walls hung with sumptuous tapestries, the floor inlaid with mosaic of sapphire and amethyst. Now Wellesley leads you to a curtained alcove and, at his curt signal of haughty command, the great drapes of gold satin are whisked back. You stand on a balcony high above the city, with all its Babylonian magnificence of stone temples, high and sheer as cliffs, of ziggurats and obelisks, terraces and staircases, of processional avenues broad enough for a marching army, of gilded towers and soaring turrets vanishing into a glorious canopy of cloud.

'A splendid sight, is it not? Yet you know none of this could have come into being without the influence of the Genii. No, no, we have never seen them; but they communicate with us by various means. Glasstown, for example, is to be renamed Verdopolis, by decree of the Genius Branii, who is entering on a new path of wisdom, and learning the mysteries of an ancient tongue.'

Branii, you say: yes, I see. And do the Genii interest themselves impartially in all the kingdoms?

'Their influence extends to us all,' says Wellesley, turning and opening a door on to a street where elegant carriages bustle between bow-windowed shops – stationers, jewellers, bookshops, toyshops – 'though each has his particular province. Branii we remember in our most sacred— What shall I call it? Story – myth? He it was who lifted us out of chaos, and brought us through the heavenly realm to confer with his sister Genii – Tallii, Emii, and Annii; and they were all clad in mystic white robes as they made their solemn choice, and gifted us with life.'

Tallii, you ask – would that be Charlotte?

'I have heard the name in connection with her. She is the presiding spirit of my own kingdom. She is magnificent – but you must beware, for you can hide nothing from her: she can see straight into your heart. Ah – I would not approach too close to those gratings, if I were you. Better to be safe than sorry. An unhealthy air emanates. Those are the dungeons. Whose *dungeons? I find it difficult to say: they are to be found everywhere in the Verdopolitan Confederacy.*

All one really knows is that terrible things happen down there.' He shudders, and for an instant those impermanent features are overlaid with another face, white, small and anguished. 'Indeed, I know from experience. The least of it is the food – the burned porridge and rancid meat – and the terrible biting cold: oh, there is worse than that . . . In fact it was the death of me.'

Dear, dear, you say – but of course you were released, or escaped?

'No, no: as I said, I died of it,' Wellesley says matter-of-factly, even cheerfully, while overhead a quick night passes with a flash of humid tropical stars. 'But, of course, the Genii restored me to life.'

You ask, Can they do that?

'Oh, they always do,' Wellesley says, doffing his hat to an imperiously beautiful woman in silks and diamonds who alights from a carriage before a grand town house and directs at him a look of queenly yet secretly wounded scorn.

So (how can you put it?) do you mean no one truly dies here?

Wellesley regards you with amiable puzzlement. 'No one truly dies anywhere, do they?'

Suddenly the city, the bay, the sky and the world begin to fold in on themselves. Wellesley manages a graceful wave and smile of farewell as he elongates, spiralling, like paper being twisted into a spill. 'Even the Genii,' he mouths, 'must sleep.'

'Oh, say that again, Banny, you sounded so funny!'

Branwell glares at Anne, dancing around him on the moorland path, but he cannot glare her down, now. She is still the youngest, still squeaky and abbreviated, but she has left littleness behind, has climbed on to a modest stool of assertion from which she can meet his eyes.

'I've told you,' he says gruffly, 'you mustn't call me that, you must call me Branwell.'

'Why?'

'Because it's more respectful,' he snaps, and on the last word his voice cracks and flutes again, and Anne hisses with laughter.

Branwell stamps ahead, massacring bluebells with his stick. 'Sometimes it's very tiresome being with girls,' he mutters, experimentally raising and lowering his treacherous voice. 'Boys have to go through certain things as they grow up, and girls don't.'

'No, the peasant girl – Mina – she remains true to him, even after he marries Helen Victorine,' Charlotte says, stroking Emily's hair. 'And even after Helen dies of neglect.'

'Another sacrifice to his ambition. But then that's always been there in Wellesley's character, hasn't it? And now that he is Marquess of Douro . . . You feel hot. Are you starting a fever?'

'No, no. I had a little pain in the stomach earlier. Tabby's pastry, I think. Branwell, by the by, says you can't die of neglect. He says there must be a scientific cause.'

'It *is* a cause,' says Emily indignantly. 'It must be the most fatal thing of all—'

'Hush – there's Aunt.'

They lie still and silent as the patten-clicking footsteps reach the landing and pause. Candlelight draws a glowing line under the bedroom door; there is a listening censorious moment. Then the line is erased and the footsteps withdraw.

'So will Mina ever marry anyone else?' Emily resumes.

'No. She is devoted heart and soul to him, even though it's hopeless. She even helps to nurse his children. I . . .'

'Don't stop, that was so nice. Charlotte – what's the matter?'

'I'm so sorry, I think I've . . .' Dreadful embarrassment, to wet the bed as if she were a little child, and with Emily sharing – and then what will Tabby say about the sheet? Hastily, carefully, Charlotte slides out from the covers. Then she sees: the summer night is light enough for that. The stain on her nightdress – too dark to be anything else . . .

'No – Emily, don't come near me. I've got something wrong with me. I think – I think I must have what Maria and Elizabeth had.' Plain white terror at that thought, with no border of surprise or grief: as if you had known all the time, the knowledge tucked away in a neat fob of the mind, that this must come.

'Stop it – what do you mean? Let me see . . .' Panic in Emily's voice, perhaps simply at the names of Maria and Elizabeth: seldom mentioned now except with a kind of superstitious awe – in a few years they have taken on an air of magpies, wearing green, new moons. 'Oh! Lord, is that blood? Does it hurt? Where is it from – your privy bit?'

'It must be. It just came. There was an odd feeling and then – Oh, Emily, there might be infection, be careful.'

'Oh, I don't mind – poor you, poor thing, come here. There. You know, Charlotte, I don't think it is what – what they had. I know I was only small, but I remember that very differently. It started with coughing, and then they got thin.' Emily's eyes gleam solemnly. 'And at the school, didn't the big girls used to talk about things like this? I didn't understand it at the time. Well, I still don't. But I think it's something to do with getting to be a woman, like your breasts growing.'

Charlotte's throat clenches. 'Hush.'

'Well, they are, aren't they? A *little* bit. And they're for feeding babies, and babies come from down there. Really, I think that's what it must be.'

Can this feeling that entwines itself with reassurance be disappointment? Disappointment that she is not dying? But, then, at least she knows about dying. She doesn't know about this.

'It's still doing it, I think. I'd better ask – I'd better tell Aunt . . .' Wild shivering horror as she pictures creeping out on to the landing, bumping dagger-gowned, besmirched, into Papa – but Emily grips her wrist authoritatively.

'Not Aunt. Tabby. You stay: I'll go and get her. She'll know what to do.'

And Tabby does. Grumbling mildly about her back and her feet, she brings a stub of candle and a strip of cloth and shows how to make the little clout.

'Stuff without a nap is best, but we've none in the basket just now. I'm past this mesen, and I dare swear your aunt is an' all. Don't fret for the nightgown. I'll put it straight in copper. Is it grinding in your belly? A hot bottle helps, if it gets too bad.'

Charlotte hovers light-headedly between relief and a peculiar, speculative shame. But what does it mean? Is it something – something like Emily's suggestion? She can hardly find the voice to ask.

'Eh? It's just your monthlies starting. Nowt grim and nowt grand. Why, hasn't your aunt talked to you about it? Hey, well, I suppose not. It's when you start growing to be a woman, and big enough to have babies. Now never tell me you don't know about how babies are born.'

'Oh, yes.' That is, she has seen pregnant women, and seen a lamb drop slithering and steaming into life, and has made the unthinkable connection . . . 'But I don't want to have babies.'

'Neither do I,' cries Emily, fiercely.

Tabby chuckles. 'Daft, you don't have to. Not yet at any rate. Nor never, if you don't want. But happen you'll think different when you're older.' She looks sharply from one to the other. 'Now surely you know how the babies get put there.'

Something exciting about this unprecedented, candid talk by candle-stub in the bedtime quietness – but now Charlotte shrinks from hearing more. 'Yes, of course. Thank you, Tabby. I'm sorry for getting you up.'

'Oh, I don't properly rest any road, not what you'd call real rest, with my back. Now come to me when you need a clean one. It'll dry up and stop in a few days. You'd best tell your aunt you've started your courses.' A shrewd glance. 'Nay, I'll tell her if you like. Now, don't sit up late talking a lot of blether. I know you.'

The departure of Tabby and the candle seems to advance the night alarmingly, so that they huddle together in the wide empty darkness.

'You were right,' Charlotte whispers.

'I wish I hadn't been, in a way.' Emily's voice is hollow with a grey wonder. 'It's horrible, isn't it?'

'It's not so very bad, you know.' Emily must be thinking: *Me next.* 'Just a small bit uncomfortable. I shouldn't have made such a fuss—'

'No, no, I mean the whole business with the babies, and being a woman. That's what Tabby meant, didn't she? It's true, isn't it? You know, like when we saw those horses on the way to Keighley. And that picture someone drew in the back of that library-book. And that girl at school who used to talk about her brother's wiggler. Dear God. Is it the same for all boys? Men, I mean. Like Branwell?'

'It's everyone, it's – all these things are just natural, I'm sure,' Charlotte says briskly, feeling suddenly so dizzy that she braces herself against the mattress as if it were spinning in space.

Emily sits up, hugging her knees. Often Charlotte will wake in the deep night for a moment or two and find Emily sitting like this, her profile a silhouette slitted with eyeshine; as if this were the real purpose of bed and sleep just an occasional choice. Charlotte adjusts the clout. Strange that the approach of womanhood requires infantine contrivances.

'Not for me,' Emily says; and then, as if in a few moments' silence the matter has been fully and satisfyingly discussed: 'No, no, not for me.'

She has been crying, certainly, crying with all the passion of a wounded young heart; but now, though pale, she is quite composed, and there is even a kind of pride about her, something lofty and exalted that transcends her quaint rustic dress.

But are you sure? Charlotte asks her. *Have you truly considered what it means to endanger – no, to surrender your reputation in this way?*

'How foolish we would think a man who left a naked flame

burning in his barn or hayloft, and went away with no thought for the consequences,' says her father from the pulpit, his words visible as dragonish puffs in the freezing air. 'Yet we are no less foolish – more, indeed, more perilously foolish – when we suppose that sin is a thing without consequences: that we can turn away, and close the door upon it.'

I am sure, Mina answers, *I have thought of it all, and I have no fear.* On the other side of the pew Anne, surreptitiously blowing on her fingers, listens to the sermon in tight suspense, as if it might take any fabulous turn, while Branwell hugs himself and tries to find a comfortable position for his newly elongated legs. On Charlotte's other side, Emily gazes into her own distance. They all know Mina, of course; but Charlotte has the strongest bond with her, and with the man she loves – the splendid, fascinating, flawed man who has forsaken her.

You mean you would give *yourself to the Marquess of Douro? Your love is such that you would entirely* give *yourself, regardless of the consequences? For you know what the consequences may be . . .*

I don't care, cries Mina, *I would do it gladly – gladly. I would abandon myself to – abandon . . .* Her voice, and her image, grow faint as Charlotte finds Aunt's hard eye upon her. She turns her head towards the pulpit.

'. . . We may sweep our sins and transgressions out of sight, so we think; but nothing within or without escapes the eye of our Lord God. So let it be understood, not as a dire threat, but as a loving reminder that the wise father gives the erring child, when we read: "Be sure your sin will find you out . . ."'

But to become his mistress – to surrender yourself to his base uses – is this not to set yourself at a miserably low worth?

The girl shakes her head with a slight, secret smile. *I can call nothing miserable except being apart from him.*

Charlotte's goose-fleshed thrill at those words is easy enough to disguise as a shiver. Except ever-impervious Emily, everyone in the church is shivering, sniffing, clenching their chattering teeth. Even Papa's voice, normally so steely, has become thin and strained as if the cold air cannot carry it.

Or as if he is falling ill.

'. . . My address has not been of its usual duration – but I think I must end here. A little temporary weakness of the breath.' Branwell, nodding, jerks his head up in surprise. Now a shiver of a different kind seizes Charlotte as Papa descends unsteadily from the pulpit, as the congregation stirs and murmurs, as Mina fades, ruefully smiling, and mouthing: *You will not forget me, I hope? No matter what happens?*

What happens is that Papa stumbles and nearly falls, until John Brown's burly arm supports him; and Charlotte realises that the future is not a vista or a prospect but a grasp, hard, irresistible, inescapable.

2

Gods and Mortals

So this, after all, is what madness feels like. Generally surprising, including the fact that though mad you are not too mad to know you are mad.

Also, the pain of it. Poetry speaks of the flight of the mind and the scattering of the wits: images of airy excess, even of release. But actually madness is narrow and dry and closes you in. It is a dungeon. It is an attic, locked and stifling, where you choke on your own screams.

'Miss Brontë, *what* are you *thinking* about?'

Was that the beginning of it? As well talk of the beginning of a mountain, or a cloud. But certainly in that simple moment Charlotte felt the sizzling brand of revelation. What *was* she thinking when on a drear day last term that dull-eyed mouth-breathing lump of a schoolgirl thrust her head across the desk and asked that fatuous, abominable question?

Things that cannot be spoken. She was thinking of the Duke of Zamorna, cloaked and spurred, shrugging off his wife's ministrations after the attempt on his life, and wondering if he would be scarred. She was thinking that if she saw that same grammar-lesson on the pluperfect tense once more she would be sick – actually be sick, then and there on the schoolroom floor. She was thinking – oh, other things: all unspeakable, and all revealing her as unspeakable. This girl asking the question, for example – why was she alive when Maria and Elizabeth were rotting? As for her lesson, it didn't matter whether she learned it or not: for all she was a lump, she already had the proper roguish curls and dimples and an uncle with connections and in four or five years' time a man would wish to marry her, and that was all that mattered. Envy, of course: Charlotte had none of these things.

Yet if that were *all* that was enviable – if that was the height of female aspiration – what did it say about the world? If having your dimples and curls assessed and approved and then matrimonially sequestered by some bland young curate represented earthly heaven, how unfathomably deep must hell reach below it? That was what she was thinking, but she should not have been thinking it. All her thoughts were bad. Even Zamorna and Lady Zenobia Ellrington and the kingdom of Angria: she should not think of them because they were not real, meaning they had no physical existence – yet how so? She had seen Zamorna standing at the schoolroom door and he had been *real* down to the last grizzled hair and the last twist of gold braid, while all the row of sighing pinafored misses and their slates and chalks and the very grammar-book in her hands were grey, insubstantial things wavering through cold dawn mist. She had seen him bending over her bed, often. Lately, she had even begun to feel his breath on her face.

What am I thinking? I am thinking that I must give Zamorna up, him and everything that goes with him. And the thought fills me with fear and rage and the cry: *Why me alone?*

What am I thinking? I am thinking that if I am not allowed to think any more – if even the mind is invaded – there is nowhere left to retreat to. Except, perhaps, madness.

And so this is what it feels like. Very much a bodily business, even though the mind leads. Charlotte has not touched food in two or three days – it is hard to imagine the desirability of eating, that strange insertion and absorption of foreign bodies. She is deadly cold: kneeling before the fire, she can see the leaping flames inches before her eyes, and feels nothing of them; almost tempting to try picking one like a flower. But she doesn't stay long enough for that – she is continually roaming about the school-house, from room to room, from house out to grounds and back again. It is like a fever patient stirring and tossing and trying to find a comfortable place in the prickling bedclothes; except that the twitching limbs are Charlotte's mind and she is trying to find a place for it in the world. A place she is afraid – madly afraid – does not exist.

It is the Easter vacation, but Charlotte has stayed on to look after the school while her employer, Miss Wooler, attends the deathbed of her father in Dewsbury. Probably she should not have agreed to this, given her longing for home and her state of mind – but it is dutiful, and duty is one of those things by which Charlotte recognises herself in the dark, distorting mirror of adulthood. The school is a red-brick box full of echoes, perched on the hill above Dewsbury's mill-chimneys. From the upstairs windows she can see streaks of snow still on the high moor, like wounds that refuse to heal. By day she mechanically oversees tasks for the handful of pupils remaining there for Easter; the rest of the time she is alone. Dazzlingly, deafeningly alone. Once – was it last night? – when the little lumber-room at the end of the passage seemed temporarily the safest place in which to sit, hug herself, weep and laugh into her shielding hands, she felt Mina Laury close by. It even seemed that the girl gently touched her shoulder; and she smelled flowers, the exotic musky flowers that grew on the volcanic slopes around the bay of Great Glasstown and that Mina loved to wear in her hair because Zamorna, when he was only Arthur Wellesley, had given them to her as a boy's love-token. It was as if Mina, tenderly hovering, wanted to know what was wrong: how had she come to this?

And Charlotte could only shrug her away. Because Mina was, is, part of the problem. The riddle facing Charlotte: that rich nourishing life of the mind that created Mina feeds her; this bare life of mere reality starves her. Solving the riddle is enough to send you mad.

She is crouching Cinderella-like in the darkness by the ashy parlour fire, wrapped in a shawl, unable to manipulate the bellows in her papery hands, when Miss Wooler returns. Miss Wooler, as ever gliding and nunlike, lights a candle and brings it close.

'Oh, my dear. Oh, my dear, look at you, you are not well at all. How . . . ?'

How, how has she come to this?

Papa's illness: it was real, frighteningly real, and Charlotte's shock was mingled with shame – because she had not quite believed in it, at first. After all, he did like to coddle himself, to remark to hovering solicitous Tabby: 'I do wonder whether I haven't caught a little chill, after my wetting yesterday. And then my dyspepsia . . .' But this was not to be cured by possets and sympathetic murmurs. For months, it seemed, after he had descended wheezing from the pulpit, Papa was a sickly shadow. At the lowest, he could not sit upright in bed: Tabby and Branwell had to heave him up for the doctor's examination. Once Charlotte approached the sickbed and found her father's eyes, unspectacled and shrunken, coldly staring at her as if he did not know who she was: or as if he did not much like her.

'A pleurisy.' Eager collector of words that she was, Charlotte could not help admiring the grave slither of this one, even as it appalled her. Mr Andrew shook his head. 'The inflammation is very severe. Of course, Mr Brontë's constitution has been generally robust up till now—'

'Up till now,' chimed Aunt. She had the air of a woman readying herself for anything.

And then came the morning of the madman knocking at the door.

'Does the parson live here? I wish to see him.'

Charlotte was in the kitchen helping with the bread: she heard Tabby at the door answer, tartly even for her: 'Well, you mayn't. He's poorly in bed.'

'I have a message for him.'

'Oh, aye, who from?'

'From the *Lord*.'

The voice rose to a strange singing note. Charlotte went to the door. An old man, stout and gaitered and ruddy, but hatless and with wild grey snakes of hair tossing in the wind, turned his horribly blue eyes to her.

Tabby snapped: 'Lord who?'

'The *Lord*. He desires me to say that the bridegroom is coming and he must prepare to meet him – that the silver cord is about to be loosed and the golden bowl broken – the pitcher broken at the fountain – the wheel broken at the cistern.' He took a deep breath, as if about to say something more, but only made a little whimper, turned sharply round, and was gone.

'Who is he?' Charlotte gasped out.

'Don't know,' grunted Tabby, who knew everyone in three parishes. She shut the door. 'Never seen him before. And if I see him again, I shall tek the broomstick to him. Coming to a house of sickness and spouting such stuff. Why, whatever are you greeting for?'

Charlotte turned her head irritably away; somehow Tabby could detect tears before they fell. 'What he said – it wasn't stuff, it was scripture . . .'

'Aye, and I've often heard the like from Baptists and Methodies when they get Bible-crazed. Either that or they go writing it up on walls. Pay no heed to him, Miss Charlotte. There, now you've got flour on your face.'

Charlotte was sure Tabby was right – Tabby, who could find an ill omen in the shape of a potato – but the sing-song voice would not leave her head.

'Papa isn't going to die,' Branwell said later, when she told the others. 'He isn't. That's just *stupid*.' He kicked out at a dining-chair, sending it and the cat sitting humped beneath it skittering: unhappiness tended to make him savage. 'It's a stupidity.'

'Poor pussens, come here.' Emily gathered the cat in her arms and appraised Branwell coolly, mouth grazing its fur. 'He is going to, you know, Branwell. One day. Everyone is.'

She was just being cruel because she was angry on behalf of the cat, Charlotte told herself. Nobody could actually carry such thoughts around. It would be like filling your pockets with gunpowder.

And Papa did not die (not then), though he was slow to recover and when he did he looked older; pared and attenuated, like an over-sharpened pencil. (Careful, don't press too hard, beware of that *snap*.) And Mr Andrew said he had heard of an eccentric farmer who went around delivering those little homilies at people's doors. And yet, and yet . . . the whole business could not simply be put away with the dosing-spoon and the leech-jar. In a way, Emily had seen the shape behind the screen. Soon Charlotte and Branwell were invited, significantly, to drink tea in Papa's study. Aunt was there, genteelly inclining her mob-capped head as if they had just been introduced. This was serious.

'Miss Branwell and I have been discussing the future. With particular reference to my late indisposition, and its attendant anxieties. God saw fit to spare me this time, but some day His will may be otherwise. Rather like the Haworth earthquake – on which I have written, I fancy, to some effect – there is to be found in this event an admonition. Branwell, as the upcoming man of the family, and Charlotte, as the eldest, you too should, I believe, share in these discussions. You are old enough to appreciate our position. The children of a clergyman of slender means, alas, must prepare themselves to earn a living in a suitable way.'

The eldest: oh, how she felt it again, the dizzying inescapable thrust of it, as if she clung grimly to a beam swung out over an abyss. School, school. She knew before the word was spoken. That had been the point of Cowan Bridge, after all: to fit her to become a governess. The intervening years of forgetting had been too beautiful – yes, she grasped it now – too beautiful to be trusted. Exactly like a vivid dream: with that mind-tussle on waking, one half vehemently insisting it *must* be real, because . . . because if not . . . Yes, you knew this would come. Papa was talking of requisite accomplishments, while Aunt peered into the teapot as if it were full of stolen money. Charlotte looked down at her hands and thought: what if virtually your whole life had been a dream, and you suddenly woke up, and realized you were a baby at the breast? It did not seem vastly unlikely.

'The school to which I have applied,' said Papa, 'is, I can confidently state, of a very different character in every respect from the – er – the previous institution . . .'

Which we do not name. It was an odd sort of discussion – as everything, really, was already settled. Branwell lounged, looking bored: a sure sign that he was uneasy. Then Papa disentangled himself from another endlessly coiling sentence and looking straight, tentative, half smiling at Charlotte, said: 'And I know you set a value on education, Charlotte. You love learning.' True: and how truth loved, like a bulky wrestler relying on his weight, to pin you down. No good straining to lift your shoulders and say *but*. You had to lie flat and submit.

So perhaps the madman's message had not been for Papa, after all. And perhaps it had not really been about death – or not that kind of death.

'I'll write to you – and I mean I'll *write*,' Branwell said. 'Not just Branwell presents his compliments et cetera. Everything that happens in the Confederacy and Angria: all the developments with Rogue and Zamorna. And you must write back, and I mean really write—'

'You know I won't be able to. I'll be at school. All my time will be taken up with studies. I've got to leave all that behind, finish it, forget it.' She spoke with the dogged, thrusting misery of someone who longs to be definitively contradicted. I've lost my purse, it's gone for ever: no, it isn't, it's here, see?

But Branwell only said with an awkward shrug: 'Well, as to that, I shall have to knuckle down to my own studies too. I can only give it a part of my time. Oh, Charlotte.' He took her by the elbows and steered her to the window-seat; then stood regarding her with one leg hoisted up on the fender, his hands in his pockets. He was full of these sudden jerks and postures lately, as if he were dipping in and out of a new self. 'When you come back, you can take it up again. Our infernal world won't go away.'

'Sometimes I wonder whether it oughtn't to,' she said.

Branwell's redhead colouring meant he could not disguise the momentary flux of emotion. Blood fled from and returned in force to his cheeks, as visible as a gulping gullet. But then, recovering, he chuckled. 'Now I know you're glum: the puritan strain is rising. Besides, don't you know the day will come when we shall all be able to do as we like? The day I make my fortune?' He stuck up his chin, stalking up and down in front of her. 'Well? Surely you don't doubt me.'

'No, no.' She found herself laughing, just a little: like a sip of weak tea. 'I merely wonder how, exactly, the fortune is to be made.'

He came scuttling close, his pale face approaching hers. For an instant it seemed about to bark out in terrible fury: to lash her with black revelation. And then that person was gone and instead, arch and delicious and droll, the old Branwell pronounced with half-closed eyes: 'By my *brilliance*, of course. What else is needed?'

So she packed, and somewhere near the top of the trunk – a thing not to be forgotten – was that memory of Papa being lifted up in bed by Tabby and Branwell. Poor Papa. Think of his burdens. Therefore get rid once and for all of this question: what will it be like at Roe Head School – will I be happy or unhappy? Because this is not an important thing to consider. If you must think of it, then thrust it down, keep it hidden. There was a story – she could not remember where she had come across it in her reading – of a young Roman boy who had stolen a fox cub and hid it under his tunic; and rather than reveal what he had done, he let the animal gnaw away at his insides. It was a story of virtue and fortitude, and it had horrified her from the first moment, and set up a clanging bell-tower confusion of right and wrong. But in the carrier's cart that took her, alone, to Roe Head, Charlotte clutched the question to her like that fox, without a murmur.

'The Misses Wooler – well known to me, both by reputation and acquaintance,' Papa had said. 'They take few pupils into their house, not above a dozen, all of older years, and the regimen is both genteel and liberal. In short . . .' In short, Roe Head was nothing like Cowan Bridge, and everyone said so, and there was nothing to fear on that score. And yet when Charlotte climbed down from the cart and faced the high grey house she would not have been surprised at all to find Miss Andrews and the Reverend Carus Wilson emerging from the porch-shadow and crying with relish: *Ah! You've come back to us!*

'What *is* that in the way you talk? Is it Irish?'

Charlotte avoided the girl's look, which was like a dog's cold, questing nose. 'I wasn't aware of – of talking in any way particularly.'

'Oh, there's nothing wrong with being Irish, you know. Indeed we have treated them shockingly – don't you think? It's no wonder they rebel. Are you Irish – or are you Scottish, perhaps?' An inquisitive pause. 'Don't you like me asking you questions?'

'No.' The dark, bouncing girl was called Mary Taylor, that she knew; she wanted to know no more. 'It's rude.'

A laughing challenge. 'Well, why don't you tell me so, then?'

Because, because . . . in that there might be connection: exposure. And Charlotte was here for one thing only. Studies, work. Compared with Cowan Bridge, the teaching at Roe Head was rich and imaginative. Charlotte stepped into lessons as into a pair of comfortable old shoes. Miss Wooler, the proprietress, who seemed to move on castors and who spoke with endless musicality, like a thoughtful bird, was a soothing and smoothing presence, and she ran the airy house without privations. So, if Charlotte could only keep her head bent over her books (all too physically easy – her short-sightedness was conspicuous here, where games were allowed, and she had the early humiliation of being tossed a ball she could not even see) then she might yet reach the other side.

And if come evening, when the other girls grouped and fizzed and chattered, she preferred to hide herself behind the schoolroom curtain, hug the fox, perhaps silently weep a little at the sharpness of its teeth, that was her own business. She certainly did not want anyone to draw back that curtain. But when at last someone did, there was not so much intrusion as revelation.

She had been allowing herself to think of Zamorna, opening a court ball at Verdopolis, and it was – perhaps – the sheer beauty of the scene that made the tears well from her closed eyes. Then she felt the disturbed air, the light on her eyelids – and she looked and gasped. The girl standing before her *was* from Verdopolis. Nowhere else did you find that mixture of delicacy and elegance, that length of white neck, that nimbus of gold ringlets. Evidently she had stepped out of Charlotte's head, and Charlotte's surprise was only that of, say, finding a four-leafed clover: it was a thing that had to happen some time.

Then Charlotte wiped her blurred eyes, and the girl said, in quite an ordinary voice: 'Oh, dear, I'm sorry to disturb you,' and the glamour faded, a little. Charlotte still knew why she had thought the girl a visitant from the world below, as they called it (below *what* was a different question). It was because she was everything Charlotte was not – even down to the single pearly, decorative tear that ran down her cheek as she quavered: 'Is it so *very* bad here?'

A new girl. Charlotte made herself brisk. 'It isn't bad at all. You mustn't take any notice of me. It's very good here.'

'But it isn't home.' The other sighed.

And there, for all her admiration, Charlotte pitied her innocent weakness. 'Dear God,' she said, 'I never expected it to be like home.'

And so she found herself, in a curious way, in the middle again. Not this time with family: with friends, you would have to call them, though the idea was as remote from her as joining the circus. Being friends, she found, was a much more strenuous and artificial business than being a sister. Even deep into the warm, arm-linking, confiding world of it, you kept coming across great unmapped swathes of territory where you had to toil and go slowly. She might not have allowed herself to be drawn in, if it were not for the sensation of finding herself liked. That was beyond anything. Now she understood why on Haworth fair-days men glugged liquor until they were blind and how solitary farmers in one-eyed homesteads up on the heights came to live for their laudanum-dose. If the sensation was anything like that of finding someone liked you, no wonder they craved it to the edge of their own destruction.

In the middle. Not in the matter of achievement: there indeed her movement was as swift and sure as Mary Taylor's way of climbing the young oak (forbidden) in the Roe Head garden – a first judicious scramble, and then unerringly to the top. Academically Charlotte rose to the top of the school and stayed there. The middle ground of friendship, between Ellen and Mary, was rather between hope and fear.

Ellen Nussey, the vision who pushed back the curtain – how to describe her? She was flesh and blood after all, but of a special kind. When Ellen walked across a room, she seemed neatly to walk the one thin strip of safety, with muddy clutching mess on either side. She was not a niminy-piminy miss: she was too quiet, serious, gentle for that; but she knew where to walk, and you felt she always would. 'Numerous,' she said mildly smiling, when speaking of her family, 'mine are numerous.' Twelve children, Charlotte discovered, with Ellen the youngest, and the eldest practically a generation older. She imagined the deft adjustments of balance that entailed – or, rather, she did not have to: it was all there visible in Ellen, who dropped into life like a leaf on to the moving stream. Perhaps it was possible to be like that, Charlotte thought, and longingly tried to imagine it: no more the clenched and warring feeling. She failed. But she could hope.

'Wellington?' cried Mary Taylor, when Charlotte waxed warm about her hero. 'Pooh, what do we want with him meddling in the country's affairs? Yes, meddling, he should never have taken office. He was all very well as a soldier. But soldiers should stick to their bloody tyrannous work, not come marching all over our liberties.'

Shocking. Charlotte flinched and shrank, drinking it in because she had to. Hadn't such things already been decided, when Papa and Aunt would discuss them vivaciously over the spread-eagled newspaper? It was just radical talk, and that only ended one way: she knew by heart Papa's memories of Luddites looming murderously out of the dark. And without these great figures, aristocratic idols rising harsh and broad-chested to do what they must, surely there would be chaos. She saw again Papa lifted and propped in his sick-bed. The horror of it: for she had always thought of Papa as, in his gaunt way, a handsome man – but how ugly that lolling, that glimpse of sad white breastbone, the downward arrow of coarse hair. Cover it up: set right the marble plinth.

But then Mary Taylor's family *were* radicals, as she was proud to declare. They even lived in a house called the Red House, actually built not of stone but of brick – that was *outré* in itself. There was something hard and jaunty and fearless in Mary – even when she looked at the schoolroom clock you felt she wanted to get to the back and examine its workings. Mary made you think, and sometimes Charlotte was afraid of where the thoughts might lead.

Being in the middle you also saw what you lacked: she could not be as spirited as Mary or as ladylike as Ellen. Yet there was something neither of them had and which struck Charlotte as an almost absurdly inconceivable absence – like possessing a head and body without a neck. They had no imagination.

'How can you *see* all that?' they would marvel, when she analysed a book illustration, elaborating its details, setting free its storied significance. And the only possible reply – which of course she could not make – was *How can you* not *see it?*

Once something struck her by its resemblance to an episode in Zamorna's life, and she found herself talking about him, garrulously and familiarly, until Mary's baffled look stopped her.

'No, go on. It's wonderful. It's just so queer I've never heard of him. My history must be weaker than I thought. Was he Italian? Florentine, perhaps?'

And then Charlotte had to confess that the person she had been enthusing about was not real at all: he was imaginary. (Why *confess*, as if there were something wrong about it? Ah, there's the thread that leads into the labyrinth of madness.) Mary wanted to know more, but Charlotte closed up.

She was literally in the middle one day – walking arm in arm with Mary and Ellen in the wood behind Roe Head – when Ellen said: 'I heard Miss Wooler talking to Miss Catherine about you, Charlotte, and she said you had brilliance.'

It was that word that left her gaping for a reply, because it was a word so much associated with the world below – with the ladies of Zamorna's court, dazzling in their bejewelled beauty and vivacity. But of course this must be a different brilliance – of the mind, as Mary went on to confirm.

'So you do, and a very good thing to have in this world, where somehow we disposable women have to get on and find some sort of worthwhile life. No, Ellen, you needn't squeak, we *are* disposable. And we are allowed very few weapons. Money is probably the best thing to have, but failing that, brains. Far better than having good looks.'

'As I haven't,' said Charlotte, lightly.

'That's right,' Mary went on, vigorous, stripping off a twig for a switch. 'Women who rely on that alone do themselves and other women a great disservice . . .' She argued on, lashing at branches and sending the rooks above clattering and croaking in disdain, while Ellen tightened her gentle pressure on Charlotte's arm.

No: there was no need to rush to the mirror that evening, to search in anguish for confirmation or denial. After all, you always knew that you were smaller and slighter than the other girls, that your skin had none of that bloom, that you were the only one who refrained from fully smiling to keep those awkward teeth covered. You already knew. But knowledge wears different guises. To know in the quiet private sitting-room of your self that you were plain (ugly, call it ugly) was different from being told so. Different, to have the door flung open on the livid fact so that it tumbled out like a secreted corpse.

'Charlotte, stop. Sit down. Chat. Do nothing.' Mary grinned helplessly. 'Be vacant for a minute.'

School was over, but Charlotte worked on, kneeling by the window to catch the last daylight. The French blobbed on the page, sang nasally through her mind. Different rhythm from English, absence of rhythm, rather: you missed the feeling of foot striking ground. 'No. No, I don't want to.'

'Why? Surely there's nothing wrong with relaxing a little.'

As ever the word 'wrong' gave her a pause of attention, like a dog hearing its own name. 'No . . . I know. But I want to carry on.' This is what I'm good at; or all I'm good for. 'I want to make the best use of my time here. It's costing Papa money. And this is my preparation for what I must do in life. It's like you were saying the other day, Mary. Disposable women.'

'I suppose. But it might make more sense if we were allowed to do some real work in the world. Law. Medicine. Anything. Instead you know as well as I do what it's likely to be – governessing to some rich mill-owner's spoiled brats.'

'Though not all such places are quite like that,' said Ellen, with a tactful cough. Several of their schoolfellows were the grown brats of rich mill-owners: they would go forth into well-stuffed and fringed and upholstered lives. Ellen's own late father had been a manufacturer and the family lived in a house called, impeccably, The Rydings, but one got the impression that, being so numerous, their fortunes were spread a little thinly; and Mary's father was a businessman who had gone bankrupt and slaved to repay his debts. Charlotte, the poorest of all, knew very well that Mary spoke the truth. And yet – look at Miss Wooler. There was a respectable, independent woman who lived by her intellect. She lived plainly, narrowly in some ways, but there was cultivation, there were books and music: there was something to be admired. And aspired to? Did it require some other sacrifice to attain that placidity of Miss Wooler's, whose very gown, white and unwrinkled, seemed to rustle more quietly than anyone else's? But Charlotte did not voice these questions: she was afraid Mary would retort that even to run a school Miss Wooler must have a little money of her own. And she wanted to keep the admiration, as one might an heirloom without wanting to know whether it was genuine or fake.

'I have known some governesses valued, you know, quite treasured like one of the family,' Ellen pursued.

'Yes, until the children are all grown, or until the governess can't see or gets slow in the legs, and then, poor dear, she must go to the parish, though with our *very* kindest regards.' Mary stabbed the fire savagely. 'No, not for me. I'd rather die.'

'Don't say that. Don't ever say that.' It burst sharply from Charlotte before she could stop it. Mary, for all her qualities, was too careless with words: she flung them about as if they didn't touch on life, as if they bore no plumes or barbs. She turned from the window: the stirred blaze hotly fanned the air, fingered her cheek. 'I'd rather have life. Even if – even if you have to put your hand in burning coals to hold it.'

'Yes. Sorry, Charlotte. I understand,' Mary said. They knew about Maria and Elizabeth: indeed sometimes she was afraid she had bored them with the subject, and she thought she detected a wry glance between Mary and Ellen now. But it didn't matter: she didn't expect anyone external to understand, meaning external to Branwell and Emily and Anne. That was when she missed her brother and sisters most, or missed them most consciously. You were easy, even comfortable on this new voyage of friendship – and suddenly you realised, with a mental shudder, how far out you were from shore.

'But what *would* you like – really, if you could shape your future, and it didn't have to be governessing and whatnot, how would it be?' Mary, unabashed, returning to the attack.

'The sea,' Charlotte said readily, 'a house by the sea, where we could all live – my family, I mean. And the garden would look out over the sea, and we would each have our own chair there.'

'The sea? Why the sea?'

'The sea is extremely pleasant,' Ellen said, stroking her own soft restless hands, with themselves. 'Scarborough – take Scarborough. It is particularly admired for its air and situation – nowhere more healthy. Prettily set out too. I am excessively fond of the sea.'

Why the sea? She couldn't say. Perhaps because the sea, as she pictured it, went limitlessly on and on – like freedom.

It's as if they're characters in a book, Ellen marvelled once, when Charlotte was describing her family – Charlotte thinking in return, *Well, yes, but we all are, aren't we?* But now came the challenge: tell us a story. An invented story – nothing so pale and pedestrian as reality, warmed over like an invalid's broth: carve it new and steaming. In the darkened dormitory Charlotte told.

'The body, gaping with all its wounds of murder, was certainly consigned there; and there the guilty party supposed it would remain. How could he suppose that it would ever reappear to accuse him? But in the deep dead of night, a sound was heard – a low, grating, dragging sound, making its way through passages and corridors, approaching ever nearer – and then a laugh, a wild, gibbering laugh like the mirth of hell itself . . .'

'I don't think we should invent horrors,' Ellen said later, quivering, downright. The screams of one girl had brought Miss Wooler down on them in stately reproof. 'It isn't right. Lord knows, they are plentiful enough in real life.'

'That's why we invent them,' Charlotte said. 'To take the edge off the real ones.' But then, seeing Ellen's solemn pale face on the pillow beside her, she felt remorse. She remembered Aunt: *It is better to be good than to be clever.*

Being short-sighted, you were used to the fuzzy process by which apprehension became comprehension. What's that – a stain, a shadow, a leaf? In a few peering moments you sorted the possibilities down to the reality. And so it was sometimes in those evenings, when she read or wrote to the last minute, and the growing dusk and the feathery murmur of young voices became one, she encountered a feeling. What's this? Not happiness, no, eliminate that: but perhaps, just for now, content?

'Who else did you suppose?' Branwell said, turning from the bow-window of Miss Wooler's parlour, and laughing at Charlotte's look.

'I couldn't tell – when she said a visitor, I could only think, I don't have visitors . . .' He looked several inches taller. Going awkwardly forward to kiss him, she had a sudden strange sensation of being found out in an imposture. She felt bristle against her lips. 'But how did you get here?'

'Walked. What's twenty miles to a young athlete?' He pounded his narrow chest. 'Not in the least winded. Did I tell you I'm going to take up boxing? There's a Pugilistic Society meets in the upper rooms at the Black Bull. They have a fellow come over from Bradford who once beat Gentleman John Jackson and *he*, you know, used to spar with Lord Byron. So when I shake his hand I shall only be two handshakes away from Byron – think of that. Well, it's a fine prospect here. How do you go on? Still at the top of the class?'

'I won the silver medal for achievement again this term.'

'Capital, capital,' he said, examining one of Miss Wooler's own watercolours above the fireplace. Suspicion that for Branwell her achievements could hold only so much interest. She was, after all, a girl; and even his gawky unfinished maleness stood out in these virginal apartments like blood on snow. 'Perspective's not right in that. Did you know I'm training in oils now? Mr Bradley says I'm ready for it. You can do much grander things in oils. And, of course, if you're to be an artist you absolutely must master the technique. I'll get you to sit for me when you come home. Well, I'm starved, when's dinner? Yes, I'm to dine with you. What ambrosia do you delicate maidens live on? Is it decent feeding here, or tripes and scrape?'

'You will do very well at table, never fear,' Charlotte said: though it was only lately that she had been able to eat the meat here. It was perfectly wholesome and well-dressed: it was just that the texture between her teeth had brought back Cowan Bridge – had brought back so many things. 'As long as you don't mind dining with an entire roomful of girls.'

'Not a bit of it. I shall be like a half-holiday for 'em,' he said cheerfully. That was Branwell: there was no shrinking in him. Unaccountably for Charlotte, who felt close to him in many other ways, he actually relished meeting people. For her the experience was like being pulled naked and screaming into the world anew every time.

'Well, and how is everyone at home? Is Papa's health still—'

'Uncertain, aye, meaning pretty well all in all, except when he takes a fancy otherwise.' This was daring: they acknowledged it with mutual widening of eyes and tightened lips. 'As for Emily, she is taller than me, which is not to be forgiven, though Anne still scarcely throws a shadow. And they're very thick together, of course.' He waved a dismissive hand, as if he would say, *Girls*. And yet: 'That's where I miss you, Charlotte. Where the infernal world misses you. Emily and Anne play their part, but it's fitful just now: I have a strong fancy they're starting to explore a new world of their own, and from what I've picked up it's altogether too romantic and elfin for me. Now *I*'ve been putting the whole chronicle of the Twelves in order, right from the beginnings. And what do you think of this?' He reached out and dramatically touched her hand. 'Great Glasstown destroyed!'

'No. No, you can't – you haven't—'

'Oh, not yet. I wanted to see what you thought about the way it should develop. It's the work of Alexander Rogue, you see. He raises a revolution.'

'It would be him.' She scowled: she could see him now, spare and dapper and smiling that ingratiating smile. 'That low demagogue.'

'Ah, but isn't there a fascination in him too? I suspect him, by the by, of out-and-out atheism. Well, he will lead the hordes that cause Great Glasstown to be cast down and levelled to the dust. Until . . .'

'Yes?'

'Well, I don't know. There will be some sort of restoration.'

'I see. Yes – the Genii might restore it.'

Branwell winced. 'I don't much care for the Genii intervening now.

It smacks too much of magic. You know, the childish solution. It's more likely that Douro will rally some loyal forces, settle the political divisions between them, and put things right at last. But, in the meantime, what a cataclysm! Think of it – the towers of Great Glasstown crashing in flames!'

She did think of it: she had seen the picture, as soon as he spoke of it being destroyed. And in that moment she had split right down the middle. There was a Charlotte on one side who moaned in shock and grief and loss; and a Charlotte on the other who said, *Good: it should be destroyed. And sow its fields with salt so it can never rise again.*

'You have done so very well at Roe Head, my dear Miss Brontë. You have truly garnered the laurels. This, my sisters and I agree, should be given to you to keep.' But this wasn't right, it couldn't be ending. Miss Wooler, with her faintly theatrical gentleness – as if really she might at any moment throw loose her coiled hair and reveal herself a bandit's bride – pressed the achievement medal into Charlotte's hand. It was ending. 'You have equipped yourself admirably to impart learning, if such is to be your future: indeed, I hardly know what else I can teach you.' Charlotte, mouthing thanks, sagged at the knees. No, tell me I know nothing, make me learn more. But perhaps this was the way of endings: the human mind rejected them outright. Not now, it's not finished: like those interesting dreams you wanted to go back to after the bell or the sunlight had closed them, and that you could never open again.

'Let's run.' Her last day at Roe Head, lessons over: now, finally, she saw a time to do what she had always shunned. She nudged Ellen and Mary, and set off running full tilt round the gardens. It was summer. The trees sprinkled light until you blinked, half blinded with it; and she couldn't tell if her friends ran with her.

So, home; and better perhaps if she had never gone back at all.

She brought with her a perceptible difference of having been away. Like that smell, not unpleasant, about the clothes of someone who comes in from outdoors. What exactly is it? You can't create it. It exists only in relation to indoors. And indoors eventually eliminates it.

Oh, she was glad, of course. Being with Emily and Anne again: the sheer unstrenuousness of sisterhood. Even if you snapped and quarrelled it produced a different kind of hurt, like digging your finger-nails into your own skin: you were not at the mercy of it. And they were a little awkward with each other at first. Together Emily and Anne had an odd, brightly conscious look about them, like children who have hidden something in the room. Then Charlotte was to squeeze the last drop out of her precious education by passing it on to her sisters – and it began, or she began, with fearful stiffness. Nothing could be more natural than their huddling round the dining-table with books and pens and paper – when had they done anything else? But how unnatural – 'Now, Anne, let us hear you read. Yes, from the beginning, please.'

It was Emily who rescued her at last, covering her hand with its finger rigidly indicating a page and saying: 'Charlotte, it's all right. I want to learn it. I like it.'

So she stopped administering it like a dose. But the reversion to pleasure worried her. Stories and verses crept on to the back pages of exercises – Emily's, Anne's; then her own. Branwell's writing-box opened to reveal thrilling and disturbing new movements in the world below, Rogue and Zamorna staking out the new kingdom of Angria, conflict, rivalry, love. Back here there was nothing to gainsay it: no friends to point you outwards to the world, no Miss Wooler to stand as an example of industry and discipline. Instead she had to be those things to herself. Charlotte avoided the mirror even more; the eyes in there pinned her so savagely.

While convulsions shook the world below, she brought her own sort of revolution to the parsonage. Ellen was invited to stay.

The ground had been prepared for this unprecedented step. Charlotte had made visits of her own during the holidays – to Mary's rackety, bracing nest of radicalism at the Red House as well as the soft-creaking gentility of The Rydings – and that meant, in due form, that a return visit could be expected. Still, it marked a great moment when Papa and Aunt, in solemn conclave over tea, agreed to extend the invitation. Nobody ever stayed at the parsonage. There had to be assurances that Papa's inviolable round of habit would not be encroached upon.

Other preparations Charlotte tried to make herself, as best she could. While they were used to Tabby's cooking, which rested upon a single fierce belief that food should be cooked *through*, she dropped a hint that not everyone relished gluey potatoes and vegetables boiled to limpness. Tabby shrugged. 'If you want to go down with the gripes, that's your affair.' As for Branwell, she knew he would go out of his way to make Ellen welcome: probably the only difficulty would be in shutting him up.

But she needed to know how Emily and Anne felt about the – well, what? Visitor? Interloper? Usurper? It was nearly, if not quite, a question of bursting out: 'You know, I don't love Ellen any better than you.' Differently, not better. Probably no species of love, she thought, could ever resemble theirs. It was as if they had grown up together on a desert island, knowing where the crocodiles haunted the lagoon, sharing outlandish fruit on palm-leaf dishes.

But the love, being a living thing, was not unchanging. While Charlotte went out into the world and Branwell, putting on the vestments of manhood, pursued his separate studies, Emily and Anne had drawn closer together. You could even see it physically: one's hand slipping under the other's arm almost without volition; a space automatically left when one sat in the window-seat. The kind of habits associated with twins – yet Emily and Anne remained very separate, very different.

Branwell used to joke about Anne's diminutive size – covering the crown of her head with his hand and crying in bafflement: 'But where's Anne?' – and she was still slight. Quiet too – but not oppressively so, Charlotte thought: it was the quietness of the observer rather than the brooder. Once Tabby brought a vase of narcissus from watering in the kitchen and set it back on the mantelshelf: Anne, writing at the dining-table, glanced up, rose, walked through to the hall, and came back with a stray bloom that had fallen on the floor. 'Well, I knew there were eleven before,' she said, at Charlotte's look.

'You counted?'

'No, I just noticed.'

She had a faint, dry, fetching smile, milky skin, and hair of a rich red-gold, like Branwell's tastefully revised. Some people, Charlotte thought, you could only imagine as they were at that moment – they were caterpillars, their future selves involving unguessable transformations. But in Anne you could see the woman she would become: the wife and mother gently, watchfully tending a family of auburn-haired clear-skinned children. Or else – more likely perhaps in this world of disposable women – the dependable much-loved aunt, conveying her pretty looks, lavendered and tissued, into a reproachless middle age.

Anne was eager for Ellen's visit. 'But I do hope she won't find it draughty here. We are so very exposed. Didn't you say The Rydings is quite sheltered?'

'Oh, she knows what to expect,' Charlotte said, noticing how Emily smiled thinly through these little anxieties. Only much later, though, when they were going to bed, did Emily come out with it.

'I hope,' she said, flinging her long limbs down, 'that your friend doesn't *expect* anything in particular.'

That was Emily's way. She would suddenly answer a question or finish a sentence that had been started hours ago, as if her mind followed a different clock from everyone else's. Charlotte lay down beside her and tussled with the knowledge that if she did have any misgivings about Ellen's visit they concerned Emily.

It wasn't a matter of wild eccentricities – though she could have wished Emily would refrain from sharing her breakfast porridge with Grasper, her hideous terrier. Call them social lapses, or rather absences, of a kind Charlotte had never noticed before she went away from home. Talking, for example. At The Rydings, she had found her own taciturnity conspicuous, and it pained her until she realised that the continual talk going on meant very little. From the moment of rising to the snuffing of the last candle, the whole family engaged in this game of conversational cat's cradle. If Mercy Nussey saw three magpies in the garden, she had to tell Sarah about it, and Sarah then had to tell Richard about it, and then they would try to recall what it signified in the old rhyme, and Mrs Nussey would be consulted, and she was sure it meant a boy, which was odd as Mercy was convinced it meant gold, but she was sure Mama was right – only it was so very odd that she had thought it was gold, was it not? and George agreed that it was odd, decidedly odd . . . What was crucial to this talk was that you did *not* invest any of it with emotion or weight or even much sense. Ellen's brother Henry, who was down from Cambridge and destined for holy orders, had the most remarkable command of it. When he entered a room he was already saying: 'Well, well, hm, hm, here we are,' and saying it, too, as if it were absolutely felicitous and fresh. Even after a heavy dinner he was still indefatigably rolling out the *indeed*s and *how very true*s. It was as if silence were nakedness, and every moment must, for decency's sake, be verbally clothed.

But Emily recognised no such imperative. She could go for hours without speaking. In the world of The Rydings, this might be a mere sign of *shyness* – in itself, in that world, no bad thing, as consonant with proper maidenly modesty. But Charlotte knew it was nothing of the kind. Just as much as the attention-seeker, the shy person cared desperately what other people thought of her (oh, how Charlotte knew about that). Emily really didn't care. And when Ellen did arrive for her visit, Emily was perseveringly nothing but herself. Luckily Ellen was too well-bred to react when Emily spent the whole of her first day gazing into the middle distance, and responding to Ellen's timid civilities only with a sort of nodding quarter-smile, as a tolerant person might respond to the ramblings of a drunk.

And it was typical of Emily that, after all, she rather took to Ellen. That night before bed she turned to Charlotte as if struck by a new thought and asked: 'Does your friend ever talk nonsense? You know what I mean – real nonsense?'

'No,' Charlotte said truthfully, plucked at by several kinds of loyalty.

'I didn't think so,' Emily said, with decision. And the next day, when they all went for a ramble on the moors, Emily helped Ellen to the smoothest paths and, when they scrambled over the beck, made sure there were stepping-stones for Ellen to cross. Which she seldom did for short-sighted, undextrous Charlotte.

And Charlotte did wonder – loyalties gnawing again – what Ellen must make of it all. Well, this is how we are: you mun tek as you find, as Tabby would say. Yet when Ellen spotted one of her secret manuscripts (are they secret? well, yes, this proves it) and asked what it was, Charlotte flourished it out of sight and said it was nothing. And Papa – so courtly, yet with his hard, nutlike bite of humour regaling Ellen over breakfast with a black tale of one of his old parishioners, 'Deceased, my dear Miss Nussey, as you will shortly comprehend,' whose widow had left his body lying upstairs for a week before she reported his death. 'The poor woman had often had occasion to complain of her husband's idleness and disinclination to labour; and so, though an *apparently* fatal stroke had felled him at last, still she wanted, to adopt her own robust vernacular, "to mek sure he weren't just lying there shamming".' And then when they walked on the moors, and Anne said proudly: 'This is the place we call the Meeting of the Waters,' Charlotte felt herself seeing from two perspectives, to her discomfort. Yes, that was what it was called, and it loomed large in their lives, and great and unforgettable things had been talked of here. Yet after all it was only – as Ellen must see – the confluence of a couple of moorland streams, strewn with slab-like stones, amid a stretch of colourless turf. So did everything depend on how you perceived it? Did that leave anything real?

At the end of Ellen's visit, they managed an excursion. They all, literally, dropped money into a hat (Branwell's – it won't look much, Charlotte needled, because your head's so big) and found it enough to get them over to Bolton Abbey in a phaeton, or what the Haworth livery-stable was pleased to call a phaeton. It went on wheels, at any rate; and the passage of a pleasure-vehicle through workaday Haworth, where trains of pack-mules were the usual traffic, was arresting enough to bring people out of their doors to stare. Only stare, though: no one waved or gave them a greeting, except little wry-necked Mr Greenwood, the stationer, acknowledging his best customers. Charlotte wondered if Ellen noticed that too. Soon, however, Branwell took vivacious charge of Ellen's entertainment, half hanging out of the carriage to point out the scenery. 'Look there – Miss Nussey, I beg you, throw an eye, as the French say – yonder you will see the castle at Skipton, and *there* lived Lady Anne Clifford, and Samuel Daniel the poet was her tutor – and who was *he*, why one of the sweetest poets of that illustrious age of Elizabeth. Try this – "Care-charmer Sleep, son of the sable Night, Brother to Death, in silent darkness born . . ." Now if *that* doesn't raise the hairs on your arms, then I give you over for ever . . . Well, Anne, what means that niminy-piminy look? Do you object to the notion of ladies having hairs on their arms? Because you assuredly do, fine and fair as they may be, and the involuntary raising of 'em is the one sure guide to the worth of a line of poetry.'

Ellen, Charlotte fancied, was a little fascinated by him – which raised all sorts of unsettling ideas for, after all, this was *Branwell*, this was her brother . . . Then when they put up for breakfast, at the Devonshire Arms in Keighley, his high spirits were temporarily cut down. A sporting gentleman, all sideburns and striped waistcoat, called his friend out to whistle and murmur in disbelief at their ramshackle carriage. Charlotte felt Branwell's inward wince, and understood it. It was the same with those little arts of ladyhood that the other misses at Roe Head cultivated so easily: you knew they were worth nothing, you despised them – yet you felt you could despise them so much more comfortably if you possessed them.

'D'you not know "The White Doe of Rylstone", Miss Nussey?' At Bolton Abbey, squiring Ellen about the grounds, Branwell was back on form. 'Wordsworth wrote it after he came here – aye, here. We tread perhaps the very spot where the muse descended.

"'From Bolton's old monastic tower,
The bells ring loud with gladsome power."

'Oh, it's splendid stuff.' He sprang up on to a stumpy fragment of wall, red mane flashing, and gave forth in his light, twangy voice.

'"The sun shines bright; the fields are gay,
With people in their best array
Of stole and doublet, hood and scarf,
Along the banks of crystal Wharf,
Through the Vale retired and lowly,
Trooping to that summons holy.
And, up among the moorlands, see
What sprinklings of blithe company!"'

One of today's blithe company, a lady stiff with silk and gauze, remarked in Charlotte's hearing to her husband: 'Yes, Irish, I think. There is always something a *little* vulgar in their vitality.'

Charlotte glared and hated, and hastened to take Branwell's arm when he got down. And deep inside she patted the little yellow goblin of thankfulness that she had won the speaking prize at Roe Head for the purity of her English.

They had made such an early start that Charlotte felt exhausted when they climbed aboard the despised carriage for the homeward journey. All around the plaid rugs were being shaken out and the hampers put up and the parasols folded. She thought: There are only two sorts of people in the world – not the rich and the poor, not the virtuous and the wicked, but the successful and the unsuccessful. Drowsing upright as they rattled along the stony road, she half dreamed of archaic barriers ahead, of gates in biblical walls, a torch thrust in to show their faces, the growled negative: no admittance.

Ellen, before leaving: 'You have such a remarkable family, Charlotte. So singular in their devotion to each other. Really, an example of true Christian living.' Charlotte was surprised at the last: whatever we are, she thought, we are not that. 'I feel – I do feel I understand you better now. I wish I understood more. You are all so fearfully clever. I should never want to be a bluestocking – but I should wish to be a little more clever.'

'It's better to be good . . .' Charlotte muttered. 'Hm? Oh, nothing.'

Papa survived the experiment in hospitality very well: he was even not averse to its being repeated some time. Aunt was strong in thin-lipped approval of Ellen's manners. 'They might stand as an example to anyone. Too many girls nowadays are pert and forward – an intolerable failing in my young days in Penzance. Or else they are stand-offish and reserved. I hardly know which is worse.'

Anne was quietly trying out a new Ellen hairstyle. And Emily made her pronouncement. 'Yes, she is very tolerable – very tolerable indeed, all things considered.'

'What things?' demanded Branwell.

'I mean, tolerable as people go.'

Branwell gave an irritated laugh. 'Pooh, Em, where did you pick up this cheap misanthropy?'

Emily was listening, but as so often there was an equivocal moment in which you didn't know whether she would reply or just wander off like a cat.

'Is it misanthropy to not like people?' she asked, with a look of genuine enquiry.

'That's a fair definition of the principle,' Branwell said scoffingly.

'Oh, well, it's not a principle. It's just from what I observe. What I know.'

'You hardly know any people.'

And then Emily, catlike, stretched and walked away, saying: 'But I know myself.'

Gambling had become highly fashionable in Great Glasstown, and such sophistications were rapidly spreading to the new uncouth kingdom of Angria. Charlotte, in chronicling them (yes, she had been tempted back, she had paddled a while in the shallows telling herself she could always get out and the next thing she was fifty feet under, floating-haired, rapturous), had pictured vividly that dramatic moment of the card turning over on the baize or, better, the bony tumble of dice from cup: that perfection of suspense in *not knowing* what the spots would say.

So different from the way the dice of your life fell now. Cheat's dice, you might say, as they rolled and stopped and unerringly displayed the unwanted number.

'Miss Wooler writes most encouragingly,' said Papa, all myopic gallantry, holding up the letter. 'All things considered, I think the terms could hardly be better. But of course you need not decide yet, my dear.'

Roll the dice again: they fell no better.

'Two guineas a lesson seems, I dare say, a great deal,' Papa remarked to Mr Andrew, who had been called in to renew his old acquaintance with Papa's dyspepsia. 'But this is no mere drawing-master. To be taught by Mr William Robinson of Leeds, who was a pupil of Lawrence –

this must lend the strongest weight to Branwell's ambition. And, yes, my own, for him. My son is to be an artist, and anything I can do to that end, any sacrifice I can make . . .' Papa spread out his beautiful long-nailed hands, expressing whole worlds of renunciation. And quite soon Charlotte was spreading out her two frocks and three petticoats on her bed, ready to pack, and expressing nothing at all.

And nothing to do, now, except reckon up the impressive sum of your ingratitude – because, after all, in going to be a teacher at Roe Head you were returning to the familiar, and you were avoiding the other, unknown fate of governess, and Emily was coming with you to be a pupil at the school so it was hardly as if you would be alone, and altogether . . . Altogether it had worked out well, hadn't it? How could it have led to this quivering, shivering madness on the hearth-rug, if not through her own fault?

Emily's first day at Roe Head was also her seventeenth birthday. Charlotte, watching her walk into the schoolroom that morning, and feeling sick and dizzy with her own unwanted transformation, had a sudden wild wish to run to her, to throw a shawl about the two of them and say: *No. This is no good. We're going*. But there was nowhere to go, given that there was no reaching the place she really wished to get to: the past.

Emily looked seventeen and more with her pallor, her gravity, her height. And yet she might also have been any age, compared with the row of misses coldly scrutinising her entrance, their eyes darting wasp-like at the old plain dress grown short in the sleeves, the home-made hairstyle. It was not just that she looked out of place: she seemed to issue from a different world. As she approached the big table with its red velvet cloth and stacked books she somehow transformed it: you could fancy it a throne or an altar or, perhaps, an executioner's block. Something from the world below, in fact – not Glasstown or Angria, but the new world that she and Anne were developing. *Gondal*: Charlotte had visited it, finding it impressive but enigmatic, a place of tragic queens haunting misty glens. Emily brought it with her into the schoolroom on that brash summer morning of her seventeenth birthday. Her eyes fell on her schoolfellows with absolute, void incuriosity, as if they were so many bare hatpegs. And Charlotte, reluctant teacher, thought achingly: Emily, you must try – pretend, bend, surrender a little. That's the first lesson you must learn.

* * *

'You know, you needn't be afraid of approaching me,' Charlotte said, falling into step with Emily on the walk to church.

'What?'

'I mean – don't mind what the others say. If they think I play favourites because we're sisters—'

'Oh! That.' Emily half smiled. Very rarely did she smile fully, and when she did the effect was almost dismayingly intimate, like a moan of pain.

'Well, do they?' Everything about Charlotte's role as a teacher was an anxiety to her; she walked to the schoolroom desk on a high wire in a howling wind.

'I don't know. Perhaps. They're mostly idiots so I suppose they might think that. I don't listen to them much.'

Or talk to them. Charlotte had seen Emily in the evening schoolroom. No sheltering behind the curtain as she herself used to: it was not needed. Emily was wrapped in her own thick curtain of solitude even as she paced with her swinging stride around the room.

'Miss Wooler says your work is very good,' Charlotte said helplessly.

'The work is quite interesting. It's just what it takes away from. The time. The time to be yourself. To live . . . *You* know.'

'Yes, I know . . . I'm sorry I can't be with you more. After school.' Or, as she might have said: *I'm sorry I can't be Anne*. 'If it's any consolation, I have a little bedroom adjoining Miss Catherine's, and she comes in nightly with her hair all down looking like a sacrificial victim, and gives me awful warnings about the ways of men.'

Well, almost a two-thirds smile. 'Is that what we have to prepare ourselves for? Turning into Miss Catherine? Lord. No, don't be sorry, Charlotte. Without you here –' Emily's tone was thoughtful, but still conversational '– I would probably die.'

'Well, of course you know your sister better than I do,' Miss Wooler said. 'I hope if it were something specific about this establishment that is making her unhappy, she would be able to tell you about it. But, really, it may only be a question of time. I have known the most timid and retiring girls settle in at last.'

Blank impossibility of explaining. Certainly timidity did not come into it. The same Emily who with every day at Roe Head was growing more pale and withdrawn had just last year taken the hot flat-iron and pressed it into the flesh of her forearm, because she had given a drink of water to a slobbering stray dog, and it had bitten her, and might be rabid. Charlotte had only found out afterwards, when they were undressing for bed, and she had yelled at the sight of the cauterised wound.

Not fear. And neither was it – Charlotte dared to be sure – the same shadow that had crept over Maria and Elizabeth. Emily had no cough, and though she was thinner there was no loss of her wiry strength, especially when they went on walks beyond the grounds. Above the meadows, above the trees, the distance was crowned with moorland, and when she had that in sight Emily looked as if she could go on walking for ever.

And there, perhaps, you had it. Homesickness – except that in Emily's case the sickness was real, and debilitating. It was not that she harped on home, bewailed her lot, refused to co-operate with her new situation. She just faded. The colour was leaching out of her personality and leaving something dusty, mothy.

While Miss Wooler was still inclined to trust to time, Charlotte knew better. For once, a knowledge she did not particularly crave or enjoy.

'Emily will endure it – that is certain. If she has to, she will endure it.' Private tea with Miss Wooler, kind, flattering elevation, and yet how Charlotte did not relish it, the priestess-like passing of cups, the solemn obligation to bread-and-butter: how she wanted to fly from it all to the ends of the earth, where there was no eating or drinking or conversation.

'Endure?' said Miss Wooler – not sharply: serious and puzzled. 'My dear Miss Brontë, what do you mean? What is to be endured at Roe Head?'

Everything, of course. 'Nothing, of course.' In the grounds of The Rydings there stood a tree that had been struck by lightning and split right down its trunk. That was how Charlotte felt: now there are two of me. One was the schoolteacher, authoritatively gliding the smooth firm path of reason. The other a morally dishevelled creature, cleaving to Emily's side before they flung the magic shawl about themselves and disappeared into the forbidden realm.

'Miss Brontë, why doesn't your sister ever sleep?'

The question was impudent, and meant to be, as Miss Lister's innocent smirk confirmed.

'That is nothing to do with your grammar-lesson. Now show me your book.' She ought to give a black mark for rudeness; indeed she wanted to. But for Charlotte discipline was complicated by her fear of being disliked, or disliked more. 'What do you mean, exactly?'

Later, Emily shrugged in reply. 'I don't spend *all* night at the window. Some, yes. I usually get a little sleep towards dawn. But look – when else can I have my mind to myself? I need to see Augusta Almeda's coronation and the outlaw Douglas and the southern isles, and in the day I can't see them. That's why.'

'You have to do without all that now.' It was meant only to be an unspoken thought, and Charlotte was startled to find it issuing from her lips.

But Emily, unsurprised, merely shrugged again. 'I can't. That's all.'

At mealtimes Charlotte began watching Emily's plate. She did eat, though she was helped to very little and was always the first to finish and to ask to be excused. At last Charlotte succeeded in following her unseen up to the privy. She stood in the passage, listening to the retchings, waiting.

'Emily—'

'Good God, what are you doing there?' Emily dragged a backward hand across her bloodless face. She was caught off-guard and flustered – a rarity.

'Does this happen often?'

'Who's asking the question? The schoolteacher, or my sister? Is it a rule? Have I broken a rule? Do I have to wear the black sash?'

'Emily, I'm worried.'

'Don't. It doesn't happen all the time. It's just sometimes it – it won't stay in me. I've got to get it out.'

'And yet you can always stomach Tabby's cooking,' Charlotte said, ducking behind a weak joke.

'Yes. Yes, that's what makes it so strange,' Emily said thoughtfully. She leaned against the passage wall, her cheek waxy white on the dark panelling. 'Well, there it is. I dare say you have to go and report to Miss Wooler now.'

'Oh, Emily, don't.'

'I do understand you're in rather a difficult position,' Emily said more brightly, and punched the panelling a rapid series of blows until the blood trickled and dripped.

'What are you doing?' Charlotte groaned, holding her.

Emily sucked her knuckles. 'Giving myself a reason for these,' she said, as tears – rarer still – ran thickly down her face. 'It's just – when you realise what you want from life, and how little, how very little it is – a quiet room, a pen – the few people you love nearby – an open door to walk through – the sky to look at – and that's it, nothing else – and the fact that this is *too much* to want in this world. It makes you see, oh, this world sets a mighty high value on itself, and how hollow the great noise . . . how hollow . . .' She suddenly wrenched herself away from Charlotte, pulling out her handkerchief and blotting eyes, knuckles, a hasty mixture of tears and blood. 'I'm *not* going to give up, you know.' Accusingly – as if Charlotte had said what was in her mind.

'So, you're just going to carry on like this instead.'

'Why not? We're carrying on talking, and that's doing no good either.'

Miss Wooler, plump fingers dancing, came to the end of a Haydn sonata, which bowed itself out with civilised good humour. She sighed, turned to Charlotte and shook her head. 'The next thing I fear,' she said, 'is that your sister's being ill may make you ill.'

'I'm quite well, ma'am.'

'For now. I think I had better write to your father, or perhaps enclose a letter with your own. Has she told you she wants to go home?'

Charlotte hesitated. She felt herself holding a precious fragile thing, and for a moment not knowing where safely to put it down: Emily's pride.

'Not in words,' she said.

When she had the answer she made sure to rise early in the morning and go into the dormitory to Emily's bed. First waking was when Emily's misery was most exposed; the day allowed her to man her defences.

There were eleven pupils just now: the odd number meant Emily had been given no bedfellow, though it was hard to imagine her accepting one in any case – she might simply drag up a rug and lie curled on the floor. Charlotte found her lying on her side, her eyes on the curtained window. She was so flat and still that each blink of her dark eyelashes seemed like a large, convulsive gesture. Emily's profile was unequivocally beautiful. When she faced you, she appeared somehow blurred, indeterminate, as if even her looks refused to be pinned down.

'Emily.' Charlotte sat down on the bed. 'I thought I'd tell you before everyone else is up and making their racket. Miss Wooler has written Papa, and Papa has written back. And he and Aunt are convinced that your health and spirits are suffering here, and that it's best if you return to Haworth as soon as possible. Miss Wooler agrees, and so – so you are going home.'

Even as she began to speak, Emily's hand – sleepier, as it were, than her head – had burrowed mole-like from the bedclothes and clasped Charlotte's. It stayed there, warm and hard as a kettle's handle, as she listened. At the end it tightened a little.

'Charlotte,' she said, speaking low but very distinctly, 'do you think it's best?'

'Yes, I do.' As she relinquished Emily's hand she had a sensation of tearing and then of swift scab-like sealing. Their separate selves, each going its own way.

Except, Charlotte thought, I didn't choose mine.

In place of Emily, Anne. The pittance Charlotte earned would still be put to good use, paying the fees to educate a different sister so that she in turn could go forth and educate other girls for a pittance, perhaps preparing them to earn their own pittances by educating girls . . . So *ad infinitum*, or rather *ad nauseam*. Ironically, Charlotte could have said something of this of Emily – it would surely have elicited the skewed smile – but it was not suitable to Anne, who took bitter remarks to heart.

And, besides, Anne came willingly to Roe Head. She came white, mute, nervous, and there was no doubt that the staring misses were thinking, *Here's another awkward dowd of a Brontë* – but it was all too easy to misjudge Anne. Charlotte wondered if she were sometimes guilty of it herself.

'I want to learn,' Anne said, when they had their first full talk on the way to church. 'I want to learn everything. I want to be completely . . . equipped. Yes, equipped for life.'

'Like going into battle?'

'If you like. I shouldn't mind, you know, facing something of a battle. To test myself. There's something about being the youngest that makes you seem always, well, *lesser*. Even to yourself. Papa was doubtful about my coming at first. He sat me down and took my hands and said, "Anne, now are you sure? You know you have never been away from home before." And for a moment I thought: That's true, that's very true, I should have thought of that. And then I remembered that it was the same for everybody – before you went away from home, you had never been before, and Emily and . . . well, Maria and

Elizabeth too. I saw that it would be very easy to get into the habit of making an exception of yourself.'

'And how is Emily?' Charlotte didn't mean the tart emphasis. (Or did she?)

'Oh, she seemed much improved when I left – although Branwell said she still looked like a yard of pump-water.'

'Branwell? Is he home, then?'

'Oh, yes, he came back last week.'

'But he is to return to London? To the Royal Academy?'

Anne looked uncomfortable. 'I don't think so. I don't believe his application was successful – but I'm not sure.' She raised her eyebrows ruefully. 'The youngest again, you see. Don't trouble her head with these grown-up matters. All I know is that he arrived home unexpectedly, and he was closeted with Papa for a long time, and he looked very down in the mouth after. And Aunt says there has been a change of plan and that he is not going to study in London after all, at least not this year. I couldn't ask him anything myself – he'd only have laughed me off. You know how he is.'

Charlotte said, yes, she knew: but suddenly she didn't know anything; all the landmarks of her present life had shifted. Branwell's going up to London to present himself to the Royal Academy, to enrol as a student at the Schools, to forge his career as a painter – this had been at the centre of everything. She had partly reconciled herself to teaching at Roe Head by the thought that she was making a contribution to that end – the expense of Branwell's training – and that it would be worth it to see him established. And those expensive lessons with Mr Robinson of Leeds, and that impressive smell of linseed and turpentine clinging about Branwell's coat, and Papa's judicious noddings as he surveyed the new canvas – they had seemed to lead so unerringly to one satisfying conclusion that Charlotte could only think that Anne had it wrong.

(And yet – let the mind whisper it only – what did Papa, or indeed any of them, know of painting? And hadn't she noticed how frayed Mr Robinson's cuffs were? You could put that down to artistic carelessness: or you could conclude that he badly needed the fees, and if that meant encouraging unrealistic expectations in a paying pupil, then so be it.)

She wrote home, but Papa's reply was grandiloquently evasive. You hunted the truth in vain through that forest of subordinate clauses. The answer must await the Christmas holiday. Meanwhile Charlotte applied herself to the task of not revealing or admitting, to herself or anyone, how much she hated teaching the misses; and Anne applied herself to the task of fitting in, somehow. She did it. She could never fit in as the others did – like guns bedding into a gun-case, Charlotte thought, marvelling and despairing, or that drawer in Papa's desk where the pot of silver-sand had its own little waiting, precisely measured, hole. But neither was she all awkward edges and bumps. She walked arm in arm, pleasantly, with another girl. You did not have to explain her or make excuses for her. It was even possible, for long periods, to forget about her.

Returning to Haworth for the Christmas vacation, Charlotte felt as if some trick had been played on her. She had been away, earning her bread, becoming a person whom the world must, even in the most perfunctory way, acknowledge: swimming in the cold element of change. Yet she found home almost eerily unaltered. Oh, Emily seemed an inch taller, and Branwell had cultivated a thin whisker, which he kept tugging at as if to make it grow longer. But everyone regarded her with a bright, smooth inexpectancy, as if she had just been down to the post office. Emily eagerly opened her writing-box to show Anne the latest chronicle of Gondal; Branwell spoke of great doings in Angria. Was Roe Head dreaming, and this waking – or the other way round?

Being short-sighted, Charlotte was accustomed to using her hands if she dropped a pin or a thimble. You knelt and spread out your fingers and set them gliding in careful expanding circles over the floor until your skin received that little cold message. And she began to do something like this as she observed Branwell: she detected the little interruptions under that smooth surface. The Royal Academy project was not mentioned. When she did casually ask him about it, he only said: 'Oh, that. Old news. Didn't suit. Other plans afoot now.' He was breezy, but there was a shrill note to the breeze. When his turn came for duty at the Sunday school Papa had had built down the lane, he groaned and seethed with impatience.

'They're such dull, idle little devils, it drives me mad. It takes an age just to hear them through three verses. I swear they drag it out to tease. And then it's perfectly obvious that none of it means a damn thing to them – as why should it?' His voice was defiant, but he glanced nervously over his shoulder in case Papa was in earshot.

'Don't let Anne hear you talk like that,' Charlotte said. 'She'll think you're in earnest.'

'She's been with Aunt too long. She'll start to smell of brimstone and hellfire if she's not careful.' His grin was strained and savage. 'Besides, who's to say I'm not in earnest?'

Later, in church, she saw him moodily cuffing the Sunday scholars into their pew and then sitting apart, tugging his whisker and staring at the wall. When the sermon began he sniffed and took a book from his pocket. A virginal apparition moved against the high barred windows: snow.

'I've a mind to go out and see how it's settling on the top moor,' Branwell said that evening.

Anne glanced towards the closed study door. 'Papa will be worried.'

'Papa won't know.' At the window Branwell's high shoulders twitched in irritation. 'Papa doesn't have to know everything, for God's sake. I'll slip out of the back kitchen. If he asks, I've gone to bed.'

It was past ten – long after Papa and Aunt had made their nightly withdrawal from the life of the house – when Charlotte, reading at the table with Emily, heard the back door; then the heavy footsteps ascending. She took a candle and went after him. 'Branwell.' His bedroom door was ajar. 'Have you no light?'

'Hardly need it. I've still got this white dazzle before my eyes. Come in, come in.' He was sitting on the bed, looking exhausted, cheekbones protruding, long swoops of damp conker hair over his high brow. 'Snow's thick everywhere. Great sculpted heaps of it. There's a kind of tremendously wasteful beauty about it all. As if someone should paint a great masterpiece of a fresco on a wall, then take a sledgehammer to the wall before the paint was dry.' He gave a short, extinguishing laugh at that; shook his head. 'Well, you've been reading the new Angrian chronicles, I hope, not wasting your time with frivolous fantasies. What think you? Does Northangerland surprise you?'

'His daring surprises me.' Yes, she had been wrapped up in Branwell's latest reports from the world below – fighting the pull of it, almost lost. Though she had not been too lost to notice the way Branwell's handwriting kept changing violently, sometimes in mid-sentence. 'I admire it in a way – I admire *him* in a way, but he is growing so powerful. And he can be so destructive.'

'Oh, yes.' Branwell nodded in satisfaction, his pale eyes locked on the candle-flame. 'He is growing powerful.'

Charlotte set the candle on the night-stand. 'Branwell, what happened? All this while I've been thinking . . . When I went to Roe

Head to be a teacher I knew that you were about to go off into a different world yourself; everyone was talking about London and the Royal Academy, and it helped, thinking we were all doing something new – and now nobody says anything about it—'

'That's because there's nothing to say,' Branwell put in sharply, and then, staging a yawn: 'I found certain entry requirements not met. That's all. What a great fuss you're making about a straightforward matter.'

She watched him. 'There's no such thing as a straightforward matter.'

'True, true. Oh, true.' He fell backwards, coldly laughing at the ceiling. 'Hand me those tablets of stone. Oh, my wrist hurts. Took a bad blow at the boxing club last week. Old Moses must have been a proper bruiser, you know. Lugging the Commandments down, handfuls of great big bloody gravestones . . . But, really, nothing happened in London. My dear Charlotte, you must restrain this urge towards the melodramatic interpretation of events.'

'Why? Doesn't it tend to be the true one?'

He closed one eye, laughing again without mirth. 'Schoolteaching has given you quite a taste for catechism. Why this and why that. When are you going to write something? Zamorna needs you. He's recalcitrant in my hands.'

'So you did go to London?'

'There you go again. What will my punishment be if I don't get my exercise? Sorry, tasteless I know. Charlotte, about the school – do you hate it very much?'

'I don't know.' I lie a lot with Branwell, she thought randomly. 'I try to see it as a necessity. As it is.'

He put an unsteady hand to his brow, as if he were shielding himself. 'I'm glad you like the new story. I have several more in the offing. In one I think to send Charles Wentworth – young gentleman of outer Angria, good family, but thoroughly provincial – well, he makes the journey to Verdopolis. Floating with excitement he is – for he knows all about the great city, you see, or fancies he does: always been a great reader, living out in the dull wilds, and he's read everything ever written about the place. And in fact it gives him a queer feeling when he gets there – when he actually beholds those palaces and steeples that have been present to his imagination for so long. And now here they are; now here *he* is – but that's just what he can't manage to put together.' Branwell sat up, hugging his knees. The candlelight pitilessly fingered his flinching face, a doctor seeking pain. 'He is conscious that he is not at all what he thought himself. Take him away from his province, where he is accustomed to be generally admired, and set him among these great avenues crowded with men of consequence, and he is quite an inconsiderable person. And the sense of this rather stuns him. He wanders about. He drinks, to take the – well, to take the glare off the terrible magnificence. His people have supplied him with money: how soon it goes, in a city like this! And he has letters of introduction, to forward his career in Verdopolis – but the letters stay in his pocket. Because once he presents them, why, then the reality must be faced, whereas at least this way I – he can slide and slink about the streets and be hidden.' Charlotte had sunk down on the bedside chair, but still he did not look at her. She had a strange sensation of his talking to her from the other side of a screen or partition: she could almost touch it. 'And when he steps into the Temple of the Muses – when he gazes on the great accretions of grandeur and genius laid out before him, a masterpiece between every blink – so superb and so unreachable – those paintings . . . then he feels like a child who has been proudly waving his cardboard sword, suddenly finding an army marching past, gleaming and clattering, with their terrible blades and potent guns . . .'

'Is that how you . . . Is that how the story ends?'

With a convulsive movement Branwell twisted round and blew out the candle she had set on the night-stand. 'Hurts my eyes. The end – I don't know. I haven't decided on the end yet. Sorry, Charlotte. God, I'm tired . . .'

As she closed the door behind her she thought she heard him say again, 'Sorry', but it might have been the sigh of snow at the window, dragged by its own heaviness from the sill.

Another Christmas vacation: snowless this time but viciously cold, the hall riddled with skewering draughts as Charlotte stood before Papa's study door, the book in her hand, her heart thundering as she readied herself to knock, enter – ask. That meant a whole year had passed, but she didn't account it a whole year, not in terms of being alive. For much of it she was not truly living at all.

And when she was truly living, it was dangerous, clandestine, wrong.

Mary Taylor said: 'Here – from Father – another shocking new French novel. Best hide it away. The girls might be corrupted just from seeing the cover. Well, well, you don't look entirely crushed and spiritless yet, which is something.' She had come to see her at Roe Head with her sister Martha, who was equally dry-tongued and pawky, but who somehow turned it all to fun: it was like the same note played on different instruments. Miss Wooler allowed Charlotte to give them tea in her parlour, where their glinting darkness seemed conspicuous among the fancy-work and tea-roses.

'That is something, certainly,' Charlotte said. 'As it's generally agreed that schoolteaching will turn me either into a drudge or a snarling harpy, perhaps the latter will be my fate. I think I prefer it of the two.'

'Fate is the word,' Mary said. 'As in fateful or fatal. As in dreadful and direful—'

'Oh, Mary, you exaggerate.'

'Of course I do, that's what I'm for. Oh, I dare say I shall be prodded and shooed towards the same gate when Father can't keep me any more – though I'll kick and bite before I go through it. But really, Charlotte, a position like this – is there any profit in it?'

'What I earn pays for Anne's schooling. So that's a saving for Papa, and that in turn means helping Branwell towards . . .'

'Towards what? Believe me, I mean no disrespect to your brother, I'm sure he is a brilliant fellow, but it might help if you knew exactly what these sacrifices were for. Is he training up for a profession – for the law, or the Church?'

'Not the Church, above all not the Church. He has no inclination that way – even Papa sees that.'

Martha said: 'You need to be like Henry Nussey to go into the Church. He's taking orders, you know. You have to have that *blink* – about one per minute – and that way of bending at the waist like a pocket-ruler and that voice that goes up and down like a see-saw.'

'Well, Branwell has none of that,' Charlotte said, smiling reluctantly. (She always did – a smile seemed to invite danger, like dangling your purse.) 'And as for the law, I doubt that would suit him.'

'But what about what would suit *you*?' Mary said, studying her so closely that for a moment Charlotte felt them to be schoolfellows again, and almost wanted to shrink behind the curtain.

'A thumping legacy from a long-lost uncle,' Martha put in, 'or a marriage proposal from a good-looking duke – the sort of things that would suit us all, Mary. But we disposable women have to be realistic in this life, you know. Else we get itchy and discontented and start contemplating the kitchen knife and wondering whether it wouldn't look nicer between someone's shoulder-blades.'

'I should want this duke to have some brains as well,' Mary said.

'And even then I wouldn't be sure. I wouldn't be my own woman any more.'

'Just a twopenny-halfpenny duchess,' sighed Martha.

'I know this is not a wonderful place,' Charlotte said, 'but neither is it contemptible. Miss Wooler is kind, and – and besides, what other sort of place *is* there? I am a woman, and I have no money or connections – and, as you once instructed me, Mary, I have nothing in the way of looks either.'

'Lord. Did I say that to you? I suppose I did. What a little beast. You should have ducked my head in the chamber-pot.'

'No, no. You did me good. As Martha says, we have to be realistic in life.' But there was a little guilty pleasure (Charlotte could not in fact imagine any other kind) in seeing Mary's discomfort, from which she emerged pink-cheeked and a little strident.

'Well, there ought to be – there must be some other sort of place. Not just teaching brats or trimming hats. And if there isn't, then we must make it somehow. And now I sound as if I'm belittling what you're doing, Charlotte, and I'm not, not at all – I'm simply saying it's a heroism that surely isn't called for.'

Charlotte frowned, perhaps at hearing her inner thoughts, those tongueless eunuchs, given such voice; turned brisk. 'Oh, nothing so grand as that. It's just – well, I know the word is dusty, but it's duty.'

'Take out the *s*, and it *is* the same word,' cried Martha, delightedly. Mary did not smile.

There must be some other place . . . Oh, yes, there was, and Branwell had tempted her – after all, didn't the devil have red hair? – tempted her back into it. Nearly every waking moment of the vacations she spent in Angria. It was wonderfully sweet, though she knew it was wrong. Or, rather, she knew it was wrong because it was wonderfully sweet. And perhaps Branwell was not really to be blamed. Weren't you very ready to be tempted? Wasn't the devil, in other words, inside you?

'Teach me to be good,' she had begged Ellen Nussey at The Rydings. Ellen was good, you could see it in her calm, luminous gaze and her patience when her brothers and sisters talked over her and the way she read her Bible with attentive interest, as if it were not a terrible drama but a well-written book of instructions: so that's how it's done. 'Teach me how to be like you.'

'Those are different things,' Ellen said smiling. 'I *wish* I was good, and that's about the best I can say of myself. But I do believe that when you realise you are not good – when you see in your heart your weakness and backsliding and don't try to cover it over – then you have made the first step.'

Charlotte hung on her words: clung physically, as if she might absorb some of that goodness leech-like. Comfort me with scripture-readings, stay me with sewing for the charity basket . . . But then she pictured what Ellen must mean by weakness and backsliding. A touch of vanity about those blond curls, perhaps; a little flash of possessiveness, hardly amounting to jealousy, when Charlotte spoke of Mary. What would Ellen think if she could look into Charlotte's soul, and see its dreadful capabilities?

Like:

Her loathing of her duty. Absolute detestation of teaching verbs and substantives to the misses, who detested learning them. Hatred of the whole thing.

Her impatience with Anne, who from somewhere – a doleful seed planted by Aunt, perhaps – had got Calvin into her. Haltingly she confessed to pious creeps and hellfire horrors. Sin, sin. Here was another one – what had Anne to do with sin, Anne who never spoke a hasty word? Charlotte shrugged her off, and shrugged on guilt: after all, she of all people ought to understand how you could be your own torturer.

Her longing for home – which was snagged and knotted by a feeling that home represented defeat. Sometimes in the evening when the north wind got up about Roe Head she would listen to its keening and buffeting and follow it, in her imagination, across the moors to Haworth. Once she wrote her name on a thin ribbon of paper and let it go out of an upstairs window, just on a whim, just so that she could fancy it bowling across the sky and ending up flapping on a thorn outside the parsonage door. And once she came to the sentimental edge of wishing she could send her thoughts there on the wind – only to recoil. Because they would not all be nice thoughts, not by any means. Because sometimes when she thought of Emily, comfortably occupied at home, safe in her willed escape, her lucky incapacity, she turned momentarily faint with envy, and hate.

Her longing for the infernal world – a sick longing, she knew that. When something was amiss bodily, you had symptoms: and the symptoms of her imagination were alarming. More than once, when she lay on the couch in the dormitory after lessons or sat on the garden-bench in twilight, and allowed Angria to become real and engulf her, she grew frightened. The misses came by, chattering, comparing ribbons, and it was as if they were behind thick glass; and Charlotte was held fast, paralysed, by the intense clasp of the dream-world, so that it seemed impossible to bang on the glass, or ever to get back to the other side of it. Impossible – and undesirable. This was sickness.

And what would Ellen make of this: the way she hugged that sickness to her at every possible moment, like a drunkard reaching for his secret pocket-flask? Until at last you no longer trouble to keep the flask out of sight. So she sat at her desk while the misses drooped over their grammar-books, and (the devil inside) succumbed to the temptation, and drew a sheet of paper towards her and closing her eyes – to shut Roe Head out, to make it not real – began feverishly to write. It could only be a sketch, a snatch – Zamorna's confession of infidelity, perhaps, and his wife's hot tears shining like dropping pearls in the Verdopolitan night – but it was something, it was everything . . . And then to hear the sidling, snickering approach to the desk of Miss Marriott – much esteemed for her dexterity with curl-papers and her talent for laughing shrilly at nothing for minutes on end – and to hear the arch enquiry: 'Miss Brontë, why ever are you writing with your eyes shut?' And then to picture with exhilarating clarity her answer – lifting up her pen, and behold it is a pen of fire, and scribbling and slashing it all across Miss Marriott's stupid pretty face until she is crossed and scored and blotted out from the page of life . . . What would Ellen think of that?

She would think – quite rightly – how bad, how very bad. Also, perhaps, how mad. (Which would be prophetic of her.)

And that was why, now Christmas had come round again, she was standing outside Papa's study with her great question hovering before her like her own condensing breath.

Again Branwell had played his part, if unwittingly, in this decision. Though he had continued with his painting lessons, he seemed to devote just as much time to writing. (As she knew, to her blissful cost, whenever a letter from him arrived at Roe Head. Before opening it she would weigh it in her hand, stroke it. She knew that Northangerland and Zamorna and Augusta Romana di Segovia waited within. It was like touching the outside of a wasps' nest, warm and pregnantly vibrating: perilous.) And he had begun applying to their old venerated *Blackwood's Magazine.*

'You mean as a contributor?'

'I mean as a saviour. Oh, not that it has gone sharp downhill or anything of that shape – that would be doing it too brown.' He was full of racy phrases like this lately: they must have come from the other publications he subscribed to, sporting magazines devoted to boxing and ratting, with drawings of muscular rakes squaring up to each other in tight breeches. 'Only I fancy it ain't as fresh as it used to be. It needs new blood. It needs someone like me, who's read it for so long he can copy the house style as like as fourpence to a groat – only I'll give them originality too, brilliance and daring. You'll observe I'm not letting false modesty hold me back.'

'But can you do that?' Charlotte had said wonderingly. 'Can you set yourself up as a writer?' *Is it allowed?* was what she almost said.

'Of course, where do you think writers come from? They ain't born that way, like dauphins and Prince of Waleses. They are what they do.'

Charlotte experienced a thrill that was, for once, not guiltily illicit. Instead it seemed to open proper possibilities: to throw a bridge across to the shores of the real and acceptable.

So, to the study door, the knock. Papa's high, strong voice saying, 'Come in,' after a moment. And the little sour lick of wonder: what it must be like to have that power of deferring entry, of making others wait though there was nothing to wait for.

'My dear Charlotte, this is not like you. To trespass upon the hour sacred to the vagaries of my digestion – and yet, you know, I am finding an agreeable novelty in it.'

Papa at his most twinkling and emollient. Promising, though it could quickly change. A meagre fire shone red in the grate like some small flayed thing. On his desk, copies of the *Leeds Mercury* and *Halifax Guardian*, passages vigorously marked: he was forever engaged in spirited correspondence, not an issue that left him unmoved. Charlotte set down the book.

'Ah, what is that you have there? Surely not one of my own poor effusions?'

'Yes, Papa. Your *Cottage Poems*. I have been rereading them with great pleasure; and they have chimed with an idea – a thought of my own that has been growing on me lately. Especially when the term at Roe Head ends, and I think of the likely shape of my future, and – and I find my spirits a little lowered.'

'My dear, are you not happy at Roe Head?' And then, with the quickness of a slamming door: 'That is, have you something specific to complain of in your treatment there?'

Go on, don't look on that as a setback. 'No. No, there is nothing in particular – I realise I am quite well placed—'

'I am intensely relieved to hear of it. It is what I would have *supposed*, knowing Miss Wooler and her establishment as I do; but still, I am glad to have your assurance that you are content with your position there.' He smiled benignly, expectantly, his hand straying to his watch-chain.

'But thinking of the future, Papa – now I know very well how we are situated as a family, and that I must earn my keep, at least for the time being. But the future is a great thing – I see it like a great sea stretching out, and I wonder if this is the *only* vessel in which I can undertake to sail it. And looking over your poems again, I wonder if I might not in some degree follow your example—'

'My dear Charlotte, you have taken up quite a wrong idea about my little publications. That was long ago. They were locally printed, with no profit to me, nor with any thought of such: moral instruction for the poor, suitably sweetened with entertainment, was their sole aim.'

'Yes, Papa – but you loved writing them, did you not? I remember you telling me how the minutes and hours would fly by, and you were so wrapped up in them you neglected to eat.'

'Did I now? It's been a while since I even thought of them. Certainly literary composition is a pleasurable and fruitful exercise for the mind.'

'And might it not be something more? You know we have all loved to write since we were small, and I believe that in itself has given us some facility. Lately Branwell has been seeking to contribute to *Blackwood's*. It seems to me that here is a possibility – more suited to my temperament and inclinations than schoolteaching – a different vessel in which to sail. If I were to apply myself wholly and earnestly to writing, it might prove a sound enough ship, might it not?'

'My dear Charlotte, this is disturbing. I am almost inclined to censure Branwell, if it is he who has put these ideas into your head, though I dare say he meant no harm. Branwell's manifold talents may possibly – I only say possibly – lead him at last to make a figure in the world of letters; but you should not suppose that this is any kind of avocation on which you as a young woman may found your future. Perhaps, indeed, I have been lax in not warning you with sufficient gravity against the indulgence of these propensities. The urge to scribble I have always regarded leniently – yes, with understanding, from my own case; but it must always be set against the sterner duties and realities of life.'

'Papa, those I do truly comprehend. I could hardly have worked for my bread this past year if I did not.' Careful: keep that mutinous tone down, notice the quartz glint in his eye. 'What I – what I am wondering is whether I may not have an ability, a resource that might be of use in that real life, even though it springs from the imagination. Women have written before—'

'So they have, but seldom has it been their sole occupation. Nor would it be healthy if it were. My dear Charlotte, you must not permit yourself to be seduced by this illusion even for a moment. The profession of letters, which entails a degree of public exposure, must always be a dubious one for a woman to enter, unless she is duly safeguarded by reputable independence or by marriage – which are also required to secure her against the notorious instability of the author's livelihood. The stipend of the teacher or governess may not be liberal, but it is regular. But beyond that, there is the danger to her character – I would go so far as to say, to her soul – in choosing to apportion so much of her time to the dreaming of dreams, the weaving of fancies. There is a temptation in this even when it is a male hand that wields the pen; for a woman, who is by nature more vulnerable to the snare of morbid romancing, the peril is dreadful.'

'Papa, I hope and believe I would never be unmindful of my duties, if I were to pursue writing seriously—'

'That would be your intention, no doubt. But we are weak and fallible mortals, Charlotte. Sooner or later the unwholesome spell would work on you. The world on the page would appear so much more beguiling than the flawed and fallen world in which we must live. Discontent, gnawing discontent would be the result.'

He spoke so forcefully, readily – as if he had this whole argument already rehearsed – that her own careful preparation went for nothing. The advance guard turned tail, the squares began to break. She tried to seize the falling colours. 'I understand you, Papa: but I cannot wholly distrust authorship –' she patted *Cottage Poems* '– when I have your example before me. If I can be aware of the dangers, yet still aspire—'

'Then you will turn into a self-tormentor,' he rapped out, reddening, 'a species of person with which I have very little patience.' He slid one of the newspapers towards him with a rigid finger. 'Have the goodness to return that book to its proper place.' And you to yours, of course, you to yours for ever and ever.

* * *

That battle was a defeat, but it was not the end of the campaign. There remained the letter.

She had talked with Branwell about this, and he had been breezily reassuring.

'Oh, don't flinch from that, Charlotte. Your great men like to be solicited with correspondence, you know, literary men especially – it reminds 'em of the fact that they're great. I have a notion to send a few things to Wordsworth some time soon, and see what he has to say. After all, his time can't be much occupied – he never writes anything of account nowadays. I might just hint that to him, while I'm about it.'

So: the letter, its contents incessantly redrafted, at last carried ceremoniously (well, just in her hand – but it felt so) down to the post-office, and despatched. No going back now. Hard to tell whether she felt cheered or discouraged by the man's blank, indifferent, Haworth glance at the direction on the letter before it went into the bag. *Robert Southey, Esq., Greta Hall, Keswick.* Yes, I am writing to the Poet Laureate. I am sending him some of my verses, and seeking his opinion on them, and on the possibility of my becoming a writer; and it seems dream-like and absurd that I'm doing this – and it doesn't modify life a whit. The yellow reeking fleeces still swung up to the high warehouse doors; and in the sky the frail winter afternoon was being crowded out by vast, authoritative swathes of blue-blackness.

The rest of the vacation was devoted to waiting for an answer. Of course you didn't want a too swift reply – that would suggest a mere dismissal, your work returned unread. But if the silence went on too long, the fear must grow that you weren't even worthy of an acknowledgement, that you had terribly insulted and presumed . . . *Return that book to its proper place.* Distraction was provided by looking after Tabby, who slipped on the icy street and broke her leg. Charlotte, Emily and Anne insisted that she stay at the parsonage while she recovered: they would help nurse her and share her work. Branwell agreed, though all he did was read her the newspaper in the evenings, shamelessly inventing as he went along – the young Princess Victoria eloping with a bandmaster, startling discovery by navy that Portugal is not there any more. As long as his routine was undisturbed, Papa was agreeable: it was Aunt who had to be persuaded, even beseeched, not to consign Tabby to her sister in Stubbing Lane and take on a new servant. Perhaps she felt the work was unladylike – sewing, bed-making and light cooking were the only approved tasks – but there was something bitterly affronted in her glance as Emily blackleaded the range or Anne hurried by with the slop-bowl. Disposable women, Charlotte thought: when they were of no further use, you disposed of them. Aunt, of course, had her little private income.

And Mr Southey remained as mute and distant and mysterious as one of his favourite mountains, right up to the end of the vacation and beyond – the beyond that was Roe Head, teaching, monotony, and steadily increasing misery. (Increasing? Call it rather a narrowing and squeezing of existence – as if, having stopped growing, you found the process going painfully into reverse.) When at last the letter came, the garden at Roe Head was long-fingered with sticky buds, and they clung and tapped at her as she walked round and round reading it, as if asking, *What does it say?*

It says . . . well, it says I certainly have a faculty for verse. That's one of the things it says.

'Charlotte, the ground is quite damp,' called Miss Wooler. 'Have a care you don't take cold.'

And it says, also, that this talent is not at all uncommon nowadays. But it does not discourage me from the actual writing of poetry, for its own sake.

'Miss Brontë, how ever can you read that same letter over and over?' squawked Miss Marriott. 'Isn't it dreadfully dull?'

And it says that Mr Southey's habit is always to warn young men of the perils of a literary career, let alone a young woman. And it says – all this is put very kindly, by the way – that he sees great danger for me in my being continually absorbed in daydreams, as they are likely to make me discontented with real life.

'Charlotte, I've brought your shawl,' said Anne, and touched her hand. 'Don't strain your eyes.'

And it says – it says . . . Darkness had filled the cold spring garden, and the letter in her hand was only a pale shape like a great moth. But she had the words by heart now.

> *Literature cannot be the business of a woman's life, and it ought not to be. The more she is engaged in her proper duties, the less leisure she will have for it, even as an accomplishment and a recreation. To those duties you have not yet been called, and when you are you will be less eager for celebrity . . .*

She felt a little faint, and reckoned that this must be the simple result of there being no blood at her heart, because all her blood, for an hour or more, had been in her burning, pulsing cheeks, in a pathological blush of mortification.

So: there was her answer, set out like a commandment in Southey's surprisingly angular script. Why surprising? Well, she had imagined everything about him as serene and rounded: the great poet, intimate of Coleridge and Wordsworth, full of years and honours, his mind deep and reflective as the Lakes. She had been wrong about a lot of things. She had even pictured his face, noble, lined, yet retaining a child-like brightness. Now she saw that the sage of Keswick wore instead the stern, carved face of Papa; and it seemed probable that, turn where she might, she would find that face replicated everywhere. An infinitude of Papas, feeling for their watch, waiting for her to go back to her place.

She put the letter away safely, where the misses could not get at it for curl-papers. Some weeks later she took it out and reread it and carefully wrote on the outer cover: *Southey's Advice To be kept for ever Roe-Head April 21 1837.* That was how she celebrated her twenty-first birthday.

That was, perhaps, the penultimate step on the path to her madness by the ashy hearth. The last was when Anne fell ill, and Maria and Elizabeth began to look out from her pain-rich eyes.

They had been much on Charlotte's mind lately. In dream, in thought, or in the place in between the two where she dwelt more and more as term succeeded term and hope became a husk. The most vivid dream was of going home and finding Maria and Elizabeth there – not dead, but grown to young women. Changed, though: cold, smart, affected, looking about the parlour with dainty disdain. And as for Charlotte – oh, my dear, is this it? What happened? Is this all there is to you? Their attention picked her up and dropped her, like a piece of inferior lace.

Waking, she carried the dream about with her. There could be none of the usual pleasure in shrugging it off, for what could one say? Oh, thank heaven it's not real: thank heaven they're dead after all.

For a while Anne hid her malady. This was not Emily, frankly and single-mindedly abandoning her hold on a life that was not her own choice. Anne, as she had said, wanted to learn, she was doing well here. But soon the fever and the tight breathing could not be concealed.

The walk to church exhausted her. She had to sit down on a stone wall, hoarse and puffing. Charlotte sat beside her. She looked down at the thin stick of wrist between cuff and glove. Remembrance and terror swirled her about, while she found her voice saying quite calmly: 'Anne, you are rather poorly. I shall ask Miss Wooler to send for the doctor.'

And the doctor said, yes, a tertian fever, an unhealthy season (incredible that the Christmas vacation approached again, as if time were falling apart too) and we must take care, yes, a lowering diet and rest – and now how was Miss Wooler's excellent father? He was sorry to hear it – and though he was sure Mr Wooler had very good medical attendance, if he could ever be of service . . .

'Consumptive?' Miss Wooler said, about to bite into a slice of bread-and-butter. It was very like her, white-and-gold, wholesome and bland. 'My dear Charlotte, I understand your concern, but the physician said nothing of that. Nor do I see anything to suggest it – and your sister complains of no such symptoms.'

'That's the trouble,' Charlotte said, sitting by Anne's bed that night. 'You complain of so very little.'

Anne smiled wanly. 'It's best to be uncomplaining. Who was that man who did all the grand gardens? Brown, Capability Brown, yes. I always liked that name. I'm going to adopt one like it. "Uncomplaining Anne" – that's how I shall go down to posterity.'

Charlotte shook off her own smile. 'Don't. Don't talk about posterity. And – oh, surely we are allowed to complain sometimes, aren't we?'

Aren't we? The question danced in echo through her mind and through the days, as Anne seemed to get no better, and Miss Wooler glided smoothly about recommending little treats for the invalid, and Charlotte found Roe Head melding into Cowan Bridge and fancied the ponderous tread of Carus Wilson along its corridors; and at last she burst sideways into rage.

'I am afraid you are making altogether too much of your sister's indisposition, Charlotte: you are fairly tormenting yourself with it,' Miss Wooler said one evening, when Charlotte had been reading to her, and not concentrating. 'Now I happen to have a very warm interest in hearing the conclusion of this chapter, if properly read, and—'

'I have a very warm interest, ma'am, in my sister's health,' Charlotte cried, throwing the book down. Suddenly everything had changed: consequences were only crumbs, to be swept off the table. 'I have seen too much illness in my family to be easy with this. I had supposed you would understand.'

'Charlotte, this violence is uncalled for.' Miss Wooler drew in her skirts and pouted mildly, as at a lapse of taste.

Charlotte's mind-sky filled with fireworks. 'Everything is uncalled for in your world, isn't it? Anything unpleasant, put it away, pretend it doesn't exist, because you mustn't be made uncomfortable even for a single second. Well, I'm sorry, ma'am, but it's true . . .' Incredibly, Miss Wooler was crying. For a moment Charlotte had a sensation of being on stage, of footlights and painted scenery. But, no, these roles were real. And something about those mewing tears goaded her to new fury. 'If I torment myself, it is because I saw my elder sisters die of a consumption – and I will not have that dismissed as if it were of no account. Nor will I sit tamely by and not speak of it, because I am made of flesh and blood, ma'am, flesh and blood not marble and china and damnable embroidery . . .'

It didn't last long, this combustion, and physically it amounted to no more than gestures, a slam of her hand on the tinkling tea-table; yet her feeling afterwards was of an awesome blast that left everything around her scorched and stunned, including herself. Contrition was there somewhere, but for the moment it was blotted out by an absolutely novel feeling: power. She had never known it before.

Miss Wooler wept and wept. 'I am really – really unequal to demonstrations of this sort. I hardly know what to do.'

'Neither do I, ma'am. But I know we are better apart – that's all.' She lay sleepless that night, gazing into an incandescent red landscape strewn with great boulders of fear. Two days later, Papa stood windblown and harried in the hall. Was it, could it be Cowan Bridge all over again? Surely life did not allow such ghastly pointed symmetry. There was a brief and dissonant quartet: Charlotte protesting that she knew nothing of his being summoned, Miss Wooler crying that she did not know what else to do, Papa trying to squeeze in his elaborate compliments, Anne claiming that she felt much better. The Misses Marriott and Lister goggled from the schoolroom door. Oh, those Brontës: shocking frights, you know, but vastly entertaining.

And at the last, after the packing, Miss Wooler beckoned Charlotte into her parlour and said, very simply, without tears, staring out of the window: 'Dear Charlotte, I don't want to lose you.'

Charlotte said: 'I don't want to be lost.'

And that was how it was: she went home early, with Anne, for the

Christmas vacation, but she would be going back to Roe Head. Miss Wooler had said all that needed to be said. And, besides, what else was there for her?

What else, indeed? Answering that question – or dwelling on it or brooding on it or wildly hurling it around the room – was what brought her, at last, to her knees by the mad hearth. And that was in spite of the vast relief of finding Anne recovering once she was back home, and the thing she had feared only a fear after all. That this did not content her showed, perhaps, what she had always suspected, that she was a very bad person. A wicked one, even – when she packed her trunk again and looked out at January thick-slabbed with dirty snow and thought: Why me? For Anne was not to return to school: her health being insecure, it was agreed that she had learned enough to equip her. It was agreed, yes, Charlotte agreed. Only the devil in her could have produced that unvoiced howl: so they are all to be blessed with the freedom of home and the freedom of the mind and the pen and the world below and I, I alone, must go back to tedium and drudgery . . .

And upheaval. Roe Head was only leased, and Miss Wooler shifted her school to a smaller, thriftier house up on Dewsbury Moor, close to the family home. There was something muffled about it, as if the fogs that could be seen roiling around the foot of the hill had infiltrated the house and were living in its attics. Down in Dewsbury Miss Wooler's father was very ill. Often she had to go to him, leaving Charlotte in charge. Once she came back from such a visit, sat down to tea with Charlotte, enquired after the day's lessons and the state of Miss Fleming's boil, and then, with careful, absorbed, accurate flicks of her finger, edged her saucer off the table until it smashed on the floor.

'In my judgement,' she said, looking glassily down at the fragments, 'there can be few things worse than making someone feel guilty for being alive. I also remark how very strange it is that the person we most love in life can inspire in us the fiercest feelings of hate.' She put up her hands to her buttery hair, to her peach-downed cheeks, as if to reassure herself she existed, then stooped to clear up the broken saucer, murmuring: 'Please never allude to this again, Charlotte.'

It was the Easter vacation when it finally happened – or, rather, the vacation that was snatched away from her because Mr Wooler was dying and Charlotte was needed to take charge at Dewsbury Moor. How inconvenient of Mr Wooler to time his mortality like that: yes, such was the sort of wicked person she had become. But the trouble was, she had made an appointment. Come the vacation, she would have the time and liberty to enter the infernal world again. Now that prospect was lost, and along with it went her mind.

But *they* could enter the infernal world, of course, that was different; *they* could spend blissful hours and days strolling the shores of imagination – them, Branwell, Emily, Anne – and how she hated them for it even as she ached for love of them and need to be with them because only they understood, only they were capable of understanding; it was as if you were a little knot of islanders who spoke a language unknown to anyone else on the globe, and untranslatable. So to this roaming and shivering, this *unhinging* (how accurate that word, for this feeling of being split almost to severance) and the fumbling at the bellows – *I can't make a fire* – and the ultimate blasphemy – *I want a fire* – as she found herself cursing Maria and Elizabeth for dying and leaving her exposed to all of it.

'Oh, my dear, I really am afraid you are not at all well. Whatever is wrong?'

What's wrong? She stared at stooping, sympathetic Miss Wooler, and felt the act of staring as palpably as if her eyeballs were being peeled. It was all wrong from the start, but more than ever wrong now, wrong to dream as she did of Zamorna, Zamorna coming to her and transforming everything – not that it *was* a dream, that was the trouble, it was the realest thing ever—

'Charlotte, your gown is torn . . . And your shoes, where are your shoes? How . . . ?'

How, how, had she come to this? You've seen how. Charlotte sat down heavily by the hearth – *I must do without the fire* – gave a gasp, and then listened to herself saying with quiet resolution: 'I must make a decision, ma'am.'

The doctor was firm, even stern.

'Home, and rest, and no agitation. The condition of your nerves allows for no delay. Miss Wooler, if you value your employee's welfare, you will let her go at once.'

'I hope I may consider myself something more than Miss Brontë's employer,' Miss Wooler said. Kind, kind: they wouldn't be kind, Charlotte thought, gazing with peeled eyes at the bowl of wrinkled warm milk, if they knew what I was really like. 'You think, then, no danger of an organic condition . . . ?'

'It might quickly be brought on, by such an overstrain of the nervous system as this. Rest, quietness, recuperation. There is no alternative. Miss Brontë, you must absolutely put aside care for a while. Have you perhaps a favourite recreation? Drawing, perhaps, music. Some pastime that is, above all, absolutely removed from the workaday world.' And now she was really worrying them, she thought, but she couldn't help it, couldn't help the great jagged laughs that ripped from her and rose and rose to affront heaven.

3

Love and Other Doubtful Expressions

'You don't have to do it, you know,' says Charlotte. The *Leeds Mercury* lies open on the table, and open also is Emily's writing-box, and Emily's hand is poised above the finished letter, about to shake the silver-sand. 'You do know that, don't you?'

Like Papa, Emily will not deal in hints and indirections. She looks enquiringly. 'What do you mean?'

'I mean I'm better now.' Even upside down the block letters stand clearly out of the advertisement: WANTED . . . YOUNG FEMALE. The effect is faintly ogreish. 'So I'll be able to work again.'

'Oh, I'm not concerned about that,' Emily says, and pours the silver-sand. 'It's me I'm thinking about.'

Without knowing Emily – and knowing her is a demanding requirement – you might think that she is, if not exactly hard-hearted, then a long way from tender-hearted. Unlike, say, Anne, whose eyes immediately fill with surreptitious tears if she sees or hears someone crying or even if, during the reading aloud of a story, crying is mentioned.

'I'm interested in seeing whether I can do it,' Emily says, shaking the sanded letter. 'I want to measure myself against it. So it's simply my choice.' She takes out the sealing-wax, then goes to the fire to light a spill. Long-backed, narrow-waisted, she crouches and pauses there, and adds, slightly muffled: 'Besides, I do have to, Charlotte. Even though nobody tells me so.'

Later, thinking about Emily's announcement, Charlotte finds herself digging through several layers of feeling: the thin crust of surprise, the soft rich soil of sympathy and admiration and anxiety as to how she will get on, and the horrible slick clay of triumphant gloating that at last she will find out what it's like. And right at the bottom, something strange, hard, jarring: something almost like jealousy. Something like: martyrdom's all I've got, don't take it from me.

* * *

'I absolutely and positively could not be better placed,' Branwell says, taking Charlotte's arm and leading her away from the coach-stand. 'Careful, steep kerb here. Well, after all, you can smell it, can't you?'

'Coal-smoke, yes, and soot, and something worse – is there a tannery nearby?'

'Money, I mean, dolt, money. That's what comes spouting out of those mill-chimneys, when you look at the matter properly.' He nudges her back as a huge dray pounds by, throwing up sheets of mud. Two ragged boys clinging to the tailboard shout out, with extraordinary urgency and clarity, as if this were desperately vital information, that she is a poxy whore and he is a bum-fucker. 'Look over there. Bricks and timber. They're building all the time. New men, new money. Bradford is the place to be for a fellow like me, Charlotte. Mr Mill-owner doesn't just want his house on the outskirts with the carriage-sweep and the Gothic pepper-pots. He wants pictures to put in it. He wants phizes on the walls. He wants portraits of himself and Mrs and all the infant Mill-owners, to remind himself how splendid he is. So it couldn't be better.'

Branwell's studio is on the top floor of a narrow, darkly respectable house belonging to a beer-merchant. The smoky view of stepped streets and blank warehouse walls dispirits Charlotte, but he is all enthusiasm.

'Capital arrangements. My own sitting-room here. Bedroom – all bed and no room, as you see. And here, where the light's best, I do my work. Landlord splendid fellow. Look here, all new brushes, sable only. Aunt helped, bless her. And a new maul-stick – feel that – chamois-tipped. Oh, did he make you jump? That's my new lay-figure. I call him Felix.' The lay-figure, a jointed dummy used as a model for the set of the body and the folds of clothing once the face is filled in, is slumped on the sofa. 'Had a devil of a time with my landlord's maid when he first came, all boxed up. I opened up and had a look at him and just then I remembered I had to step out to get a letter off, and while I was out the maid came up to bring the water and coals. What does she see but an arm and a leg dangling out of a wooden case – and so she starts screaming and she's still at it when I come back. Well, I can see the conclusion she's jumped to, and plainly she's not in a way to listen to a reasoned explanation, so I choose the perhaps unfortunate expedient of dragging Felix out of the box, and shaking him before her eyes and then, you know, turning him upside down and banging his head on the floor. To show he's not made of flesh and blood . . .' He watches Charlotte's smiles appreciatively, hungrily, as they turn to laughter. 'Took any amount of smelling-salts to restore her. She still looks at me as if I'm a monster. Sit, sit. There's a nice little cook-shop round the corner in Darley Street where I can send for a meal for us.'

Charlotte sits. She looks at Branwell, who is so much himself and yet so altered by the sheer fact of his altered setting. 'Banny, isn't this strange?' Strange above all that it is a sort of household, but with no Aunt or Papa: separate; free. She finds herself sitting right on the edge of the old horsehair sofa, as if some excitements, some hectic performance were about to begin.

'It's mighty strange, isn't it?' His wondering smile answers, mirrors hers; then dims just a little. 'Why did you call me that?'

'I don't know. It was just – thinking how far we've come, I suppose. Since we were those children in the little study. And yet it all seems a wink of the eye . . .' She shakes herself. 'So, you have commissions?'

'One. So far. Clerical friend of Papa's. A fat, pleasant, windy, unconscionable humbug, as we do not, most emphatically not, say. Charlotte, promise me you won't ever marry a curate.'

It is her turn to pause. 'Why did you say that?'

'Oh, because it's what the daughters of poor clergymen so often do, if they get the chance,' Branwell says, raking a hand through his permanently unsettled hair. 'And some of them, God help them, set such a low value upon themselves that they actually leap at it – they think life has granted them some tremendous favour, to have this dull prig in a high collar deign to take notice of them.'

'That can't be how all curates are,' she says – feebly enough, because at root she agrees with him.

'Humbugs all. And the worst thing is . . .' He passes a hand over his face, as if actually wiping away the scowl. 'The worst thing is I am off on a little hobby-horse of mine, which is tedious for you, and that's about enough of it. So – you're going back to Dewsbury Moor after all.'

Charlotte takes the inert stiff hand of the lay-figure, shakes it. Peculiar impulse to jerk it off the sofa, fling it violently across the room. Because you can, perhaps. Dear God, what does that say? 'Yes. I see nothing else for it. And, besides, I'm better now. I shall manage well enough.' Finding his scrutiny a little uncomfortable, she rises and goes to look through the sketchbook on the table. 'And this – is this what you want, Branwell? I know, I know it was your idea, and you had a great deal to do settling it. But what about – well, do you still apply to *Blackwood's*?'

'Despair of 'em,' he says, with a short laugh. 'They're so wretchedly timid, won't take a chance – nothing new, nothing daring. Nothing nothing, in sum. Never got a reply from Wordsworth. But then, of course, he's not going to take kindly to competition anyway, now his inspiration's dried up. The way I see it is –' he holds out a cupped, expressive hand '– the moment will come. It *must* – else there's no reason for the desire to scribble ever being planted. In the meantime, the thing is to keep writing. You can still show me yours, by the by, Charlotte: I'll be very interested.'

Her pastime. Her forbidden pastime. Charlotte takes the inert stiff hand of the lay-figure, shakes it. Peculiar impulse to jerk it off the sofa, fling it violently across the room. As a substitute for Branwell, perhaps? Branwell who has naturally been set up by Papa and Aunt in a studio to pursue his artistic calling. And who condescendingly proposes to look over her little amateur work. And yet how she loves him. She feels sick and afraid, as if she is made of poison.

'Branwell, whatever happened to your toy soldiers?'

'What?' His laugh is prompt, harsh. 'Lord knows. Lost, broken, I suppose. Or put away in the attic. What on earth made you think of them?'

'I don't know.' Put away in the attic. 'Simply wondering, I suppose – does the same thing ever happen to people?'

'I am Miss Patchett. You, I take it, are Miss Brontë.'

This is very good so far, keep it like this: exchanging of information. From a great cold height Emily observes her hand being shaken by Miss Patchett's hand. Worlds colliding. Still, very good.

'Yes. That is –' Not being the eldest, she has never been Missed '– Emily Brontë.'

'Only the style *Miss* is used here, for pupils and teachers alike,' remarks pretty, worldly Miss Patchett, passing swiftly through surprise, puzzlement, comprehension, irritation and assertion in a few efficient instants; and Emily thinks of a sparrow bathing in a wet wheel-rut before the next coach rumbles on. 'Well, you'll be tired after your journey. You've supped, I hope. The girls are just gone up. Are all your gowns like that travelling-dress?'

'This is one of my two.'

Miss Patchett sighs and goes to look at herself in the pier-glass above the fire. Her parlour is a piping hot, plush, crannied little place – as if a cat should furnish its own room. For several moments Emily sees, in the mirror, Miss Patchett's long whiskers and elliptical jade eyes as she licks her paw – as she puts back a stray curl and sighs again. I know: I see it. Country parson, limited income, no society. One comes across this so often. One sympathises. It's just a pity nobody knows how to make the *best* of themselves any more. Miss Patchett is not as young as she looks. The fire hisses like a little pet dragon.

Quick view of the darkened schoolroom, once a barn: part of massy, sturdy Law Hill house, entrenched on its hilltop, is still a working farm. Wish from a part of Emily that it all was. Manage better surely with sheep, cows, fowls, than these: opening of the dormitory door, noise-gust of concentrated girls hitting her.

'You will share this bedroom with Miss Hartley. She is currently supervising the girls' retirement for the night. This is one of the duties you will perform by rota. At present we have, as I believe I mentioned in our correspondence, above twenty girls boarding.'

Twenty, no, double that or triple it to amount to that monkey multitude beyond the door. Bubble of babble, giggle, gabble swelling until Emily feels it will burst and send blobs of talking femininity slapping against the walls and trickling down.

'Well, Miss Hartley will be here anon to inform you further about your duties. I'll have your box brought up. I think, Miss Brontë, that we shall get along pretty well.' From Miss Patchett, handshake, contained smile, or brief purring leg-rub before off to the bird-hunt with stiff raised tail. 'You are, thank heaven, no chatterer.'

Emily is unpacking her trunk when her fellow-teacher comes in. She is carrying a candle. She does not set it down but waits a moment, listening, at the door leading to the dormitory, then flings the door open and darts back, crying: 'Very well, any more noise and I'll come among you with this when you're asleep and set light to the place. Think on it. Think how merrily those curtains will go up. Is Hartley mad enough to do that? Is she? You know she is.'

Miss Hartley, red-rimmed eyes, rueful lips, thirtyish, acknowledges Emily with a quick stare and then dives like a swimmer on to her bed. Pulling off her stockings supine, scratching incidentally as she goes, she says: 'La Patchett told me you were coming. Are you related to her?'

'No.'

'In that case, she's a bitch.' Miss Hartley unhooks and unlaces; the carapace of gown slides and thinly pools. Emily does not know what to do, where to look. There is so much of Miss Hartley. 'You're going to loathe it here, you know. God, let me see.' She takes and consults a watch from a stand beside the bed, a large silver pocket-watch. 'My father's, this was. It was meant to go to my brother but he died. Consumption. Father said to me, "You may as well have it, it doesn't matter now." So: yes, I can manage being awake the next three-quarters of an hour. That's what I've got. It's about how much time you get for yourself, if you're lucky.' She topples back on the bed. 'Then it's the blessed interval of being asleep, and then duty begins when you open your eyes, and it doesn't stop for a second until you find your bed again. Did I say you're going to loathe it here?'

'This is Miss Brontë,' Miss Patchett announces. 'Needless to say, you will all, day and boarding girls, accord her the respect that is due to her position at Law Hill.' The schoolroom is crawlingly attentive: drop a lump of food among the ants. Emily skims across the alien faces, forty-odd. Surely an unnecessary duplication.

'It was better when Miss Maria was here. That was La Patchett's sister. Younger. Gentle ways and – well, anyway, she got married and La Patchett was mad with jealousy. Oh, you could just tell. And she's been odd ever since. In fact, for all the curls and the new clothes, you know, she's the perfect old maid.'

Emily, trudging alongside Miss Hartley back from church, asks curiously: 'What do you mean by old maid?'

'What do I mean by . . .' Miss Hartley rolls seething eyes. 'For pity's sake. You never speak a word for hours, and then when you do it makes no sense. I mean, of course, what everyone means. A woman who couldn't get a husband.'

'Oh . . .' Winter evening, light almost gone. Shapes of bare trees – you couldn't call them black or grey. Instead colour was cancelled, everything given to form. 'Oh, that. I thought you meant something important.'

Miss Hartley starts to splutter something, but Emily removes her hearing, fixes her attention on the house up above: yes. Her heart lifts. Yes, there he is, waiting for them by the gate. Hanno, the school dog – guard dog supposedly, but general petted favourite. Let them all fuss and pat. She keeps titbits in her pocket, and sooner or later she will get him to herself. Then she can have long minutes of feeling half alive. Hanno likes to frisk around but then, soon and quietly, he puts his hard-soft jaw down on her foot or knee, and they stay like that. Long minutes. So different from the long hours.

And then that dismal day when he goes missing. Emily anxiously pacing the schoolroom, while her form of young creatures – whoever they are – see her abstraction, and let their slates and pencils droop, and begin exchanging whispers. And suddenly, beautifully, from the window she sees Hanno, being benevolently tugged home by the lad-of-all-work. She has to share it.

'Good news – there is good news. They have found Hanno. It looks as if he decided to spread his wings a little, and try new places and – well, no matter, he's back, I've just seen him.'

There is a murmur: part relief, she can tell, but also something else; vinegar in it. Someone speaks up. 'Lord, Miss, anybody would think it was one of *us* that had gone missing, the way you carry on.'

'Oh, no, no,' says Emily, cheerfully, thinking of squeezing Hanno's chops later, and giving him the saved soup-bones, 'I care for Hanno a good deal more than any of you. As you must know.'

This is just information; and that's what she is here to dispense, after all.

Fog and dark, and Branwell's boots slithering on the slimy cobbles as he struggles to reach the top of Darley Street without falling down again. Fun, though, the falling, and his friend and fellow-artist Thompson (portraits, accurate, a bit lifeless) is there to pick him up.

'Damn it to bloody hell, Brontë, I've a mind not to invite you to any more drinking-parties.'

'Symposia,' Branwell corrects him. 'To be sure the literal meaning is the same but, still, it's different, you know. Educative. Never was such a set of fellows. Leyland, now, have you seen his sculptures? Of course, you introduced us. Fine fellows. Except that one who – you know, he reckoned himself from London—'

'The one you picked a quarrel with, yes.'

Branwell chuckles, then stifles himself. 'Hush, hush now.' His lodgings. 'My landlordy. Lady and lord. Mustn't wake them. God, who put all these stairs here?'

Thompson, who is yawning, all the fun gone out of him, propels Branwell upward and steers him on to his bed. 'Well, Brontë, you're lucky,' he says, before leaving. 'You've discovered something about yourself, and that is you have absolutely no head for liquor.'

On his bed Branwell laughs long and loud, for no reason; then being horizontal alarms him and he flounders up. With tremendous labour he finds tinder and flint and lights a candle and goes through to his painting-room. The whisky has made him see so many things clearly and afresh: it will be interesting to discover how his work appears under its enlightening influence.

On the easel, almost-finished portrait of wealthy coal-merchant's wife. Branwell raises the candle. Flat fish eyes stare past him. Dear God, the proportions are all out – and where's the moulding? He lowers the candle, which has begun to tremble. But then, look here, what do they expect? His terms are very modest, have to be if he is to get any work at all and – well, what *can* you do with such an ugly old crow? 'Eh, you can't polish a turd,' he says aloud in Tabby's voice, and a giggle shakes him again. He scrabbles among his paint-pots. 'Ugly old crow, ugly old turd.' Up comes a brush laden with umber. He daubs and slashes, singing now, 'For unto us a turd is bo-orn.' He dances on tiptoe, arm flourishing and swirling. 'For unto us a-ha-ha-ha a turd is given . . . And his name shall be called *Shite-begot . . . Kiss-my-arse . . .*' There, a great improvement. Standing back to admire, he knocks the candle – not over, not quite over, manages to right it with fumbling fingers and dwindling chastened laughter. Imagine the oils catching, imagine the blaze. Lord. He carries it reverentially back to his bedroom. When he blows it out, the blackness is total and lasts twelve hours.

'I'm sorry you're so unhappy at Dewsbury Moor, Charlotte,' says Ellen, in the middle of describing the new London modes.

Charlotte stares. 'I – I hope I haven't been complaining of it.'

'No, the reverse. You skirt round it. You'll talk of anything except that, even the new fashion for trimming bonnets, which I know very well you don't care a jot for. I wish I could help.'

'You do. Oh, you do,' Charlotte says, squeezing her arm. You keep the sane and decent side of me alive, just. As long as there is this, this soft, gold-haired skin, these walks around a walled garden, these assurances that a good, straightforward person finds her worth liking, then rampages are kept at bay. Just.

'I hope Miss Wooler isn't putting too much on your shoulders again.'

'Oh, she never did that. It's just me. The fact is, Ellen, I don't mind – that is, I can bear being a teacher. That, after all, is the only possible future for me. But I make an indifferent nursemaid. And now Miss Wooler is to look after her elderly mother and her little niece at Dewsbury Moor I have a strong suspicion that such will be my additional duties. Should I protest at this? No, because that would be ungracious to Miss Wooler, to whom I owe so much. So really it would be better to leave now, on friendly terms . . . Oh, Ellen, did you not see any ladies at Bath who might want a paid companion – a selfish, unaccommodating and uncompanionable companion, that is? I am well qualified for such a post.'

Ellen has been staying at Bath with her doctor brother – Ellen's brothers have spread themselves through all the professions – and has acquired a certain promenade saunter. The other change is the family's removal from The Rydings to Brookroyd, a smaller house a few miles off. (Less exposed situation. Better air. All right, cheaper.) Here Charlotte's brief stay coincides with that of another of Ellen's brothers. The Reverend Henry, he of the comfortable hums and haws and general imperturbability, is up from his new curacy in Suffolk. The word suggests to Charlotte something juicily bucolic: the very opposite of stony wind-scoured Haworth.

'I almost fancy I would *sink* in Suffolk – I imagine rich spongy greeny-browns benevolently sucking the shoes from my feet.'

'Well, now, hum, Donnington is a pleasant fertile spot, to be sure, but rest assured, Miss Brontë, there is no such danger to be apprehended there, believe me.' Rather handsome is Henry Nussey – tall, fair, glossy locks, fine curved lips; between his brows a sharp cleft that somehow has the effect of a question mark on a page. Ellen and Charlotte have been drawing together, and after dinner Henry takes up the portfolio, sifting and judiciously admiring. 'I know very little of drawing. But it is an elegant accomplishment, and perfectly capable, I believe, of improving the mind. These botanical sketches, Miss Brontë, are I think the product of your skilful pencil.'

'The product of my impatience. I was trying to get a likeness of Ellen, and couldn't, and so I gave it up and fell to flowers because they're easier. They're not even real flowers, or recognisable as such.'

'Oh, Charlotte, they are,' puts in Ellen. 'That's surely a heartsease.'

'Ah, the wild pansy, or *Viola tricolour*,' says Henry. 'The Latin names of the common flora make a diverting subject, I find – a refreshment for the mind in the intervals of more serious study. Though, hum!, the Latin is frequently not such as a classical scholar could look upon without a blush.' He makes a small sober rumble, presumably the equivalent of a laugh.

'*Viola tricolour*, I like that,' says Charlotte. 'I can see her – yes, I can see her in a play. Viola Tricolour, a lady of republican views.'

'I'm afraid I don't know the play to which you are referring, Miss

Brontë,' says Henry, with magnificent blandness, holding up a watercolour landscape upside down. 'The drama has not been my study. Not that I have any strict doctrinal objection to theatre-going, I hasten to add, as long as the piece is calculated to effect a moral improvement in the spectator's breast.'

Later Ellen goes to the piano.

'Hum, ha, now we shall have some music,' says Henry. Charlotte has to admire: imagines him waking in the morning and remarking in just that mildly appreciative tone: *Hum, ha, now I am getting out of bed*. 'You do not play, Miss Brontë?'

'I do not play, sir. Being short-sighted, I was obliged to lean so far forward to see the music that it was deemed bad for my posture.'

'Posture, indeed, yes. Still, unless there is some actual danger to health, these proscriptions upon womanhood are, I feel, rather regrettable. Surely it is better to be sensible, useful, rational.'

'There, Mr Nussey, we are in full agreement.' Odd how sometimes she finds herself dwelling on the strong white column of his neck.

'I flatter myself that we often are. When I was engaged in debate with my brother Joshua earlier, I observed your attentiveness to our theme – the conversion of the natives of New Zealand to Christianity – and I fancy you were inclined to my side of the argument.'

'Yes . . . that is, I was certainly interested in the . . .' What *was* she thinking of, while the Nussey brothers earnestly and drearily thrashed it out? Probably the beginning of her new story. She only has it in her head so far: the danger will set in once she begins to commit it to paper. If she does. 'I'm sorry, Mr Nussey, please remind me of the question at issue.'

'Oh, ha, the great question, Miss Brontë, of missionary endeavour to the savage tribes of New Zealand,' he says readily. 'I use the word "savage" advisedly, for besides being fierce and warlike, they are much inclined to cannibalism. But they have shown themselves notably receptive to Christian teaching; and so the great peril opens alongside the great opportunity. For it is our first duty to them, as I was explaining to Joshua, to ensure that they are not exposed to the doctrinal errors and corruptions of Roman Catholicism. It is vital that we forestall such a tragic reverse. There, I believe, Miss Brontë, from observing your expression, I have your agreement.'

Charlotte just murmurs something. The reply she wants to make is: *No, I think it is rather more vital that they stop eating each other*. But something holds her back, something as feeble and clingy as vanity: for

Henry Nussey seems to think well of her, and no matter who it is she can never dismiss that. After all, it is too unbelievable to be dismissed.

Miss Hartley pads nightgowned and goosefleshed down the passage towards the spare room with the thin ooze of light under the door. If that is the senior girls in midnight conclave, she will have to break it up; but she suspects instead . . .

'Oh, my Lord.'

She is huddled, asleep, on an old springless couch, papers underneath her cheek, a pencil gripped in a clawlike hand. Her bare feet are purple with cold. On the floor beside her a candle is guttering – a crazy candle made, Miss Hartley sees, out of a number of saved candle-stubs, awkwardly melted together into this drooping, pooling tower.

'What are you doing?' Avoiding the hot wax underfoot, she shakes Emily's arm. 'Wake up. Look. Look at that. D'you want to burn us all in our beds?'

'Not particularly.' Emily sighs. She blinks, shivers, sits up. 'Well, it lasted quite a long time.' She extends a bare foot and extinguishes the candle by smothering the wick under her toes.

'*Now* what are you doing? For pity's sake, you'll hurt yourself—'

'Can't feel a thing. Can't see a thing, now.'

'You ought to go to bed properly.'

'Why?'

'Why? Because you'll be fit for nothing in the morning otherwise, and that means more work for me.'

'Oh. That.' Stiffly Emily rises. 'Yes, of course.'

'Come on. Give me those—' Miss Hartley is only going to help her with the papers, which are slipping from Emily's frozen grasp – but she is furiously batted and barked away.

'No! Don't touch them, don't ever touch them, do you hear?'

Miss Hartley shrinks back. 'All right, all right.' Lord: there's no helping her.

Clutching the papers to her chest, Emily limps down the passage, and Miss Hartley follows, thinking: What on earth can those scribblings be, to make them so important? Well, there is only one thing she can think of: love letters. Miss Hartley, thirtyish, disabused, sucks in and bites on the cold brittle air. Yes: it would explain a lot.

It is unlucky, perhaps. After a long imprisoning spell of bad weather, the boarders at Law Hill are at last allowed a walk outside the grounds, shepherded by Emily. And there, on a shoulder of hillside as clear as a green stage, they come upon the hawk devouring a new-killed pigeon. Feathers and blood everywhere, and each time the hawk pounds its beak into the pigeon's body there is a little fluty squeak.

'No, no, it isn't alive,' Emily assures them, as they wail. 'You hear the same sound when you pluck a chicken. It's just—'

'Oh, Miss Brontë, it's horrid, make it stop!'

'It wouldn't signify if I did, now. The pigeon is dead, and the hawk is simply getting its food. If you were a hawk, you would do the same.'

One pupil gives a low, insulted glare. 'I would never do anything like that. That's nasty. I shall tell Miss Patchett you said so.'

'Do. Tell her over the chicken-and-ham pie,' remarks Emily.

But another girl, a quiet one who seems to have taken to her and who reminds her just a little of Anne, threads a soft, tentative arm through Emily's and ventures: 'You would have to do it if you were a hawk, wouldn't you?'

'Yes. Because it would be in your nature.'

'So would it be better to be a hawk, or a pigeon?'

'A very good question,' says Emily, 'and one you must answer for yourself.' She won't go so far as to tell what she knows about the hawk hunched among the shower of bloody feathers: that it is not just blind nature. That he glories in it.

Next day, bribing Miss Hartley with the offer of taking over bedtime duty for a week, Emily secures the dreamed-of time to go for a walk alone. Climbing the high hills, feeling the moving, spinning earth beneath her feet – you can feel its infinite slowness and its unthinkable speed at the same time – Emily forgets about Law Hill, literally: it is an effort to remember its name or what it looks like. Neither is she conscious of cold or tiredness; only of a wish to go higher, a benign urging of the hills to multiply, to excel themselves.

At first when she spots a house she is affronted: even here, on these pure heights, the invasion. But she relents. There is nothing vaunting about this battered old hall. It seems rather to be going into the land, as a tree will grow round a nail, and taking on the characteristic hue of the moors – which is somehow not open-air, more dun and shadowed. Even the moss and bracken and turf have a subdued, secretive look, like vegetation surviving in a cave. The snow lying in the lee of walls and ridges surely never fell; it is just an element of this place, as much as peat or stone. No signs of life, but it is not lifeless.

Then, the dreadful descent: it must come, the world, the school, the talk (try to block it out and still hear, instead, the scurry of wind through thorn, hum it like a tune), the people who loom in her view like dolls thrust in your face by a boisterous child. But to make it better, this. Final glance up at the far heights, with their white strips of snow; compare this cobbled courtyard, last week snowy, now black and soggy with thaw. In other words, out there it is still last week. In other words, time does not mean anything – or, rather, its meaning is quite different from what you supposed. Here is a discovery, like some unsuspected physical aptitude . . . What? Miss Patchett is calling up the stairs to her, pointing in horror. What? Oh, her skirts. Crusted with mud. Yes, what of it?

'Six inches,' Miss Patchett cries. 'A good six inches.'

As so often, it is difficult to know what to say, so Emily has recourse to facts. 'More like eight,' she says, studying them judiciously, before carrying on up the stairs.

The tea-drinking has not been a success. That is, Miss Brontë, invited to the rare hospitality of Miss Patchett's parlour, has drunk a cup of tea, but that is about it. Apart from a single remark, before the maid closed the curtains, that the snow is quite gone now from the hills, she has spent most of the time gazing at the door.

Miss Patchett gathers herself. 'Miss Brontë, may I ask you frankly? Are you – are you happy in your position?'

'Yes, ma'am,' says Emily. Perhaps that will mean she can go now.

And she is in fact very happy today. This morning an image of Augusta Almeda going into banishment liquefied into two lines of perfect verse – no, not perfect, but better, closer to the ideal than ever before. She has carried them with her all day. Indeed, she has literally lived on them. That was why she didn't eat any dinner: didn't need it.

Branwell is home for the weekend, as he often is, but not much in evidence at the parsonage. Nor does he attend the meeting of the Haworth Masonic Lodge, where his friend John Brown, the sexton, misses him. Brown tracks him at last to the church, where Branwell is moodily playing the organ. Devil knows where he picked it up. Brown remembers him starting to learn the flute: then, suddenly, he could do this. A bit showy in execution, but very competent. He recognises a snatch of melancholy Handel as he coughs and approaches.

'Heard you come in, old squire,' Branwell says, not looking up from the keyboard. 'Ears like a bloodhound, you see.'

'Face like one and all, I'd say, just at the minute,' remarks Brown. 'What's plaguing you, then? Is she pretty? Is she worth it? Or haven't you got to the meat in the pie yet?'

Branwell laughs briefly, throttles off a last congested chord. 'That wouldn't be so bad. There's a remedy for it, after all,' he says, dipping his fingers into his waistcoat. 'This, though. This is a different matter.' He twiddles a penny, making it disappear and reappear like a conjuror. Devil knows where he picked that up either.

'If you're short, I can spare a little. But I do mean a little.'

'What? Don't tell me *your* business is failing, John. I never supposed dying would go out of fashion. Come on, let's go down from here. I can hear the rats rustling too clearly.'

'I thought you were doing pretty well in Bradford. Your father—'

'He said so, no doubt, and that's partly because I tell him so, and partly because – well, I am *his* son, and therefore I *must* be doing well, nothing else is conceivable, and so we go along.' Branwell flings himself down in the family pew and, after a brooding moment, puts his feet up. 'Home from home. Can't think of how many times as a boy I picked my nose and wiped it under this seat. Probably the snot's holding the joinery together. The thing is, John, I'm not doing well enough. I've done some reckoning up, which isn't like me, I know, and – well, I've got six months of earnings and six months of debts, and one should be bigger than the other, and it ain't the right one, and so now shall we talk of something else? This –' his naked redhead's eyes flash balefully up at the pulpit '– this is rapidly becoming as tedious as a sermon.'

Brown sits opposite him and pulls out his flask.

'What's that?'

'Drop of whisky – what d'you suppose? Buttermilk? Go on, it'll help.'

Branwell, reaching, pauses. 'In here?'

'Your father's not here, is he? Now tell me true, because I don't know about it. Everyone hereabouts admires the portrait you made of me, and I do too—'

'You would,' says Branwell, sharply: miserably. 'Because you believe in me, and because . . .' He doesn't finish that part. 'Look, there are any number of fellows round about, doing what I do. Painting faces. Trained at the Royal Academy Schools, some of them. Bradford, Halifax, Leeds. If you want a portrait, you don't have to look far. You can even get a good one, in certain quarters.'

The last remark is like a scattering of broken glass in front of you: go on, walk across that if you can. Brown prefers to ignore it. 'Well, if, as you say, your accounts don't square up, then it's only sensible to consider your future. What if you carried on for another six months? Would it just be throwing good money after bad?'

Branwell takes a drink from the flask. 'My God, I can't imagine another six months of it.'

'Well, then. You tried, but it didn't answer. Just a question of telling your father. Best done sooner rather than later, I reckon. He won't be waxy with you, will he?'

'Hm? Oh, no.' Branwell takes another swallow. 'He never is. That's part of the problem, perhaps. There's this sort of grand, towering sorrow instead, that makes you feel like the lowliest little worm – because at the same time this awesome being loves you, and you're not worthy . . . Ha! Now where have I heard that before?' He gestures obscenely at the pulpit. 'Funny. We can dispense with God, but we can't dispense with fathers.'

'Here, turn about,' Brown says, as Branwell goes to take another drink; but partly this is his own discomfort. He has a taste for bawdy, but Branwell's blasphemous talk faintly alarms him. 'What about these debts? Will you be able to clear them? Like I said, I can spare a little.'

Suddenly Branwell looks not just touched but actually stricken. 'No need for that, old squire,' he says hoarsely, 'but God bless you for it.'

Ah – which? thinks Brown. The one you don't believe in? But he doesn't say it: older than Branwell though he is, he avoids the paternal with him. It is curious: he likes Branwell, even though much that the young man says goes over his head. And then the family . . . Brown has sharp words for those in the village who speak disrespectfully of 'Old Ireland up at the parsonage'. And yet if you were to dig deep, sexton-like, for what he really thinks, you would find this: the doting old fellow should have set the lad to some proper profession or trade early, and made him stick to it; and with the money he'd save, he could go for a little spell in Harrogate or York, buy new dresses for the girls, and see if he couldn't get them husbands. What they needed was Sir Roger knocking at their front door. You only had to look at them.

'I can't believe it. I must be dreaming. I keep pinching myself – but then they could be dream-pinches, couldn't they? No, it can't be real.'

'Oh, stop it, Branwell. You make it sound as if I were marrying the Archbishop of Canterbury.'

'Or marrying anyone, come to that.'

For several blinks Charlotte regards his shoes as he paces the parlour. 'Or marrying anyone, as you say.'

'I don't know what to think. The axes of the world have shifted. An era has ended.'

'I haven't been there *that* long.'

'No . . . it's just the idea of – you not doing what you ought to do. Charlotte, the perennial slave of duty.'

After a moment she says: 'Well, that's the thing about slavery: absence of choice.'

The shoes stop.

'You veiled that reproach very tastefully,' Branwell says.

'No, I didn't, it was rather naked.'

'Such language. Now I see why you think you're unfit to train the infant mind.'

'Not unfit, unwilling. Oh, I know I shall still have to do it, one way or another, but I've had enough of Dewsbury Moor, and Miss Wooler understands. I shall still do what I ought to do, simply because I have no choice – oh, look, I don't mean that. I mean I don't reproach you, Branwell.' And she means it. Reproach him: what for? For not having made a comfortable, sister-maintaining fortune by the age of twenty-two? No: rather, she thinks, I envy you. I envy you the significance of your burden. If I fail, it doesn't much matter to anyone, but your failures would be splashy and consequential, you can point to the great ripped hole in life and say, *I did that.* Of course, this is assuming . . . 'This is assuming that you weren't joking earlier. When you said you'd soon be home permanently yourself.'

He sighs, opens the piano lid, fingers a single note, nods.

'The portrait-painting – the studio – is it not . . . ?'

'Not.' He closes the piano lid, with a glacial neatness that is somehow louder than a slam. 'Possibly this is the time for a change of subject. Has Emily written you this week?'

Charlotte busily occupies herself opening her writing-box, knowing he does not want her to look at him for the moment. 'No . . . No, I fear from what she said in her last letter that she simply hasn't the time. Three teachers and such a big school – really, I don't see how she can carry on at Law Hill. Didn't you notice how she was at Christmas? So thin, and she hardly spoke a word—'

'Oh, being thin and not speaking are the defining characteristics of Emily,' Branwell says, presenting a freshened, jaunty face.

Charlotte doesn't care for it. 'That's just playing with words.'

'Of course – what else are they for? Charlotte,' suddenly his voice hardens, 'don't you have any faith? Oh, I don't mean that kind, though I've got my suspicions there. I mean faith in what we might do – what might become of us. Why did you ever have that vision of the house by the sea, and the chairs and whatnot, if it wasn't going to happen? Now, you saw that clear as clear – I remember you telling us about it. And a thing that has once existed cannot, by its nature, cease to exist, because nothing in nature can be destroyed. Shelley's position, that, and *he* was an atheist. So—'

'The house by the sea existed only as an idea, Branwell. It's different, and you know it. And that belongs to, well, when we were children.'

'Nothing wrong with that.'

Charlotte takes out pen and knife and begins sharpening. 'Isn't there? Sometimes I think we were too happy as children.'

Branwell, astride the piano stool, challenges her with a stare. 'Happy. Hmm. Losing our mother – and then there was Maria, and then there was Elizabeth—'

'I don't mean the circumstances. I mean what we made in spite of them. Or because of them, possibly, I don't know. But surely most children want to leave childhood behind. They strain to get free of it. And instead we loved it all. It was wonderful and, yes, I would have it back tomorrow, with everything that goes with it. And that in itself cannot be right.'

'Would you have had it otherwise, then? No world below? No writing?'

'They don't necessarily go together.'

'Hmm. That's what I thought when I read that new tale of yours.' He points to the writing-box. 'Story of Elizabeth Hastings. Quite an oddity—'

'I didn't show you that.'

'No, I just read it. When did we ever have to ask? Oh, it's a full, strong measure of a tale, I warrant you, but – well, she's just a plain little miss that you might meet in Keighley High Street. Hardly seems to belong to Angria at all.'

'I know. That's how I could bear to write it.'

'It's funny, isn't it,' Branwell says watching her, 'how we don't get along so well any more?'

She cannot hide her shock. 'What do you mean?'

'Well, we'd still die for each other, obviously. But now there's this sort of pulling . . . Do you remember when you were growing up being bidden to kiss Aunt? And in a way, yes, you wanted to, it was Aunt and it was right. But once lips touched cheek your whole body strained the other way . . .'

Remembering, she smiles ruefully. 'Probably we understand each other too well.'

'You know, Charlotte, my heart was never really in the portrait-painting. Stiflingly mechanical after a while. It's lucky, really, that I've spotted I'm on the wrong road before I'm too far down it. No, I'll make my mark in another way. You'll see. And I'm sorry about the – the getting-married nonsense. What would you want with a husband anyway? Anyone short of a Homeric hero would just be an encumbrance.'

Well, a good try, she has to give him the credit for that. And it alerts her also to the fact that if she ever does marry, it will have to be someone like Branwell; so even the pain of quarrels can be kept within the circle of self, no worse than biting your tongue. However, all this, she reminds herself, is as remote and fanciful as Verdopolis and Angria. We must only think of the real.

Miss Patchett sent Emily home.

Not in disgrace, or anything like that. In the civil little note she directed to Mr Brontë, she did not speak of dispensing with her services, or finding her work unsatisfactory. Indeed she seemed to grope for some acceptable formula. Emily's health – yes, there was that. Emily was worn, pale, stick-thin. Yet she was insistent that she wanted to stay.

Perhaps the deciding moment for Miss Patchett was seeing one of the older girls, in the courtyard, convulse her companions by disarranging her hair and flitting in a ghostly glide across the cobbles, moaning sepulchrally: 'Look out, I am Miss Brontë, the phantom of Law Hill! Speak not to me, for I cannot answer!' That moment – or the succeeding moment when Miss Patchett found herself smothering her own smile.

So she told Miss Brontë that it was for her own good, and Miss Brontë looked back at her in that way she had, as if you were telling some tremendous lie and she was wondering why; and in her civil little note she hit upon a phrase that seemed, at least, partly appropriate. *I cannot stand by and watch,* she wrote, and left it at that.

All of them at home, then, and without employment: such is the burden of Patrick and Miss Branwell's tea-table colloquy as spring swells the streams, stirs up the typhus, and points out, with a long, didactic finger of sunlight, the threadbare patches on the tablecloth.

'The difficulty of three girls,' sighs Patrick. 'Boys, or let us say men, can make their way in life so much more successfully. I do not at all mind having them at home, of course, Miss Branwell. If I were more comfortably circumstanced, that would be my absolute choice. But my income is not getting any larger, and I am not getting any younger, and so it is all rather troubling. Branwell – I do not fear for Branwell. His talents must secure him a position in the world sooner or later. And Charlotte insists she will take up teaching again – and she is ever dutiful. Emily's aptitude for an occupation outside the home is, I fear, rather more to be doubted. It is not that she is at all idle, or addicted to luxury. I believe she is doing most of Tabby's work; and she was asking me the other day about the diet of the common people of Ireland, and whether it is, as she had heard, mainly composed of the potato. When I answered in the affirmative, she said that it seemed an admirably simple and economical way of living, which she would be happy to adopt at any time; and I did not doubt her.'

'In my youth in Penzance, the potato seldom appeared at the dinner table, I am afraid, Mr Brontë, now and then, with other garden stuff; but it was not esteemed in those days in polite circles.'

Patrick bows his acquiescence to Miss Branwell's gentility. 'I believe Emily was suggesting that, in lieu of employment, she was quite prepared to make equivalent sacrifices. One respects this, of course. Still, it is a worrisome business.'

'And then there is Anne.'

'Yes – oh, dear me, yes, there is poor dear Anne.' Patrick shakes his head fondly. 'Who still says she is determined on doing it.'

'I beg your pardon, Mr Brontë, but it is not a matter of saying; Anne *is* determined, and so there is no doubt that she will do it. What the result will be is a different matter, to be sure.'

'Well, she may surprise us yet,' he says – but conversationally, moving quickly on, as one does from an unmeant compliment.

Anne: families are narratives, and when you come along at the end of the story it is possible to believe one of two things – that you are its grand climax and summation, or that you are an afterthought.

Anne – being a listener – has often heard about the *ones* in families: oh, he's the clever one; she's the one who takes after her mother. And Anne has never had any doubt about which *one* she is. The youngest one: the quiet gentle one: the one the others look after. She has no real quarrel with that – those are aspects of her, undeniably. But she wishes the others would see past those things. She cannot help but notice that, even so strong-minded and unconventional as they are, when they look at her they draw the easy, lazy conclusion.

Even Emily, who is so close to her.

'No, Emily, I *want* to work as a governess.' Not simply the immemorial cry of the youngest – I want to copy what you're doing. 'I think it would suit me. I really do.'

'I wish you didn't have to do it,' says Emily, darkly; proud of her, but fierce and sombre – and none of it quite right.

'But I don't feel that I have to,' Anne explains. 'I want to. It's my choice.' And again – she can tell from the tender head-shakings – this is interpreted as putting on a brave face. And sometimes Anne wonders about this notion of putting on a brave face, as if it could only be a sort of mask. Can't you have a real brave face? Yes, no doubt she will feel homesick, miss her family terribly, be lost and adrift, and all the rest. But. Just occasionally at the parsonage, she has a suffocating feeling: wants to throw open doors, even smash windows and feel the air rush sucking in between the jagged fangs of glass. Just occasionally, she does not want Emily's long sinuous arm around her neck, locking her in place. She likes it too much.

'What makes you think it would suit you?' Emily demands.

'Well – in the first place, I like children.'

Darker yet, Emily almost smiles. 'You've never known any.'

In May Charlotte goes to be a governess with a wealthy family at Stonegappe, near Skipton – or, at least, one Charlotte does. She happens to be the real one; but for a little while there was another potential Charlotte, and in the coach to Skipton the real one imagines the quite different journey of her double.

Well, she is travelling all alone in the public coach, to begin with, and the potential Charlotte would never have been suffered to do such a thing. Even before her marriage, there would have been the most punctilious care not to see her exposed to indignities and hardships. More to do with what is due to her as a future curate's wife, perhaps, than from any excess of tenderness. But, still, not to be sneezed at. The coach is draughty, the seat-cushions gritty with old dustings of flea-powder.

And then, where she is going. She knows something of her new employers, Mr and Mrs Sidgwick, who have fortunes on both sides, and of the fine house bought with them; but otherwise, this is simply a job, an anonymous hole into which she will be slotted. The destination of the other Charlotte is quite otherwise. It is all to be prepared for her – perhaps not exactly like a bower but with diligent attention to her tastes and requirements. And it is not on steep, sharp Skipton heights, but in luscious lowland Suffolk, lucky land of soft folk, suffused with suffocating succulence.

'Miss Brontë, is it?' At the Skipton inn-yard the manservant mutters the question with dull indifference, one employee to another, and flings her box into the waiting gig. He is, quite naturally, not much interested in her. But the other Charlotte is eagerly anticipated, much discussed, her arrival at her new home looked out for: what will she be like? Nothing grand awaits that other Charlotte, but nothing negligible either; she will be a figure of some influence and importance in her sphere.

As for the box, it contains the real Charlotte's two plain stuff dresses, her patched and cobbled underwear, and a few treasured books; and all this will have to last an unspecified time. Contrast the other Charlotte, who not only has her trousseau, but can expect a liberal portion of comforts to be supplied to her for the foreseeable future.

Stonegappe shoulders into view: a thumping great thrustful take-it-or-leave-it place, queening it over hilltop gardens and terraces, big enough to lose ten governesses in. The real Charlotte leans forward in the gig, trying to compensate for the climb, wondering. Wondering what this will be like and at the same time wondering what it would have been like for the other Charlotte, arriving at the parsonage-house in Donnington in Suffolk as the new wife of the Reverend Henry Nussey.

'Bastard beasts always shit on t'carriage-sweep,' says the manservant, as the gig pulls up outside the house and the horse performs a prompt, noisy evacuation on the fresh-raked gravel. 'I s'll have to answer for that. Master and mistress'll be on to me straight off. Nuisance, really. Fucking buggers.' His tone is at once bright and relaxed: it is hard to tell who are the fucking buggers, the horses or the employers.

She still has the letter he wrote her – in fact it is in that box the manservant is shouldering down. Why keep it? A reminder, perhaps, of the fork in the road, of the other person she might have been.

The housekeeper shows her to her room, stopping every now and then to give her a good, thorough stare. Along the passage doors stand open revealing the little frugal bedrooms of the maids. Charlotte's room is bigger and has a window-seat and a view, but the same narrow penitential bed. Neither fish nor fowl, the governess, that strange social mermaid. She sits on her rock, the hard bed, awaiting the summons from her employers.

The other Charlotte, of course, would have slept in a double bed. Was it that? No: no, she believes not, though her imagination tends to hurry across that bridge, not looking down. Certainly when the letter came her reaction was not: dear God, how repugnant, how could he even think I would accept? It was more a vast surprise, temporarily eclipsing every other emotion.

> *My reasons for venturing thus to address you, Miss Brontë, will become swiftly clear when I inform you that I am now tolerably settled at Donnington, that the house, garden &c are fitted out to my satisfaction, and that after Easter I hope to begin that project I mentioned to you, of taking in pupils. It is at this stage of my life that I feel circumstance and inclination point most strongly towards matrimony . . .*

Curious how, even as she mended a pen and moistened the ink and prepared to write her refusal, what capered about her head were all the reasons to say yes. Security: and no need to teach resentful girls; and no guilt at being a burden to Papa; and a relief of pressure on Branwell. *Do not therefore accuse me of wrong motives when I say that my answer to your proposal must be a decided negative* . . . she wrote, while ring-a-rosy they went around her: comfort; and a useful life; and they could have Ellen to live with them; and Henry is a good decent man; and, after all, this is someone who wants to marry you in spite of everything, in spite of what the mirror tells you . . . *As for me, you do not know me. I am not the serious, grave, cool-headed individual you suppose* . . . But you could become her! cried the reasons, with a last despairing whoop, as the letter was finished, sealed, sent.

'Mrs Sidgwick will see you now.'

As for the other reason – the reason why she turned him down – that is as simple and elusive as a scent on the breeze, a glance, a word.

So, farewell to that other Charlotte and her possible, impossible existence. And yet . . . when she enters the capacious drawing-room of Stonegappe to be greeted by her employer, she has an odd feeling that her double exists, after all, and is hovering just at her side. Because that is where Mrs Sidgwick directs her eyes as, from the sofa, she remarks that Miss Brontë was expected a good hour ago, and laments this necessity of finding a temporary governess, and hopes that Miss Brontë is a good hand at plain sewing. Yes: it is clear, from Mrs Sidgwick's way of seeing her now, that she is not going to see her at all.

At Stonegappe there is an atmosphere of wealth, and no qualms about displaying it. Mr Sidgwick has added to his manufacturing fortune by marrying judiciously: Turkey carpets muffle the well-fed family's footsteps, many gilded mirrors reflect their keen, prosperous faces.

At Blake Hall, not far from Roe Head, Anne moves in a different world: old family, old money, more dusty idiosyncrasy; splendid drawing-room, but above she cannot help noticing the dismal old lop-sided chandelier, like something that has climbed up there and hanged itself. The Inghams treat her with well-bred courtesy, when they are aware of her. Handsome Mr Ingham is devoted to horse and dog and gun; pretty Mrs Ingham spends a good deal of time dressing.

As for the children – Charlotte, bent over the heaps of sewing that occupy her free time, sets her mind to the question of which of the four little Sidgwicks is the most repulsive. Twelve-year-old Margaret: a combination of heavy stupidity and ladylike mincing ('Miss Brontë, did no one ever correct your *posture*?'). Ten-year-old William, a bully who already has the loud, hard laugh suitable to smoking-room stories. Seven-year-old Mathilda, slightly less robust than her siblings, carving out a niche for herself as a kind of wheedling tattle-tale and informer. Four-year-old John Benson, fat, fraudulent picture of innocence, who has found out that pretending not to know better grants you all sorts of immunity. No: it's an impossible choice. They are repulsive individually, and repulsive *en masse*. Of course, this aversion to the children reveals her to be a thoroughly unnatural woman, but she knew that already.

At Blake Hall, the Ingham brood are younger, with three still in the nursery. Cunliffe and Mary, six and five respectively, are Anne's charges. She feels touched, even slightly humbled, on being introduced to them, on shaking their little hands and seeing their wondering scrutiny: who is she, what will she be like? It is a great responsibility and she is quietly proud of it. And she is careful to equip herself with understanding. It is only natural if at first they resist her and do not seem to settle. They are having to make an adjustment just as much as she is. She looks forward to getting to know them, watching over their development. Doing some good.

Charlotte: 'William, you are not to go near the stable-block, I've told you. And once you try to do it, John will copy you, as you well know. Do you want to get him into trouble?'

'I don't much care,' says William, with his cool, fixed smile. 'You know, when I go away to school I shan't have any women telling me what to do. There aren't any women except skivvies, and that's how it should be.'

'It's your father's order that you don't go near the stable-block. Because it's dangerous.'

'Father won't be angry with us. He'll just put the blame on you. Come on, John. You don't want to be ruled by petticoats, do you?'

They are too quick for her. But she is more determined than they anticipated. When she catches up with them in the stable-yard William gives a little moan of disbelief. Then he stoops, and for the first time she comprehends that phrase 'an unholy light in the eyes', just before the stone hits her temple.

There is blood. John starts to gurgle in amusement, but his brother pales, curtly stops him. A stable-boy appears, and stares; the servants are not usually her allies, suspecting her of giving herself airs, but this is unignorable. Charlotte, mopping with her handkerchief, sees through the swirling pain a chance to seize a little power.

'I told you, it's dangerous here.' She keeps her voice low, level. 'Let's go in now. Come.' Stiffly, great-eyed, they obey.

Later Mrs Sidgwick, visiting the schoolroom and managing to see Charlotte instead of the air just beside her, gives a little bleat. 'Miss Brontë, what has happened to your head?'

'Oh – a blunder, ma'am. A low branch in the garden-walk. I wasn't attending.'

'Dear, dear. Well, if your time hangs so heavy upon your hands that you must needs be wandering around the garden, I can assuredly find you some more sewing to do. Mathilda's dolls need dressing, for one.' Mrs Sidgwick – pregnant, light-haired, nose on the generous side, mouth on the mean side, resolved to be no more than thirty, and after five years of the resolution looking a little worn and strained by it – glances wonderingly around the schoolroom. 'Dear me, one forgets how roomy – almost half a house here that one never has the use of. Well, Miss Brontë, I leave you to your domain.'

When she has gone William yawns hugely and says, scowling: 'John, I think it's monstrous dull around the stables, you know. We won't go there any more.'

No victory, only a ceasefire, a withdrawal to safer positions. But Charlotte is glad even of that, knowing full well she can never win the war.

Anne: 'I do not wish to see it, Cunliffe. Take it away – put it back where—'

'But it's still *moving*, Miss Brontë. Isn't that funny? Mary, look. See its legs. Isn't that the funniest thing?'

The funny thing is a mouse caught in a trap and, as the boy is delighted to observe, not quite dead. Shivering, Anne wishes she were Emily, who would make a swift, merciful despatch; and she wishes her pupils would not display this savage side to their natures. But then, she reflects, they belong to a world of hunting and shooting: Mr Ingham regularly flings his bagged birds on the dining-table or even the sofa, where Mary lifts and waggles their sad wool-necked heads. It's natural, or rather inevitable. (Not the same things. Anne is a word-hoarder like her sisters.) Anne still believes in the measureless human possibilities of her pupils. If you can just foster this, suppress that, influence, balance . . . goodness will gradually emerge. This is her solid, unshowy belief. She holds to it all the more firmly because she knows the wild clawing tug of its opposite: that it is all fixed, that evil moves like a pulse under our skin, impels us in red-cheeked riot to watch the death-twitch and laugh.

Mrs Sidgwick, Monday: 'Really, Miss Brontë, it is part of your duties that *you* discipline them. If they misbehave, then you have full authority to be strict with them; they know they are not to come crying to me about it.'

Mrs Sidgwick, Tuesday: 'Upon my word, Miss Brontë, this is a sad tale I hear from poor Mathilda, of your unwarranted severity. You should recall that they are only children, after all.'

Mrs Ingham, Thursday: 'Any trouble of the disciplinary kind, my dear Miss Brontë, refer them straight to me or Mr Ingham, no matter what it is, no matter how slight. They must know that they cannot get away with the slightest disobedience to the governess.'

Mrs Ingham, Friday: 'Oh, my dear Miss Brontë, I don't know, we really cannot be plagued and fussed with every little thing. If they will not sit down to their lessons, you must simply make them.'

At Stonegappe there is much clattering down of boxes and flourishing of dust-sheets: annual removal to Swarcliffe, country place of Mrs Sidgwick's elderly father. Sudden anxious incomprehension on the part of John Benson, the youngest: what's going to happen? What about Miss Brontë? Relief that she is not going to be left behind, swathed in gauze with the schoolroom shutters closed, makes him uncharacteristically tender.

'I love you, Miss Brontë,' he remarks cheerfully at the dinner-table, as she is tying his bib.

Almost choking, Mrs Sidgwick cries out: 'My dear, love the *governess*?'

Mr Sidgwick, hard and clear-cut and quite sensible except in his devotion to his family, shakes his head and barks a laugh. 'Natural affection of the childish heart, my dear. You must accept it.'

'I hope I do accept it, Mr Sidgwick, when it comes simply to affection. But I must voice my doubt whether that word – that expression – is at all appropriate. I'm sure you of all people, Miss Brontë, would entirely understand.' And she manages to look a good three feet to the side of Charlotte, so that Charlotte feels her existence pared to the merest sliver. An apple-peel or rind, bound for the pig-bin.

'Do you know what, Miss Brontë?' confides Cunliffe, beaming. 'We're not going to do anything you say today. We've made a plan. Isn't that funny?'

'They have, to be sure, a great flow of animal spirits,' says Mrs Ingham, later, looking twinklingly bemused, or more so than usual, 'but I cannot think, Miss Brontë, that tying them to the desk leg with string is the proper way of restraining or directing them.'

'I beg your pardon, ma'am,' Anne says, her voice hoarse from unaccustomed shouting. 'I was perhaps a little desperate, wishing them to apply themselves to *something*, for a little while. Even their alphabet, which they hardly know—'

'Oh, as to that, you must do as you please – though it's as Mr Ingham always says, good breeding will always come before mere book-learning.'

At Swarcliffe, great galleon of a house moored amid rippling woods, Mrs Sidgwick ascends to the temporary schoolroom to instruct

Charlotte in the new situation. Here, Charlotte understands, Mrs Sidgwick's clan annually gather: the shrine of her beloved, venerable, failing, wealthy papa.

'Now, there will be a great deal of company this evening. It may be that Papa will prefer to rest quiet; but then again he may wish to have the children down after dinner, to display their accomplishments. If so, make sure they are properly dressed, and for each a short recitation – some verses of Dr Watts, say – will do very well. They quite dote on their grandpapa, you know, Miss Brontë, and he on them: of all his grandchildren, I rather fancy they are his favourites.'

The children have already been gloomily discussing this familial duty: Charlotte heard them earlier. ('Grandpapa smells of pee,' William lamented. 'When he kisses me he puts his fingers under my bottom,' Margaret moaned. 'When he dies we shall have a new carriage,' Mathilda countered. 'I heard Mama and Papa talking about it.')

'As for you, Miss Brontë, you will of course recollect that this is an evening occasion, and if you are summoned down, your dress must be suitable for social presentation, but not such as to give a misleading impression of your position in the household, and thus cause embarrassment to either party. However, I have no fears on that score.' Mrs Sidgwick gathers up a smile. 'One thing I will say for you, Miss Brontë, and that is that you never betray yourself by an ill-advised attempt to shine in company.'

Anne, having learned her lesson, makes no appeal to Mr and Mrs Ingham: she carries on contending with Cunliffe and Mary single-handed even to the day when Cunliffe, clambering over the desk and whooping mad and monkey-like in her face, makes hay with the repeated words *silly cunt silly cunt*, and Mary's paroxysms of laughter are such that she claps a hand to her burping mouth. 'Going to be sick.'

Anne is brisk. 'Quick into the bedroom, then, get the pot.'

But Mary, instead, with sidelong winking winces at her brother, totters accurately to the desk and to Anne's workbag and, yanking it open, she directs her fluid yellow yell right into it.

Well, now Mrs Ingham is brought in, though Anne still feels a little abashed, and Mrs Ingham still looks aristocratically weary about the whole thing.

'I should hope, Mary, that you have made a proper apology. Cunliffe too. I dare say you were egging each other on: it's no excuse, though

I'm sure you meant no harm. Now I am concerned, Miss Brontë, about those papers I see in your bag. I rather fear they are not to be retrieved, given the – the circumstances. I must know if they are important – letters, documents, things of that kind?'

'Oh, no,' says Anne; and as her employer's pretty pony face still insists, she adds, with the most dismissive plain shrug: 'Verses, that's all.' Later she does try to retrieve them. It's not absolutely necessary, because her poems are retained in her head, secret jewel-box. Still she passionately believes, quiet one though she is, that words written on a page are sacred.

Now – now that Charlotte has bribed, wrestled and bludgeoned her charges to bed – there's a space to be by yourself a little. This is the precious moment when you trim the schoolroom candle, draw up the chair, and dare to think. Reading or writing are out of the question, because your hands must be occupied with sewing in case Mrs Sidgwick makes a sudden appearance – even at Swarcliffe, where she is generally downstairs being vivacious in company. But solitary thought, yes, that vice can be indulged.

Plunge of gloom, then puzzlement, as the schoolroom door opens. A tentative movement: questing red tip of a cigar.

'Hello? Where is everybody? Is it a game?' The gentleman comes unsteadily in. Seeing Charlotte, he brightens. 'Well, here's *one*, at any rate. Where did the rest go? Damned peculiar, I call it.'

'I think you have made a mistake, sir. This is not one of the reception rooms. This is the schoolroom for the Sidgwick children.'

'Damn me. I'm upstairs, aren't I? Ridiculous mistake to make. I do beg your pardon.' He advances a little further into the room, bowing: dark, fleshy-faced. A touch of Zamorna (the forbidden) in his wiry brows. 'I've had too much of our host's excellent wine, that's what it is. And pardon me again for mentioning such a thing in this . . .' He gestures loosely around.

'Abode of innocence?' Something – perhaps that prohibited thought of Zamorna – makes her suddenly bold. 'Don't apologise for that, sir. I wish I could drink a little wine up here myself.'

After a startled moment he gives a low appreciative laugh. 'Damn me.'

'However, it might be worse. I suspect you may have been indulging in the excellent wine to help you tolerate the less than excellent conversation.'

'To speak the truth they are a rather dull set, though of course one doesn't . . .' He chuckles again around the glowing cigar; steps a little closer. 'So you're the governess, are you?'

'For my sins.' Strange pleasure, this running towards the cliff-edge of rebellion: of course, you will pull up.

'Sins? Oh, I doubt you have any of those on your head.'

'You might be surprised.'

'You're a funny little thing,' he puffs, and steps closer – closer so that for the first time the candlelight falls full on her face, and his bleared eyes take her in.

'I may be funny, but I'm not a little thing, sir, I'm a woman,' she says, conning his expression. The cigar-glow fades. 'No doubt now you will wish to rejoin the company downstairs.'

'Ah. Think I'd better.'

The cliff-edge turns out, after all, to be no more than a gentle slope. At least, however, he did see her, briefly: preferable to the usual invisibility, she supposes. And she tries to smile to herself; but feels only the sensation at her cheek-muscles, like pulled strings.

'Miss Brontë? Oh, there is no pleasing her. She quite tyrannises over us, you know: sometimes I say to Mr Sidgwick, "I am half afraid to venture up to the schoolroom, though it is my own house."'

'Miss Brontë? Well, she is a good little thing in many ways. No, as I tell Mr Ingham, I will not hear a word said against her. But it has to be confessed, she is rather the old-fashioned parsonage mouse – I fancy she, you know, pens little verses and whatnot, which is so quaint – and altogether I do not think she is quite equal to the splendid animal spirits of our youngsters.'

One evening, after a particularly grim recitation of her shortcomings by Mrs Sidgwick, Charlotte allows herself to look again at Henry Nussey's letter: to blow again into momentary life that phantom other Charlotte who accepted him. And to try to pin down the real reason that other Charlotte never existed.

Love, then. Just this, the thing she can never feel for Henry Nussey. It is a lot of difference for one emotion to make to a life. And what does she mean by love, anyway? People use that word and mean all sorts of different things by it.

But she knows what she means by it. She knows, as she watches the clearing of timber from the schoolroom window at Stonegappe; and just as sometimes she will follow a bird in flight and imagine herself the bird, so she enters that contorted trunk, lifted and flung, landing in the flames and cracking and twisting and splitting and feeding the fire, becoming part of the fire, becoming the fire, becoming it.

'Well, Miss Brontë, of course you always knew that it was a temporary arrangement – still, I dare say you will not be sorry to leave, though in very truth, and despite the fact that we have not always agreed, and you have not always set yourself to give that modicum of satisfaction which one has a right to expect from a governess, I shall actually, in spite of everything, be rather sorry to see you go.' Thus Mrs Sidgwick, adopting several personae and as many expressions in the course of the speech.

Charlotte: 'Yes, ma'am.'

'Well, Miss Brontë, believe me, Mr Ingham and I are very sorry about this, but we shall have to let you go.'

'Oh, ma'am, no.'

'I'm sorry—'

'I'm sorry I haven't given satisfaction, ma'am. May I not have another chance? There must be something I can do better—'

'I'm sorry.'

Anne swallows her failure. How does it taste? Bitter, bitter. The littlest one again, stretching beyond her reach. But she is still Anne; emotional apothecary, she investigates that bitter taste, assessing whether it can be made refreshing, searching for its medicinal properties; there must be something. Packing, she slides her thin, precious pages between her two gowns. There must be something.

There must be something better than this, is the thought-refrain that Charlotte takes away from her first experience of governessing: something better. It goes with her back to Haworth and it is still with her when she makes a journey, at last, in unbearable exaltation, to the sea.

Ellen's doctor recommends sea air for her health, and distant, still-benevolent Henry has friends at Bridlington and arranges for Ellen and Charlotte to go and take a holiday there. The journey itself includes a novelty, exciting and faintly alarming – part of it is by railway. They grip each other's hands, laughing tensely, at every jolt: the speed seems unearthly, a sort of diabolical trick.

But all of this is forgotten when she reaches the sea, which has been waiting for her for so long.

Ellen shows exemplary or Ellen-like patience. But one evening on the cliffs the dark and chill finally draw a protest from her. 'Charlotte, please. It's very late and Henry says there are disreputable types about the Quay at night. You can't stay looking at the sea for ever.'

'Why not?'

These are the questions we do not ask, and Ellen regrets that her friend has no sense of it.

'It will still be there tomorrow,' she says, gently tugging Charlotte's arm. 'The sea won't go away if you leave it.'

Charlotte turns to her, and in the indistinctness of dusk Ellen perceives something part-smile and part-shiver. 'Do you know?' Charlotte says. 'That's exactly what I'm afraid of.'

4

Saving the King

'They are mere boobies and chuckleheads, Anne, that's all I can conclude from what you tell me of 'em, and not worth a single second's regret.' Branwell was firm. 'Well, did you ever hear one of that family ever say a clever or fresh or even mildly interesting word, hey? I'm willing to bet you never did.'

'No . . . but then not everyone can be as clever as you, Branwell. And, besides, cleverness isn't everything—'

'Of course it is. What – you're not going to trot out that old adage of Aunt's?' He sucked in his cheeks and fluttered his eyelids. '"It is better to be good than clever." What reeking bilge that is. If you're mortal sick and apply to the doctor, you don't want him to say: "Really I don't know how to make you better, I know nothing of medicine at all and in fact I'm the veriest dimwit, but I am a thoroughly *good* person." You want somebody with brains who knows what he's about. But look here – you think this is just Branwell being sceptical as ever, but you'll find Weightman saying much the same, and he's in orders. Yes, Papa's new curate. Capital fellow, in spite of the cloth. Ah, look, see, you fire up at that. He wouldn't take any notice of it, that's how he is. Now, have you finished that shirt-collar for me?'

Devoted sewing (or at least, unavoidable sewing) by the parsonage females, equipping Branwell for his new venture. Which is quite harmonious and appropriate, altogether: he is to be a tutor in a private family, up in the Lake District. The situation, meaning the geography, could hardly be better – Branwell is already in Wordsworthian ecstasies over it; and as for the situation, meaning the job, well . . .

'It is, after all, how I began my own rise to such very modest eminence as I can claim,' Patrick says comfortably to Aunt.

'Goldsmith – Marvell – Swift – that's how they started out,' Branwell says enthusiastically to Charlotte.

'Well, he is much more suited to it than any of us,' Emily says hopefully to Charlotte; while Anne, overhearing, tilts her chin.

Charlotte, meanwhile, tries for witchery with her needle, to sew into his cuffs and bands charms and enchantments. Let him stick it out, let him succeed and impress, let him above all not be like me.

Patrick has had a curate to assist him before and, past sixty and desperately narrow-sighted, can hardly do without one now. But William Weightman is more than just a convenient addition to Haworth. He is that exotic curiosity: a person everyone likes. Not only around the parish but at the parsonage – and that is what makes him like some rare spice harvested from desert flower-petals and costing a fortune per ounce. He is so popular there that people are already talking about which of Old Ireland's girls he might marry. To be sure, they are odd, proud, gawky girls all, and someone of Mr Weightman's attractions could easily do a lot better – but still it is a *possibility*.

Even Emily, who likes no one that she cannot remember always liking, peeps at Mr Weightman over the high stone wall of her reserve.

'Yes, this is all very well in its way,' he says, accompanying them on their walk up to the moors, 'only it is too messy.'

'Messy? Are you afraid of a little mud on your boots, Mr Weightman?' Even to draw Emily out thus far is an achievement.

'Mud, no: I mean that all this ruggedness is unsystematic. A great stretch of hillside there, and here a little ragged clump of trees, and there what I feel impelled to call a tussock though I cannot remember having used such a barbarous word before, and yonder another hill – it all needs rearranging somehow. It needs folding up and compressing – say into the size of a garden-plot. Then you could get your inspiriting ruggedness all in one dose, without having to go to a lot of trouble and tire yourself out.'

'What you propose is mere domestication.'

'Absolutely. I would roof over the sky if I could.' He observes Emily's expression. 'You take everything very seriously, I think, Miss Emily.'

She nearly allows him a smile. 'Everything except you, Mr Weightman.'

Mr Greenwood the stationer remarks to Mr Andrew the surgeon – probably the only person around who would understand – that the new curate is like a clergyman out of Miss Austen. Certainly he seems to come from a warmer, gentler world, a world of opening possibilities, clear views, bright sidelights, though he is from the north himself.

'Appleby in Westmorland. It is very pretty there when it is not raining, that is one Tuesday in June, alternate years. Also we have a bit of a Norman castle, which is always a nice thing to have. It was built by Baron Ranulf who was known as *le mesquin*. Miss Brontë, your expert knowledge of French will supply the translation.'

'I wish I were expert . . . is it not "wretch"?'

'Exactly. Ranulf the Wretch. Isn't that a delightful title to bear down to posterity? I like to imagine that he had a more tolerable young brother, say, who was known as Rollo the Faintly Disagreeable.'

He is remarkably good-looking too, Mr Weightman – clean-cut features, inky eyes, a complexion any woman would envy. Perhaps that is why Charlotte finds herself referring to him as Celia Amelia, because it seems absurd that a man should possess such charm and beauty. Perhaps also it is a reminder to herself: keep your distance.

Oh, he is a flatterer, she knows that. He even has Aunt bridling and simpering; and when Ellen visits he trains on her the whole battery. The trouble is (or the troubling thing is), you cannot accuse him of mere empty insincerity. When he praises Charlotte's drawing, he does not leave it at that: he is eager to have her draw his portrait.

'I warn you, sitting for your picture is dull work; and ten to one when it's finished, the sitter declares, "Oh, it's nothing like," and glares as if you have wasted their time.'

But Mr Weightman says he will take the risk, and disposes himself in academic gown and elegant profile, only occasionally swivelling one long-lashed eye in her direction. 'You have played me false, Miss Brontë. You told me this was dull work. Instead I have complete leisure to rest, to reflect and philosophise, whilet having my appearance sedulously dwelt upon by the bright eyes of a charming young woman. Surely this is some appreciable way towards paradise.'

'Not when your neck goes stiff.'

He laughs. 'Now I need never fear going off on a flight of fancy. You will always bring me down with one clean shot.'

'Oh, I am not entirely averse to flights of fancy, Mr Weightman,' she says, with a little stifling feeling in her chest.

'I know. Why, what means that look? I am an observer of character in my own way. Now neither you nor your sisters have ever blushingly shown me a book of hot-pressed paper, proudly labelled Elegant Extracts, with bits of Addison and Cowper written out in a twirly hand, and pasted vignettes of narrow-waisted ladies and gentlemen going to be married in churches the size of sentry-boxes. But that is what generally passes for the imaginative temperament among young ladies. Your tastes are much riper and more serious. I would even suggest, if it were not ungallant, too serious.'

'Never mind the gallantry, Mr Weightman – as you know me so well, you know I don't care for it. Say what you mean.'

'Only that the exercise of the mind need not be solemn. No one can live epics and breathe in heroic measure: life must contain a little light verse also, as long as it be well crafted. Well, confess – when you receive a valentine, is there not a specific pleasure in that, which you would not feel if someone addressed you with a Horatian ode?'

'I couldn't say, Mr Weightman: I have never received a valentine. Nor, lest I sound pathetic, have my sisters.'

'Never received . . . But what have the young gentlemen of Haworth been about?'

'There are none.'

'Keighley then, Skipton, shame on them all—'

'Mr Weightman, you must recollect that we have of necessity never really moved in society. And besides that – well, as Tabby would say, what you never have you never miss.'

'That isn't true,' he says gently. 'Forgive me for questioning the wisdom of generations of grannies, but that statement is coldly and horribly untrue.'

'Cold and horrible – pretty apt for Haworth. But tell me, Mr Weightman –' she is more uncomfortable than she cares even for the one dark eye to see '– about the Elegant Extracts and so on. You surely cannot be describing the tastes of Miss Walton. That lady of Appleby with whom you are supposed to have an understanding?'

His lips curve as she sketches them. 'How am I to answer that?'

'Well, the truth might be one way.'

'No – as well as drawing me, you have drawn me out shockingly, Miss Brontë, and I must retain a little mystery, else you will be bored with me.'

Small chance of that. In February Ellen comes to stay, and Mr Weightman is always entertainingly at their service, arranging walks and musical parties and charades, inventing word-games on the spur of the moment. He is to give a literary lecture one evening to the Keighley Mechanics' Institute – won't the young ladies come and hear him? They can discreetly let him know the effect he is making by gasping in admiration, or yawning at the dull parts . . . Awkward exchange of looks between the sisters. It is difficult . . . But soon Charlotte is reminded of Maria when she was a child, banishing nightmare horrors – so calmly opening the closet door and thrusting her head into the fanged blackness, pushing back the bed-curtains with their collapsible monsters. This is what William Weightman does with the problem of Papa and Aunt and their querulous objections – dear me, disruption, decorum. They are so easily dealt with that Charlotte, setting out to walk to Keighley in the frosted evening with Mr Weightman and a clerical friend of his staunchly escorting, has a dizzy glimpse of what might have been, with just that tincture of different personality at the parsonage.

Not that he can conquer everything. It is midnight by the time they get back – laughing, glowing, shivering in starlight – and Aunt is waiting up with a pot of hot coffee to renovate their fainting female forms. Four cups.

'Oh, Miss Branwell, none for me or my friend here?' cries Mr Weightman. 'Here we are, half perished and famished and craving your pity and kindness. I never supposed you one of those women – the proud, queenly sort who like to see men grovelling and humbled beneath their dainty foot—'

'Really, sir, it is enough to have to sit up till all hours waiting, without having to listen to your nonsense as well,' snaps Aunt, red-faced – not caring for a slight on her housekeeping, even in jest.

'Mr Weightman, please, have mine,' Charlotte says, and Emily echoes her; but Aunt will not have it.

'You'll do nothing of the kind. The coffee was made on purpose for you, and as you know it is not a beverage I customarily prepare – but neither is this, thankfully, a customary occasion.' And Aunt's voice quivers with the bitterness of innovation.

A few days later come the valentines.

Ellen, as a guest, is given her post first, and so is the first to discover the valentine verse, apparently posted in Bradford. '"Fair Ellen, Fair Ellen",' she reads out in a flat voice, as if it were a circular: then she realises. 'Oh, good gracious.'

No great surprise, however, that pretty, well-mannered Ellen should receive a valentine. The surprise gathers as the others open their post.

Charlotte: 'I have a missive called "Away Fond Love".'

Emily: '"Soul Divine". Yes, Bradford too. Let me see the writing on yours . . .'

'Anne, do you have one? It must be Celia Amelia. No, I can't think how it came up, but we mentioned valentine verses, and I simply said we'd never had any . . . and now look.'

'He has gone to a good deal of trouble,' Ellen says, 'and so clever too – I never read a cleverer poem.'

'Well, Byron's laurels are safe,' Emily says judiciously, 'but he versifies prettily enough. Listen, this is a good stanza . . .'

Not a grand gesture, but then grand gestures often leave one cold, and this has simply created a subtle warmth around it, like a house-wall with a fireplace on the other side.

Anne, do you have one too?

Yes: and it is called 'Mistake Me Not'; and she joins in the general pleasure and laughter, and does not say much about it.

'A sphinx?'

'Well, if the expression can properly be used with the indefinite article. I suppose strictly one can only speak of *the* Sphinx, as *sui generis*. I'm gabbling in this dreary way, Miss Anne, because I'm afraid I've offended you.'

'No, no, not at all. I'm only a little baffled. I have never supposed myself anything like a sphinx – or the Sphinx, or anything mysterious and enigmatic like that. I can't think how I strike you that way, Mr Weightman.'

'Ah, this is exactly it. There are plenty of young women, you know, who would greatly fancy themselves as sphinxes, even though they are as obvious as daylight. But you don't, and that's part of the fascination.'

'Well, I hope I'm not quite as dull as I imagine the Sphinx to be – just repeating the same old riddle.'

'No. But here's the paradox. Miss Brontë talks with me just as long as she feels like it, and then closes the conversational door when she's had enough. Miss Emily throws me the odd word like a bone – usually meaty. You are much more easily communicative than either of them. And yet I feel further from you – I feel I am politely, even charmingly held at a very precise distance – and I'm impudent enough to wish I was not.'

'I'm sorry, Mr Weightman, if I am not – not very entertaining as a companion—'

'You really mean that, don't you? Sad, sad. Haven't I told you of my fascination? Mind, you are probably inclined to think of me as a mere flirt. But consider the possibility that even flirts are serious sometimes.'

'I think – well, I know I am shy. But that is something I struggle with all the time, because I don't want to give in to it, I want to beat it at last. I hope I am not reserved . . . Really, I prefer to hear your talk rather than my own, Mr Weightman. I cannot offer you anything of interest.'

He studies her closely – he is studying her all the time, as they sit out a game of forfeits, but only occasionally does she allow herself to look up at him. Just as Augusta Almeda, imprisoned in the Gaaldine dungeon, carefully limited her sips from the pitcher of sweet water her disguised page brought her.

'If you tried, you would be surprised. It only takes a very little to interest me. I am incurably curious. My landlady at Cook Gate, for example, eats no fish. It is served at dinner, but never does she partake. I am so infernally curious that yesterday I had to ask her. Well, she cannot abide any fish, she tells me, since she was mortally ill once after eating a bad lobster. "Oh," says she, shaking her head, "it was a shockingly bad lobster." The way she said it somehow suggested that the lobster was not only poisonous but morally delinquent. Hard to see how, really. Not much a lobster can do in the way of transgression.'

Anne, after several long, floating moments, finds herself saying: 'It might have a crabbed disposition.' And risking another sip of that sweet water.

He is laughing. 'So it might. A selfish shellfish, perhaps. Oh dear. Thank you.'

'What for?' No more looking now.

'For giving me a little. For putting up with my insolence. For not thinking me just a flirt, after all.'

'No. I don't think that . . .'

'You're going to say *but* or *only* or *except*. I can see 'em coming. It's all right, fire away.'

'I only wonder whether – whether flirting is always as harmless as the word sounds. What is meant to be taken lightly may – may not be taken so.' The physical act of speaking these simple words leaves her breathless and oppressed, as if waking from a nightmare.

'Oh, surely not. I mean, surely not with me. Whom do you mean? Not Miss Brontë, she has the measure of me. And it can't be Miss Emily. I always feel with her like a kitten crawling over its dam, nipping and clawing and making a brave to-do – but you know the mother only needs to give that single swipe she forbearingly withholds. Surely not your friend Miss Nussey. She is too sensible—'

'I meant – I only meant it as a general principle,' says Anne, feeling as if she sits in the middle of a grass fire that is moving inwards. 'Look, we should rejoin the game.' Or perhaps he has never left it.

Mr Weightman says: 'Anne, what are you afraid of?'

'I'm not afraid of anything. Well, yes, I am, I'm afraid of lots of things.'

'But nothing in this particular situation.' They are walking down the lane to the Sunday school, slithering on melting blackened slush, like snow gone hopelessly to the bad. Natural therefore to take his arm. Natural, unnatural, flinging her into far spinning worlds.

'No, nothing.'

'Meet me, then. There, it's out. I want you to meet me at the Sunday school, once all the heathens, pupils I mean, have gone home, and be alone with me for a wee while, and talk nonsense with me. Just that. Anne—'

'You shouldn't call me Anne.'

'Arabella then, Anastasia and, I don't know, Antirrhinum. Yes, I know, it should be Miss. I was just hoping you might not be Miss any more, with me.'

'I am the eternal miss,' she says; and they laugh, and in their laughing their heads come close together.

'You will be there, won't you?'

'I can't. I'll be missed at home.'

'Then go home, and come straight back to the school. To fetch the gloves you left behind. See? It's easy. Try. Try the exquisite pleasure of surprising yourself.'

Anne shakes her head. But he doesn't seem to mind that: even seems to draw a conclusion from it.

She hears, but does not hear, her Sunday scholars recite: they might as well be reading from the newspaper. At the end, her favourite pupil wants to stay behind to talk about her new baby brother, and whether perhaps God will let this one live; but Anne is too distracted. Soon she is slithering back up the lane. Her hands are cold without her gloves.

In the hallway she hesitates. Voices from the kitchen; thoughtful juicy tick of the clock on the landing, like someone sucking a comfit. Aunt has been poorly and housebound with a cold, and she decides to go up and see how she is. That's one decision.

In her room Aunt lies sleeping, propped up in bed among the framed samplers and texts and silhouette portraits, snoring neatly. Anne smooths the coverlet, then stirs the little fire. Aunt's room: in a way, this is Anne's home of homes. Here she slept as a little girl; here the long quiet afternoons of sewing, with the light tilting and draining from the ceiling. Here, in Aunt's absence, they had explored her collection of the *Methodist Magazine* – soon coming to smile, and even laugh, at the gulping language, the incredible conversions and apparitions. Still, Anne always knew that laughter was only a response, not an answer. She knew, and she knows, that you laugh at your peril.

Anne warms her ungloved hands at the fire. Then slowly she sits down in Aunt's chair, leans back, and watches and listens. She watches the decline of light on the ceiling, and she listens to the regular rhythm of Aunt's snores, measuring the time away.

Once Emily comes up and looks in. 'Oh! You're here,' she says. 'We were wondering—'

'Yes,' Anne says, smiling tensely, 'I'm here.' And Emily with a nod leaves her. You don't have to explain anything to Emily: she doesn't believe in explanations.

Once Aunt stirs and opens her eyes, though she seems to be still dreaming. 'Maria,' she says, looking at or through Anne; then is instantly asleep again.

Anne sits on, while the winter day dies.

Why, then? Various reasons lie to hand, but like the objects around her in the half-light they bloom and blot and seem to elude the grasp. Because to go would have been wrong, simply wrong: there is a reason, though only semi-solid. Because she was afraid? That idea looms promisingly, then ripples away. Afraid of what? Not afraid of William Weightman in that way, of what he might do, no, no. Afraid of herself, perhaps. Afraid that, after all, he only means what he says, just to meet and talk nonsense. Nothing more. Yes, that reason fits solidly enough into the hand: though she does not much want to hold on to it. She wipes a truant tear with her sleeve, irritably. How much easier this would be to make sense of if it were happening to someone else: someone not real. Or someone scarcely less real than Anne herself feels, as her still sitting figure becomes only an aspect of the darkness.

Time for Ellen to go home. The Nussey carriage stands before the parsonage door (needs a lick of paint but, still, a carriage is a carriage, and the coachman makes sure to look about him disdainfully), and William Weightman is there to hand Ellen in, to help with the bags, to declare that she is taking a piece of his heart with her to Brookroyd.

'Oh, there are pieces of *your* heart all over the West Riding,' says

Ellen, quite at home with this sort of talk. She is waved and well-wished away; Mr Weightman sighs, and shepherds them into the house.

Anne hangs back. 'Mr Weightman – I feel I should explain something—'

'My dear Miss Anne, please say nothing. There is no need. It was a very proper admonition for my impertinence,' he says, smiling. And goes in.

'Yes,' says Patrick uncertainly, laying down the newspaper: he must hold it against his nose to read now. 'Yes, I don't deny it sounds a desirable position. A good deal further off, though, my dear, almost as far as York.'

'But not so very far, Papa,' says Anne. 'And the children are rather older, which I think I would like better. And I know that Mr and Mrs Ingham, though I did not suit them, will give me a character.'

'I should hope so,' he says, a little hotly. 'Well, I am compelled to admiration at your determination to return to employment so soon, but I wonder if it is a little hasty. All I ask is – my dear little Anne, are you sure?'

Stoutly she answers: 'Yes, Papa.' And silently: Are you sure I'm your dear little Anne?

'Confess it, Mr Weightman, you are simply piqued that you have met someone who will not play your trifling games,' Charlotte says, wielding the eraser. The nose is right, the lips, but she just cannot get the shape of that chin. Almost wants to scribble, obliterate: give up on it as a hopeless case.

'Harsh as ever. And you may be right, as ever. I just wonder – no disrespect – is it your aunt's influence? I know she had much to do with her bringing-up. It's as if – as if someone is always standing over her. And I have the urge to pull her forward out of the shadow.'

'Shadow – sir, you are romancing. Anne is simply her own self. And the fact is she is much too serious and sensible for a light-mind like you. Nothing more mysterious than that.'

'A pity,' he says, after a while.

'What is?'

'Oh, lots of things, too many things.' Something about the profile alters: a lifting, a clearing of the brow. 'Too many for a light-mind to think of, at any rate.'

* * *

Branwell wrote home glowingly of his situation as tutor to the sons of Robert Postlethwaite, Esq., of Broughton-in-Furness. The spot was idyllic and it sounded as if he had swiftly made himself indispensable to the family. In fact Patrick had been talking of him in exactly those terms to Mrs Barraclough, the watchmaker's wife, the day before Branwell arrived home: unannounced, and unemployed.

'I don't understand. What possible reason could Mr Postlethwaite have for dismissing you?'

'On my honour, Papa, I can't think where I failed to give satisfaction. I won the confidence of the boys – we were going famously through Virgil, and making pretty fair progress with Homer, though their Greek was much more rudimentary when I took them on. I was introduced into the Postlethwaites' social circle, I was even given one or two confidential errands by Mr Postlethwaite. No one could have been more surprised than me when he announced he would be dispensing with my services at the half-year. All I can suggest is . . . well, the gentleman does have an intemperate side. Once or twice, at such times, he made slighting references to my name – my ancestry – which I am afraid it is not in my nature to shrug off. So perhaps . . .'

Patrick, turning to his study window, beat down a furious, scarlet, Irish flush. 'I see. It is regrettable . . . but of course such things are not to be dismissed tamely . . .'

Later Charlotte asked: 'Why were you sacked, Branwell?'

'It wasn't so much a sacking as a – a mutual agreement that the time had come to part. Oh, look, Charlotte, it hardly matters because when I was up there I wrote to Hartley Coleridge and he replied and actually invited me to his cottage at Rydal Water and I spent the day there, yes, discussing my verse and my translations of Horace and he was vastly encouraging and seems to think I have it in me to be a writer. Yes, Hartley Coleridge – magisterial fellow, a little other-worldly as I imagine his father to have been, and perhaps no stranger to stimulants neither but – oh, brilliant, brilliant.'

'If he approved your work, then of course he must be.' Jealousy, laying its cold metal bar across her neck.

'I shook his hand, of course, which means I am one handshake away from his father's, and from Wordsworth's and Southey's. Now I'm going to send him my full Horace translations and see if he can help me place them with publishers, and so I've been forging away at those night and day and – well, yes, I dare say I neglected my tutorial duties. That's why.'

Later, John Brown asked: 'What happened? You weren't such a noddy as to get caught tippling, were you?'

'No, I was sober day and night, there was no help for it. The truth is, old squire – and strictly not a word anywhere, I beg you – there was a delightful little piece who did the sewing and the laundry, and I found that she was obliging in other ways too. Well, pretty soon she starts to get plump in the wrong places, and Mrs P. notices, and there's a hell of a to-do. Now I can't be sure if it was me who caused the swelling, for there's no denying she was a girl who spread herself around a good deal – but old man Postlethwaite seizes on me, and as I didn't care for the way they were treating her, or me, I wasn't accommodating in my answers. And so, goodbye and good riddance. But look here, I'll pay you back what I owe you very soon, because I have other irons in the fire, don't you fret.'

Later, Branwell said to Emily: 'It's a pity, how I just missed Anne. Handsome situation, though, Vale of York – and I hear Thorp Green's quite a grand establishment. How will she manage, do you think? Mind, I don't see why she shouldn't manage pretty well, pretty well all round. All things considered. Well –' he sighed gustily '– plainly you want to ask me why I was sent away by the Postlethwaites.'

Emily looked at him: following his speech like someone playing a party game where all the words are spoken backwards.

'Oh,' she said brightly, as if realising her turn had come. 'Oh, sorry, Branwell, I don't care.'

So: Branwell back at Haworth, with those carefully stitched collars needing replenishing . . . and that carefully stitched reputation too? Surely only jealous carpers and nay-sayers would suggest it. Nothing of the blush in Branwell's behaviour. If anything, more strut and flourish. When Mary and Martha Taylor arrive for a visit, he thrusts in like a fox in a coop, demanding that they be better entertained than poor Ellen, calling on William Weightman to help him. At all costs, no ladylike dullness.

'Ladies don't necessarily enjoy ladylike dullness, as you call it,' Mary tells him, 'but often it is forced on them by men, who want them to be a species of large, animated doll.'

'Oh, we're there, are we?' says Branwell, smiling at her. 'Well, that should make it less dull, at any rate.'

Mary Taylor is now possessed of, or rather encumbered by, remarkable beauty: it seems to make her uncomfortable and less herself. By contrast her imp-like sister Martha has, as it were, her hands free: she bursts with unselfconscious curiosity.

'Is it true about the valentines? Only Ellen told us, of course, but then you wonder how much she slanted or embroidered or even suppressed. It is my firm belief – and Mr Weightman is a very pretty fellow by the way – it is my firm belief that Ellen didn't tell us all – sometimes I think behind those big blue eyes she is quite sly – I say it is my firm belief that one of you has already been favoured with a proposal.'

'You and your firm beliefs. You sound as if you're standing for election,' Mary says. 'My firm belief, by the by, is quite otherwise.'

'Why?' says Charlotte, perhaps a little quickly.

'If that were the case, you would have told us. Besides, my impression of Mr Weightman is that he can probably make every woman imagine that he is a little bit in love with her.'

'You have him exactly,' says Charlotte; realising how much she has always valued Mary's sharp sense, and relishing being with her again; and unaccountably wanting to kick her just a little bit.

'It's a pity we missed Anne,' Martha says. 'She must have decided on a new place mighty quickly.'

'There is a great deal of decision in Anne's character,' Emily says, 'but she doesn't shout about it.'

William Weightman is, as before, perpetually available for entertainment – chiefly, at the parsonage, conversational and musical, cards not being encouraged there. But there is a backgammon set from Aunt Branwell's dusty muslined youth, and also a chess set over which Mary likes to preside, taking on all comers.

'It is the pure meeting of minds, or contesting of minds, which is even better,' she says to Mr Weightman, as she invites him to another game. 'Everything outside the mind, the merely material and consequential, the physical, the emotional – all is irrelevant: when you play chess, it doesn't exist.'

'That's interesting,' says Mr Weightman. 'Then that very physical bang you gave the table, just after I took your queen, must have been an illusion.'

'The loss of a queen,' Mary says glowering, half smiling, 'is not to be borne with fortitude. Here is another fascination of chess. The queen, the only specifically female piece, is the most powerful on the board. Bishops and knights are male; rooks and pawns, neither really. The important pair are the queen, without whom everything is lost, and the king, who can't do anything. He just lumbers about from side to side, incapable of deciding any move, and just requiring to be defended and saved all the time. Isn't there a rather interesting parallel here with life?'

'But the king feels so nice and heavy when you pick him up,' says Mr Weightman. 'That must count for something.'

'What exactly is your contention, then, Miss Taylor, drawn from this example of chess?' says Branwell, who has been watching the game. 'Are you saying that women have more power than men, or that they ought to have more power? And are you happily declaring that men are useless lumps, or regretting that they are?'

'It is *so* often the case that one must regret it,' says Mary; and though he is not the one seated opposite her at the board, they exchange baleful skimming glances, like players about to begin a game.

'Tell me, though –' the next day, and the whole party taking the moorland path for their walk, and Branwell high-shouldered and bottled-up and asking '– this business about men.'

'There is no business about men,' snaps Mary. 'And trust a man to suppose there is.'

'Now I know I have you rattled,' Branwell says happily, 'because you're resorting to meaningless aphorisms.'

'I *mean*,' says Mary, struggling after him up a steep slope, 'that as soon as the mere question of women's role in the world is raised, men immediately assume they are being criticised. Branwell, wait.'

'May I give you my hand? Or will that be perceived as condescending to female frailty?'

'It depends. Would you do the same for a male friend?'

'Assuredly.'

'All right, then.' She grips his hand and strides up level with him. They are almost of a height. Something similar in the set of their lips: a wry question.

'But when you say *men*, are we to take this as meaning all men? All over the world, of every kind, ever?'

'If you like. Every general statement must by its nature involve imprecision.'

'So is it the mere fact of being men that makes us so? In other words, we're born like it and can't help it? Dangerous doctrine, Miss Taylor. Let us skirt the theological ground – that God made us that way – and simply consider common decency. Would you scorn anyone else for the way they were born – with a deformity, say, or a limp, or a constitutional weakness? Is this not mocking the afflicted?'

'Perhaps. But I'm sure you have known people with a constitutional weakness who begin to make much of it, and trade on it, so that it becomes their excuse for everything instead of just some things. That, I think, is closer to the general male position.'

'Does it not occur to you that being a man may also be a burden?'

'Oh, dear me, yes, such a burden – a burden to be free to choose your own life, and to have independence and power and responsibility—'

'Yes.' He stops and confronts Mary with a look. The piping wind conjures red snakes from his hair; his pallor is dramatic. 'I thought you a woman of imagination. Can you not imagine how that can be a burden?' He takes her arm and gestures at the long brown heaves of moorland below them. 'Imagine somebody takes you to the top of the hill and shows you a world spread out before you and says: "That's *yours*, all of it, as far as the eye can see: now, enter into possession of it. But that comfortable corner behind you? No, you must leave that."'

'Well . . .' Mary hesitates, watching his face . . . 'I would like the chance to *try* the burden, at least. But wait – I can imagine it, yes, Branwell – wait for me . . .'

'Lord above, now they'll be quarrelling all day,' complains Martha.

'Quarrelling?' says Emily. She shakes her head with a stoic sort of gloom. 'No, no. Mary is falling for Branwell, I'm afraid.'

Martha gasps and stares; Charlotte manages not to.

Emily tears up a fan of bracken and eyes Branwell and Mary through the fronds. 'I wish I had Papa's pistol,' she says.

'Emily! The things you say!' shrieks Martha.

'And which would you shoot?' enquires Charlotte.

'Oh, neither, I suppose.' Emily sighs; but points the bracken pistol-like and adds: 'It just needs – bang! – to be stopped somehow.'

William Weightman seems to notice something also. That evening he makes way for Branwell at the chess-board.

'Now, at least you may be sure, Branwell,' says Mary, smiling, 'that when I checkmate your king I shall feel a *little* sorry for him.'

Later, at the piano, she ignores Mr Weightman's call for something jolly and plays again 'Oh No, We Never Mention Her' – Branwell's favourite song.

'You see, I can send a valentine too,' Mary adds quietly, as she gets up from the piano. Quietly – but Charlotte, seated at a little distance, hears it, and so certainly must Branwell, who has been turning the music-pages; and who looks, extraordinarily, as if someone has just spat in his face.

* * *

'Well, there we are, I have made something of a fool of myself, but it's over now,' Mary says, wiping her cheeks, 'and I shall do my best to see the experience as educative.'

'Oh, Mary, I'm sorry,' Charlotte says.

'Why are *you* sorry, Charlotte?' The old spirited Mary flashes up. 'None of it was your fault. You did nothing – any of you – to foster any illusions about what Branwell felt for me. It was me who laid those addled eggs – and brooded on them – and hatched them.'

'If they were addled, you couldn't really hatch them,' puts in Martha, who is brushing her sister's hair in the girls' bedroom. 'Sorry. Only sometimes a little pedantry helps to take your mind off it.'

'Well, it was all my fault at any rate. I created it.'

'Branwell too,' Emily says yawning. 'He must have given you some reason.'

'Ah, but that's just it. I should have been happy with little hints and intimations of his regard, and just sat nursing them, and not making any demonstrations of my own. God, I feel a fool.'

'Oh dear.' Martha brushes more vigorously. 'Well, after all, it's not as if Branwell is very much of a catch. Sorry, Mary. I mean, sorry, everyone, but – I'm trying to make things better. It is rapidly borne in on me that I am not succeeding.'

It has happened vividly and very quickly, like a mayfly's life. The tart exchanges shading into flirtation, the flirtation ripening into something more – and then Branwell's abrupt withdrawal to cool looks, commonplace conversation, and a disinclination to be alone with her. Only the tactful interventions of Mr Weightman have kept it from downright rudeness.

Strange – and yet, even before this evening's nightgowned confessional, not entirely incomprehensible to Charlotte. She hardly needed Mary's husky explanation that she had told Branwell, simply, how she felt about him. She knew Mary's honesty and directness. And she knew also – not from experience but from the richer experience of dream-life – that if ever she felt so, she would have to speak it out too. And suffer that same cool, disdainful retreat.

'We are not supposed to say,' Charlotte pronounces now. Her own voice crackles on her ear, harsh and sibylline in the midnight silence. 'Anything we feel, we are not supposed to *know* we feel. If we do know, there is something morally wrong with us. If you like a man – not even love him, but like him enough to be drawn to him, to think you might possibly love him – you aren't supposed to know that either. You are supposed to go drooling about like an emotional infant.'

'It's true,' Martha says. 'That's the way the world wags. He's supposed to corner you in the arbour, and press his suit, and then you go into a flutter as, to your timid surprise, you discover an answering sentiment in your heart.'

'Breast, usually,' Mary says, half laughing.

Emily has prowled scowling to the window and leans there, tugging at her hair, her long white toes busily moving as if writing on the floorboards. 'What has the world got to do with your feelings?' she says sharply. 'Your meaning ours, mine, anybody's. That's the last castle. It can't be taken.'

'Well, I'm better now, and I feel stupid even talking about it, and thank you for your forbearance – especially as he's your brother,' Mary says briskly. 'The absurd thing is, the ridiculous height of it is, I am not in the least set upon hooking a man, as he no doubt sees it, and never intend to marry at all. Absolutely set against it. Other ideas entirely.'

'What other ideas?' Charlotte asks – casually, but with passionate curiosity.

'Hush – Aunt,' hisses Emily: and she shades the candle with cupped unburnable hands, and they breathe in arrested silence, while the slow pattens clack near, pause, move on.

'We'd better go to bed,' says Martha; and so they do, and only then, horizontal and hugger-mugger, does Mary draw a long breath and answer – if it is an answer: 'I want to go far away. But the trouble is there isn't anywhere far enough.'

Branwell's room. Evening hour when Charlotte would often come in, talk with him while the syringed gold or iced purple would spill over the window-sill. Today, the same yet different.

'I have a new tale.'

'Excellent.' Branwell visible only from the back: hunched over his writing-box, squeezed on to the bedside table. His face flicks round. 'Angrian, I hope?'

'No, not really.'

He makes a bored boiling sound between his teeth, bending over his papers again. 'Well, I'll look over it when you're ready.'

'Oh, it isn't written at all yet,' Charlotte says. 'It's in my head – but complete, or as good as. It's about a man who is a clerk in a counting-house. And he is a quite a well-paid clerk, and he has some prospects – but he feels he deserves better. Indeed he probably does deserve it.'

'Dull so far,' sings Branwell, his back to her, 'dull dull, yawn yawn.'

'But instead of receiving his deserts, he is always passed over – he never feels that life treats him as it should. Which makes him angry. It is an anger he is powerless to express. He has an aged mother relying on him, as well as a family of his own. And the manager of the counting-house is a Tartar, who takes a delight in lording it over the clerk, and making him feel the inferiority of his position. All day the clerk must keep his anger and disappointment buried in his breast. But when he goes home in the evening, things are different. For a little while, power is in his hands. He has a son, a small boy who adores his father, who hangs on his every word and look and would do anything to please him. And this is where the clerk finds recompense for his bitter life. He does not beat the boy or abuse him. But he is cold and exacting and impossible to please. Painstakingly, proudly, he withholds his love from the boy. And in that the clerk knows the power of a king.'

Branwell stirs. 'Your writing is taking a dismally workaday turn, Charlotte.'

'Oh, I haven't decided whether to write it out yet. But there's truth in it, wouldn't you say?'

'Perhaps. Not that I've ever understood what's so interesting about truth. I was right, though, wasn't I?' He almost turns to her: light chalks his cheekbone. 'About us not getting on any more.' The chalk is rubbed out. 'I think I'd like you to go now.'

'Branwell—'

'I really do think it, Charlotte.' Voice raw, splintering.

As she reaches the door he adds: 'Don't feel sorry for the boy, by the by. It's better for him in the long run.'

Branwell alone, opening the trunk at the bottom of his bed, needing something to tide him over, reality just too strong for him at present. Cool rotundity of the little bottle beneath his fingertips. Praise the laudanum. First tried it on a trip to Liverpool with a friend last year, when he came down with neuralgia. Friend recommended. Opium, good servant and bad master: look at Johnny Chinaman stealing into those waterfront dives after his dose. Sickly-sweet smell as he uncorks the medicinal genie. Just those odd occasions when only this will do for what ails you. Sit and wait, wait for the quiet beautiful flourish as the folding screens of the mind are put back. Now, in this subterranean light, you can look at things that otherwise are not to be borne. Now you can approach again that grey stone house up on the brow of the Lakes, taste again that mountain air, taste again those dazzling views (for now the senses have much to say to each other) across the high fells and your pride, yes, in your position, Mr Postlethwaite hearty and frank, and Mrs Postlethwaite remarking so flatteringly to her friends on young Mr Brontë's talents and how we are lucky to have him and, oh, the pride of that day with Hartley Coleridge (father the most eminent of opium-eaters, which surely goes to show something) when the conversation moved and chimed like music, and now dare we let the creeping light inch forward and envelop this figure? Yes – it's all right – she looks as she did at first, lovely Agnes, something so winning, almost absurdly enchanting about her dark rolling eyes as she passes through the hall with her bare white arms about the laundry-basket, and soon, oh, yes, we can see and taste this, those bare white arms around his neck and her tolerant chuckles, no, there isn't anybody, well, perhaps young Jacky up at the mill, why you mustn't be jealous over a bit of fun, and now you do remember, sir, I sadly need those new shoes. Now the dose is emitting its brightest glow – can it make this tolerable? – the sight of himself hanging about the back door of Agnes' cottage, and then by lamplight her dark eyes no longer bewitching but narrowed with irritation, yes, yes, I am for sure but I shall see if I can't get rid. Enough is enough, sir. You take it all wrong. Now Mr Postlethwaite standing very *pomposo* before his desk, gripping lapels, nostrils flaring and hairy, really Mr Brontë making a fool of yourself over a serving-girl and, tut, the good name of this family, at once Mr Brontë do you hear at once. Bearable? Yes, you can even laugh about it as you see yourself packing your bags – after all this was just an episode, amusing to recall . . .

Except Agnes, except Agnes, who found him at the last silly. *Oh, sir, you're silly.* That twist of scorn. Not bearable. Because of the wanting, such wanting – like with that girl in Bradford, her little sister crying in the next dismal basement room and the sooty chimney-piece where he laid the money. Knowing, of course, it was all a matter of the money and yet, oh, the wanting. Because when you were in that embrace then surely you were the desired and admired, you were Northangerland and king and conqueror: you were the man you should be. You were the man – ah, the dose has done its anaesthetic work, because now he can touch this terrible blister of truth – you were the man you are afraid in your heart you can never really be.

At Brookroyd, Ellen kissed Charlotte and studied her at arm's length and said: 'Now, tell me it's better than Stonegappe, at least.'

'It's better than Stonegappe.'

'And the Whites – they are a more amiable sort of people than the Sidgwicks?'

'Generally more amiable.'

'They let you come here for a half-holiday, after all. I think that was good of them.'

'Certainly; and I only had to grovel for it, and will have to make up for it with an eternity of sewing. What is it, Ellen? Are the Whites paying you a retainer to speak up for them?'

'Oh, Charlotte, I'm sorry. I was only trying to look on the bright side for you.'

'Oh, Ellen, you are too good. You ought to reproach me for my foul temper. I indulge it with you because I can get away with it. And if you can't reproach me,' she reached for George Nussey's riding-crop, 'here – at least do me some physical violence. I deserve it.'

'Indeed I won't, and you don't. What about the children?'

'There again I must count a small blessing. They are not quite so ungovernable as the little Sidgwicks; and I even find myself, to my astonishment, almost liking the baby. No, the fault, my dear Ellen, is with me. I was unhappy in my last governess's place, and now I have a place that is pleasanter in most ways, and I am still unhappy, and no doubt if I had the best governess's place in the world I should be unhappy. Such is my perversity, indeed, I should probably be unhappiest of all there – knowing that most depressing knowledge, that this is the best that can be hoped for. Talk of something less tedious than myself. What about the gentleman?'

The gentleman, as they always called him, was a suitor. Henry Nussey was all in favour of him: Ellen sometimes spoke with a smiling tremor of the refined tenderness of his sentiments. Yet the gentleman never seemed any nearer to an actual proposal. And Charlotte had a peculiar suspicion that Ellen liked it that way.

'Henry had a communication from him lately, in which he declares himself unchanged, and I think it as well to leave it so for the time being. Here is something more surprising: Mary Taylor is leaving England.'

'Not entirely surprising, but gratifying. Good for her.' Mary's father, worn out by working to repay his debts, had died earlier that year: the lively rackety family of the Red House was splitting up.

'Yes, but to go all the way to New Zealand . . . Well, that is her ultimate aim, she says, as soon as it can be arranged. Out there a woman can earn her own living in a way she never could here, according to Mary – not just teaching or seamstressing or dressing bonnets, all of which she would hate like black poison.'

'That sounds like Mary . . .' Charlotte shook her head. 'I wish I had her daring.'

'Not I. To be half the world away from home and no means of easily changing your mind and returning, or even going back on a visit – well, unless they find a way of making railways cross the oceans. Which reminds me, do you hear much from Branwell?'

'The odd letter.' Charlotte restrained herself from saying, *With Branwell, no news is good news.* He had another position now: clerk-in-charge for the Leeds and Manchester Railway, at a small station unpromisingly called Luddenden Foot. She found the very thought dispiriting: but when Branwell had first secured the job, he had launched into eloquence.

'To be a clerk upon the railway, you know, is no dull, plodding sort of business. Think rather of mariners taking ship in Queen Elizabeth's time. Those adventurers were making a new world – and so, assuredly, is the railway. It's changing the country before our eyes. So really when I take up this post I pass through the gates of the future, which is potent and . . .' What else was it? Terrible realisation: that now when Branwell spoke, after a while you stopped listening.

Hard to identify, exactly, when the buried seed became a shoot, and when the shoot was tall and firm enough to be seen.

There was this, when Charlotte came back to Haworth for the summer vacation, and found she had missed Anne, who had had to take hers earlier.

'No, she's not happy at Thorp Green, though of course she doesn't complain,' Emily said. 'I fancy they are a demanding sort of family all round. But they do seem to value her in a way. Perhaps she keeps the peace. Aunt and Papa remarked how tired she looked. It's not just the work, Aunt says, it's living in another establishment, where you can never be sure of the wholesomeness of the provisions or the airing of the beds. *You* know.'

And then news from Miss Wooler in her retirement: her sister was unable to keep Dewsbury Moor going, and the school was closing.

'A sad day,' Papa said. 'Girls' education in the district will not be the same without the Misses Wooler.'

'Perhaps someone will come along to replace them,' Charlotte said. 'A pity it can't be the Misses Brontë.'

And then the uncurling of the shoot, as the question began to pass among them: why can't it?

'Running our own school, like the Misses Wooler. You, me and Anne.' Emily fixed her eyes on the idea. 'Yes. Oh, dear God, yes, I can see it. We would be together. Work and home would be one. Oh, it's just too good to happen. I'm glad, in a way, that it's impossible, because then I won't have the torture of thinking about it.'

Charlotte said: 'Why impossible?'

'Well, the money, of course. Even the most modest of little schools would need money to set up. I've got, let's see, three halfpence in my drawer, how about you?'

And yet there was a possibility, after all. Aunt, with her small private income and her dedicated frugality, had amassed some savings. These savings would come to her nieces in time – but she might consider a loan, an advance, if the enterprise were sufficiently promising and sensible. So Papa explained to them, rather as if he were Aunt's legal agent, while Aunt sat enlaced and mittened in her penitential chair and shook her head faintly at any suggestion of thanks.

'Of course this is to be viewed not in the light of a gift or favour, but as a serious commercial proposition,' Papa said. 'I think I speak for Miss Branwell when I say that any such project must not be undertaken without great care, forethought, and deliberation.'

And then the shoot went luxuriating in all directions. Charlotte tended and watered it. She could hardly sleep: she kept waking to check its growth and vigour. Anne wrote saying she would do anything for them to have a school together. Miss Wooler wrote offering her the furniture of Dewsbury Moor, then even raised the question of her taking over the defunct school itself. Aunt began to speak definitively of a hundred pounds. Back at her post with the Whites of Upperwood – Bradford merchants, wealthy, well-meaning, insecure, just conceivably a little afraid of her – Charlotte wiped the snot from her sleeves and the sick from her shoulder and mentally crossed off each day's governessing like a prisoner marking the dungeon wall.

Freedom loomed, but its shape was still indistinct. Dewsbury Moor

– well, that was the place of her madness and, besides, Miss Wooler made it clear that the offer was only to her, not her sisters. Perhaps if nothing else, then . . . but surely something else . . .

When it came, it turned the whole budding plant around, as if responding to some strange new sun.

'Brussels. *Bruxelles.*' Charlotte, with Mary Taylor's letter in front of her – or, rather, on the bed beside her as she reads it again by the light of the last scrimped stub of schoolroom candle – tries over the word in a rapturous whisper. How the authentic pronunciation transforms it. Odd to think how the French suppose we live in Angleterre, that we go down to Londres. Or some of us do. Others stay in the same little place for ever and ever. Not knowing better.

Mary's letter is exciting and excitable – even the look of it on the page, the wild festoons of looped *y*s and *g*s, writing turning into decorations. Mary's plan of emigration holds firm; but in the meantime she has travelled with her brother to Brussels, where Martha's bristling spirits are to be smoothed at a continental finishing-school. And oh, Charlotte, what we have missed, what you must not miss. Mary gabbles of galleries and crows over cathedrals. And what you can gain here economically but with no sacrifice of quality – for the schools and seminaries are so uniformly excellent – proficiency in languages, French, Italian, German, and then music and drawing and, besides, the place is an education itself. If you want to make a success of the school idea, then come here first, study, absorb. Then you can come back to England confident, cultivated, finished, and you will have your diplomas to flourish before your impressed clientele.

How much of this is actually in Mary's letter and how much a conclusion drawn by Charlotte – never mind. Folding the letter safely away, folding herself into bed, Charlotte is already composing in her head the other letters: to Emily, to Anne, above all to Aunt. The one to Aunt occupies her over three evenings, as well as the unsleeping word-shuffling nights. Which suggests careful calculation, when in fact every word burns to the touch, with the incandescence of real meaning, of listen, please, please.

'Brussels.' Patrick, taking tea with Miss Branwell. 'It is curious, the first association the name has in my mind is still the great ball before the battle of Waterloo. Well, well, it will be a very great change for them. I hope they will be equal to it.'

'I think they will. I should not have agreed to advance the funds for the project if I had not been entirely convinced by Charlotte's reasoning. The fact is, Mr Brontë, if they are to undertake a school for girls, they will face a deal of competition; and they must offer languages. A continental education is their best hope of enhancing their qualifications and prospects, and it appears that Belgium offers the best combination of economy and decent standards. I could never be happy seeing them exposed to the extravagance and corruption of Paris, and I still fancy the German cities too remote and uncouth, though no doubt I am old-fashioned. The good report of the Taylor girls reassures me above all. Their brothers are happy to see them placed there. They have cousins living in the city. We would not be sending the girls quite among strangers. All in all, I think the scheme is creditable.'

'To be sure, Charlotte has pressed it very eloquently; and though it troubles me to think of them so far from home, I admire the courage and foresight that arms them for the venture, and could almost wish . . .' Patrick applies himself to his tea and does not say what he could almost wish. 'But Emily, now. I confess I am surprised at her agreeing to the plan. Again it appears that Charlotte has written most persuasively – but Emily's intense attachment to home, her actual revulsion from other places, give me some anxiety.'

'Oh, I don't think Emily has agreed to it lightly. She has, I believe, shown good sound sense. For economy, two must go; and again, for economy, it must be her. Emily earns nothing: no money is lost by her removal, whereas to take Anne out of Thorp Green would be to sacrifice her income. It is this attention to the practicalities of the scheme, Mr Brontë, and how they may best secure their common future, that has compelled my admiration.'

'And stimulated your generosity, Miss Branwell,' says Patrick, with one of his little bows, 'for which I will not embarrass you with the thanks your disinterested benevolence can hardly require.'

So they are as circuitously courteous with each other as ever, over this unprecedented conversational topic. Only now and then do silences intervene between them, like lopped boughs falling, crashing, bleeding sap.

'Brussels.' Emily trims the lamp-wick, turns the ashes on the fire, and resumes her seat at the dining-table. 'Very well. The sooner the better.'

It is Christmas Eve, evening. Charlotte has returned to Haworth today after giving notice and taking leave of her employers, the Whites of Upperwood. (The parents loaded her with good wishes and the children cried, and Charlotte carried the guilt of knowing how much she despised them all the way home in the coach like a hot, heavy dish righteously burning the fingers.) Anne is home for the holiday likewise; Branwell apparently wishing to get home but unable, apparently, to leave Luddenden Foot. And Papa and Aunt have retired.

So it is the three of them, seated around the dining-room table, and feeling, somehow, and on the edge of putting into words, the rightness of it. The ghosts of Maria and Elizabeth laid at last, perhaps? Or the living ghost of Branwell, the king who never seems to come into his kingdom?

'This is how it will be,' Charlotte says. In a gesture unusual to them, they have all three joined hands. 'I speak prophetically.'

'This is how we will sit in the evenings, when work is done,' says Emily.

'Except we will have our writing-boxes out, won't we?' says Anne. 'When we have our own school, we will have time to write?'

'Certainly. We shall manage it so,' Charlotte says. 'This is how it will be – I don't know where yet. Prophecy fails me there. It might not be in the house by the sea, not yet.'

'But it will be *our* place,' Anne says. 'That's what matters.'

Though Mr Dickens – whose works in their monthly numbers are eagerly awaited by Mr Greenwood the stationer – has already begun his grand reinvention of the Christmas season, here there is not much to be observed. A few references in Patrick's family prayers, a gift of stockings sent down to Tabby, lame and temporarily retired to her sister's house in the village. But Emily has her own ritual, as Charlotte finds when she wakes in the night and misses her.

'Emily, what are you doing down here? You'll catch your death.'

'Just settling Keeper.'

Emily's brute of a dog barely lifts his bear-like head from the kitchen floor at Charlotte's entrance.

'He looks settled to me.'

Emily shrugs. 'Well, settling everything else.' She moves about the candle-lit kitchen, a white-gowned streak, touching things, slightly rearranging them: kettle, flat-iron, bellows. 'At Christmas I fancy the house is . . . most itself. And I like to think of everything in its place, and comfortable. Well, didn't the Romans have those little household gods? *Lares et penates*. I always thought that made a lot of sense.'

'You heathen.'

'Most Christians are, I find.' Emily tidies the knife drawer with precise delicate movements, as if playing the piano. 'Are you afraid?'

'What of? Damnation?'

Emily gives her dawning smile. 'Everyone's afraid of that. And isn't it curious that they can all picture it so clearly? Like a place they already know. No, Brussels, I mean, going abroad, all of it.'

'Afraid, no. I would never have suggested it if . . . Well, yes, I am a little apprehensive; sometimes I wonder what it will be like and my mouth goes dry – but not afraid.' This is true: Charlotte's doubts are only the shade cast by the great noontide blaze of excitement.

'When you first wrote me about it,' Emily says, 'my impulse was to throw the letter on the fire.'

Charlotte watches her. 'But you didn't.'

'I am actually very eager to go. I would go tomorrow – tonight – if we could.'

'Because then it would be over sooner.'

Emily straightens the pot of spills above the range. 'Yes. And then the object would be achieved. The school: an end to trouble, you and Anne having to be governesses; all of us settled together.' As if addressing the household gods she turns slowly about the kitchen, coils of candle-light and darkness slithering round her, and says distinctly: 'I'm going away now so I won't ever have to go away again.'

For a few moments Charlotte feels stiff, heavy-tongued, as if struggling to break free from a spell. 'Emily – I do understand. Look. When we're there – if you really can't bear it, you will tell me, won't you? Promise.'

Emily takes up the candle, and in her eyes there is something of the bloom and glitter of those knives. 'I promise I will let you know.'

Christmas Day, and Emily helping to pin up Anne's hair before church. 'You haven't told me how you're getting on at Thorp Green.'

'Haven't I? Surely I have. I was saying the other day – when Aunt was asking – how I'm getting on very well, and—'

'Anne. This is me asking. Stop being Anne.'

Anne exchanges a glance with herself in the mirror, and you may perhaps read in the glance the words: *Stop being Anne? I can't, now.*

'I do get on very well. Pretty well. No, say very well, because, after all, I've been there a year and a half now, and that . . .'

'That is longer than any of us has ever stuck at anything,' Emily says, kissing the top of her head, 'as you are too kind to point out.'

'No . . . I was just going to say I've surprised myself. I wanted to prove something – but I'm not sure I have.' Anne looks away from that woman in the mirror, who is being too familiar: makes you uncomfortable. 'Thorp Green is a good position and I know it. But they are an unhappy family in many ways. And unhappy families seem to spread their unhappiness out so that it touches other people. None of which, by the by, matters at all. The things that matter are here. Papa looks better, I think. Less tired. I suppose he is still . . . I suppose Mr Weightman still performs a fair number of duties?'

'Yes,' Emily says yawningly, 'in between his other self-imposed duty of being delightful to every woman in sight. No, no, I do quite like him. He's very good. Anyhow, Anne: what do you think? The right decision?'

Anne sways with the jolt, then carefully places her feet on the pitching deck of misunderstanding, until it steadies. 'You mean Brussels? Of course.' There is really no such thing as a right or wrong decision. That is a refinement of sophisticates. The main thing is to get a decision made.

'Only I was just wondering – whether perhaps for those six months you could be here at home. Give up Thorp Green. It would mean losing your wage for that time, but Charlotte could probably persuade Papa and Aunt to that: you know how she is. Then when we come back, we start up the school.'

Anne shakes her head: very gentle but firm, very Anne. 'No, Emily. Let's stick to the original plan.' She rises, goes away from the mirror. 'You have to think about what you can bear.'

Emily performs her customary toilette – a short scowl into the mirror, a raking through of her wiry hair. 'Charlotte's very excited about this thing, you know. Brussels, all of it.' She shakes her head, sombre, eyes unlighted.

'Is that wrong?'

'With Charlotte, I think perhaps it is . . . Do you remember on the moors when we were young, how she was frightened to run downhill? And yet you know I have always suspected that Charlotte would leap right off a cliff – if there was something down there that she really wanted.'

PART THREE

But thou, poor solitary dove,
Must make, unheard, thy joyless moan;
The heart, that Nature framed to love,
Must pine, neglected and alone.

Anne Brontë, 'The Captive Dove'

1

Disharmony for Four Voices

January, and snow making folded linen landscapes of the Vale of York, and Anne returning to Thorp Green Hall. Returning to the expected things, even the dreaded things; but bringing something new with her.

Mansion was the only proper word for Thorp Green, lofty and solitary amid its lawns and shrubberies, parkland and prospects, ha-has and summerhouses. The terrace was just made for a gathering of horses and pink coats and dogs; the broad drive cried out for a procession of house-party carriages. But such things were not to be seen there, not now.

The Reverend Edmund Robinson, proprietor of the estate, had been suffering from ill-health for some time, and it set severe limits on the social life of the family. That accounted, in part, for the unhappy atmosphere in the great house. So you might have put it if, like Anne, you were inclined to be tactful in expression.

But Anne was also observant, highly sensitive, sharply honest. Hence the expected things, the dreaded things, that she could not shrug off or keep at a decorous distance. They rubbed like a nutmeg-grater at the quick of her self.

The servants, with their hard look, part wariness, part calculation: result of service in a place where wars were fought, alliances forged, advantage always to be sought.

The children: three well-grown girls, Lydia, Elizabeth, Mary – the eldest sixteen in age, thirty in worldliness, six in responsibility; and the only boy, Edmund, praised and indulged by his parents, as the boy must be, alternately babied and teased by his older sisters, so that his temper was perpetually raw and clamorous.

'Oh, Miss Brontë, what do you think? Is it not the very thing?' Lydia, showing off her new ringleted hairstyle. 'It's how hair is being dressed in London this season, you know. You quaint thing, how you do stare!'

'I should think she does.' Elizabeth, waspish. 'It isn't a style that becomes *you*.'

'And is it really true, Miss Brontë, that you were never in London in your life?' Mary, barely fourteen, and the most pretentious of all. 'Lord, I can hardly imagine it!'

But a little later, when a quarrel developed, Anne was courted, tugged this way and that.

'Miss Brontë, it's been dreadful while you were away. Elizabeth has been telling tales on me to Mama. And I'm afraid Mama has been foolish enough to believe them so *if* you should hear of them don't believe a word, not that you will, I know, because you are always so sensible.'

'Miss Brontë, Lydia is being beastly to me, I wish you would speak to her about it, because Mama takes no notice at all – or else she takes her side. I stood up for you the other day, you know – Lydia and Mary were saying you dress like a fright, and I told them you just dressed properly for your position.'

Then there was the re-meeting with the Reverend Mr Robinson. Difficult in various ways. Impossible not to wince in pity at the decline in his health: he was only in his forties, but turned sallow and gaunt. Only the very blue young eyes remained, so that when they pierced you from that harassed wedge of face it was as if he was looking at you from a lost past. But his temper, never easy, was made worse by his illness.

'Miss Brontë.' As she passed the closed door of his invalid's study-bedroom, Mr Robinson opened it and called after her. 'I did not know you were returned.'

Anne dropped a curtsy. 'Yes, sir. Late last night.'

'Really. Well, I trust you had a good journey. It is rather a pity you did not think to come in and see me. It is not as if I am overburdened with company. But there, perhaps my condition makes you uncomfortable: perhaps you are one of those people who cannot abide illness, hm?'

'Not at all, sir.' Anne knew, as he knew, that if she had knocked on his door for such a reason it would have been reprimanded as over-familiar, inappropriate and so on. 'I hope you find yourself a little improved, Mr Robinson.'

'I wish I could say I do, Miss Brontë.' He frowned. 'Well, pray don't stand about idle. I'm sure your pupils require your presence more than I.'

And then Mrs Robinson.

Hard to say what the dread was here. Mrs Robinson did not tyrannise or patronise or find excessive fault. Sometimes she was positively warm. 'My dear Miss Brontë, come and sit beside me and we shall have a comfortable little cose.' Or she might just barely acknowledge you, with a misty glance and a full-hearted sigh: 'Miss Brontë.' It depended whether she was being a vivacious woman, or a lonely misunderstood woman, or one of the many other variations. Perhaps that was it: you never knew, almost literally, where you were with her.

'We are bound to get on well,' she had said to Anne long ago, 'for I have a great taste for knowledge, myself: I yield to no one in my love of books.' And indeed sometimes in the evening Mrs Robinson's needlework-box was taken away and a little pile of books placed beside her chair instead. Then she would pick up a book, open it, read the title-page, read perhaps half the first paragraph, close the book, lay it down, sigh, and say: 'There are no books I like nowadays.' The next day, perhaps, might be one of her days for romping with her daughters: they would play mad, squealing, ticklish games of hiding things in each other's clothing. Anne could not help regretting this, because it made the girls unmanageable for the rest of the day; and it must have shown. 'Look at Miss Brontë, giving us that stern look,' Mrs Robinson said once, her hair coming down. 'Really, Miss Brontë, if you're not careful those books will turn you into a dreadful grave-airs.'

Once, in genial mood, she confided to Anne: 'I can honestly say, Miss Brontë, that I feel more like a friend – a sister even – to my girls than a mother: that's how close we are.' Lucky she did not hear, as Anne did, what scathing things her friend-sisters had to say about her behind her back. Still, sometimes their plain disrespect could not fail to get through to her: then would come the chilling, awesome retreat, Mrs Robinson mounting to a cold marble throne of melancholy maturity, beckoning Anne to her as handmaid.

'This is the great pity of being a relatively young mother, and retaining – well, so many people tell me it is true that I must believe it – retaining so much of the bloom of youth. One is not attended and obeyed as one would wish, and I cannot find it in my heart to be stiff and severe with them, as you do.' Mrs Robinson was about forty, and looked rather as any forty-year-old woman with pretty eyes and good skin might hope to look – no more, no less: a margin, Anne guessed, she found anxiously narrow. 'Of course, one might expect that a father's natural authority would mend matters. But there, between ourselves, Miss Brontë, I am too often sadly disappointed, and I do not refer only to Mr Robinson's present ill-health.'

A divided marriage, then. Yet an hour later Mrs Robinson might be drooping on her husband's arm, and declaring: 'You know me, Edmund, I have never been able to bring them to order as you do, and I am afraid Miss Brontë is too much of a tender-heart for it.' Then Mr Robinson would bark fiercely at the girls, and they would hate him, and despise him a little also for his palsied hands and the flecks of foam at the corners of his mouth; and they would protest their ill-usage to Anne, and then later to their mama, who would gently sympathise, and by bedtime they would be whispering that it would be a good thing when Papa was gone and Mama could find someone better.

Like a game. Yes, perhaps that was what Anne really dreaded, the return to these games. In a way she understood them. For all their wealth, the Robinsons were quite cut off from the world at Thorp Green. Turned in on themselves, the family invented things to absorb and entertain them. Yes, Anne understood that.

Understanding made it a little better. It was one of her consolations, kept in pockets of her mind: to be touched now and then, like Tabby touching her fairy-loaf and her lucky thimble. Memories were another: some quite recent. The Robinsons took a summer holiday at Scarborough, and Anne's vision of the sea was something she kept tight hold of: not so much the beauty as the astonishment – this is the place, this is the very place I want to be. The sight of York Minster was there too, tucked in with her faith, which had too often been a sharp, sore thing with her, until she learned to hold it more gently. Gondal and Gaaldine and the world below – yes, though they were a little worn and thin to the touch now. But writing, yes, verse and stories and the everlasting refreshment of words, that was a consolation.

And now, another. The future: not as a vague arena of promise, but as an appointment. When Charlotte and Emily came back from the Continent, they would all start a school together. For that, Anne thought, waking to each jangling unhappy morning, I can bear this. That was enough and plenty, that was the greatest good: look no further. Anne had found that it was not possible to live entirely without consolations – though it was possible to live entirely without illusions. Possible: even, perhaps, necessary.

Charlotte could see only glimpses of London from the train window, intimations of immensity, lights uncountable. They had left Leeds at nine in the morning, and now her tired pricking eyes interrogated the darkness of February night. She wanted desperately to sleep and also to stay awake for ever.

'Remarkable,' Papa said to Mary Taylor, 'for those of us who remember the coaching days, and how you would have to break such a journey overnight. Indeed, when I first came to England a man proposing to travel from the north to the metropolis would often make his will first.'

Mary was returning to Brussels, accompanied by her brother Joe, after a short stay in Yorkshire: natural that they and the Brontë girls should travel together. Not entirely necessary, then, that Papa escort them, but it was a thing that, in his punctilious way, he insisted upon doing. He had scarcely stirred beyond Haworth in twenty years, yet here he was undertaking a tremendous journey and quite at ease with it: repeating *com-bee-an-der* and *see voo play* from a little ancient phrase book, and disembarking at Euston fresher than anyone.

Their lodging for the night was of his choosing also – a place he had used as a London base when he was young. The Chapter Coffee House, right in the old booksellers' quarter of St Paul's Churchyard: an odd, brown, panelled, creaking, dusty, gravy-smelling gaiters-and-hair-powder sort of place. From there, Charlotte woke to her real experience of London. They had a couple of days to spare before their ship sailed: she wanted to take it all in. Even if, as it turned out, she was almost made sick by her greedy appetite. Joe Taylor knew London, or at least the sights, and was eager and tireless. Come then: the Abbey, the galleries, to be sure, all of them. She felt as if she were a child who had gone to hide in a game of hide-and-seek, and then forgotten to come out; and now you came blinking out of your hidey-hole, and there was all this going on, and it had been going on all the time while you drowsed behind the curtain. She got up early, to miss nothing – but no matter how early, in London the day already seemed half used, the coats of the horses already steaming, the flowers in the street-sellers' baskets already wilting. Chimneys rising above chimneys, as if houses had been built on top of houses; above, coal-smoke created a dark, foggy day, though somewhere behind it was a wintry bright one. St Paul's transfixed her: for a strange few moments she revisited the forbidden Verdopolis. At the Royal Academy exhibition she had to be restrained from putting her nose right up to the paintings: the vortex of Turner's brush-strokes pulled her in. They were still spinning around her mind that evening, when she actually was sick.

'Well, it will prepare your stomach for the sea-crossing, at any rate,' said Emily. She stalked about the room, business-like, folding clothes, competent traveller, even slightly bored. Only around the base of her right thumb there was a ring of red indented links: as if she had been biting.

'This,' Charlotte said weakly, 'this is where living begins. Isn't it?'

'No,' Emily said, with a cool bare glance. 'It's a pause.' And for a moment the rumble of wheels outside turned into the sound of drums, threatening war.

The next morning, the packet-ship for Ostend carries them away from London Bridge Wharf. Guttural pounding of steam-engine, panicked stampings and groans from the livestock on board, thin cheers from the passengers. On deck Charlotte, breathing in experimental half-lungfuls, watches London wrap itself in grey tissues of distance. Crossing the sea. There must, she feels, be something magical in so significant an act: surely it opens new, undreamed of possibilities of change. Surely you can even leave your self behind, leave it to wither on that shrinking shore.

Brontë, thinks Madame Heger. Quite a euphonious name, considering: most English names strike her as a grim collision of consonants.

And that is all she thinks – for now.

She is the directrice of the Pensionnat Heger. Large school for young ladies, situated in the rue d'Isabelle in Brussels: fronting on to the street, blank and formal as an excise-office or a prison, but with its own secret life behind – a real, enclosed little world of pretty court-yard and fruit-treed garden, and a gingerbread summer-house and balconies. Whichever way you look at it, as far removed as is possible from the grey stone and rigour of the West Riding. Here, a whiff of incense and garlic: of Catholic girlhood. Soft dark eyelashes, rustling gowns, guilt confessed and transformed. A kind of slightly stirred, rosy languor about its well-appointed rooms, its airy dormitories. Feel it especially when the young ladies are out in the garden, as they often are – free exercise, good meals, no puritanical deprivations; that is the style of the Pensionnat Heger. Now it awaits its latest pupils. Certainly they will be curiosities – grown women, English, Protestant – but the Pensionnat Heger is known for its powers of assimilation. It will manage very well. For it is managed very well.

Industrious Madame Heger is lingering just a little over breakfast

– a second cup of coffee, a stretching of kid-shod feet towards the fire while the English nursemaid takes charge of her three little girls: permitting herself this, because she is eight months pregnant. She has that reputed, seldom-seen glow; in fact altogether she is the picture of womanly domesticity, this plump pretty woman with her buttery skin and glossy black coiled hair and the look about her lips of nearly smiling over some gentle thought. Only a few minutes does she allow herself. Duties beckon: including, this morning, the reception of the English girls. She rises, and in doing so clips the edge of the tray at her side, and a china coffee-cup pitches on to the hearth and breaks. Most curiously, it does not shatter, but falls neatly into two halves.

Madame Heger stares a moment in mild surprise. But not the faintest superstitious thought touches her. She is a fruit of the Enlightenment: Catholic, but with an equivalent faith in reason that has made her a dedicated teacher. She rings for the maid, apologises to her for the extra trouble, and has the pieces swept away. That's better. Mess is her aversion.

Downstairs she passes through the two long schoolrooms, greets and bestows civil enquiries on Mesdemoiselles Blanche, Marie and Sophie, the teachers, distributes kind looks and words among the day-girls and boarders alike, ensures that all is well, all going smoothly. Smooth as her skin, smooth as the hair that she brushes for a good twenty minutes each night. Madame Heger cannot pass a coverlet or a drape without smoothing it: she has to do it.

And presently the bell rings in the portress's lodge, and Madame Heger goes across to the tiled hall to welcome the newcomers.

All rather charming and touching, as she tells her husband later. The tall, white-haired pastor with his halting courtesies: the two little shy pale women, making her think of, what do you call them? Quakers. And, oh, so very serious: one feels they are ready at any moment to go to the stake.

'To the stake?' Monsieur Heger, who has his cheek resting against her belly, waiting for a movement from the baby, lifts his dark quizzical face. 'What for?'

'That's just it.' Madame Heger shrugs and smooths his curling hair. 'One can't imagine.'

Charlotte was nearly twenty-six; and not since early childhood, the days of being safely in the middle, had she felt so right.

She liked it all. She liked the long lumbering *diligence* journey across

Belgium, and the way Belgium looked like a great moist market-garden. She liked Brussels, which seemed to her to have everything a foreign capital should have: endless churches and convents and little quaint gateways and embrasures and the angelus bell forever tolling down dark gullies of streets, and then a rue Royale where high-perched carriages bowled along and cavalrymen paraded, looking as if they had been half mummified with gold braid, and it was hard to tell the grand ladies from the courtesans, and a chestnut-shaded park with vaunting great bronzes of celebrated nonentities and umbrella-bearing bourgeoisie airing their hoop-bowling children and waving away wooden-shoed violet-sellers with nut-brown collapsed faces. She liked the school, which was well run and comfortable and civilised, and she liked Madame Heger, who was cultured yet approachable and – this was revelation – not an old maid.

No, there were things she did not like, but they did not thrust themselves upon her like the little Sidgwicks' grubby hands and snotty faces: they were ignorable. Their fellow pupils, for example – vain starers and gigglers and sentimental strokers of each other's hair; luckily Charlotte and Emily had a little curtained alcove to themselves at the end of the dormitory, and could be quite separate. There was mass, and the evening *lecture pieuse*, full of obscure saints doing conjuring tricks, but they were excused from them – and even looking on one discovered a satisfaction, the realisation of just how right Protestantism was. Emily was coldly amused.

'Why not just prostrate themselves before a painted stick, and have done with it?'

And, yes, of course she liked having Emily with her, she was thankful a hundred times a day that she was not alone because that would have altered everything – and yet also, perhaps an equal number of times a day, she suffered heart-clenching anxieties over her. She began to have a special corner-of-the-eye feeling for Emily, as for a child just starting to walk, or an insecure candlestick in the breeze.

'Is that what they are wearing in England?' asked one of the gigglers, early on, plucking at the drooping sleeves of Emily's frock.

Every word spoken here was perforce in French, which partly explained the searching look Emily gave her. Partly.

'Why do you ask?'

A giggle. 'Oh, faith, because I am curious to know.'

'Then,' Emily said carefully, 'you are a fool to be curious about such a thing.'

The girl produced a little shriek, and looked around for her allies. Anticipating a shrieking-fit Charlotte put in: 'You must know, Mademoiselle, that like me my sister finds it difficult always to choose the right words to express herself in French.'

It was a good twenty minutes of stoniness later that Emily spoke. 'Don't ever apologise for me, Charlotte.'

'I was only trying to get her to go away and—'

'Don't apologise for me. Remember, we are here – I am here because of a bargain. And I was to tell you if I find it intolerable. Well, this is one of the terms. If I am to stay, if *we* are to stay, then you take me as I am and don't try to change one thing about me, or cover it up or apologise for it.' Emily would not look at her. 'Is that agreed?'

Charlotte said: 'Yes, Emily.' Because harmony must be restored: because she liked it here. Learning above all – difficult and taxing as the lessons, all in French, could certainly be: there was pleasure in the difficulty, the intellectual victories fought and won. It was what she most wanted, and it was the only thing Emily wanted. For a while they received well-meant invitations to the home of the British chaplain of Brussels, a clerical acquaintance of Papa's – English conversation and gossip, and tea, and polite, hearty young fellows helping you to it. Charlotte struggled, and Emily presented her most formidable silence.

At last, when Charlotte mentioned that the Reverend Mr Jenkins had invited them again, Emily burst out, with the full force of exasperated bafflement: '*Why?*'

'I suppose the idea is that it gives us a little society.'

Emily glared as if Charlotte had replied in baby-talk. 'I'm not here for that. Are you?'

'No,' Charlotte answered truthfully. 'I'll make our excuses.'

Not here for that, no: which didn't mean there was no society here she relished. There were the Taylors, Mary and Martha, though they did not get to see them till the Easter vacation, when they walked out beyond the city tollgates to visit them at their finishing-school. The Chateau de Koekelberg: more manor-farm than chateau, as Mary remarked, and too many English pupils.

'And there you were complaining about the ignorant Belgians grovelling before crucifixes,' Martha said.

'I don't like ignorance and grovelling of any kind. But the English girls are such little ladies, which is even worse.'

'Oh, I think you are learning a few ladylike ways yourself, my dear dragon, and not before time. Just be careful of that German. It plays havoc with your face.' Martha stuck out her jaw and enunciated with hoots and sobs. '*Wie spät ist es? Es ist fünf Uhr.*'

Mary aimed a mock-blow at her, turned to Charlotte. 'Have you begun German yet?'

'Not yet. Fluent French is the first aim.'

'It is splendid and noble, in spite of what my incorrigible sister says. I mean to try Germany next – a post in a private family perhaps for a time, or a school.'

'And you still aim for New Zealand?'

'Oh, yes. I'm afraid I have the heart of an emigrant. I want to get all I can from the world.'

'But will the world leave you anything of yourself?' Emily asked.

Mary smiled. 'I can't be like you, Emily. Nor, I suspect, can Charlotte . . .' Suddenly it was as if she saw she had made them uncomfortable, and decided to do the same for herself. 'Well, tell me, news from home. Branwell: how does he do? Is he promoted?'

Dispiriting to have to answer. There had been the same pained reluctance in Papa's letter.

'Branwell is leaving his post with the railway,' Charlotte said. 'That is, it seems he has been dismissed. There was a discrepancy in the accounts of his station – a shortfall of money. I think there is no real suggestion or possibility that he was directly to blame – he has suspicions of the porter – but as clerk-in-charge, he is held responsible. It is, of course, a great pity – a piece of very bad luck.' She had a feeling of handing on to Mary some tremendously delicate single bloom: it might be received in careful fingers, or casually crushed.

'Well,' Mary said at last, 'he needed something better than that, anyhow.'

'Just what I always thought,' cried Martha. 'Such talent – so clever and gentleman-like – surely he deserved better than that, I thought.'

'I didn't say "deserved",' Mary said, with a quick bare smile. 'I said "needed". Charlotte, you look so well. I'm glad you're happy at Pensionnat Heger.'

And inside Charlotte reeled a little at that word. Happy: it felt like an accusation of some small, slinking crime.

Two days later, Easter Monday, there was some genteel hurry and urgency in the Hegers' private apartment. Presently came the news that Madame Heger had been safely delivered of a boy. When Charlotte lay down in her narrow white-curtained bed she picked out, among the already familiar weave of sounds that was the night-time Pensionnat, the thin, tenacious cry. It was typical of the Hegers' courtesy that a couple of days later Charlotte and Emily were invited to come up and see Madame Heger and the new baby: typical also of their tact that the younger girls were not to know. Though babies might have been more in their line.

Charlotte, however, had the right phrases of admiration and congratulation to hand as they went in. Madame Heger, looking more rounded and lustrous and finished than ever, turned slightly, smilingly away, giving them good morning while she buttoned her bodice. The baby drooled whitely in the crook of her arm. The incredibly shining bursting coral-tipped breast was gone as if it had never existed.

Revulsion and fascination kept the image before Charlotte for some time after. Not unlike the statuette of the Virgin that stood in the little oratory upstairs, a light always burning before it. Ugh. You had to look.

But what she liked best – well. *Like* was a word both too imprecise and too straightforward for the experience, which could contain fear, anger, exultation, incomprehension – anything, in fact.

Lessons with Monsieur Heger.

You saw him before, knew him in some sort – Madame Heger's husband, who was about the place, but whose life was chiefly elsewhere. He was professor at the Athenée Royale, the boys' school that adjoined the Pensionnat Heger – actually adjoined it, so at one end of the garden there was an *Allée Défendue*, a Forbidden Walk, where the boys might glimpse femininity through the thick trees and hedges, and the girls be thereby instantly corrupted. That was his world: but he also, incidentally, taught French literature to the girls of his wife's school. The shortish, scowling man with his arms full of books, shouldering doors open: seeming always to be pushing impatiently at some threshold.

Then he burst through it, and into the world of Charlotte and Emily.

'Mesdemoiselles.' He stood at the door of the private study, chin up, sneering, cracking an imaginary whip. 'As you are aware, I consider you, from your progress so far, eligible for my particular attention. Very well. This is not a matter for celebration. You may regret it bitterly. But I promise you, you will learn.'

Suddenly French was no longer a subject for study. It was a living thing, and so to be respected – and honoured, and wooed, and tenderly loved. Slights and insolences to it were not to be tolerated.

'Why?' Monsieur Heger crouched low beside Charlotte's desk, almost falling on his knees, his dark, mobile face creased in a rictus of agony. His hand hovered and trembled over her translation exercise, as if it were a glowing coal he was nerving himself to grasp. He spoke pleadingly. 'This – this *mediocrity*. Why, why do you do it? I want to help you. Will you not help me, a little, instead of inflicting this –' his hand came down hard on the exercise '– this wretchedness on me?'

'I'm afraid there are some errors—'

'No no no.' He sprang up and did a little drooping dance of desolation. 'It is not a matter of errors, it is a matter of you not caring. You don't care what you are writing.' He performed a mime of oafish scribbling. 'There, *la la*, get it down, anything will do.'

'Indeed, Monsieur, that is not true,' Charlotte said indignantly. 'I care a great deal about what I write—'

'But it doesn't show!' he almost bellowed. 'Don't tell me, Mademoiselle Brontë, show me!'

Impossible not to flinch at his anger, as from a finger coming straight at your eye. Emily fixed him with her coolest, remotest stare.

'Mademoiselle Emily? What is it? Ah, you are admiring my beauty, perhaps.' He flung up his pugilist's profile. 'Never fear, you will have plenty of time for that. In the meantime, you will please explain the numerous beastly absurdities in your own translation exercise.'

'You shouldn't let him upset you,' Emily said later. 'It isn't right.'

'I don't. Well, sometimes a little. Though I've noticed when I do get upset I stop thinking about speaking in French and it just comes out naturally.'

'Hm. He's trying to . . . I don't know.' Emily mockingly did one of his own mime-gestures. 'To *mould* us.'

'He'll never do that. But then – well, after all, I suppose, as a teacher, that is what you should aim at.'

'Sacrilege,' Emily murmured, picking up her grammar-book.

Monsieur Heger took them through his own special course of teaching, reserved for the most promising of the Pensionnat's pupils. It was literary; excellent. But when he set out the technique of it – reading and analysing passages from French classics, and then writing a composition on the same theme, Emily cried out: 'Copying, you mean. Where is the virtue in that? All it will do is discourage originality. It will destroy everything about us that's fresh.'

Monsieur Heger regarded her quite mildly, looking only as if he were suppressing a sneeze. 'Originality, then, you take to be the highest virtue in writing?'

'No, the only virtue,' Emily said, folding her arms.

'Ah, the only one, and no other!' Monsieur Heger made a face as if he were inhaling some elusive odour that might be nice or might be nasty. 'Interesting – and, Mademoiselle Brontë, you agree with this brief and definitive statement of literary theory?'

'I wouldn't say the *only* virtue,' Charlotte said, 'but I don't think there can be any genius without originality.'

He looked volcanic for a moment: only when he smiled did she realise how tensely she had hung on his reaction.

'A true statement,' he said. 'And what I propose to examine is, precisely, the works of original genius – and how *none* of them—' fiercely he held up a finger, locked eyes with them both in turn '– could have existed without attention to craft and style.'

This, this Charlotte liked: the writing of the essay, the last anxious glance over it before you handed it over to him – and then the response. It made her feel hugely alive. Even when it made her cry.

'This word. Why this word? Look at it. Does that seem to you the right word for what you wish to say?'

'It is the nearest word . . .'

Monsieur Heger took the cigar-stub from his crooked lips, looked at it a moment, then hurled it at the opposite wall. 'It is *that* far from the word you want, Mademoiselle Brontë. There is only one word for what you want to say and you must seek it high and low, and if you are unequal to that effort, then you are wasting my time and yours.' He peered at her. 'What's this? Why do you cry?'

'I don't *know*,' she said hotly, wiping her face.

'There, come now, don't do it. Are you taking it personally? My dear Mademoiselle Brontë, this is where you go wrong. You must be objective about your writing. Here, here.' He hunted through his pockets and, among various oddments, came upon a pink bonbon. 'That's for you.'

Now she couldn't help laughing. 'Monsieur, I am not in the infants' class.'

'Oh, well, we are all children sometimes, in our heart of hearts.' He was in his thirties, and when in beetle-browed mood looked older; but contrition brought out something very boyish in him. You almost wanted to urge him to eat the bonbon himself.

He never drew any tears from Emily, who, she said, didn't care for his opinion any more than his methods. But she laboured hard over the essays, and Charlotte saw her hungry look when she received them back. And sometimes when he read aloud the scornful twist would leave her mouth.

'This is the tragedy of Phèdre – the tragedy of self-knowledge. Tragedy, and greatness. She is burning with love, forbidden love, for her stepson. Indeed she is dying of love, though the love is also what keeps her alive. *Oui, Prince, je languis, je brûle pour Thésée.* This is the lie: that the love is for her husband. The truth comes out in the brilliant crystal of her language, both pure and passionate. *Que dis-je? Il n'est point mort, puisq'il respire en vous. Toujours devant mes yeux je crois voir mon époux. Je le vois, je lui parle; et mon coeur . . . Je m'égare, Seigneur, ma folle ardeur malgré moi se déclare.* Do you hear it? The chaste simplicity of these words: how it concentrates this confession of an illicit passion, so that we feel it with her, and are not repelled. We pity, we admire; we burn too.'

That evening Emily kept the candle burning even longer in their alcove. She was reading *Phèdre.*

'I wish they weren't so remote and grand,' Charlotte said. 'You know, princesses and mythical heroes.'

Emily shook her head. 'It doesn't matter. The feelings are the same, that's what counts. The feelings burst through everything.' She laid the book down. 'In fact, she reminds me a little of Augusta Almeda, before her exile to Gaaldine.'

Charlotte said nothing. There was a certain glint in Emily's eye when she mentioned the world below, and something in Charlotte stood warily back from it: like liquor on the breath.

'It's very interesting about Mademoiselle Emily,' Monsieur Heger said to Charlotte once, joining her in the garden. 'The way she fights me. It's the way a man fights. Hard and fierce – knock you down, perhaps – but then, when it's done, extend the hand, no hard feelings, and so you part. But when *you* fight me, Mademoiselle Brontë, it's different.'

'You mean I fight as a woman fights?'

'I hardly know. It's a kind of winning-round – so that I will be defeated almost without knowing it, suddenly, flat on my back, and you above me smiling down. Is that a fair description of how a woman fights?'

'I don't presume to speak for all womankind, Monsieur Heger.

Indeed, I don't think such a thing is possible. I would contend that there is not such a great difference between men and women as you suggest. The perilous truth is how alike we are.'

'Perilous?'

'Oh, yes. It would be a Jericho blast to acknowledge it. Walls would tumble. We would all have to alter our positions.'

He studied her, brown fingers stroking and tweaking his beard. Sometimes he seemed to like inflicting little jabs of pain on himself, as if to keep his mind alert. 'A new idea to me, I confess. And the result? Would we all be happier – men and women?'

She hesitated. 'We would be more truthful with one another.'

'Ah!' His smile was profoundly gentle. 'That's a different matter . . . But, yes, come here, come here and be eaten!'

His three daughters came running from the house and enveloped him. In a moment he was rolling on the lawn, making ogre meals of them. They were dark, fizzy little creatures: you could see both Monsieur and Madame Heger flickering in and out of their strongly marked, expressive faces. And there was Madame Heger appearing at the garden door, with her baby in her arms. The perfect family. Charlotte stepped back a little because even her shadow falling across the grass seemed an intrusion.

Their six months was up, but Charlotte and Emily were not going home. They were to have another six months at the Pensionnat Heger, partly pupils, partly teachers: Charlotte to instruct in English, Emily in music, in return for their keep.

'I think Madame's offer is one we can hardly refuse,' Charlotte told Emily. 'We will gain such precious experience for our own school, and in the meantime we can make progress with our German. Really, I don't think we could ever have such an opportunity again.' Careful, she told herself, don't overdo it: that was the way to harden Emily against you. The offer had certainly come from Madame Heger – but only after a suggestion from Charlotte that they would do anything if they could stay longer. Emily need not know this. 'It means putting off our return for a while but that's all, no drawing further on Aunt's money, no change of plan.'

Emily's silence was, for her, quite short. 'Very well,' she said – and that was it: one thing you never needed to fear was Emily changing her mind. Charlotte's stomach muscles relaxed; the toppling candlestick was righted again.

When the wobble came, it was unexpected. Charlotte was altering the sleeves of one of her gowns. Emily glanced up from her German grammar, saw, frowned. 'Whatever are you doing? There's hardly any wear on those.'

'No. But they're so wide, and you notice how much more neatly and simply people dress here.'

'*You* notice.'

Charlotte breathed deep. 'I just want to be a little more presentable.'

'It's enough that we have to copy other writers without having to copy how people dress as well. What next? Muttering over your rosary?' Emily tossed the book down and went to the dormitory window. 'I wish to God we could throw these open and get some breeze; it's all so thick and still in here, it's like being at the bottom of the sea. I'm sorry, I'm sorry. It's just that sometimes I make a mistake. I look up.' She shook her head. 'Exactly what I told myself I wouldn't do. I look up – and even through all these damnable tactful muffling curtains I see the moon. And it's the same moon that shines on home: and at this moment, I think, Anne might be looking at it too, or Branwell.'

'In a way, it's a nice thought,' Charlotte said cautiously, with a feeling of inching out on to crackling ice.

'Except it isn't true. It isn't the same moon really, or the same sun. That's the horror of it.' Emily stalked back to her bed, picked up the German grammar, found her place. 'That's why I should never look up.'

When Charlotte wore the gown with the narrowed sleeves a few days later, Emily made no comment. A few days after that, during morning exercise in the garden, one of Emily's pupils unhelpfully demanded: 'Why do you still dress in that monstrous old-world way?'

Emily shrugged. 'I only wish to be as God made me.' And then, as if speaking through the back of her neck at Charlotte behind her: 'I am not one of those people who are forever concerned with *pleasing*.'

Well, thought Charlotte: debts are always called in. She even tried to smile about it. But the smile would not come, and her eye fell on a windfall apple in the grass, and the spiked rump of a wasp rooting in its rottenness.

It was September when the first piece of news came. Of course they didn't know then that it was the first of a series. And yet it did seem to come thumping down from the sky, making a crater of disbelief and shock – making room for more.

William Weightman had died. Twenty-eight years old. Mr Weightman, dying? Somehow you could imagine him doing anything but that, Charlotte thought, with the black absurdity of grief: somehow it was out of character. And yet, as Papa's letter revealed, not so. Cholera had slowly wrung the life from William Weightman's personable young body: cholera probably caught from going among the poor and sick of his parish. He did that, conscientiously, willingly. And you knew that. And somehow it was easier not to know it, and to keep that light thumbnail sketch of his character in your mind instead. Easier, safer.

Then it was the scribbled note from Mary Taylor at Chateau de Koekelberg.

Martha very ill.

Charlotte got there the next morning, having run nearly all the way through mud; her skirts dragged like heavy armour. Mary came down to the hall. Oak beams and antlers, of all things – of all things to surround you while you heard about delightful irrepressible Martha Taylor dying last night.

'That was too long to suffer,' Mary said, with a sort of dry crossness. She fixed her gaze, as if drunk, somewhere in the middle of Charlotte's face. She had nursed Martha. She had been awake for thirty hours. 'I'm glad it stopped. It wasn't right. She was very good, of course, all the way through. She always was, wasn't she, Charlotte? I think so. Very good, Martha. Gone now though.' She began a low, square-lipped wail. Charlotte held her hand while it went on.

Cholera, incidentally, or coincidentally, had worked its way into the crowded school and put an end to Martha Taylor as it had to William Weightman. It was as if a great arm had swept from Yorkshire to Brussels, knocking away the human chess-pieces – except, of course, it wasn't as if anything of the kind. One thing had simply happened and another thing had simply happened. That was what was so terrifying. Life was simply accumulation. You kept adding on experiences, but they never added up.

It was November when the third piece of news came. In fables and fairy tales, there was always something fateful about three and third. They signalled transformations.

'Madame, if you will be so good as to grant us leave – leave to go home for a time,' Charlotte faltered. 'We have had a very sad letter – our aunt. Our aunt has died.' Saying it in French made it unreal. What could Aunt Branwell ever have to do with French? She was untranslatable. 'That is, she was my mother's sister, and she stayed with us from when we were little children, and so she is – I mean, she was something more than an aunt, if you understand me.'

'My dear Mademoiselle Brontë, of course,' said Madame Heger. Her great soft-lashed eyes scanned Charlotte swiftly and kindly, as if she were a sad letter herself. 'I understand you perfectly.'

End of a strange journey, for Elizabeth Branwell of Penzance. She did not complain of her illness, or the excruciating pain of it, until it pinned her to her bed and could no longer be hidden. Why? Perhaps because familiar Mr Andrew, the hard-working Haworth surgeon, had also died that year, and she did not like change and preferred not to see his replacement. Perhaps also because it was something she believed. Suffering must be hidden. Why? Too late to ask that.

Elizabeth Branwell of Penzance, not of Haworth, almost to the end. Always there had been this polite fiction that her residence at the parsonage was temporary, that at some time, when certain things were settled, she would go back to Cornwall and pick up the interrupted threads of her real life. But now at last, just before pain finally deprived her of speech, she told Patrick: 'I shall not go home again.'

Thorp Green, sombre among bare woods and under pewter sky. Intolerable day for someone of Mrs Robinson's lively spirits: early on she swooped into the schoolroom and carried the children off for a drive. Anywhere, my dears, anywhere. It would be a sad squeeze in the landau with Miss Brontë – so she is to consider the half-day hers. Mr Robinson will lunch and talk symptoms with his physician, who is forever about the house.

Anne takes her morning walk in the grounds. Smoky caw of rooks: somewhere in the distance the flat clap of a sportsman's shotgun. Near the stable-yard the chock of hoofs as Mr Robinson's horse is led out to exercise, voices of groom and gardener. 'Give her a good run. The master's riding days are over.'

'Aye, they are that.' And then something more, with a harsh blast of mirth.

She stops at the gravelled forecourt, arrested by a flash of red up the long drive: the post-boy. And at the sight of him Anne experiences – most unusually for her – something like hate. Poor innocent. Not his fault he was the one who brought the letter from home: the letter telling of William Weightman's death.

Every day since then she has enacted a ritual in her head. When she has a few minutes' leisure, she pictures the Sunday school at Haworth. She puts herself back in it. She watches the last pupils clattering out of the door. She places her gloves on the lectern, then leaves the school, and walks up the lane to the parsonage. She goes up the stone stairs to Aunt's room, where Aunt is sleeping off her cold. She sits by the fire. And each time she waits for something different to happen.

It never does. Each time, the denial. And after the denial comes the inevitable death.

'Bad news? Who?' Mrs Robinson asked inquisitively – perhaps kindly – when she saw Anne tearfully, hastily putting away the letter.

'My father's curate, ma'am.'

'Oh.'

'He was – was very young.'

'Dear, dear,' Mrs Robinson said, her interest drifting to her new bracelet. 'What a shame.'

And that, really, was all you could give it. Denial has produced another deprivation: she has no right to mourn, no title to grief. What a shame. Yes, shame, this secret indulgence. But she cannot help it, or is too weak-willed to resist it. (Lucidly, firmly, Anne believes herself to be a bad person in many ways.) It was her first thought when Mrs Robinson gave her this morning free: Ah, I can use the time to indulge in vain regret.

The post-boy draws nearer. She feels sorry for her little spasm of hate, and goes up the drive to meet him and take in the post herself. She is surprised to find another letter for her, from her father: it's rather soon. But she suspects nothing, and doesn't open it until she is seated in the schoolroom.

And now she sees what a very bad person she is. Here she has been brooding and burning over a person who was, properly, nothing to her. And meanwhile Aunt Branwell, who was so very much to her – who brought her up from an infant, whose name always came alongside Papa's in her prayers, who has been the closest thing to a mother she has known: Aunt Branwell, whose only place in her thoughts lately has been as an incidental figure in her morbid fancies – well, meanwhile Aunt Branwell has been dying in agony. And is gone.

The Robinsons make such a long outing that the late-autumn afternoon is darkening when they get back. But Anne is still sitting in the same place in the shadowy schoolroom, the letter a white shape on her lap. Bursting in full of high spirits, seeing her there, the girls briefly whisper, then pounce.

'Boh! Guess who it is!' Lydia comes up behind and puts her hands over Anne's eyes. Elizabeth grabs and imprisons her hands. Mary sits on her feet. 'There! Now you're our prisoner, Miss Brontë. You can't get away. We've got you, you're caught fast and there's nothing you can do and nowhere to go! Isn't that a good joke? You're laughing, aren't you, Miss Brontë? I can feel you laughing!'

Branwell growls, 'Don't talk to me about peace and release. It was hideous.'

Though Anne got home to Haworth in time for Aunt Branwell's funeral, Charlotte and Emily, with the long crossing from Brussels, were too late. Now they have gathered to pay their respects at Aunt's grave in the church, close to their mother's.

'It ended, Branwell,' Anne says.

'Oh, to be sure, it ended, after unimaginable agonies.' Branwell stalks to the family pew and flings himself down. 'Just like with poor Weightman – only a week or two of unthinkable suffering. Mind you, Papa managed to justify it, of course, Aunt and Weightman both being thoroughly good Christians and offering their pain to God. Very greedy for pain, you know, this deity, gobbles it up, simply can't get enough of it.'

Charlotte says, 'Oh, Branwell, don't.'

'Why? Never tell me you've turned pious.'

Why? Perhaps because she just doesn't want to think about it: wants to think about good things instead. The letter she has brought from Monsieur Heger to Papa, commending their brilliant progress at the school, urging him to consider their return. She stirs guiltily under Branwell's scrutiny. 'I just don't think you should torture yourself with these things,' she says.

'Self-torture is one of life's few inexpensive luxuries,' he grumbles.

'I don't know why we should lament,' Emily says. Being back at Haworth she looks healthy, serene, almost happy. 'The pain has stopped. That's the best we can ever hope for.'

Branwell turns his hollow gaze on her. 'Whose pain do you mean, Emily? Aunt's, or yours?'

'I don't think we should quarrel at a time like this,' Charlotte says. Her voice sounds different, artificial, to her own ears. But she feels somehow disconnected from them: as if she is still partly across the sea. And torn, tangled, baffled as the four of them are, she feels they need something: some corrective. Monsieur Heger, now, he would know how to reconcile these stormy contradictions: his mind would hold them like a cupped hand. And the image of his hand, cupped, is suddenly very strong for her and makes the church and everything fall away.

The Robinsons have been very understanding, allowing Anne a couple of weeks' leave for Aunt's funeral and the settling of her affairs, but they are glad to have her back at Thorp Green at the end of November. Glad in the sense that her presence is missed – as balance and counterweight, as target and ammunition.

Mrs Robinson gathers Anne's arm in tender solicitude, and in full view of her daughters with whom, it is clear, she has had a falling-out. 'Miss Brontë, I grieve to see you in mourning, though allow me to say you look so very neat and comely in it. Do tell me how your excellent family bear up. Your sisters, they came back from their studies on the Continent to pay their respects? I am gratified, but I am not surprised. Simply from knowing you, I am convinced they must be as dutiful as they are clever. I hope, when you write to them next, you will convey my most heartfelt sympathies and compliments. Let's see – Emily and Charlotte, those are their names, I think? It is quite a pleasure of mine to picture them – I almost feel I know them.' Her daughters are very soon hanging affectionately round her, pouting with jealousy.

Mr Robinson is concerned for Edmund. Nothing but temper-fits and pretended stomach-aches, as would befit a much younger child. 'I fear you've nursemaided him, Miss Brontë, and that's why he's so troublesome. Well, it's done now. What he needs to set him straight is a good strong masculine influence.'

'That,' says Mrs Robinson, with a sigh, 'is certainly what's missing in this house.'

And this surely should be one of those moments when, as mere governess and employee, you quietly take yourself off. But the Robinsons never let her. Miss Brontë, where are you going? Miss Brontë, I hope we don't make a stranger of you. They would lose their audience.

'What Edmund needs is a tutor, a male tutor,' Mr Robinson says, going to the side-table with its tray and decanter. In his illness he has adopted a compensating energetic way of lunging and bashing at things, applying a disproportionate element of will to small physical tasks. The pouring of his brandy is a clumsy, noisy affair that has Mrs Robinson closing her eyes in exquisite endurance. 'He needs to be guided by a man, and – pardon me, Miss Brontë – but it is past time he was introduced to a classical education.'

'Oh, sir, I know Latin, if you'd like me to start him on that,' Anne says.

Mr Robinson grimaces, drinking. 'Latin. Whatever was your father thinking?'

'You are excelling yourself in being disagreeable today, Mr Robinson,' says his wife. 'If you must take out your ill humours on someone, then pray let it be me, not Miss Brontë. Heaven knows I am used to them.'

Later it is Mr Robinson's turn to seek Anne out, to appeal and confess, to have the cushion of self plumped up. 'Miss Brontë, I spoke hastily earlier. Your good sense, of course, will already have apprehended the reason and, I hope, excused it on that account. I have a great deal of trouble to bear – and this business of Edmund adds to it most vexingly. The fact is, boys at his age naturally resist petticoat government. And my infirmity makes it difficult for me to supply the deficiency myself.'

'Of course, sir. I understand.' And she really does. Anne's trouble, perhaps. Doesn't stop her seeing, though.

'Lord knows what we are to do. We are rather isolated and quiet here. Of course, that doesn't matter so much for a woman. But a man may not find it easy to settle, unless he has the right temperament for it. It is a difficulty.'

'My brother.' This is the carefully considered, slow-cooked suggestion Anne presents. Careful consideration, too, about which one to approach, before finally settling on Mrs Robinson. Less likely to see presumption in it and, as she laments, tired of Mr Robinson fretting about the matter – even talking of sending Edmund away to school, which she cannot countenance, her boy is too high-strung and sensitive . . . 'He is a classicist, and has been a private tutor before. As for the amiability of his temper, there I have, of course, a sister's partiality, but I really think that Edmund would draw well with him.'

'Your brother . . . Well, it is a thought, Miss Brontë. Certainly there would not be the disquiet that accompanies the introduction of a complete stranger . . . I shall consult Mr Robinson. Of course we should have to be convinced that your brother is entirely suitable for the post. But I shall be very glad, my dear Miss Brontë, if we can find such a comfortable solution.'

It seems to Anne to solve so many problems. It will give Branwell employment, and introduce him to that higher social sphere where he surely belongs. It will lessen her loneliness and help her to bear Thorp Green until they open their school. It will be good for Edmund, and thus good for the family. And, as a very bad person, Anne is desperate to do something good.

Aunt Branwell's will is proved, and her nieces each find themselves richer by three hundred pounds, invested in railway shares. Well, they need not fear fortune-hunters, but it will be a great help towards the project of the school.

It is the Christmas holiday, and they are all there as Patrick, consulting a copy of the will – he has to use a magnifying-glass to read now – distributes Aunt's personal keepsakes. For Charlotte, the Indian workbox, for Branwell the japanned dressing-case, for Emily the ivory fan, for Anne the watch and eyeglass . . .

'The residue to be divided as I see fit. There are, I believe, various items of jewellery and so on. I shall leave that to your choice.'

Branwell sniffs. 'This is wretched work. Won't you keep something yourself, Papa?'

'No, no. I need nothing to reinforce the memory of a just, principled woman who lived and died an exemplary Christian.'

But Patrick does miss her. When an important question requires attention – as does, now, the question of her housekeeping keys – he misses the stately rite of the tea-table discussion. And once or twice there glances across him, like a bar of light from a cold sun, something he recognises with difficulty as fear. If she can go out of his life, others can too. He even glimpses the possibility – and slams the door on it at once – that he might eventually be left alone.

The housekeeping keys, yes, Emily happily claims them. John Brown's young daughter Martha won't have to manage the housework alone now.

Emily moves among the things of the kitchen and cellar, the needed things. For the past eleven months there has been a kind of metallic ticking in her blood and now, bliss, it stops. Instead she feels the essence of these things. *Lares et penates.* The old gods, Dionysus, Eros, they could reach into you, enter you, why not these? Flour, fine softness carrying the memory of the hard grain fighting up towards the sun. Kindling, black, sharp, bristling, intense: already a fire. Earthenware mixing-bowl: its perfect shape; it is shaped like winter mornings, yolky flappings of beaten egg, granny-like kiss of oven heat on the face.

Shape of her world as she likes it, forming around her. Yes, she misses Aunt, but death is death, and this is life. When the long journey from Brussels was over and she stepped down from the gig it came surging up through the soles of her feet, and for a moment she swayed and looked at Charlotte as if she should surely feel it too. Like when the Crow Hill bog burst like an earthquake but in reverse: an earthsettle.

Her trunk is unpacked, and that is good too. Her room will be the old children's study. Narrow bed, no fire – irrelevancies. Dog Keeper here, cat Tiger: feel them in the blood, square strength, luxurious stretch, even as she bends over her writing-box. Travelling abroad, Brussels, Pensionnat Heger – well, that was a thing she did because she had to. Done now. Now she can concentrate on the important, on the real. Writing-box open, gaze deep into Gondal.

Bitter end-of-year weather, but the four of them venture on the after-dinner walk up the path to the moors, gloved and hooded, shaking off the stuffiness of indoors.

'The Meeting of the Waters,' says Branwell. 'What do you say? Can you get that far? Seems appropriate, you know, before the parting of the ways.' He is in ebullient mood. The letter confirming his appointment as tutor to Edmund Robinson at Thorp Green has arrived. He will travel there with Anne after the holiday, and so everyone will be settled.

'I can certainly get that far, and before you,' Emily says, long legs outpacing him.

'Wait, don't leave us behind,' calls Anne. 'There'll be fog – we mustn't get separated.'

'It's too windy for fog,' Charlotte says. 'You've got governess's disease – feeling desperately responsible for everything. I remember it.'

At the Meeting of the Waters the icy streams, brilliant and bleak, come together and mingle; and Anne thinks, Is it governess's disease, or simply the way I am? I am, thinks Branwell, about to make a new start and perhaps indeed this will be the true start and if secretly I am a little terrified from time to time it's surely natural to feel so. To feel so eager and alive, thinks Charlotte, is mighty strange, but perhaps I shouldn't mistrust it, for Monsieur and Madame Heger sing our praises and say we should go back. Go back, yes, I knew she would have to go back, thinks Emily, I remember her saying if anyone likes her then she can't help liking them in return – danger, danger in that, Charlotte, the thing that's needed is to need no one. No one need know about what happened before, there I shall simply be Mr Brontë the tutor, and if I could just flatten this lump of fear, fear of what, of myself perhaps, come if little Anne can do it then surely, and look at Charlotte preparing to go back to Belgium completely alone. Alone, I think that is Branwell's trouble, he doesn't do well alone, and that railway job was terribly isolated, so if I am with him at Thorp Green I think it might make all the difference, though I hope that isn't pride or vanity in me, after all I know Branwell doesn't think much of me. Alone, thank God, I shall be free to be alone, to walk and wake and write and think and none of that damned dormitory and people, stupid inquisitive people, poking their fingers into your head. Alone, but I shan't be alone, there will be Monsieur and Madame Heger, remember Dewsbury Moor where I really was alone, I fear I don't do well alone, I wonder if I shall always be alone.

2

The Secret Lives of Married Women

'Tell me, Miss Brontë, was your brother never at university?' asks Mrs Robinson.

'No, ma'am,' Anne replies. 'He was educated at home by my father, who was a Cambridge man.'

'Really? Surprising.' Mrs Robinson consults the pier-glass. 'He just has something of that air.'

'Mama, we will be going to the hunt ball, won't we? I shall absolutely die of frustration if we don't.'

'My dear Lizzie, you are not yet seventeen. Hardly an age to talk of dying of frustration.'

'It is when you have to spend your precious youth *mouldering* here. It's all very well for you, Mama, you've *had* your day.'

Mrs Robinson turns on Anne a look of wry, smiling patience. Anne often comes in for these. She is far from a confidante – but a chorus, perhaps, bearing witness. As later, when Mr and Mrs Robinson have one of their marital debates.

'I notice a distinct improvement in Edmund's behaviour lately. He is more inclined to listen and take heed,' Mrs Robinson says. 'Don't you think so?'

'Perhaps. Yes, a little,' Mr Robinson says, with a shrug.

'Mr Brontë seems to teach him a wide curriculum: he is full of odd bits of knowledge. I fancy that may have been Edmund's difficulty, you know – he was simply dull and bored.'

'I see. Well, thank you for heaping another reproach on me. Perhaps you think I enjoy being forced to live like this – unable to be active, to be the father I would wish to be to my son, to be—' A fit of coughing stops him.

'You make it very hard for me, Mr Robinson. I am almost afraid to talk to you: I try to cheer you and divert you with conversation, but my only reward is this continual ill-humour.'

Certainly Anne has gained credit for the introduction of Branwell – who really does seem to have worked wonders with his pupil. Anne, who has never been able to get more than half an idea into the curled heads of the Robinson girls, tries not to feel jealous.

'Edmund has been reciting to me today, Mr Brontë, and reciting very well: I commend you,' Mrs Robinson tells him. 'No, I didn't set him to it – this is what I found so remarkable – he simply wanted me to hear it, because he likes it. But you are of a poetic bent yourself, sir, I think. Oh! No, just recognition of a kindred spirit. Time was when I dreamed over poetry for hours together, even forgetting to eat and drink. But life deals harshly with such inclinations, I fear.'

'Harshly, ma'am?' Branwell gives a grey smile. 'Usually it crushes them underfoot.'

'Mr Brontë, I hope you'll forgive my mentioning it, but you seem a little low-spirited. I do hope Mr Robinson has not been severe with you again.'

'No, ma'am – and if it were so, I hope I should have sense enough not to be cast down by it, and make due allowance for the effects of his illness.'

'Allowance, to be sure, one must make – though it is not always easy. But, come, I shall exercise a woman's prerogative, and press you. Are you quite well? Your lodging in the village, is it comfortable?'

'It is quite comfortable, thank you, and very quiet. Well – if anything, a little too quiet. If ever I do suffer a little in the way of low spirits, it is when I am alone there in the evenings. But that soon passes off, as I think of returning here in the morning.'

'You know, Mr Brontë, I can't think what objection there could be to your coming up to the house of an evening, and joining us *en famille*. Lord knows, time often hangs heavy with us likewise, and Mr Robinson's hour of retiring is of necessity so early . . . You play the piano, I think? Yes, I was asking your sister here or, I don't know, she happened to mention it.'

Anne plays also, of course, but she lacks Branwell's manner and – now stop it. Put aside this jealousy. Think of the positive. You have achieved something – you have found Branwell a place at last where he fits in and his talents are valued. And never mind that voice crying, *What about me?* Train yourself not to hear it, like the pitiless ticking of a clock.

* * *

'Genius. Very well, Mademoiselle Brontë, I see this is your preoccupation, let us talk of it some more. We shall quarrel, mind.'

Charlotte doesn't mind. It is like air to her, this exchange, these fascinating short hours with him; the rest of the time she is swimming under water, only waiting to burst the surface and gasp it in. 'I mean that surely the power of genius lies in the fact that it is untrammelled. It doesn't have to plan or weigh or revise or refine. It simply speaks out – it roars like a fire, or sweeps on like a flood—'

'Oh, come, you must examine your received ideas, Mademoiselle Brontë. Aren't they a trifle stale? Roaring fires and sweeping floods. Every churchyard gloomy and every warrior valiant. It is precisely this vagueness and inexactitude that will hamper your efforts to write with vigour and freshness. And I don't just refer to your exercises with me. You have ambitions beyond that, don't you?'

'I have scarcely dared to have those ambitions, since I was told that I . . .' Charlotte looks forward, then back; nerves herself, and makes the leap. 'Yes, Monsieur, I do – and I would be glad if you would help me try to realise them.' There, she has landed, she has not disappeared into the abyss. Back on the far bank Mr Southey shrugs and evaporates. Papa is still there, though: shaking his head. She fixes her eyes on Monsieur Heger's. Odd how, away, you forget quite what they are like, in their rich darkness: how you only think of blue eyes as piercing. A received idea.

'This is as I thought. But again we must fight. I must take issue with your flood, for example.' He leaps to his feet and goes to the study door. 'Suppose the river has burst its banks, and the flood-water is about to come in. Shall I let it in?' He flings open the door. Madame Heger's neat-backed figure can be seen gliding down the passage. 'Swoosh, here it comes. Soaking your skirts and my trousers and, possibly, unbalancing that high stool. And then just slopping about and becoming a deep puddle. But with the same volume of water – no, less, much less – discharged at high pressure through a narrow pipe, I could knock you off your feet. So with genius. It must be concentrated, not dissipated. What do you fear? That you will lose your power?'

'Perhaps, yes. That is, if I have any power—'

'Oh, please, no modesty-games. You have it, Mademoiselle Brontë, and you must know it. Now, look. You want to write, yes? And not just little time-passing feminine nothings, you want to write *well*, yes?' Yes, yes. 'Then you must be prepared to strip yourself naked. There can be no hiding. No hiding behind rodomontade, or high-flown ideas about genius and inspiration, and just letting it flow, and all the rest of that rubbish. You must take pains, and more pains, until you can stand up before your reader and say, "This is me, the best of me, I have done everything possible to *make* it."' Suddenly his scalp lifts. 'I remember having a similar conversation with your sister Mademoiselle Emily – well, not conversation, I spoke and she set her face against me. I wonder if she took any of it in. I have hopes.'

A finger of absurd jealousy prods her.

'She was not, then, to be persuaded to return? Ah, well: I know the strength of *that* will. I should not like to have it pitted against me in earnest. I think she would be as unsparing of others as she is of herself. But I'm afraid, Mademoiselle Brontë, that you may be lonely without her. Of course, your French is now so fluent that you can mix with the other teachers without awkwardness. Besides that, Madame Heger joins me in hoping that once the day's work is done, you will join us in our apartment, and consider yourself *en famille*, so that . . .'

'Thank you, Monsieur – but I wonder if this is not a received idea also?' She smiles, though the smile feels disconnected from her. 'That a woman who is alone must be lonely?'

'I'm not saying that all received ideas are untrue. Only that we must examine them.' The look he gives her is sombre but gentle; then abruptly he stretches and smiles. 'It reminds me. My dear late father. Though our name points to German ancestry, he always had the strongest aversion to the Teutonic. He was only ever in a German town once in his life, when business took him to Hamburg – and there a hackney ran over his foot. Somehow this act confirmed all his prejudices. And after this – such is the lasting association of ideas – if ever he saw someone with a limp, he would say, "German, I should think – poor devil!"' He chuckles, consulting his watch. 'Well, I must go and introduce mathematics to some small boys, who I fear will decline the acquaintance. Thank you, Mademoiselle Brontë, for the –' he taps his temple '– refreshment.'

She stares at the place where he was, thinking of that last word. Refreshment: like a little cup of coffee or a tisane. Not, as it is to her, meat and drink and air and sun and life itself.

Charlotte tries it. She has felt dubious about it from the start, but the offer is kind and must be responded to once or twice: just to see. So, at the hour when she and Emily used to withdraw to their curtained alcove, the hour when Mesdemoiselles Blanche, Sophie and Marie gather to hate each other affectionately round the schoolroom hearth, she joins Monsieur and Madame Heger *en famille*.

Very comfortable their drawing-room, and not without its fascinations – the books piled on the prie-dieu chair like an emblem of mind overcoming superstition – and no one could say there is anything the least bit stiff or formal here. The two elder girls, rosy from bathing, come in to chatter and to lean drowsily against their papa's or mama's knees, or indeed Charlotte's, and show off their little crumpled drawings; the lamp glimmers, voices gently swell and fall, and Madame Heger shares what is plainly a recurring joke with the nursemaid about stockings, and Monsieur Heger disposes himself in a particular chair and says, 'Claire, I don't think those endives are fresh at all, where are they coming from?' and Madame Heger goes and pinches his nose and briefly caresses his face and says, 'Constantin' (in the working daytime they never use these Christian names, of course), 'you said that last week and then you forgot and pronounced them excellent, it's when you smoke too many cigars you lose your palate'. And Monsieur Heger sits up looking frowning humorously pouting round as if to find someone to back him up – and Charlotte perching on the settle by one numb segment of buttock looks down at the book she has brought with her, and will not look up.

No. This doesn't work; and if she wants to fly from it to the ends of the earth, then that simply shows – well, it's rather as Emily said, I'm not here to socialise. I'm here for other reasons. The personal has nothing to do with it.

Better the dormitory. The bells heard far off, delicately registered, as if the ear has a pulse like the wrist; the long line of white-curtained beds, dream-shapes. Lonely – yes, perhaps. Lonely too the schoolroom, the teaching, the supper in the long, lamplit refectory bubbling with gossipy French. But her lessons with Monsieur Heger – him teaching her French, and now her beginning to teach him English – well, then she is not lonely. A simple equation. No need to think about it.

Madame Heger is thinking a great deal about it.

Now Madame Heger labours under several disadvantages – those of being content, fulfilled, reciprocally in love, a model mother, and successful in her chosen career. Sickening, perhaps? But surely fair for her to say: I worked for this. I value it. I won't see it threatened.

And she knows about overthrow. This placid, decorous woman, smoothing the tablecloth, patiently guiding the first class through their alphabet, glancing neutrally at her neat reflection before setting out for Mass, has always the imagination of disaster.

The world is as it is, Aunt Anne-Marie used to say. This was not a kind of verbal shrug but a very specific warning. One must be vigilant, one must conserve and preserve, one cannot rely on hopes and dreams. It is a fallen world, in which with luck and dedication one may salvage something. Salvage and salvation. All along the rim of this world, a red, slithering abyss. Closer than you think.

Madame Heger's father was an *émigré* from the French Revolution. He got out early, in 'eighty-nine, when moderate men were saying what a good thing it was. Not Monsieur Parent. He could see that looming red rim. He settled in Brussels, gardened and botanised, married judiciously, and watched as his view of human nature was terribly demonstrated across the border. Given the right circumstances, this is what will happen. All you had to do was make a concession – say, 'Very well, this once it will be allowed, for particular reasons, but after that we will be rational, we will rein in' – and off it went, the murderous carnival.

His sister, Aunt Anne-Marie, was a nun in a convent at Charleville: one of those pockets of resistance to the march of revolution. She managed to escape across the border in a peasant's costume and arrived at her brother's house with her wooden shoes full of blood. She was saved. She was properly thankful but – as she later told her favourite niece Claire Zoë Parent, the future Madame Heger – she could not exult. Other nuns were going to the guillotine – some defiled first: dying two deaths.

'For the guillotine they always cropped the victim's hair short,' Aunt Anne-Marie told her. 'And you will always hear it said that this was a typical piece of cold efficiency – so that the blade would not be impeded. This is nonsense. The guillotine blade cut straight through bone. It would not be impeded by such a thing as hair. It was not practicality they were after: it was humiliation, it was that extra little refinement of cruelty. Why not?' She spread out her splendid smooth bare hands. 'Once you grant a licence to enthusiasm, it must run its destructive course. You cannot call it back.' Aunt Anne-Marie's own hair, after the suppression of her order made her a laywoman, was still nun-like in its plain simplicity. Papa always kept his hair defiantly tied and powdered, long after it had gone out of fashion. Together, they saved something.

Aunt Anne-Marie began a school in Papa's house. She believed strongly – not passionately, that way lay danger – in the education of the young. Teach, guide, conserve, save. She taught Claire Zoë. From her earliest years Claire Zoë was accustomed to the murmur of repeated lessons, the demure filing into class, the neat lines of the copybook inviting you to do your best. Two of her sisters became nuns, but there was never any doubt of where Claire Zoë's vocation lay.

When she was eleven years old forty-seven thousand men died violent deaths around a country village ten miles outside Brussels: Waterloo. Thousands more were wounded and were brought into the city to the military hospital at the Hôtel de Ville: more than could be treated. Aunt Anne-Marie flung open her schoolrooms to accommodate them. Claire Zoë helped with the fetching and carrying. An orderly tried to unpeel the blackened bandage round a soldier's head: a lid of skull lifted. And Claire Zoë, seeing, thought of the cauliflowers that would come into the city early in the morning, heaped in baskets, and how sometimes the cart would wobble on a kerbstone and a cauliflower drop on to the road, and the sound it made. Aunt Anne-Marie was right. The world is as it is. Once things break out there is no stopping them. Learn, teach, understand. Conserve, preserve.

When she was twenty-six years old, and just in the process of setting up her own school with a small legacy from Papa, there was another breaking-out of gunfire and blood: the revolution for Belgian independence. Fortunately it was on a smaller scale: four hundred and forty-five dead bodies. What she did not know at the time was that her future husband, a young teacher, was one of those manning the barricades and narrowly escaping death. And he could hardly have appeared as a future husband then, being already married. But a few years later there were more dead bodies in Brussels – eight hundred and sixty-four, from a cholera epidemic this time – and among them were the young wife and child of Constantin Heger. When Claire Zoë first met him, he looked, literally, as if he would never smile again.

And he did: and that she sees, realistically, as the combination of healing time and the happiness of his second marriage. But she knows the shadows are always there. Indeed who knows that better than Madame Claire Zoë Heger, who every month has several of what she thinks of as her uncomfortable nights – nights when she wakes sweating from visionary nightmares of chaos and loss, and has to get up and light the lamp and check that everything is all right; ears straining for her children's breathing, fingers tensely testing locks. Luckily Constantin is a sound sleeper.

His own bad times can be prompted by the slightest thing – a sad anecdote, a stirred memory; suddenly he is down the well, his groans coming faintly up. Then not even his faith sustains him. Then there is only Madame Heger.

'Oh, my darling, I shouldn't say it, but life is black – black!' he whispers; and she pulls his bristly head on to her breast, and lets him whimper there. For this is something Madame Heger has learned, early on: an essential difference between men and women. When women leave childhood behind, they do so permanently. She has watched it happen in her classes: it is not necessarily to do with puberty, though occasionally it can be. It is a crossing, as from sea to land: there. But men must still be children sometimes. You have to allow them it. Otherwise they are somehow blocked and baffled. And it is not much to ask, after all, and they are so thankful for it. Rather like the sex: it is almost pitiable how much they want such a commonplace thing. Anyone would think you'd granted them a fortune.

So, along with so much else, they have this in common – the darkness inside. But he doesn't know it, because she prefers to keep hers hidden. She prefers to be on watch, scanning calmly from the heights. She loves him – not wildly or consumedly, that would be dangerous – but with a certain faithful minuteness: she loves as a Dutch painter paints. And that includes looking out for perils in his path. Knowing him better than he knows himself.

From the beginning he has always made a strong impression on those girls at the Pensionnat whom he undertakes to teach. No wonder: that is his style of teaching, personal, powerful, emotional. She has never minded the way they take to him. They are young girls, and it is the way of young girls to idolise. It has never gone beyond that, and she would not expect it to: he is so much older, and by no means conventionally handsome. But still, she has stayed on the watch.

Because you never know what might break out. There is this element in him – not a bad one, really. More to do with helpless generosity. She knows the story of his father, who had been the wealthiest jeweller in Brussels until he lent a large sum of money to a desperate friend and never got it back. There is that largeness of sentiment in Constantin: the possibility that he might generously, disastrously do something against his own interests. She always remembers Aunt Anne-Marie. Once you grant the licence, you cannot call it back.

And so to the difficult question of Mademoiselle Brontë. Madame

Heger likes her, admires her courage and intellect, wishes her well. But: Madame Heger knows a revolutionary when she sees one.

Conserve, preserve. She is a true realist, in that she is able to be realistic about herself. Not long after Mademoiselle Brontë's return to the Pensionnat alone, without her sister, Madame Heger finds herself pregnant for the fifth time. Now, Constantin adores their children and is delighted. But childbearing takes its toll on figure and spirits, and Madame Heger is five years older than her husband. Mademoiselle Brontë is not yet twenty-seven and, though no one could call her a beauty, presentable and trim-figured. This is how the realist must see the case: these facts, added up. And if that was all, there would be no need of closer surveillance, the risk is so slight.

But there is more to it than that. When the Brontë ladies first arrived, Madame Heger said something about their looking ready to go to the stake. What for? Constantin had asked. Well, now she has an answer.

In Mademoiselle Charlotte's case, for you.

But it is something that she will never tell him and, more importantly, that he must never find out for himself. It isn't that she doesn't trust him. But he is a man and his father's son and it is possible that he might with a great shudder of generosity give away not a fortune but himself.

I worked for this. I value it. I won't see it threatened. This is not only her marriage and family but her school. No scandal has ever touched the Pensionnat Heger, and there would be ruin if it did.

She has no doubt that Constantin doesn't know what he is doing when he singles Mademoiselle Brontë out for confidences, praises her attainments, makes her gifts of books. He is just being himself. But now that she has begun to observe Mademoiselle Brontë's tingling silences and sudden spates of words, the flat, dead glance she turns on everyone else at the Pensionnat and the way it singes into life when Constantin appears, Madame Heger must ask herself: does Mademoiselle Brontë know what she is doing?

Well, she wants to give her the benefit of the doubt. Madame Heger, strong supporter of female education, is a firm friend to her own sex. Yet life has led her to the conclusion that men often stumble about in a fog of intention, or move like sleepwalkers, while women know, they know very well, what they are about.

'What is it exactly about the Carnival, I wonder, that sets your back so straight?' laughs Monsieur Heger, as they turn into the rue d'Isabelle.

'Is it just the Protestant in you? Never mind. I'm sorry it was such an unpleasant experience.'

'No, no. Is that how it looks? I'm very grateful, Monsieur, for your taking me to it. It was thoroughly instructive,' Charlotte says.

He laughs again. 'Exactly what it is not meant to be. It represents slipping the leash and letting go. Turning everything on its head. The tradition of *l'abbé de liesse* – surely even in England—'

'The Lord of Misrule, yes. I understand it. In fact, I like the Lord of Misrule; I think I would follow him before most other lords. I suppose what disgusts me— But I fear I will offend your faith, Monsieur.'

'My faith is secure a million times,' says Monsieur Heger, though his chin jabs up and his teeth tighten on his cigar.

'Well, it is something like hypocrisy—'

'Ha!' Smiling teeth, frowning, champing.

'Well, I don't know how else to put it. Because Lent is coming, when you all have to deny yourself, you have a big feast in which you indulge yourself. But surely all that mummery and guzzling is just an acknowledgement that Lent makes no sense. If you're going to deny the flesh, then do it consistently, because you believe it to be a good thing. Not because some nonsensical calendar tells you to.'

'So, Mademoiselle Brontë, you think there is no moral or spiritual authority beyond your own private conscience.'

'Yes. Which I suppose is a definition of being a Protestant. Sorry, Monsieur Heger, we've fallen back to these old positions.'

'No no no, I'm rather fascinated. Everything in me rises up full-armed against what you say. But when *you* say it I must give it attention. I must drop my weapons and unbuckle my breast-plate and come forward bare-chested to meet it.'

'Oh, tut, Monsieur, if you used those figures in an essay I would have to scribble violently in the margin as you do – "Far-fetched image, get rid of it."'

'Am I really so harsh?' He shakes his head and smiles dejectedly. 'Don't answer that. But the carnival, you know, and the masks – isn't it a great outlet for the feelings, once in a while? To be masked, to be other, to be – for a little stolen but permitted time – not yourself?'

Charlotte stares down the sharp-edged valley of the street towards Pensionnat Heger. 'Why would you ever want to be not yourself, Monsieur Heger?'

'You've mistaken a general question for a personal one.' He strides on, trailing cigar-smoke.

'No, wait, I think it sounds wonderful – but then you would have to go back to being yourself, eventually.'

And what's really in her mind: the horrible bottom half of masked faces. Above, all is stylised and smoothly sculpted; below, you see chins wagging on hinged jaws and the wet red puckering eagerness of mouths.

'Would you?' He bends on her a look almost purely curious, as if he has never known anything like her. 'But what is that? Don't we have many selves?'

'Do you, Monsieur Heger?'

He flushes slightly. 'Ah, we will make a Catholic of you yet. Now you are seeking confession.'

She tears her eyes away from his, feeling on her own face the hot clinging of a mask.

'Louise is so fractious lately. Do you think she's unwell?'

'She overtires herself a little, always trying to keep up with Marie. Also,' Madame Heger watches her husband tugging at his cravat, 'she did say that she hardly ever sees Papa.'

'The monkey. She sees me after dinner. Other times.' He gives up on the cravat, goes and stirs the bedroom fire irritably. 'Perhaps I should make a little more time. Do you think so?'

'Well, I do worry that you work yourself too hard.'

He gives her a crisp, dubious look. 'That's always been my way, Claire. Nothing's changed.'

'I know that. I think even the little ones understand. But, you see, we all want our fair share of you.' She goes over and unfastens his cravat. 'Me too. I don't want to see you exhaust yourself. Squeezing out every last drop. You must leave me a little – a little juice in the lemon.'

He laughs, his face softening. 'You could have chosen a sweeter fruit.'

'Oh, no.' She kisses him. His hands come up. She sucks and chews his lower lip in the way she knows. 'Oh, no, I couldn't.'

What with all the teaching he has to do, Monsieur Heger's time is very much occupied, so he will have to discontinue the English lessons. He is sure Mademoiselle Brontë will understand.

'Yes.' In the schoolroom Charlotte stares blindly at her class. Shifting and twittering, a birdlike vagueness. 'Yes – yes, Gabrielle, what is it?'

A sigh and a moue: Mademoiselle Charlotte is so prickly lately. 'That sentence. I don't understand.'

'Of course you do.' No, I don't. I don't understand.

'It's nothing, Constantin. A mere piece of stupidity. Mademoiselle Blanche is being ridiculous again, and I told her so.'

'I'm sure you did nothing of the kind, you're too soft-hearted. What is her complaint?'

'Oh . . . it's about Mademoiselle Brontë. She says we favour her, treat her differently from the other teachers, all this nonsense. No, I did tell her it was nonsense, because I do not like to hear Mademoiselle Brontë abused in that way. It's quite untrue that she gets special treatment – and if it were true, I hope we would have the justice to admit it.'

'Just so. Of course, Mademoiselle Brontë mustn't be allowed to think she *is* treated differently, because that surely would create unfairness.'

'Perhaps. Yes, I suppose so. But then, after all, she is far from home, and so perhaps we do indulge her a little. I don't know.' Madame Heger sits down, cradling the small roundness of her belly. 'I must confess it wears me out when Mademoiselle Blanche cries so.'

'Monsieur . . .' Charlotte comes upon him in the *Allée Défendue*. He frowns, turning, reluctantly quitting thought. 'Monsieur, I believe I have you to thank for the gift of this book.'

'Hm? Oh, that. Why, where did you find it?'

'In my desk. Along with a tell-tale aroma of cigar. You will never be able to commit a murder successfully, Monsieur.'

He laughs. 'Ah, my dear Mademoiselle Brontë, as I've told you before, you are too imaginative.'

She is glad to see him laugh – he is abstracted lately – but she holds the cold thought: *You have never told me that before.*

'Now, what is this I hear about you and Mademoiselle Blanche? Is it true you are not on speaking terms with the poor creature?'

'We – pursue our separate lives, Monsieur.'

'And so will never get to understand each other better. Come, I urge you to make the effort. You rub along well enough with the other teachers, do you not?'

She stares at him. 'I suppose so. It's not a thing that much concerns me, Monsieur.'

'Come, remember Terence: nothing human do I consider foreign to me.'

'This is Mademoiselle Blanche we are talking about.'

There is impatience, or more impatience, in his quick smile. 'You ought to mix with them more, you know. I don't like to see you so solitary.'

'If it is your wish, Monsieur.'

'Well, yes, it is my wish.' The frown almost cancels out the smile. 'But only that. It's not a command, for heaven's sake. We don't stand as master and pupil any more.'

No. How do we stand? I don't understand.

'You are studying late, Mademoiselle Brontë.'

Madame Heger, entering the refectory, silent as a cat. Charlotte moves the blotter over the paper, even though Madame Heger knows very little English.

'Not studying, Madame. A letter.'

'To your excellent father? Please present my compliments, and those of Monsieur Heger, if so. We were most concerned to hear of the trouble he is having with his eyesight.'

'No – my brother.'

'Ah, the one who is a private tutor. I hope he prospers in the post, Mademoiselle Brontë?'

She has never noticed it before, but Madame Heger has a way of standing just a little too close to you: soft breath and gently swelling bosom; it is almost as if she is about to embrace you.

'From what my sister Anne tells me, he is greatly valued by his employers, and very happy. I have not his word for it – he is not a good correspondent.'

'I'm not surprised at his success, if you will allow me to say so. I have seen for myself the attainments of two of his sisters, and I cannot doubt that he shares the family intellect. When you set up your school in England – which surely cannot be long now – perhaps he may join you in the enterprise. Do girls' schools in England commonly have visiting male masters?'

'It is known. Not common.'

'I always feel it makes for a better atmosphere in a school. More realistic. After all, the pupils are preparing for the world, and the world contains both men and women. To be sure, there are dangers where the pupils are older but seldom, I think, dreadful ones. More often the problem lies in someone misinterpreting and romancing and building something up in her head that simply isn't there. Well! I must let you finish your letter. Don't stay up too late, my dear Mademoiselle Brontë: remember your health.'

Well: she is still sure of what she has written in her letter to Branwell. Madame Heger doesn't like me. And I don't understand.

'Now I discover your brother trained as a painter, Miss Brontë. Edmund was showing me a sketch he made for him. *Very* spirited.' Mrs Robinson gathers Anne's arm as they walk down the oak avenue. Flattering, but not likeable: somehow there is always a feeling of being taken into custody. 'I used to dabble that way myself. Have you ever been his subject, I wonder?'

'A couple of times, ma'am.'

'Your features, I fancy, would be hard to capture – there is something so subdued about them. In fact sometimes, my dear Miss Brontë, I hardly know you are in the room. But there, that's you – better than some bold-faced baggage. Really I think we are very fortunate to have procured someone of your brother's talents. And so unsuspected! To be sure, you are of a bookish turn yourself, but still . . . Of course, Yorkshire is an uncouth sort of place, where the gentleman of parts is not likely to be recognised. Talk of lights under bushels, Miss Brontë. Lord above, I know what it's like – to be buried.'

At Pensionnat Heger a landslide of trunks and bags stands piled in the cool interior; outside summer heat presses and glares at the windows. The Hegers go to the coast for the vacation, the other teachers and pupils home. Only Charlotte and the housekeeper will remain.

The sea, the sea. She wishes she could go to the sea. She knows she ought to go the sea, and take the packet-ship home, instead of staying here like a – well, what? Dog in the manger? Cuckoo in the nest? No, there are no images. There is no way of conveying how she is feeling, except that she cannot imagine any other kind of life. And she can't understand it.

In the hall Monsieur Heger shrugs on his white travelling-coat while his daughters swirl excitedly round him. As so often, he seems to see Charlotte even though his eye is not on her.

'Mademoiselle Brontë, I hope you found the book,' he says, coming over to where she is lingering by the stair. 'I thought it might help occupy your time.'

'Thank you, Monsieur. It was a kind thought.'

'Well, I am not easy in my mind about leaving you here alone. I was going to say I don't think women bear solitude as well as men – but I remember you persuading me that men and women are more alike than we suppose, so I'll hold my peace.'

He shakes her hand. She supposes there is a goodbye: she is not quite aware of it. She is thinking about men and women, the things they share and the things that divide them and whether, as he questioned, they would be happier if they acknowledged them. And it occurs to her that for some on both sides this is an irrelevance: that there are people who are destined to be unhappy.

'Miss Brontë, I declare you are looking quite peaky of late.'

'Oh – I'm sorry, Mrs Robinson.'

'My dear, I don't mean it as a reproach. Come, tell me, are you unwell? I shall quite bully you until I am satisfied. Dr Crosby can surely be persuaded to leave Mr Robinson's side for a while—'

'No, no, I am just a little unwell – for the present.'

Anne feels her blush burning. But Mrs Robinson, sinuously seating herself with a tinkle of bracelets, is quite untroubled.

'Oh, *that*. Come, we are women together, Miss Brontë, we needn't be shy of mentioning it. How right they are to call it the curse. It quite puts me out of order for half the month. Sea air I find the best restorative, you know – and we remove to Scarborough soon.'

'Oh, yes, I do look forward to that, ma'am.'

'Escape from the dullness of Thorp Green, eh? No, no, I'm only teasing. It is a heavenly spot, isn't it? Those delicious cliffs and that glorious sea . . . You know, I might have married a captain in the navy, once upon a time. There was never anything approaching an engagement, but there was the degree of attachment that made it at least a possibility . . .'

Once embarked on a tale of her old conquests, Mrs Robinson can be safely half listened to while you think of other things. But Anne, who likes to command her thoughts, finds them today scattering like shooed chickens. And though it is her time of the month, it isn't just that – this feeling she has; or rather, it's like a terrible amplification of it, oppressive and grinding, and altogether – incomprehensibly – a sensation of being on an intolerable brink.

Charlotte walks a lot, to fill her days, and to try and tire herself for the terrible bed-time and grovelling supplication at the altar of cruel sleep, the god who refuses to come. Brussels in August blazes. Nothing could be further from the cold, dour north than these sunstruck boulevards with the gnats teeming in the inky tree-shade, the great-bellied water-carts always groaning by, the straw bonnets and black lace mantles. Yet she keeps thinking of Scotland: of that doomed magnificent cavalier Montrose, taking up arms for his king, executed, and dismembered. (It was Maria who first read the story to them in the children's study: dear God, Maria. Only a child then, but already more sense, more sense than I will ever have.) They cut up his body and nailed the parts up in various places, as an example. A hand in Aberdeen, the head in Edinburgh. Why does she think of this? Somehow she feels, as she walks and walks, that something similar has happened to her without her knowing it: that there are chopped bits of her everywhere about this city, in the park, at the Gare du Nord, in the Chapel Royal, on the ornate gabled fronts of the old merchants' houses around the Grande Place. Perhaps this walking is a way of gathering herself up, putting herself together. Yet she is always torn in pieces again by the time she returns to the Pensionnat Heger.

She talks to no one. Mary Taylor has gone to Germany, and most of her English acquaintances in the city have moved out for the summer. Once she hovers before the door of the seamstress who has made her several dresses in the neat French, rather than clumsy English, mode and who is a pleasant talkative body. But she moves on. Madame Heger was the one who recommended her. Curious to think of. She is sure Madame Heger would take no such friendly interest now. She can't understand why.

If she has any communication, it is with faces. Often she goes out into the streets in the very early morning; at that hour the faces of the people she passes seem oddly naked and vulnerable. In them she fancies she reads their late sorrows and troubles – the marital quarrel, perhaps; the vigil by the sickbed; the dreams of fulfilment to which the waking day has presented such a drab, metal-tasting contrast. Sometimes she goes down to the flower-market. What fascinates her is not so much the great trestles and pallets and baskets of flowers, in such profusion that the eye can scarcely travel six inches without being struck by some new variation of colour, as the flower-sellers. Contrast again. Next to the blooms, they look like the drabbest afterthoughts of creation – poor, thin, old, ragged. In every respect the flowers seem to have the best of the bargain of existence. Except perhaps in the matter of consciousness – but that is a dubious advantage.

No matter how early she sets out, how long she walks, still she finds herself undressing in the empty dark dormitory with a throb of mutinous wakefulness, as if she were a punished child sent to bed with sweet afternoon exhaling temptingly at the window. And here, sometimes, as she lies in the prisoned heat and watches the white curtains stir like sluggish ghosts, she finds something impending: like a person in the next room bearing news, like the first cold nudges of toothache.

The world below. Angria opens before her mind, a hum rises from Verdopolis . . . No, no. Remember Dewsbury Moor, remember what it's like to be mad and alone.

But am I not mad and alone anyway? Lurking here, banished and confined to this dismal attic of experience?

You chose it. Charlotte. No one put you here.

Who said that?

She sits up, bare-legged and in her shift, sweat tingling on her upper lip. The figure standing in the dormitory doorway is tall, broad-shouldered and imperious. He steps forward. Large strips of him are completely visible, though he has holes and gaps, too, through which the light shines. The light of reality, presumably.

You wouldn't have thought that about me, once.

It is Zamorna: indistinct, but absolutely characteristic.

'Go away. You're not real.'

Oh, you have changed. What has done this to you? Or, rather, who has done this to you, Charlotte?

'No one has done anything. There's nothing wrong with me, I'm just . . .'

Desperate.

'Yes.'

That's why I'm here. He moves closer, growing taller, his hair waving more luxuriantly. *That's when I always used to come to you, isn't it?*

'It's different. You wouldn't understand. You're so – so magnificent and grand and perfect. You wouldn't understand that something can be wonderful and painful at the same time.'

He draws a deep breath, a sorrowful breath, his great chest swelling.

I understand, he says, *that I am supplanted.*

'I don't understand,' says Charlotte; but Zamorna, like Montrose, like herself, is torn into shreds before her eyes, and the pieces go whirling away into the endless dark.

Priests and nuns. You see them everywhere in Brussels, and Charlotte's eye falls on them with a kind of settled, resigned aversion, like drunks or jeering street urchins. Such mummery and quackery: astonishing that a man of Monsieur Heger's intellect can be enslaved to it. These are Charlotte's feelings.

And yet here she is kneeling in the confessional, and a priest is rattling back the little door on the other side of the grating, and she is saying, because she doesn't know what else to say, 'Father.'

How did she get here?

Well, a circuitous route: her longest walk ever. She went to visit Martha Taylor's grave in the Protestant cemetery outside the city gates, and then she walked further into the country, and there was nothing but flat fields, and the ring of the horizon was like a noose. And she came back into the city and walked all round the park and along the rue Royale and then down the plunge of stone steps to the rue d'Isabelle and still she wasn't tired, and the towers of the church of Sainte Gudule rose up before her and the *salut* bell was ringing and so, for somewhere else to go, something else to do, she came in. And she saw people waiting to go into the confessional boxes and she thought, Well, something else to do . . .

How did she get here? Desperation, of course.

'Father. It's difficult – you see, I'm a foreigner. English, and brought up as a Protestant.'

'You mean you are a Protestant?'

'Yes. And I feel I want to confess but I don't know how it is done – confession, I mean.'

'It is not done at all, if you are a Protestant.' The priest is gruff with her. 'Confession is a matter of the utmost seriousness. It touches on the welfare and ultimate destiny of the soul. It is not a pastime for the idle and curious.'

'Oh, but I'm not idle and curious, I – I am in earnest, Father. I am in great need . . .' Her voice breaks; she swallows the sob, but there is an alert movement on the other side of the grating. 'I need help.'

'Very well. It may be that something is pulling you back to the true Church, and if I can be the instrument of that . . . Yes. I will hear your confession, my child.'

Coldness of stone seeping into her knees. 'What one confesses – I know it is supposed to be sin, but I can't be sure what constitutes sin in the eyes of your church.'

'Sin is sin.' Gruff again. 'Look into your heart.'

'What I feel for someone . . .' She stops. Though their voices are so low, she seems to hear them booming and echoing about the bell-tower above, her words clanging out across the city, the fields, the sea. 'It is not anything I would do, it is not an action. It's more of a wish – but not the sort of wish that could ever come true. It's not . . . If you wished someone were dead, that would be a sin, would it not? Especially as that might actually happen. But this is a wish – simply – that someone had never existed. Is that a grave sin?'

'Do you feel it so?'

The sob rises again and she cannot answer. But the priest takes her choking silence as acknowledgement, contrition – soon he is urgently murmuring that she has made the right beginning, that the true Church is waiting for her, that she must come to see him every morning and he will oversee her conversion . . .

She gets away, promising that she will. Well: she has already told one lie, anyway.

'Constantin, I worry about Mademoiselle Brontë,' says Madame Heger, sitting up and trimming the wick of the bedside candle. She hates to see a candle smoking.

'I know you do, my love,' he says sleepily. 'Because you're kind.' She is too heavily pregnant for love-making to be comfortable, so tonight she has relieved him by manipulation, which always leaves him mightily relaxed like this. It occurs to her that, despite its being in the marriage bed, this may still constitute the sin of onanism; but there, she doesn't believe in troubling her confessor with every little thing.

'No, I mean more than ever. When we got back from Blankenberg I was shocked at how thin and pale she looked. I didn't feel easy about leaving her alone here over the vacation in the first place, but you know how strong-willed she is. Well, I asked her how she had got on, what she had done. Nothing, she said, and then, with an odd look, said she did a lot of thinking.'

'That sounds like Mademoiselle Brontë. She has a formidably developed mind.'

'I know. But what about her heart? Is that developed in the same way, I wonder?' Before he can answer she goes on, gently stroking his arm: 'I said, just in conversation, that at least she would not lack for company now. She looked all round the schoolroom in the grimmest way, and said she cared nothing for that. And I didn't know what to say.'

'You think she's unhappy here? Why, then, does she stay?'

Madame Heger has a strange sensation of trying to hustle something savoury safely into a larder over the nose of a hungry cat or dog. Carefully she says: 'This place has been good for her: she has learned much, gained strength and independence. But I'm afraid that now it is no longer good for her, that she is living as an outsider and a solitary and so becoming a prey to morbid fancies – and yet she doesn't realise it. She doesn't see the change. I think –' hurry, close the larder door '– I think we have perhaps not been helpful in that regard.'

'But, Claire, we've done everything possible to make her feel welcome. To feel that she is not far from home and alone, that she has a special claim on our attention. Haven't we?' Sighing, he sits up. 'I see. The solution is really the problem.'

'She *is* far from home and alone. And there's only so much intimacy with us that can ever be – appropriate. So, if anything, it must be rather a torment for her, being with a family who can never really be her family. Especially when her real family ties are so strong. I'm afraid this may be at the root of her present – well, I must call it her awkwardness. Come, lie back comfortably, Constantin, you're tired.'

'I must confess, I don't feel easy with her of late. Always seems to be some great cloudy question gathering that I can't answer. Of course, she's English, she's Protestant: they enjoy biting on stones. But still – I don't understand, thinking of everything you've said, why she stays.'

'No.' She draws close, caressing him. 'Never mind. Oh, my love, hello, what's this? You are full of life tonight . . .'

Anne boards the York coach, lifting her skirts from the dark, crystalline slush, the horse-dung slither of the innyard cobbles: going home for Christmas. The four words bear something, at least, of their traditional spell, as she spreads her cloak and settles herself for the journey – even if all is not as it should be. There is Branwell, for instance – or rather, there isn't, because he slipped away while the luggage was being put up, and now the coachman is crossing the innyard doing slow, delicate uncoilings with his whip and Anne, anxious, pulls down the glass and looks out for him. Anxious because he is not himself, or he is some self she cannot quite recognise, and surely capable of missing the coach altogether.

Suddenly he is flinging open the door, and looking annoyed with her for her anxiety. 'What's the matter? I only stepped over to the public. They'll still be fussing with the traces for an age yet. You know how these coachmen like to make themselves important. Not that it's any sort of spanking turn-out. In truth, I never saw a shabbier. But then all this has pretty much had its day, and not before time. They should be opening the railway line to Keighley soon. And then we'll see.'

He does not say what we will see, but he seems, in an irritable way, pleased with himself. That is also a rough description of how he has been at Thorp Green lately. He teaches Edmund separately, in the library, and some days Anne hardly sees him; and when she does, he is sometimes grandly condescending to her, as if he were one of her employers. And yet at other times he seeks her out almost humbly, asking her to take a walk in the gardens with him, and when she does so holding tight and pale and silent on to her arm, so that she almost wants to say: Don't worry, it's all right, whatever it is can't be so very bad. Occasionally, too, her former pupil comes to her in the schoolroom, and mumbles that Mr Brontë has been cross with him and it isn't fair; but soon enough it will be Mr Brontë gave me this, Mr Brontë let me do that. Wonderful Mr Brontë.

That is the bad side of her saying that, of course; and remember, she was hoping to beat that down, and do something good for a change, when she brought Branwell to Thorp Green. And again, sometimes it seems she has. He is still much prized in the family – that is, Mrs Robinson speaks warmly of him and his influence on her son, the girls put up their noses while trying to catch his attention, and Mr Robinson seems to tolerate him while glaring covertly and balefully at all the youthful strength he lacks. So, perhaps she should rest content. Stop looking *into* it.

Can't help it, though. She notices when the coal-scuttle is nearly empty, swiftly calculates how long before cold will set in: not her own room, any room. She foresees and forestalls, and there is this about Branwell now – well, when he delves in his coat-pocket and pulls out a bottle, all she thinks is, Yes, of course.

'Lord above, Anne, don't give me that finicky look. Surely a man's allowed to warm his blood with a nip or two when he's making the coldest, dreariest journey this side of perdition. Your trouble is you've been governessing too long.'

Yes, I have: but unlike you, I never had a choice about what I was to do. Oh, the bad Anne is terribly to the fore today: please, restrict her to thoughts, and don't let her speak.

Branwell uncorks, sips, lips pursed in precision. The coach starts to move, tipping about with jerky inconclusiveness, as if it might just decide to shudder perpetually on the spot and never go anywhere. 'Ah, the restorative tot or tincture. Nobody thinks twice about it when it's a huntsman – or a coachman, come to that, or a sailor with his drop of grog. And yet there you are, saying—'

'I haven't said anything, Branwell, since you got in. Not a word.'

He sips again; all manner of expressions test themselves on his face. 'You needn't come the martyr over it. Anyway, I know a disapproving silence when I hear one.' Suddenly he laughs uproariously. 'Hear one. Dear, dear. As if you can hear a silence.'

Yes, you can, thinks Anne: it's the loudest noise there is.

'A man must break out a little when it's holiday. I never touch it when I'm at Thorp Green, you know, nobody could accuse me of that. I'm always responsible.' He yanks down the glass and thrusts his head out. 'What's the matter, why the devil don't we get on? At this rate it'll be full dark before we reach Keighley. I hate travelling in the dark.'

'We'll make up time when we get on the high road. It will be all right.'

'Dear Anne, you're too good for this world.' He puts up the glass and sits back, pale, cheekbones agitating. 'Why don't you just tell me to keep my ill-humours to myself?'

She thinks. 'I don't know. Perhaps it's not my role.'

'Who chooses our roles for us, do you suppose? And can't we change them? Never mind, I don't expect an answer. Did old man Robinson see you before you left?'

'Yes. He gave me a letter to give to Papa.'

Branwell, lifting the bottle, stops and stares.

'What sort of letter?'

'Just like before, I think. Greetings of the season and so on. He said he had so little opportunity to correspond with a fellow clergyman.'

Branwell studies her for a moment, lets out a long breath, drinks. 'Clergyman. What a travesty. He's the biggest landlord in the district and I hear he hardly ever took services even when he was well. Now, look at Papa . . . How did he seem? Old man Robinson, I mean. Worse?'

'Frail. The same.'

'Edmund will be well set up when he finally goes. The girls too. You'd better teach 'em about fortune-hunters.'

'I don't think there's much I can teach them when it comes to that kind of thing.'

'Well, I say it's not so bad, their knowing a little of the world. That's our trouble. Brought up in a desert, Papa as poor as a church mouse, lots of studious rectitude and little else. That's why they can't get Charlotte back in the barn now she's been turned loose in the meadow. Probably hooking herself some continental husband with waxed moustaches even as we speak. He hates me, you know. Old man Robinson.'

'He isn't old. He's not much older than Mrs Robinson.'

'Next to her, he's a mummy,' Branwell says savagely.

The drink alters the shape of his mouth, she notices: as if there are a few extra teeth in there. 'I don't see why he should hate you.' Or why you should hate him. 'You've brought Edmund on in his studies wonderfully, and his disposition's improved.'

'I add a drop of this to his milk-and-water,' Branwell says, wagging the bottle. 'Sweetens his disposition in no time.' He gives the laugh again, a too-prominent laugh suitable to a noisy, crowded room. 'Your face. No, it's obvious, I mean, look here, it's to you he entrusts the letter for Papa, not me. Poor Papa, he won't be able to read it, the way his eyes are. Work, that is, strain. But do you think anyone will remember him when he's gone?'

'We will.'

'Ah, but who will remember us?' Branwell scowls. Anne watches the liquid tilting in the bottle. Strange stuff. You seize it to warm and cheer you, and end up deadened and cold. 'I'll tell you how it is with old man Robinson. He doesn't want there to be anything more to me than the tutor who comes in to administer Latin to his son. Just function, no more. When Mrs Robinson was telling him about my poems in the newspaper he looked as if he would be sick. And he made sure to be extra insulting to me for the next few days. God, I feel sorry for her.'

'She bears up well.'

'Ha, you women can never bear to say anything nice about one another.'

Anne watches his sharp profile in perplexity. She hadn't meant anything except the literal truth; and it makes no sort of sense to talk about her and Mrs Robinson, employee and employer, as *you women*. The whisky-fumes are strong, and she begins to wonder if she is getting fuddled as well. 'I wish Charlotte would come home.'

'Why? You hardly ever see her when she is.'

'No, but it will be different. We'll be starting our school, and I'll be leaving Thorp Green, and—'

'Leaving?' He jerks upright. 'You can't leave. I mean – it would be strange without you. You – you balance it out somehow.'

'But you know I've never been happy there, Branwell. Yes, there could be many worse situations, but – well, it's as you said, you have to be nothing more in life than a tutor, a function.'

'It's different for women, though, surely.' His glance grows vague and inward: she is sure he is not seeing her. 'Don't be in a hurry for anything. Life has a way of turning inside out before you know it . . . What the devil are we stopping for?'

Coachman's face at the window: many apologies, but this steep hill, with the ice, and to tell the truth not a well-matched team – be safer if they would step out and walk to the top of the rise . . .

'This is what I mean,' grumbles Branwell, tucking his bottle away. 'High time the railway got rid of all this . . .'

Anne takes his arm, and they walk up alongside the straining horses, and Branwell grumbles some more. She doesn't hear him. She is taken up with what she saw inside his waistcoat as he struggled to stow away his bottle. It was a ring, attached by a loop to a buttonhole, hanging on the left side of his chest. Only a glimpse, but all that Anne, observant Anne, needs: recognition clicks into place. A thin garnet ring, a dress ring, one of many that Mrs Robinson likes to try on and take off her long, pretty fingers and say, 'Well, Miss Brontë, what do you think, this or this?' and then toss them down with a sigh of 'Lord, what can it matter in this wretched tomb of a place?' (Though that mood is less on her lately: another observation.) The first startled suspicion, that Branwell has been tempted to thieving, is soon dismissed: he wouldn't, surely, and if he did, why wear the thing like that instead of selling it, and it can only be worth about five shillings anyway. The only other explanation – well, it is no explanation at all, because it doesn't belong in reality, it is an importation from the wildest fiction. Anne, climbing the bleak, crackling hill, rejects it. Because – because it is like what happened last evening, when the manservant at Thorp Green was fetching her luggage out of the closet, and as he pulled and tugged the heap of bags toppled, and slap on the floor at her feet went the game-bag.

'Oh, sorry, miss, that shouldn't be there – hasn't been cleaned since Dr Crosby took it out . . .'

He spirited it away, but too late, the game-bag had opened its leather mouth with a putrid reek and shown her its dark interior of crusted blood and feathers. Look at me. This is the way it really is.

'Thanking you, sir, ma'am,' the coachman calls down. 'If you'd like to step up again now, I can swear to you the worst is over.'

'Ah, my friend, thank *you*, I've been waiting all my life for someone to tell me that!' cries Branwell who, in his typical way, is now sunny and charming. The yawning game-bag snatched away, the ring flashing, disappearing. No, come, come, it can't be. And, yes, of course, there was Elizabeth the other day, recounting to her giggling sisters some concession wrung from their mother – 'I simply said to her, "Mama, if you don't let me have it, I shall tell Papa how you carry on with Mr Brontë"' – but that, oh, Anne hadn't dignified it with a response, though they looked over their shoulders at her and hissed hush, because it was simply nonsense, because, yes, Mrs Robinson in her effusive way makes rather a favourite of Branwell: he looks over her drawings and she likes to have him read out loud after dinner in his fine, expressive voice, and altogether it reminds Anne of some medieval lady of the manor having a troubadour about the place. But beyond that . . .

Some boyish impulse makes him, instead of handing her, lift her bodily right into the coach. Surprisingly strong, Branwell, who is slender and not tall.

'Now Tabby's back with us, we should tell her all our news,' he says. 'About how you fell through the ice on the frozen pond and were rescued by a passing colonel of Hussars, who then proposed marriage but you turned him down because there was something suspicious about his left boot, and I fought that duel with him after he challenged me to name all the Sandwich Islands, my chosen weapons being soup-tureens, but we all parted friends and agreed to meet again either in ten years' time, or in extraordinary circumstances, or in a large barrel, whichever is the least convenient.'

'Branwell, you shouldn't tease her. She'll take a broomstick to you.'

'She'd think there was something wrong with me if I didn't tease her. Tell me, do you find time for Gondal?'

'A little. Oh, I write, but sometimes I like to write outside Gondal. When I'm with Emily, I tend to get pulled back into it.'

'Emily's lucky. Everything she wants, she can find there. Here, in other words.' He clasps the crown of his head. 'Makes life very simple.'

'Does it? Because life doesn't allow you to go there all the time. And even if it did, it might not be—'

'Good, right, healthy? I sense morality hovering.'

So does she; she often does. But it is never dull and abstract, it is something terribly lively with curved teeth and watchful eyes; it will get you.

'Branwell . . .' She saw the game-bag, yes, but did she really see the ring? Can't we choose what we see? A great responsibility, seeing. You don't want too much of it. And if it's true, what can she do? Image of those toppling bags. Just a minor closet, there is a big room upstairs, she knows, full of the Robinson family's luggage, great monogrammed trunks and boxes; you could have fitted all of Haworth Parsonage into them. Anyway it can't be true. 'Branwell – we are very insignificant people, you know.'

And the Branwell she loves and has been easy with these last minutes disappears under a high, remote frown and a sandy chuckle. 'Speak for yourself, Anne.' He delves into his coat, finding what he wants, going away from her.

Well, it was managed at last, thinks Madame Heger, boarding the Brussels train at Ostend, and with luck nothing will come of it. Mademoiselle Brontë is gone home, and there is an end.

All the same, Madame Heger made sure to linger at the quayside long after the steam-ship had chugged away, long after the last handkerchief-waving friends and relations had dispersed: just to be sure. Just to be sure that the ship did not, for some bizarre reason, turn back. Highly unlikely, of course. But those Brontë women seem to shed around them a dark shade of the unlikely, and Madame Heger does not like it. Light, light the lamps.

It will probably be dark by the time she reaches the rue d'Isabelle, where she can feel her precious cares tugging her. Especially the new baby, little Victorine, whom she hates handing over to a wet-nurse. But accompanying Mademoiselle Brontë to the packet was a job that had to be done, and only she could do it. Not the other teachers, with whom she was on such poor terms, and of course not Monsieur Heger.

And the whole thing was managed, as she had hoped, without scenes. Madame Heger has a horror of scenes. It came very close that day in October, when Mademoiselle Brontë, very grim and mutinous, came and said she wished to give her notice. 'I am no longer happy here, Madame. I feel miserably neglected and useless, and I had better go at once.'

'I'm sorry to hear you say that, Mademoiselle Brontë. You have my assurance, you know, that you are far from useless: you are much valued here as a teacher.'

'Oh, as a *teacher* . . .'

Yes, what else? What more? This was what Madame Heger could not say. But of course it was all a complicated dance of the unsaid. Mademoiselle Brontë's burning tears threatened danger, a breaking away from the prescribed steps. Madame Heger was careful.

'If you really wish to leave, of course that is your choice, Mademoiselle Brontë; but I shall be heartily sorry, and I urge you to – not to reconsider but to think about this decision a little longer.'

She thought she had doused the flame. But the next day Constantin came to her fuming. Perhaps the most delicate moment of all.

'Mademoiselle Brontë says she is leaving.'

'Yes. We agreed, you know, that this would be best.'

'When? Best for who?' Barking it out – almost angry. But he never was, with her. *You are my great exception*, he had once said to her, *the place where I walk in and am still*. 'Oh, I know, I know she must go home in the end. But not like this. She's half mad with it. She says she feels so alone she has no choice but to go. I said, "No. Stay." ' He fumbled in his pocket for a cigar. There was thunder about him. She wondered if he quite understood himself. She was very calm and careful.

'I also advised her to stop and reconsider,' she said, going to take a spill from the fire, lighting the tip of his cigar. 'And I am sure she will. There is no need for haste.' Oh, but there is.

Still, though Mademoiselle Brontë did reconsider, once she had said so firmly that she was going to leave, it made it almost impossible for her to stay in the long term – without making herself appear capricious and dramatic in the way she so deplored in the other mademoiselles. So, in a way, she had done herself no favours. Madame Heger had watched and waited. Once or twice, noticing how pale and thin she had become, knowing that she was sitting for hours all alone in the schoolroom, Madame Heger had been on the point of going to her, keeping her company – but no. Better an end. And so, come Christmas, Mademoiselle Brontë was able to announce calmly that she had been long enough at Pensionnat Heger and needed to return home, and Constantin was ready with a sigh to agree. Above all because, Madame Heger suspects, the spectacle of unhappiness is in the end terribly tedious.

The train begins its long, uneventful trundle through the winter countryside, a landscape pared to a few monochrome essentials: flat horizon, verticals of bare straight trees, slashed diagonals of dikes and roads. In the same carriage a little girl is being urged to sit still by her English governess. Madame Heger hears the accent without pleasure. Still, before Mademoiselle Brontë went aboard the packet, Madame Heger did kiss her. She might not believe it, but she does wish her well: every happiness, in fact. But Madame Heger, watching the angular abbreviated figure climb the gangplank, and recalling it now with the vividness of ending, doubts that she will have happiness. Women like that simply don't get on. The world is as it is.

Well, thinks Charlotte, going into the after-cabin, I suppose this is the thing to be doing. Going home. It is the thing she has told herself to do and it is the thing that Mary Taylor, writing her from Germany, has almost screamed at her, if you can scream in a letter, to do; and even Monsieur Heger, parting from her with a touch of his old kindness, had said it was of course the thing to do. As opposed to staying at the Pensionnat Heger, where he no longer strolls with her in the *Allée Défendue*. Forbidden Walk. Everywhere there is a forbidden walk, now. So, go.

There are platters being laid in the after-cabin, and a waft of boiled bacon reaches her. She stumbles her way out. It will be freezing on deck, but never mind. A little girl intercepts her, saying something plaintively: what? It must be Flemish or Dutch, because she doesn't understand.

Charlotte says it in French: 'I don't understand.' And I don't. Lost, perhaps? The girl's white-capped *bonne* comes hurrying over, scolding and hugging. Yes, lost.

As for Charlotte, she is going home. The thing to do. Certainly not a thing that should make you feel fear. Now when – just a year ago – she made the trip back to Brussels alone, then there had been a fearful occasion: the train from Leeds down to London had been late; it was midnight when the hackney brought her to London Bridge wharf, and she got down amid a swarm of drunken watermen. Two of them nearly came to blows. *This one's mine, you fucking cunt. Fuck off, I'm having this fucker.* It was her trunk they wanted: to carry it aboard and be paid and so buy some more drink. But for a minute or two she stood on a trapdoor of terror, thinking that these oaths, these words like cudgels, would be the last words her sane mind would ever hear.

And yet that was nothing compared to the terror she feels at going home. But if she tries to pin down just what it is she fears, all she gets is: I'm afraid of finding myself there, waiting for myself. And I don't understand.

Emily says, helping to unpack Charlotte's trunk: 'I began to think you were never coming home.' And then, seeing Charlotte's deadly wrinkle of a smile, she thinks: *And, in fact, you haven't.*

Emily: she does understand. She reaches understanding by a different route, perhaps, from anyone else. Say, as the crow flies. Like that crow she saw on the moors this morning, or whenever it was, perched on the topmost twig of that solitary bare gnarled tree. The very topmost: it couldn't have got any higher. Did it choose it so? Needed to see the lie of the land, perhaps. But no, more than that, the crow was making its perch vaunting and illustrious, it was riding that tree, a bravo crow. She rode, too, and felt her life joined to it and the tree, all happening to live in the same slice of time, which picture as a wedge cut out of forever. But she does understand, she does feel for Charlotte, who is plainly unhappy for some reason not yet to be grasped – swaying about on the sharp, dizzy top of that unhappiness, in fact – yet her feeling has to exist alongside the celebratory feeling of crow and tree and life, and the heart is boundless but it is not wide.

Understand, feel for – not sympathise, that's different. It literally means to feel with – an impossibility. No one can feel what someone else feels, surely, not without invasion and tearing. Recognition, though. When she persuades Charlotte to get out of the house and come for a walk on the moors, Emily watches her, reads her, in little glances, and what she reads is familiar. You are thinking that everything, all the elements of the scene before you, the fields, the stone walls, the heights, the broken shapes of slate roofs and chimneys and clouds, look like mere husks of themselves, as if the visible world is a discarded chrysalis, from which a better world has risen and for ever departed. Yes, that's your state of mind: I know because I know it. Exultation of crow and tree is not always, nor greatest.

'What are you going to do now?' It is some weeks after Charlotte's return that Emily asks the question. She is not tied to time.

'Do now? What do you mean – today, next week, in the near future?'

Emily covers her smile: crossness always seems so absurd. 'You choose.'

'I don't know. I don't *know*.' Charlotte drops into this sudden abject weariness, like a fever patient. 'It seems as if there are so many things to be done and also as if there is nothing to be done. Does that make sense?'

'Yes, but all paradoxes do to me. The real paradox is I can't conceive of a real paradox.'

'Of course I shall have to do something. Branwell and Anne shame me by their dutiful example.'

'You don't have to win at being dutiful. It isn't a competition.'

'Yes, it is. And it's the only one I can ever win. The school, we must think of the school. But there's Papa. His eyes. Does he pretend to see more than he can?'

'He did, but it's stopped now. It was too obvious. Tabby told him off. We can't leave him, can we?'

'No. Not now.'

'Meaning today, this week, in the near future . . .'

Charlotte shakes her head, wry. The fever abates. 'I'll think of something.'

But not yet. Because what is she really going to do now? Write.

Letters.

She remarks on it brightly at first, even jauntily. Monsieur Heger, having so interested himself in the matter of her education and training, says he will be more than happy to correspond with her and learn all about the sequel, so she will be writing to him regularly, which will have the added advantage of keeping her French up to scratch. And scratch, scratch goes Charlotte's pen, in the evenings when Papa has retired and Aunt's recollected presence too – see it like fingerprints on glass when the sun comes through, just as real – and Emily at the other side of the table observes it and nothing is said.

It is the obverse that is revealing. Observe the obverse: the letters back. How few. And Charlotte's painful, patiently sitting suspense when the time for the post draws near, and the lurch up from her chair at the knock, the embroidery hoop down-flung and sadly exposed like a beetle on its back, and then you hardly know which is worse, when there is no letter or when, God have mercy, there *is* one, and Charlotte does not seize or snatch, she cradles and secretes swiftly away; with care she can make this little fragility survive and live.

It goes on a long time. Even Emily, with her view of time as a sort of affectation, cannot help noticing the drag and heft of it: the weeks becoming months, Charlotte's quill wildly wagging: just peep over her shoulder and it's as if the bird the quill came from is dying all over again, surrendering the feather in acquiescence of inky blood. Then that spectral brightness in Charlotte as the post comes and there are letters, some for Papa that they have to read out to him while he stares furiously into the unseen nearness, some from Anne and from Mary Taylor and Ellen Nussey but nothing from Brussels this time, nothing again.

'Well, of course it wasn't really my turn to write,' Charlotte says, 'and of course with all the demands on Monsieur Heger's time I mustn't be surprised if he has to strictly limit his replies. But I came across something that so reminded me of what he said about the critical and the creative faculty, and how you could not have the creative without the critical. He laid it down as such a law that I just had to challenge him a little, even though I could see his point. And you remember how he used to glare when someone challenged him, yet there was a sort of laugh ready to break out as well—'

'No,' Emily says, 'I don't remember.'

Charlotte looks at her, half smiling, jolted, as if she is in a fast carriage speeding by: that far from her. 'Don't you?'

Dear God, thinks Emily: Charlotte doesn't understand.

In the kitchen Emily finishes the ironing while Tabby, too lame and stiff now for any but the lightest work, potters about brewing tea and reminiscing. As she gets older Tabby's fund of anecdote grows darker, as if from the same stream as the German tales Emily has been reading: human experience is wild and extreme, fathers inflict tremendous cruelties on erring sons, dwellers in lonely farms lose the use of their tongues and wits, dead hands clutch keys and will not be unfastened. Emily loves it. But today she is not listening.

'What's up?' Tabby says at last, as Emily drifts to the back door and stares out at the yard. 'Got the mulligrubs, have you?'

'No. Just seeing the way the wind is blowing.'

'The usual,' sighs Monsieur Heger. 'This morbid dependence on me. Well, as you say, the less I respond, the sooner it will blow itself out. Poor creature.'

'What did you do with it?'

He points to the waste-paper basket. Madame Heger goes over and fishes out the fragments: not liking that. Not enough indifference in it.

He watches her. 'Why?'

'They can be pasted together on a piece of cardboard . . . Why? You keep the letters you had from other old pupils, don't you?'

He shrugs. 'Yes, if they are rational.'

'Well, then. It is just as if Mademoiselle Brontë were still here – she is not to be treated differently.' Madame Heger, quick-eyed, matches up the torn pieces. *I am firmly convinced that I shall see you again some day – I know not how or when – but it must be for I wish it so much . . .* 'Eventually there must come a rational one.' Another thing she learned from Aunt Anne-Marie: always keep your accounts.

'I just worry that he might be ill, and that's why I haven't heard from him,' Charlotte says. 'He does work himself terribly hard, and doesn't take care of himself.'

'Who?' Emily says.

'Why – Monsieur Heger, of course.'

'Yes. Of course.'

They are in Emily's room – the old children's study, and little changed; and just as in those old days they are talking before bed. Except that now there is only ever one subject of conversation. And Emily has decided to confront Charlotte with it – or the moment has decided itself. After all, this room has something to say too, this room where they made a world; and where now the world is thinning, desiccating. Charlotte needs to understand.

'Why did you say that?' Charlotte is sitting on the floor by the bed. She looks up at Emily combatively enough, but tucks her bare feet under her nightgown: the touched snail, drawing itself in.

'Because I had to.'

'I don't see that you had to do anything of the kind. If I talk about that subject too much, then you only have to tell me so. I'm sure I don't mean to bore you . . .' Retreating right into the shell now.

'Not *that subject*, Charlotte. Monsieur Heger, him, him, him. But you're right, in a way, to say that, because he is just a subject now, a subject of conversation. Words, words, that's all he is now. Words on the page. Well, it's not as if you're going back to Brussels, is it? You're not actually going to see him again. That's all finished. So now it's just words and sooner or later the words will have to run out.'

Charlotte's shoulders are so high and tight that Emily knows if she reached out and touched it would be like touching wood: hard, hard to protect the terrible softness within. 'Very well,' Charlotte snaps, 'perhaps I do talk of him a lot, but then he was quite an interesting man, and really there is very little of comparable interest in this dreary,

God-cursed hole in the ground. As for our correspondence, that's interesting too.'

'But very unequal.'

Charlotte darts her a vicious glance. 'You're cruel. You sail about as if you're above all the pettiness of the world but really you've got the cruelty of a vindictive old maid.'

'Yes, I dare say.' No pain: maybe later. 'What I can't stand to see is waste. Time, and effort and heart and *writing*, of all things. God knows what you put in those letters—'

Charlotte scrambles up. 'I'll show you – yes, if you like I'll show you. You'll see there's nothing in them to be ashamed of.'

'Idiot,' Emily says, grabbing her hard by the arm, pulling her back. 'I don't give a damn about that. It's the waste. Because, look – you see, you must have one drafted, half finished perhaps, if you can show me it. Another one, another useless letter—'

'I *like* writing them.'

'No, you don't. It's misery to you. And that's what I hate seeing. Because, oh, how I would hate it if pen and paper became *that* to me. If they dragged me down and chained me. They've always been my freedom. The page is where you should live – not die.'

Charlotte sits stiffly, frozenly, on the bed. 'I can't be like you, Emily. I can't find that kind of contentment.'

'Contentment? Great God, you don't know me, Charlotte.'

'Of course I don't, because that's how you like it.'

That one later too: there will be a time. When she's alone. 'If you think I'm content . . . No, no. It's because I know I can't be content, ever, that I have to find a way. A way to be in the world. Because I know I shouldn't really be in it. Like a school or a barrack where you're not on the roll-call but you eat the meals and keep your head low and hope they won't notice. It's because I'm all wrong that I have to find something right. And I found it here, in this room. We all did, didn't we? We found something that alters the conditions of life. You write. You write yourself out of it, you write it out, you write it right. But it's as if you've forgotten how.' Her arms go round Charlotte, who ducks, flexes, submits. 'Charlotte, he's taking your life.'

'He is my life,' Charlotte moans against her breast. 'Oh, God, Emily, don't ever tell anyone, don't ever speak of it. I know, I know it's wrong.'

'Wrong? What in hell's name – what's this about right and wrong, what have they to do with it?' They are half hugging, half punching one another. 'It's whether it kills you, or whether you live through it. There. There now.'

For a little while Charlotte quietly howls. Emily fingers her hair.

'Promise,' Charlotte says, when she can speak, 'promise, Emily, swear. Swear you'll never speak of it. I'm going to live through it. I'm going to stop – I don't know how. But you must swear—'

'I swear, I swear. Who do you think I am? Ah, but then, of course, you don't know me.'

Charlotte gets up from the bed, stormy creases on her cheek. 'I said some harsh things.'

'Yes, but I'm not bleeding. Also they were probably true.'

'I'm jealous of you, Emily,' Charlotte says stonily. 'Half hate you. Because you can write.' She gestures to the little rickety table, the folded papers. 'You were writing before I came in, weren't you? What, I wonder. But me, I can't, you see. Only the letters. You were right. Perhaps because I can't see the point of it, it won't lead anywhere, I can't be an author . . . But, no, really because it all pours away elsewhere. Scribbling like mad and creating absolutely nothing.' She goes to the little plain square of mirror that serves as Emily's dressing-table. Her huge reflected eyes meet herself balefully, then swing to Emily. 'I never expected love to be so like death.'

3

Lost and Found

'I'm sorry, it hasn't exactly been the quietest of visits for you, has it?' Mary Taylor said, closing the bedroom door on the babble of vehement talk still going on downstairs. The Taylor house at Cleckheaton was brimming with Taylors and their kin, all bright-faced, tireless, argumentative. A farewell gathering, but typically not a sad one.

'I get quietness enough at home,' Charlotte said.

'Which is exactly what I wanted to talk to you about.' Mary steered her to the bedside chair. 'Now, tell me. Is the school plan quite given over?'

Charlotte shrugged. 'The cards of terms are still about. Ellen still distributes them wherever she can. But if you ask me, do I think we will ever have a pupil at the Misses Brontë's Establishment, I have to say no. And, dear God, any parents who did bring a girl to Haworth would probably take one look at the place and whisk the child away. And I wouldn't blame them.' Such had been the fudged notion to which their project of opening a school had been reduced: having the school in the parsonage. Like many fudged notions, it had first presented itself as a splendid idea. Very well – they could not leave Papa, ageing and nearly blind, but with the school at home, they would not need to. Somehow they had persuaded themselves that there would be room for a few pupils, and once their fees were coming in then one could build an extension . . . The best of both worlds. Charlotte had managed to carry on believing in this chimera for quite some time.

'Well, in a way you have answered my other question. Are you unhappy at the parsonage – or, rather, just how unhappy are you?'

'Middling and a bit, as Tabby would say.'

Mary sat down on the bed and scrutinised her. In Germany she had taught, daringly, at a boys' school; and now she and her brother at last had their passage booked for New Zealand, where she intended to open a business. Such a coolness of conquered experience had been added to her old confidence that Charlotte actually felt shy of her.

'Charlotte, you can't stay there.'

'Of course I can. Oh, yes, I don't much like living at home, but I've lived in several places and not liked them. In fact, that always seems to be the way with me. I go somewhere and at first it seems quite tolerable and then—'

'This is different. This is prison. It does you no good, Charlotte, I can see it. This shade comes over you, even your voice . . . You must get out somehow.'

'Oh, Mary, I can't be like you. I can't just pack my bag and go overseas.'

'You did once,' Mary said, with a faintly hard look; and then, 'Charlotte, I don't want you to be like me. That's not what I'm saying. I want you to be like Charlotte again.'

'That doesn't seem to me outstandingly desirable.' She got up, pulling away from Mary's tight attention. At the window she parted the curtains: it was a clear night and she sought stars. But the Taylor mill was right across the yard, and the window-pane was opaque with smoke. A fierce irritation swam up in her at this, at everything. 'Anyway, why should it trouble *you*? You won't be here to see it. You'll be off to your new free life on the other side of the world, and you'll have many other things to think of.'

'Yes, and damned if I'll feel guilty about that. But I shall still think about you and care about what happens to you. Believe it or not as you like.'

Charlotte fingered the curtain, unable to turn round. 'Isn't it funny how people quarrel when they're about to say a long goodbye? As if to take the sadness off.'

Mary laughed. 'Lord, call this a quarrel? In my family it would count as an exchange of civilities. Charlotte, I'm thinking of you alone in that house. No, I know you won't literally be alone. There's Emily, yes, who would be content to live on top of a rock, and to be just as communicative. There's your father, yes, and doubtless he would be content for you to carry on sacrificing your health and spirits to support him. Then there are the geese in the yard and the sheep on the moor to furnish you with a little more stimulation . . . Don't just think of it now, Charlotte. Think of the future. Imagine what you'll be doing in five years' time.'

Obediently, Charlotte tried to picture it. In five years' time, what will I be doing? Why, very probably I shall still be waiting for a letter. She put her hands to her face. Yes, sitting there cobwebbed and staunch, still waiting for a letter from him . . .

Mary sprang up. 'Oh, Charlotte, I'm sorry – don't cry.'

But she wasn't. It was a groan of laughter that had escaped her – laughter more bitter and lacerating than any tears could be. 'No, no. I'm all right.' She shrugged Mary gently off, paced up and down the room. 'Did I tell you about that teacher in Brussels? The one with the little notes? Oh, she must have been in her thirties. No money. Terrified of what would happen if she lost her job. So to all the menfolk in her family she entrusted these little notes, to be passed among their friends, explaining her vulnerable situation, and asking if any one of them would be kind enough to marry her. Kind enough.' From downstairs hearty Taylor voices rose in good-humoured contention. She wondered where they got all their life from: she had come to view it as a scarce commodity, of which she had probably already used up her portion. 'No, Mary, I'm going to stay. I'm determined. Why? Because at least then I'm being determined about something.'

'Yes, Papa, it is confirmed. You have your new curate. The vicar of Bradford begs leave to inform you, et cetera.' Charlotte was reading Papa's correspondence to him, not with complete patience: ecclesiastical style was so windy. She imagined Monsieur Heger's wince of contempt, his hovering blue pencil. No, stop. 'It is the one you thought – Mr Arthur Bell Nicholls – just ordained at Ripon, late of Trinity College, Dublin. Your compatriot, the vicar says.'

'Indeed, indeed. Mind, I have lived so long out of Ireland, I hardly consider myself belonging to that country any more. Well, it goes hard with me to say so, but the parish sorely needs another minister. With my incapacities, the church here is beginning to be esteemed a poor thing.'

'Oh, no, Papa, people have nothing but pity for your difficulties—'

'I do not wish to be a pitiable object,' he hissed, and his long-nailed hand came down hard on the desk. 'Now, read the letter in full, if you please.'

She did, thinking, Well, Mr Arthur Bell Nicholls, whatever manner of man you are, I do not envy you your coming here.

News, of a sort to set her thinking, wryly though not ruefully: Henry Nussey was getting married. He had found a young lady to be his stay and helpmeet, to listen to his benevolent hums and rumbles, to do all the things, in fact, that Charlotte might have done. And the young lady had a little money of her own, which was always nice. Charlotte was pleased for him. It was alarming how genuinely pleased for him she was: surely only a fond old aunt or a saint could manage it. And one of those she knew she would never be.

Even the prospect of going to stay in the house where Henry and his bride would live was rather attractive than otherwise. It was in a picturesque Peak District village, where he was newly made vicar, and Ellen was there alone, overseeing the refurbishing in preparation for the couple's arrival. She wanted Charlotte to be with her. It was, as she wrote, all rather difficult: suppose Henry's bride didn't care for her taste in upholstery? Hearing Ellen's gently anxious fluting as she read, Charlotte smiled and wanted to be with her too. But she doubted she could go. Papa was still fierce in depression. Mr Nicholls the curate had arrived – no William Weightman, a gruff dark presence one nodded to and then forgot, but apparently a solid, reliable sort of young man – and begun at once taking services, which lifted that burden. But the blindness and dependence still gnawed at Papa. Unable to read, he needed to be continually fed with titbits of talk. Emily was not adept at that, and when you could not see her face her shattering silences must have been even more unsettling. So, Charlotte had better stay.

And then, suddenly, a happy shift, as if everyone had been sitting in the wrong chairs and now they moved round and got comfortable. Anne and Branwell came back from Thorp Green for the summer vacation – or, rather, Anne came back for good.

'Papa, may I speak to you in your study?'

That was the first inkling, while Branwell was still lugging their luggage into the hall. Certainly, my dear, certainly . . . Anne went in, the door was closed, and Branwell, thumping down the last bag, swore and said: 'If only we had a manservant. Well, lo and behold, Anne is dutiful as ever – report to Papa first, do the proper thing – but I can tell you, as the pair of you are goggling with curiosity, that she's quitted her post at Thorp Green. Yes. Gave her notice, worked it out, and here she is and here she stays. She's a bloody fool, as I told her, because she'll never get a better position, but there you are. You can't help some people.' Suddenly he darted to the study door and put his ear against it.

'Branwell!' Charlotte cried. 'Stop that. What's wrong with you?'

'About four glasses, I'd say,' Emily remarked absently, sorting the luggage.

Branwell came away from the study door, hands jammed in his pockets, savagely pouting. 'Really, in truth, you know nothing, you two. Any of you. I'm not sure whether that makes you lucky or unlucky, but you absolutely don't know a damned thing about this world.'

'I'm glad,' Emily said.

'Well, yes, if that's how you like it. Certainly it's nice and safe for you—'

'I mean I'm glad that Anne has left Thorp Green. That's what I'm talking about – Anne. Not you.' Emily's voice was calmly informative. 'She never liked it there.'

'I never liked it there,' Anne said, late that night, when they had the parlour to themselves: Papa retiring early from unbreakable habit, Branwell from quiet but diligent drinking. Here they were around the table again, we three; and again that peculiar rightness in it. 'And I suppose it was the thought of our having a school that kept me there, because that made it temporary. And now that we – well, it doesn't seem likely we will have the school, so there's nothing to persevere for, if you see what I mean. No, I don't mean that in a gloomy way. Simply that I may as well look for another governess post, as I've done quite long enough in that one.'

Of course; and so here was a good thing, to be welcomed on all sides. Emily and Anne quickly re-forging their old bond, and even planning an outing together. With Anne home permanently, that would be more company for Papa, therefore Charlotte could go to stay with Ellen in Derbyshire – if Emily and Anne could just have their little trip first. It was delightful to see them squeezing things into bags and reading, with mistrustful frowns, the railway timetables. They went to York, and were away for two days.

'It was lovely,' Emily said, taking the linen-basket from Tabby's arms. 'You don't have to be yourself at all. Nothing calls for it. We played Gondal all the way, didn't we, Anne?' Anne listening but, perhaps, too tired to reply.

So they were happy; and with Branwell going back to his post after a week, and seeming as happy as he ever was lately – meaning hastily amused and blackly impatient – Charlotte decided she could leave, and travelled to the Vicarage, Hathersage, Derbyshire: the address that she might have written at the top of her letters, but for – well, what? Decisions. Well, it was a thought, not a regret. (Charlotte had regrets, but they were differently born, terrible, savage things, banished to the mind's attic.)

'It's a pretty view, isn't it?' Ellen said, of the epic, mouth-drying sweep of hill and valley that opened out below Hathersage. It was good to be with Ellen again: that feeling of life being always in neat lower-case, never capitals. Charlotte saw and approved Ellen's redecoration of the vicarage, suffering a mild pang of envy at the sight of curtains and rugs. Mild, too, her complaints about Ellen insisting on their making visits.

'Dear Charlotte, I know you would prefer just to look at scenery, but I have a little acquaintance here and it should not be neglected. Besides, I'm sure you will like to see North Lees Hall – it's quite in your line, terribly Gothic and ancient with battlements and things. It was the seat of the Eyre family, the ones with those ghastly brasses in the church. But they are gone and the people living there now are thoroughly agreeable.'

'Gothic and ancient. Really, Ellen, I didn't think I had worn that badly.'

And the curious thing was she did enjoy the visit, and not just for the splendidly dark manorial house. She found that she was not actually as awkward and painful and hopelessly maladjusted to normal company as she thought. Somewhere there had been a change. And at night, facing her usual sleeplessness, she found herself taking out pen and paper. Not to write a letter.

At first she just looked at them, handled them, her old appurtenances of witchcraft. She thought of what Emily had said. She thought of Emily who, when she was not housekeeping, was always bent over her writing, drafting, copying: in her world. When Charlotte did dip the pen in the ink and begin, it was nothing much, verses that faltered and stumbled over hollow sentiments. But then at the bottom of the page she wrote a sentence that surprised her. *Is it possible to live again?* Surprising, because not so long ago she would have expected to write and wonder, instead: *Is it desirable . . . ?*

Pressed by Ellen, she stayed at Hathersage another week – though she did not need much pressing. She was in no hurry to get back to Haworth. Only afterwards did her reluctance seem prophetic. At the time, she feared nothing worse than boredom.

⋆ ⋆ ⋆

Emily: 'Why *did* you leave Thorp Green in the end, Anne? Don't worry, I'm never going to ask again, and I will be quite happy if you tell me to go and boil my head.'

Anne thought. It was not her way to leave a question unanswered. But it was difficult to pin down the moment of decision. It was something as elusive as an atmosphere, a look, a feeling of the creeping unspoken. Perhaps, though, it was this: the cold mechanical amusement that began to be perceptible around the servants, and the way its finger touched her one night. She had been called, unusually late, to Mr Robinson's room to sign the receipt for her wages, and as she came out into the dark passage she nearly bumped into Mrs Robinson's maid. Who said, with a dry chuckle: 'Lord, it's turned into a proper game of turnabout now.'

Yes, that was it. But she couldn't tell any of it to Emily.

'Human nature,' she said at last.

'Oh, *that*,' Emily said, with a significant nod; and seemed quite satisfied.

Charlotte reached home from Hathersage at ten o'clock of a balmy July night and knew, at some moment between stepping over the threshold and hearing Tabby's sigh as she took her cloak, that something was wrong.

'Your father's gone to bed. You know he'll never miss his time. No matter what,' muttered Tabby. 'Miss Anne's stayed up. Have you supped?'

'Yes.' The parlour doorway was ablaze with light. 'Emily?'

'Upstairs, studying or some such. I reckon she couldn't fancy stopping down here, with t'other one carrying on.' Tabby jerked her thumb at the parlour. 'Ask him, will you, if he won't take owt to eat? Bread'll soak it up a bit. I'll not ask, he'll only talk daft.'

The oil-lamp stood on the table beside several candles. There were more candles burning on the chimney-piece and on top of the bookcase. There was a hot, waxy smell. Branwell was sitting on the floor, legs outstretched, back propped against the sofa, staring at a piece of air about four feet from him. Anne got up from the table.

'My dear, I began to worry, how are you, did you have a safe journey? I had Tabby save some soup. Papa's well, and said to say . . .' Then Anne seemed to run out: not just of commonplaces but of everything. Her eyes glittered helplessly and she put out a hand.

Charlotte grasped it. 'I'm all the better for seeing you, and seeing you so *clearly*. What means the illumination? Have we won a battle? I didn't know we were at war. How do you do, Branwell? I don't suppose you're going to rise to a normal position to greet me, and I certainly don't intend getting down there.'

'We always have it too dark in this house,' he said, in a loud, gritty voice: he was pale, loose-lipped, eyes sliding away from hers. 'We don't have enough lights and we creep about in darkness. Instead look – look how magnificently everything is laid bare.'

'We'll be creeping about in the workhouse at this rate,' Charlotte said, taking up the candle-snuffers. It was rather dreary when Branwell tippled like this: he was not a genial drunk.

'You're the worst, Charlotte. You're the worst for keeping it dark, keeping it secret – never let anything out in the light and that way perhaps we can all go lying to ourselves all the way to the bloody pissing shite-begotten grave.'

'I had a very nice time at Hathersage, thank you, Branwell. So, the Robinsons are still at Scarborough, I presume? When do you go back to Thorp Green? Plainly you're not liking it very much at home.'

Anne caught her eye, minutely shook her head.

'Do you hear that way of talking you've got?' Branwell slithered half upright. 'That sort of snip-snap way. You don't hear it, of course, because we don't hear these things ourselves, but you know, Charlotte, I think that's partly what's kept you from getting a husband. Think about it, at least.'

'Getting a husband being, of course, my one aim in life,' Charlotte said, extinguishing candles: the light was devoured in big, successive bites. 'Especially with such an inspiring example of manhood ever before my eyes.'

Anne said: 'Please, both of you, don't.'

'Wise virgins. Ha. You know nothing. *Nothing*.' Suddenly Branwell was crying, elbows on knees, the heels of his hands grinding into his eyes. 'You're lucky. God, you're lucky.'

Charlotte hadn't seen him like this before. For a moment all she could do was, guiltily child-like, gaze at the spectacle. Then briskness shivered through her. 'Oh, Branwell, you've surely had a deal too much to drink. Tabby wants you to eat something – it will do you good, just bread and cheese, say – and then—'

'Bread and cheese.' He laughed, snorting and sniffing into his hands. 'Solves everything, you know, bread and cheese, famous for it. I need another drink.' Suddenly he was up and out of the room, moving with a blind man's purposeful absorption.

Charlotte watched him go. 'Will he get any?'

'He may have some hidden away in his room. I don't know.' Anne sat heavily down. 'There wasn't time to write you about this, Charlotte, before you were due home. Branwell has been dismissed from his post at Thorp Green. On Thursday he had a letter from Mr Robinson, telling him so. It's been a great shock to everyone, Papa especially. The reason why he was dismissed.'

'Oh, no – and he was doing so well there . . . What was it then, the liquor? It's a pity, because he doesn't do it all the time. It's not even really his character—'

'Not that. The letter from Mr Robinson was about his— Well, I'll show you it presently. About his proceedings with Mrs Robinson being discovered.' Anne closed her eyes a moment. 'That's why he's arrived home under such a cloud – and you can feel the cloud in here, can't you? A cold, clammy, lowering thing that's got into the house willy-nilly and so you have to live with it.'

Charlotte sat shakily down. 'Proceedings,' she said. Branwell's recent behaviour passed quickly before her: the irritability, the sudden bursts of elation, the distance. It all fitted. 'My God, I don't believe it.' She believed it. For a single moment a menagerie of emotions roared out from their fetid cell – wonder, envy, longing – before she banged the trapdoor on them perpetually. 'What's going to happen? Can Mr Robinson do something – you know, legally?'

'I don't know. Isn't there a thing at law called criminal conversation? But, no, he doesn't say anything of that. Just forbids Branwell ever to come near his household again. He's a sick man – and then they wouldn't want scandal.' Upstairs there was the sound of something, drawer or trunk, being overturned and emptied, objects skittering on floorboards. Anne bit her lip. 'This is how he's been since the letter came. There's no restraining him.'

'What does Papa say?'

'They've been cloistered together in the study several times, and then after a while Branwell has stormed out. Papa's said nothing to us about it.'

'Mustn't affront our virgin modesty, you see,' said Emily, coming noiselessly in with her writing-box. 'He's making his racket up there now. At this rate I shall have to work in the outhouse. At least the geese don't pretend to make sense. Hello, Charlotte. How was Hathersage? Wish you were back there? It's pretty grubby here.'

'He insists – Branwell does insist that it was a genuine attachment,' Anne said painfully, 'and that's why he is so grief-stricken over it.'

'Noisily grief-stricken,' muttered Emily, opening her work.

'Well, genuine or not, surely it can only ever have come to one end,' Charlotte said, then caught herself up: there was a road she did not want to go down. 'My Lord, Anne, you must be glad you left Thorp Green when you did. Was there ever any – I mean, did you ever suspect what was going on?'

Anne swallowed, shook her head. 'No,' she said. 'No, no. Because if I had, well, then surely it would have been my duty to do something about it.'

'Pooh, what was there you could do?' snapped Emily. 'Even if you had known all about it, it wouldn't alter anything. It wasn't your fault.'

Anne shook her head again, as if she could never quite accept that sentence. Duty, guilt, Charlotte thought: Anne's vice. Momentary irritation with her, and with Emily for being so tart and unassailable. Realisation, then, of how much this thing had disturbed them. We three gathered at the table again – but not really we three, not now. And yet now more than ever they needed to draw together, find their common ground. Probably they had all, except Papa, stopped expecting great things from Branwell. But this was a new place they were entering, where you stopped expecting anything from him at all. Except disaster.

'Well, my dears, I'm sure you collect why I wished to speak with you here, while the opportunity exists.' Papa's study: Branwell had gone over to see John Brown, or so he said. 'I know you are all acquainted with the substance of the Revered Mr Robinson's . . . note.' He seemed to find a minor consolation in calling it that instead of a letter. 'I do not propose to go into this painful subject any more than is necessary. But what is necessary, I feel, is that you should know in what terms I have spoken to your brother on a matter which does affect us all. You should know that I have addressed him severely, taxed him sorely with his conduct. I have made sure that he feels his disgrace. And that he feels it not simply as a matter of the breaching of social ordinances, but as sin. I very much regret having to talk to you of such things, my dears, but the welfare of the soul is at issue, and so I must. The entanglement into which Branwell allowed himself to be drawn was nothing less than adultery. A sin. And you know I do not bandy that word about, nor allow it to go unexamined. Adultery – encroaching upon the sacred domain of marriage for the foulest purposes. I urge you, as I urged him, to look at it squarely: to see the enormity of it.'

He isn't really looking at me, Charlotte told herself. Poor Papa can hardly see anything of us now beyond vague shapes. Ridiculous this feeling of wanting to evade those blind, flashing spectacles, as if they might burn her.

'Now, as ever, it is the task of the Christian not only to condemn the sin but to gaze deep into ourselves and ask if we can be sure we would resist that temptation. Not to judge from on high, but to judge from our own weakness and fallibility. This is what the Redeemer meant when he spoke of casting the first stone.' Turn your head away, for God's sake, Papa. 'So I hope I have spoken to Branwell more in sorrow than anger: sorrow that my son should have trespassed so grievously against all that is sacrosanct. And I hope that it is with sorrow likewise that you will view his case, my dears; not excusing the sin, but praying in your hearts that the sinner may be forgiven.'

'What about love, Papa? You haven't mentioned love.' Branwell stood in the study doorway, frowning, jaw working, but composed.

'I thought you gone to Mr Brown's.'

'I know. You were meant to think that. I wanted to listen to the sermon.'

Papa threw up his hands. 'Plainly you are well schooled in the underhand stratagems of duplicity and deceit.' That was Papa: strong feeling made his language more ornate, not less. 'I don't ask you to apologise to me for this intrusion, because you and I still have much to talk of, but you will apologise to your sisters.'

'Intruder in my own home, eh? That's revealing.'

'Before talking sentimentally about home, sir, you might think of the home you nearly destroyed.'

Branwell flushed. 'No home worth the name. A miserable home – a miserable marriage, Papa, that's the truth of it. That's why I said you should mention love because it was love I felt for that unhappy woman, and love I still feel. If you could only hear her speak of what she has endured – how that supposedly sacred bond has been the cruellest of shackles to her—'

'Stop it, Branwell, I will not hear this.' Papa hesitated. It was like a man choosing a stick: how does this feel in the hand? Yes, this will support me. 'I do not doubt, my boy, that these are the feelings you suppose yourself to possess, and that you even believe them to be in some way honourable. Indeed I suspect – I believe that you were to some degree led astray by someone far more worldly than yourself, and that it was your own natural warmth of temperament that was taken advantage of, and betrayed.' Yes, you could see him gripping hold of this, believing it. 'But, still, to explain is not to excuse. And you must not continue to speak of that woman in that way – not to me, but most certainly not in the presence of your sisters. You must undertake, Branwell, to put this whole episode behind you, to cut yourself off from it in thought and word and deed, so that it is as if Mrs Robinson never existed. I see no hope for you else.'

'That I can't do,' Branwell said dully. 'But I see no hope for me at all, Papa, so for once we are nearly in agreement.'

He was gone. Papa tilted his head: he was beginning to locate people by hearing alone. 'I'm sorry you had to hear that, my dears – and yet I'm not, in a way: let the worst be known. I perceive now what a diabolically designing woman we have had to do with. Shocking to think that one of your sex could be so . . . But there – as daughters of Eve you are, heaven knows, not exempt.'

And now Charlotte was so sure that the sightless eyes were boring into her that she had to rise, mumble excuses, get out.

Emily lying on the warm turf, looking up at the brilliant summer sky. But seeing, with lazy interest, the odd filamented bubbles that move on the surface of the eye. One of hers resembles the skeleton of a snake, another is almost a letter *d*. They're always there, even when you're not aware of them. Everything you've ever seen has been through these chain-like translucencies, and the last thing you will ever see will be too. Always they intervene between you and the world. When you see the sky you don't truly see it, you see something mediated. You need an entirely different pair of eyes to see the real sky.

Faint irritation, as a shadow extinguishes the floaters, and after a hard-breathing moment Branwell sits down beside her.

'Papa wants me to go away on a trip for the good of my health,' he says, after a minute. 'Liverpool. Take the steamer across to North Wales. John Brown says he'll go with me. Landscape, you know, change of air. Tramping about. Restores you. Works off the morbid humours. Right as rain. Do you good. What do you think?'

Emily sits up and yawns.

'You really don't care, do you, Emily?'

'About what happens to you? Yes, Branwell, in fact I care a great deal. But I can't give you what you want just now. You want to be pitied. I can't understand that. I can't think of anything worse.'

He crops up grass with hard, nervy fingers, the sound just like a sheep grazing. 'Perhaps. But then you don't know what it's like, Emily. You've never loved.'

'Well, I don't know about that. It depends what you mean.'

'I mean *really*.'

'I've never been to Glasstown *really*.'

He scatters the grass to the wind, shakes his head. 'Imagination's different.'

'Why? It's something you experience, just like experience, except it's usually a lot less tedious.'

He gets to his feet, brushing down his coat-tails and trousers. 'Very well. I'm sorry I bothered you with it, Emily. You're so sure of everything, I should have known better.'

Watching him go, she does feel sorry for him, a little, because he is obviously unhappy. But as for this grand banner of grief he wishes to bear, well, first, where is this Mrs Robinson? Throwing everything in the dust to be with him, or holidaying at Scarborough with her husband? Come now. You don't build a mausoleum over a dead sparrow.

Things you can't say. But she's used to that: that's what most things are. If you want to express them, you have to find another way.

'Go on then, say it – "Why, Branwell, why?" There always has to be a reason, doesn't there?'

Branwell flings himself back on his bed. His thin, stockinged feet poke up absurdly, or pathetically – Charlotte isn't sure of the distinction any more.

'I came up,' she says carefully, 'because you ate no breakfast, and no luncheon, and I – we were worried. Tell me there's no need, and I'll go.'

'No need – meaning you can report back that he doesn't *seem* drunk, and he doesn't *seem* to have taken a laudanum dose, so it's all right, we can cheerfully carry on pretending that nothing's amiss—'

'What do you mean, "pretending nothing's amiss", as if we all just float about at our ease when really the constant anxiety from morning till night is you?' Charlotte is taken by surprise at her own ferocity, at the way her voice drops into a rapid guttural. 'The last thing you ever need to fear, Branwell, is lack of attention. I thought you would have learned that, at least.'

He levers himself up off the bed, gropes around for the water-jug. 'God, I'm dry. The point is, Charlotte, I was hoping for a letter. I know she is watched and spied on and it's difficult for her but I thought she might manage it somehow . . . And I know that is an absurd and contemptible state to be in, placing all your hopes of even being able to draw the next breath on the fact of that letter coming, winging its way towards you and whatnot, and then when it doesn't you just want to die. But, still, if you could just understand—'

'I don't.' There – say it full out. 'I don't understand, Branwell. I'm sorry. All I can see is this. All I can think is you should never have let yourself go down this road. You must have known where it would end.'

His look is almost humble. 'We used to understand each other, once. I remember you saying we understood each other too well.'

'Once. Not any more.' Oh, such a big lie is like a debt: you know you will have to pay for it one day, with interest.

What made Charlotte do it? An ignoble impulse, really, at the root of it. You could dress it up: say she was wistful for the time when they used to read each other's work, say she was so full of admiration for the way Emily concentrated on her writing that she simply had to see the results. But honestly: inquisitiveness, underscored by jealousy. Her own efforts were still so halting, so disjointed and dissatisfying. Perhaps Emily's exterior was deceptive, perhaps her work was the same. When opportunity came, when Emily and Anne went for a walk and, most unusually, Emily left her writing-box open, Charlotte seized it, or was seized by it.

Because of course she knew this was wrong. She knew Emily's fierce insistence on privacy. Wrong, this inching the notebook out of the box, trying not to disturb the loose papers, leave traces of the crime. Surrendering to temptation. Trespassing on the sacred terrain. (But not like Branwell, upstairs in his room brooding, drinking, turning the leaves of the last book his lover gave him.) But she had to, had to do it. Maddening, the curiosity. Maddening, to see someone so contentedly in possession of what you lacked. (Branwell hurls the book across the room – he can have this but he can't have her and it's maddening, what do I want with this, what do I want with a book, poems, words?) Charlotte caressed the cover of the notebook with tentative fingertips, then snapped it open in the middle, plunging in. And actually she knew it would be beautiful – *Cold in the earth – and fifteen wild Decembers, From those brown hills, have melted into spring* – but had not guessed that it would be beautiful like this. These poems – nothing of the lady's album of verses. *When the pulse begins to throb, the brain to think again,*

The soul to feel the flesh, and the flesh to feel the chain. (Oh, the first time, Branwell thinks, she let him lift her petticoat over her head and she stood revealed for him – and it was more wonderful than imagination, it made imagination seem like the scrubbiest grey tracing of experience.) Beautiful and strong and strange. And as she read on, trembling a little, Charlotte left behind the envy and the guilt. They were still there, but she was striding heart and mind towards something more important. This notebook must be a beginning. A threshold.

Something must come of this.

But, first, she must face the tempest. She prepared herself. She was sitting with the notebook before her on the dining-room table when Emily and Anne came in.

'What are you doing?' It was a crisp autumn day, and it was unnerving to see the bright pink glow on Emily's cheeks fade so quickly and completely: a light snuffed out. 'What in God's name do you think you are doing?'

For a few moments, as Emily came at her, Charlotte thought she was going to be hit: she even had time to wonder what it would be like. Probably, from Emily, a good square punch. But instead Emily grabbed the notebook and clutched it to her breast.

And then something about this gesture seemed at once to amuse and disgust her – the two were never far apart in Emily – and she dropped the book back on the table. 'Well, I don't know why I'm doing that. You've already looked, obviously.'

'Yes. I came across it and I couldn't help but look and – and then after that I couldn't stop reading. Emily, was it so very bad? I knew you wrote. What I didn't know was how boldly, how—'

'You did not have my permission. You intruded.' Emily stood over her, firm, crag-like: it felt as if her shadow should cast you into cold darkness.

'Yes, I confess it, and I'm very sorry. But I'm glad, too, I'm glad that I was given the chance to see—'

'You were not given the chance. You stole it.' Emily turned to Anne. 'Better make sure to lock all your private things away, Anne. She'll be poking her nose into them before you know it.'

'I know I should have asked. I've been curious for a long time. And – and I've been wishing we could be as we were, you know, when we used to share our work.'

'Things were different then,' Emily snapped. 'That time is gone.'

'We might bring it back.'

'Oh, no. There has to be trust first.'

'I know, I know I've offended you, and I don't expect you will soon forgive me. But, Emily, your verse is so fine, it – it *ought* to be brought out into the light.' Charlotte tried not to wince at Emily's glare. 'It ought to be published.'

'Now I know you've gone as mad as Branwell.' Emily was about to stalk away, but Charlotte held her arm.

'Why? We used to dream of being authors, didn't we, when other girls were dressing dolls? So why not revive that dream – make it real? Yes, writing is a private thing, a private world, but it can be shared too, surely, without being destroyed.'

Emily shook her off. 'Why should I want to? I'm not like you, Charlotte. I don't long for approval. I'm not going to start sending out needy letters to the world: oh, look at me, admire me, love me.'

Charlotte was silent a moment, swallowing pain, feeling it go down. 'You did promise,' she said.

'You drove me to it,' Emily said, turning away, concealing her face. 'Well, now you've seen my rhymes and I can't undo that, so let that be an end of it. Just believe what I say, Charlotte: I am sufficient of myself.'

'Yes, as long as someone else pays for your bread and keeps a roof over your head.' A feeble delayed reaction, a kind of verbal back-swipe that she was already regretting: but it stopped Emily dead.

'Ah, well,' she said, 'at least that's out in the open now.'

'Emily, I didn't mean it—'

'You should always mean what you say, Charlotte: I always do. Now I'm taking this book away, and it's going back into the darkness where it belongs.'

Anne said: 'But won't you let me read it, Emily?'

Charlotte watched them. Felt a shifting, a redistribution of weight: it was like when the spaniel Flossy jumped up on the bed and you felt her carefully negotiating a place to sleep.

'Oh, if you really wanted to,' Emily said, with a stiff shrug, 'and if you asked. Which I suppose you have.'

'Because, you see, I agree with Charlotte,' Anne went on, lifting a quick hand as Emily glowered. 'I mean that I want that back too – that time when we shared everything that was going on inside. I don't say she was right to read your poems without your permission but I can't honestly say whether I might not have given in to a similar temptation. And, besides, I've been writing verses too. All the time at Thorp Green, it was my . . . Well, it helped me. Let me get them. Let me show you.'

Emily stroked her hand. 'Oh, Anne, you don't have to do that.'

'I know I don't have to.' Anne's gentle tone was just a little serrated. 'I'm not compensating for anything or offering anything up as a sop. I want to show what I've written, and hear what you honestly think. It just seems natural to me. We – we've been apart, haven't we?'

'Millions of miles apart, sometimes,' Emily said, with a smothered glance at Charlotte.

'And we got used to it,' Anne said. 'But getting used to something isn't the same as finding it natural.'

'Well. Of course, if you want to, Anne . . .' Emily's jaw was still tight. 'I don't think Charlotte should be exempt, mind.'

'You can gladly see what I've written lately. It doesn't amount to much. Most of my verse that was even half bearable was written ages ago, before – before I lost the gift.'

'Before you sacrificed it,' said Emily, still coal-hard and black to her.

'Yes.' Let her have that: it was probably true. The main thing is, keep on this road. Something must come of this.

At first, an incredible mutual shyness – as if they are thrown back to being children and seeing each other undressed or bathing. They say nothing, or they say nothings: that's a pretty line, that's a sad one. And then they truly begin to talk, because they have to, because they have always had to since the days of the Twelves and the Genii, whenever words and images and dreams are at stake.

Emily's so powerful. Almost oppressively so sometimes: you seem to feel the weight of the thought like a slab across you. Well: Emily not displeased. (Emily almost forgiving Charlotte but still determined that this sharing is the end of sharing, that they take this exposure no further. Charlotte tacitly acquiescing, but still prodding and shepherding along.) In Anne's, such melancholy. It disturbs, knowing her quietness, her straightness of regard: all the time, this, unsuspected – but why didn't one feel the shudder, hear the sigh? Well, sometimes in writing one takes oneself off like a garment, says Anne. Not so Charlotte. She knows it. Her work is bulbous and misshapen with self, as she sees it. Sometimes it shines, but sometimes the shine is the scaly glimmer of decay.

We three again, around the table, the shuffle of papers, the lattice of talk: this is right, something must come of this. Occasionally Charlotte is visited, as she edges her persuasions forward, by a little snub-nosed doubt: hasn't she been here before, wasn't this the same eagerness that made her press the idea of going to Brussels and of starting up the school, is it going to be another disaster? But she shoos him away.

'You must value your poems, Emily, or else you wouldn't have arranged them and made fair copies of them like this.' A good while before she ventures on this. 'Is that done just for yourself?'

'I don't know. Perhaps . . . But it isn't done for the world, that's for sure.' A vinegary glance: I know what you're up to.

But discussing, revising, sifting inevitably points to selection. And why select, if not for a purpose?

'But, Emily, you went along with the idea for the school. In fact, you made a huge effort for it, going abroad to study, you really devoted yourself . . .' Careful: she flares up at flattery. 'And yet the school was only a school after all: it was an acceptable solution, preferable to the alternatives. It wasn't an ideal. But what *would* be ideal would be – well, what we've always done. Writing. Instead of the Misses Brontë's Establishment, the Misses Brontë, authors.'

'Of course,' puts in Anne, who is learning to wield the shepherd's crook herself, 'we wouldn't have to use our real names, if we did try for publication. No need for that. We can be quite anonymous. I'd prefer it, in fact.'

'Anonymous, or pseudonymous,' Charlotte says. 'Dear me, they sound like late Roman emperors.'

Emily narrows her eyes. If Charlotte is being flippant, something must be afoot. But she says nothing. And, at last, Emily's silence becomes complicity.

The selection: twenty-one of Emily's poems, twenty-one of Anne's, nineteen of Charlotte's. It takes a deal of work and talk to arrive at this – we three around the table, busy, and busy in a way we aren't supposed to be, not sewing or mixing home-made remedies. Brewing up something entirely different. And we three are very separate now from the rest of the house. Papa, who long ago cautioned Charlotte against the tempting folly of authorship, is cut off by his failing sight and his absorption in Branwell. Daily he lectures and exhorts: what is to become of him? It is not so much the matter of getting a new position – though there is that, there is always that – as making a thorough moral reform. And Branwell looks sometimes earnest and sometimes harried, and all the time you know he is eluding Papa, slipping down side-roads of the mind to get to those beguiling and tormenting thoughts. Usually he is stupefied by evening, and Papa's early retiring leaves them in possession of the dining-room. Lamp on the table, three chairs askew: often as they work and talk they walk, round the room and back again, as if the energy of the mind communicates itself to the legs.

This is how it is. Daytime is a footsore haul across bare, flinty land, accompanied by the baleful presences of Papa and Branwell; but at night, when the men are gone, they launch, they are taken up buoyant and weightless by the dark-light sea.

Once Anne says, 'Do you think Branwell still writes?'

'Why ask me?' says Charlotte.

'Well, you two used to be so thick when you were writing about Angria.'

'Long gone. No, no. We have nothing in common now.' There, add to that debt.

Once he bursts in on them, late, benign and expansive: met a gentleman traveller putting up at the Black Bull, kept him company over a bottle. 'Splendid fellow. Thoroughly well-bred and sensible. Antiquarian, you know. Mighty surprised, as he said, to find another gentleman with a well-stocked mind in a desolate spot like this.' He bends to peer over Anne's shoulder. 'Mind, I shan't be here for ever. Hinted as much to him. Couldn't do more than hint, you know . . . Poetry, eh? Nobody writes good poetry nowadays. Everyone's hungry for novels. But where are the good novels? Oh, there's Ainsworth, there's Boz, to be sure, but really the public appetite is for such trash, and that's all the idiot publishers look for. I think to turn out a novel myself, once I'm a little more settled. Just a matter of holding your nose until the deed is done. The thing is, the one thing that you *must* have to write anything worthwhile is experience of life.' He deals out to them a blurred, condescending smile. 'My God, I've got that, all right. My God. That's where you fall down, I'm afraid. Not your fault. It's this damnable place. But there, I shan't be here for ever. No one could stay here for ever. No wonder it's turned Papa half cracked. Ha! The way you look at me. "The Weird Sisters, hand in hand". I'll leave you to your cauldron. "Double, double, toil and trouble".' He saunters, chuckling, out.

As always when Branwell goes, there is a short silence: like leaving a space on the mental page for the thoughts you cannot say.

'Now, read it again, Charlotte,' Anne says.

'"To Aylott and Jones, Paternoster Row, London. Gentlemen: May I request to be informed whether you would undertake the publication of a collection of short poems in one volume octavo. The hope of the authors is that you will see fit to publish at your own risk: however—"'

'I'm not sure about that "hope of the authors", it sounds a touch mealy-mouthed,' Anne says.

'Perhaps a direct question then. "If you object to publishing the work at your own risk, would you undertake it on the authors' account?"'

'Yes. Depending on how much it will cost,' Anne says, with a grimace. 'No, don't put that, of course. Yes, I think that's better.'

Emily draws a crow at the top of her page and says nothing.

'You're having second thoughts.' Charlotte goes into the little cold bedroom where Emily sits at the unshuttered window, her hand against the glass, feeling the butting of the January wind.

'Second, third, hundredth. It doesn't matter.'

'It does if you're going to back out.'

'You'd never let me.'

'Now that's funny. When have I ever been able to make you do something you really don't want to do?'

'Don't you remember?' Emily cocks a pale eye. 'No. I won't back out now. It's just that letter made me realise what's happening. Submitting ourselves to the world.'

'Not necessarily. It might be the other way round. It's just as you told, me, Emily: this room, what we did here, that was our salvation. And now it can be again.'

'Ah, we're going to conquer the world with a book of rhymes?'

'That's the beginning. Authors don't stop, they carry on writing. Again, like we did here, with Angria and Gondal.'

'You don't have to keep buttering me up.'

Yes, I do, thinks Charlotte. And I don't mind. I'll do anything for this.

'Branwell never used to be so absurd, did he?' Emily says suddenly. 'Only I looked at him tonight and thought: If I didn't know you, I'd think you were a fool. That nonsense about turning out a novel. As if it works like that.'

'I suppose that's how some people approach it.'

'But we've never been like that, have we? Writing to *please*.'

Charlotte stiffens: the scar of bitter words throbs for a moment. 'You don't want your writing to please people, then? What do you want it to do to them?'

Emily gives her old listening look, then bursts into laughter as if the sidelong voice has told her a funny joke. 'Burn them.'

Charlotte proceeds confidently with the arrangements, as confidently as if she knows what she is doing. Everything happens on that far-off exotic island, London. You just have to pick it up: the way to conduct the correspondence, to parcel up and send the manuscripts, the way to hand over your money. Yes: Aylott and Jones, genteel publishers of works chiefly of a religious character, will only undertake their book if they meet the cost of the printing. So there it goes, from Aunt Branwell's legacy: thirty precious guineas, for an even more precious end. The publication of *Poems, by Currer, Ellis and Acton Bell*.

Well, sheer anonymity would just be absurd: they have to have some sort of names, and Charlotte likes the idea of retaining their initials. *Bell* – they take that from Papa's curate, Mr Arthur Bell Nicholls, and they are sure he won't mind. (It's hard to imagine him minding anything much: he goes trudging about his business, black-browed, jaw set; when he comes in wet from a rain-shower you almost expect him to shake himself dry like an imperturbable dog.) As for the first names . . .

'Perhaps I could be Charles. How would you feel as Edward, Emily?'

'Ridiculous. Prefer Ebenezer. Prefer not to be a man at all.'

'But if we use female names they'll judge us differently,' Anne says. 'They'll judge us not as writers but as women – or even *ladies*, which is worse.' She shudders.

'Who will?' Emily says.

'Readers. Critics,' says Charlotte – casually, to suppress her surge of excitement. Because this, madly, is real. This is not cutting out and sewing tiny books and reviewing them in their own tiny hand-sewn magazines. This time the world is joining in the game. It's like sitting down to cards with a giant. And playing for high stakes.

So, they conjure up the ambiguous names, Currer, Ellis, Acton. They like the ring of them, just as if they were – as they are, in a way – choosing the names of fictional characters. A subject that begins to exercise them, as the poems are surrendered to the printer, and we three around the lamplit table need new spells to practise.

'Branwell's right in a way. It's novels that have the biggest readership,' Charlotte says.

'But wrong in every other way,' says Emily. 'You can't just write a novel by mechanically covering so many sheets of paper. It doesn't work like that. You'd have to bring to it everything you bring to poetry. More. You'd have to learn to stand outside it.'

'But we're used to writing long stories. Lord, what else did we ever do?' Charlotte has a pang that is not quite nostalgia: a spike of dread in it.

'But they've tended to be the kind that go on and on,' Anne says. 'Gondal and Angria tales, where one just melts into another. That's what's so frustrating about them.' She catches Emily's eye. 'Sorry, Emily.'

'Why?' Emily is crisp. 'Why be sorry for what you feel?'

'I don't know. I often am,' Anne says softly. 'I do still love Gondal, but . . . well, I've made a start on a prose tale, and it isn't at all like that. It was after Branwell – came back. I felt I had to write but – not in the dark, somehow. In the light of day. I'm not sure about it. It's very plain, and it doesn't really transport you anywhere, so I don't know if it will appeal—'

'Anne, stop apologising,' says Emily, with mock sternness – though with Emily the mock is not quite distinct from the real – 'and read it to us.'

Madly, this is real: the proofs of *Poems by Currer, Ellis and Acton Bell* have arrived from the distant island, not a little battered by the journey, for it looks as if someone has half ripped open the parcel, but clear and elegant and, oh, alarming. Print really does change everything. Those are your words there, exposed. It is as if someone very powerful and important should hearken to your private mutterings, then go and loudly announce them to a gathering of the equally powerful and important who all turn to regard you as if to ask you what *exactly* you meant by them . . . If I am feeling this, thinks Charlotte, then what must Emily be feeling?

Emily, though, seems mildly amused and exhilarated. 'It's like being on the moor when the fog comes down. Nothing for it but to try and get home alive.'

For a time the idea of the novels hangs heavily about them. In a way it is like the presence of Branwell in the house, drunk and rackety or ominously quiet: you can't quite ignore it, but to pay attention to it is to become mired in helpless frustration.

Anne's story is about a governess, and how she survives. It is real and steady and wry, and Charlotte admires while thinking, But I can't do that. Emily seems lost in a wilderness of notes. Sometimes the whole project looms up at them like an ornate folly, flawed at the foundations.

'It's different from verse. It's dancing in a public square,' Emily says. 'I hate it.'

'But the book of verses is public,' Charlotte says. 'We've published it – or rather the Bells have. This is just the logical next step.'

'I don't want to please the public. That's why I'm getting nowhere. I keep picturing some simpering miss on a sofa turning the pages and saying tut-tut.'

'Make her say something else then,' Charlotte urges. 'Make her stare. Make her uneasy.'

'The whole point is I want nothing to do with her.' Emily gouges her page with murderous crossings-out. 'I'm going for a walk. I need to get outside myself.' She whistles Keeper, rubs his brutal head. 'Yes, that's what I need.'

Anne, looking over Charlotte's work, says: 'You've written a lot.'

'Is that the best that can be said of it?'

'Oh, no.' Anne looks shocked. 'It's very strong. Only . . .'

'Come on, out with it,' says Charlotte, more breezy than she feels.

'Well, I feel as I read that we might go anywhere. Instead of somewhere definite.'

'You mean I'm still stuck in Angria.'

Anne hesitates. 'What I tell myself when I pick up the pen,' she says carefully, 'is to mistrust it. It's like a skittish horse that might run away with me. So I have to keep it on a close rein.'

Again Charlotte thinks: I can't do that. The thought is violent; and that evening she finds herself writing nothing but a mutinous string of curse-words, and then tearing the paper up. An unusual gesture: paper is expensive and, more than that, precious. But the next day she feels strangely better, clearer. And that evening when Emily begins to read out her own work and then, furious, stops and shakes her head and stuffs the papers back in her writing-box, Charlotte finds herself speaking out of that clearness, with something that – if it wasn't herself – she would call authority.

'The trouble is,' she says, looking at Emily and Anne, fixing their attention, 'we are doing this as if it's something we've got to do. A task or an imposition. Instead of something we want to do.' For a moment, just for an allowable moment, she has an image of Monsieur Heger standing at her shoulder. 'But this isn't something coming from outside, like having to be a governess or running a school or being what the world tells us to be. This is coming from us. Always before, when we've written, it's been what we do against the world and in spite of it. It's been *our* place. That's been our – defiance. And that's what we mustn't lose.'

After a moment Emily shakes her head. 'I'm trying. Perhaps too hard. And, yes, perhaps I am thinking of it as something I've got to do. Which never rubs well with me, as I dare say you know.'

'Turn it about,' says Charlotte. 'Make it something you've got to do – simply because you can't *not* do it. You can't help yourself.'

Struggling, wrangling, falling silent, walking round and round the table, they forge through the lamplit evenings, pages written, read, discarded. Getting nowhere. Until you lift your head and find that you are getting somewhere, even if the place is unfamiliar, alarming.

Voices in the night.

'He's frightening, Emily. Not just from what you show him doing, but what the reader believes him capable of doing.'

'But isn't it ill-usage that has made him so?' says Anne.

'No, Heathcliff is as he is,' says Emily. 'Like a crow on a tree.'

'I don't like the thought that someone can be beyond amendment.'

'Dear Anne, I'm not asking you to like it. Only to – submit to it. But what about your Agnes and Tom Bloomfield? Can she possibly amend him? Is there any hope?'

'She believes that it is possible. I— She couldn't go on otherwise . . .'

Another reading.

'No, Emily, it's too horrible,' says Charlotte, her smarting eyes fixed on the lamp. 'Rubbing her little wrist on the broken glass.'

'It will give me nightmares,' says Anne.

Emily looks mildly puzzled. 'But it is a nightmare.'

'But the blood running down—'

'Oh, Charlotte, blood is blood. It's shed every day.'

Another.

'Anne, when Tom Bloomfield gets the nest of baby birds to torture them, was that real?' asks Charlotte.

'It's all real,' Anne says, eyes lowered.

'There's the true horror,' murmurs Emily.

'I hesitated over putting it in. I wondered whether people would find such cruelty unbelievable.'

Emily shakes her head. 'It's the one thing that is always believable.'

Another.

'Is there really no understanding between Edward and William?' Anne asks Charlotte. 'We're back to cruelty again, but – for someone to be so cruel towards his brother—'

'Perhaps they understand each other too well,' Charlotte says.

Where are we? Somewhere. A long way from Gondal and Angria, certainly, though something of its enchanted air still faintly hums about these scenes, schoolrooms and mills and stony heights.

'No, there can't be any other title, of course,' Charlotte says. 'I just wonder what the southerners will make of the word.'

'They may make what they like of it,' Emily says.

'Wuthering is a very good word, I think,' Anne says, 'because it's precise. No other word can do its job.'

'Only one word for what you want to express and nothing else will do. That's what my – that's what I remember being taught,' says Charlotte. The right word. Are they doing the right thing? It must be right. Everything depends on it being right. Write, write.

Choice and expensive importation from the distant island: the books are here. Something has happened to the wrapper of the parcel again before Charlotte gets to it, but never mind. Here are the bound volumes of *Poems by Currer, Ellis and Acton Bell.*

Strange: no one to congratulate them but each other. Can't tell Branwell, who has retired to a sort of lofty gutter. Temptation to tell Papa – but surely all it will do will fret his mind, even make worse his consciousness of his near-blindness, shutting out the world of print. There is a faint hope there: a cousin of Ellen's is married to a surgeon who has given his opinion that a cataract operation might be successful, in due time. 'So we must wait for the cataract to harden along with my courage,' Papa remarks, with a rare quiver of humour: it takes the grim to bring it out of him. Helplessly strange moment when Papa, feeling his way around the dining-room, lays his hand unknowing on the dark green cloth binding of their book, then gropes his way on.

For Charlotte, after the first glow, a sense of impatience. Right, now the next thing: reviews, notices. Ignoring Emily's rueful look – *sending out needy love letters to the world, love me, admire me*, no, be damned to her – Charlotte haunts the Keighley circulating-library, calls continually on Mr Greenwood the stationer, who takes periodicals of all sorts. Perhaps they should have spent some more money, secured some advertisements . . .

'Have you found what you were looking for, Miss Brontë?' asks Mr Greenwood – amiable, devoted to the paper-devouring family who keep him in profit, and just a little nosy.

'No – dear God, no,' Charlotte says, laying down the *Yorkshire Gazette* and hurrying out.

She finds Emily and Anne in the kitchen: Tabby too, but so deaf now that anything can be said in front of her.

'Mr Robinson is dead. I saw the obituary in the newspaper – died last week after long illness.'

'God rest his soul,' says Anne. 'He suffered a great deal.'

Emily lets out a low whistle. 'Well, now we shall see something.'

'But what shall we do?' cries Charlotte. 'Should we tell Branwell?'

'Well, if you were in his situation, would you expect to be told?' says Emily.

'I don't know,' says Charlotte, and on the other side of the grating she sees the father confessor shifting impatiently. 'I can't imagine his situation. Where is he, anyway?'

'Gone over to Halifax, I believe,' Anne says.

'What for?'

'Oh, he can still get credit in the public-houses there,' Anne says. Noticeable how even tender-hearted Anne speaks of Branwell in this flat, disengaged tone now. Like when their favourite cat Tiger died and they buried him in the garden – and for some time you had a sad cherishing consciousness of that spot. Until eventually you just walk over it without thinking.

'He's sure to find out somehow,' Emily says, bending to rake out the oven. 'And when he does, we'll all know about it.'

Home from Halifax, crashing into the house, coat-tails streaming and tossing back sweat-soaked hair, Branwell is like a slash cut through the soft, bee-singing summer dusk.

'Letters, where are my letters? Martha, you there, Martha –' he almost yanks little Martha Brown, passing through the hall, off her feet '– what did you do with the post today? Where did you put my letters?'

'I took the post in, Branwell,' Charlotte says. 'There was nothing for you today. Come, come in here and sit down. There's still tea.'

He grips her by the shoulders. 'Do you swear it? Do you *swear* that's the truth, Charlotte?'

'Well, I think so. I could look in the teapot to make sure.'

After a staring moment he relaxes, or rather tenses further, into wild laughter. 'Oh, Charlotte, if you could only understand what I'm feeling.' He begins prowling around and around the table, as if in unconscious parody of their night-time walks. 'All of you. Shall I tell you what's happened? I got the news today in Halifax. He's gone. Her husband is gone. Isn't it the most . . . ? Oh, God, you can't understand. You'll never understand.'

'We heard,' says Anne, 'about Mr Robinson. It's very sad for the family.'

'Which family?' Branwell's laughter goes up and up: you find yourself wincing at each fresh burst. 'I'm sorry, I'm sorry, there are just no words, no set of responses, nothing one can say that will seem apt to the occasion.' He gasps, hands on knees. One gets used to classifying the smell of drink; this is of the stale, soon-be-needing-more sort.

'Branwell, have you eaten?' Charlotte says. 'I had Tabby save some cold beef. It'll eat very well with bread and butter – you must be hungry—'

'Food, I'll tell you about food, my dear sisters, because there's a secret to it and it's this – it *isn't* a necessity. We think it is because we're told so, but no. The real necessities, the things we cannot do without if we are to live and remain human, they're here – and here.' He touches his head, his breast, smiling angelically.

'But if you don't eat, you do die,' says Emily.

'Ah, diversions, delusions, illusions. Listen here. I know I shouldn't say it, but come the time, you shall all be set up comfortable. I'll see to that. There'll be an end of governessing and scrimping. And Papa—'

'What are you talking of, Branwell?' Papa is in the doorway. 'I hope this is not a reversion to the old subject. I've told you in the clearest terms that is not to be dwelt upon.'

'No, Papa, it's a new subject, or the old one overturned. For the former things are passed away . . .' For a moment Branwell moves as if to embrace his father. 'Mr Robinson is dead.'

'I'm sorry to hear it,' says Papa, at once cold and fierce, 'but sorrier still to find you rejoicing over it, sir. Are you quite lost to all feelings of shame and propriety? To crow over a man's death—'

'He is released, Papa – and so, above all, is she. That's all that runs through my mind, that's all I celebrate. I'm sorry for him, yes, and, dear God, I'm sorry for her – what she must be feeling. She's a woman of such warm affections and tender conscience, this must be breaking her in pieces. The guilt and sadness and relief all tangled up together,' Branwell half laughs, half sobs, 'well, if anyone can begin to understand it, I can, for I'm experiencing the very same. Really she hardly needed to write to me, I can see that now. It's just a matter of heart echoing heart—'

'Stop it. Stop it, Branwell, this is beyond anything,' snaps Papa. 'It is *unmanly*.'

Branwell only laughs low, in a wistful, kindly way. 'Oh, Papa, I can't tell you that you're wrong, I respect you too much. I can only say that soon – *soon* – you will see and behold the man and the gentleman I should have been, all this time.'

He is very confident; and with the same glittering, unearthly confidence he demonstrates, over the next few days, that he really can do without food, sleep likewise. Not talk, though. The house becomes a tight drum-skin on which the emotions of Branwell are beaten out in ever-amplifying tattoo, until his hopes deafen you and his fears make your head ache. This must come to something, something must come of this. Until finally the day of the knock at the door, and the bootboy from the Black Bull standing there, and deaf Tabby making him shout it twice over.

'There's someone put up at Bull as wants to talk particular to Mr Branwell Brontë.' Who is already shouldering him aside, on his way.

He is gone a long time. The unaccustomed calm and quiet in the house almost jar, as if a waterfall should abruptly cease. The first inkling comes from Martha Brown, who has been down to the village to buy soda, and who picks up the gossip like burrs. Yes, handsome travelling-coach they say, yellow wheels and red panels. No lady, though. Just someone called Allinson or—

'Allison,' says Anne. 'That's the Robinsons' coachman.'

Pen briefly suspended, Emily says: 'Come to fetch him?'

'Surely not,' Charlotte says. 'Mr Robinson is scarcely in his grave – surely the woman could not be so—'

'No, she wouldn't,' says Anne. 'You know, I can't help feeling that this is all my fault.'

'That's ridiculous,' Emily says hotly. 'Nothing, nothing in this could possibly be called your fault, Anne, and everyone would agree that to feel so is nonsense.'

'But that's what I mean. I can't help feeling it. In that way I'm as bad as Branwell.'

At last another knock. Charlotte hurries to answer it. This time it is John Brown, who is supporting a drooping, tear-streaked Branwell on one brawny arm.

'Landlord sent for me from the Black Bull. They didn't know what to do with him. Lying on the supper-room floor squealing, he was.' He grimaces at her over the top of Branwell's tousled head. 'Come on, old squire, in with you.'

Branwell lurches forward, gets as far as the stairs before sinking down with his head in his arms, crooning.

Papa's study door opens. 'Mr Brown? What's going on?' The bafflement of blindness makes him more sharp and querulous.

'Bringing Mr Branwell home, sir. Took rather a turn. He was shut up a long while with a messenger from Thorp Green, the coachman, it seems. He's gone now. Not sure what it's all about, but plainly, er, plainly something troublesome.'

'Branwell?' Papa shuffles forward, brings his face close to the shape on the stairs. 'What is this, sir? Come, be a man, be in possession of yourself, and answer me.'

But Branwell just quietly moans it as if to himself: 'Lost, lost, lost.'

'Well, you know it's been hard enough getting any sense out of him lately,' Charlotte says. 'And now . . . But it seems to be something about the will. Mrs Robinson sent the coachman to tell him about it.'

'Rather odd,' Emily says. 'Why not just write a letter?'

'Oh, it seems she's unequal to anything like that, being in this terrible state of guilt and grief. Weeping and praying. Half mad with it, apparently. I don't know.' Her gaze falls on Anne, who is standing at the window with her back to them. 'Anne, does that sound like Mrs Robinson?'

'I confess it does not,' Anne says, after a moment. 'Though she had her – pious moments.' She grimaces, as she always does when forced to speak ill of someone: as if she does not like the taste of it.

'Well, Branwell says that the terms of Mr Robinson's will make it impossible for them ever to marry. That is, if she marries him she will lose her claim on her late husband's estate.'

'That's different from making it impossible,' Emily says. 'And, besides, isn't that always the case when a widow remarries? She only keeps her own settlement. Which I dare say in Mrs Robinson's case is comfortable enough. Anne?'

'I don't think she will ever be poor,' Anne says reluctantly. 'But then she is used to living very high . . . It's all a sad business.'

'Do you suppose the will really specifies Branwell?' Emily's look is sharp. She has an instinct for untruth. 'Or is that how she's making it appear?'

'For what reason?' says Anne.

'To keep him away. Because she doesn't want him.'

Anne comes slowly away from the window, troubled. 'In that case . . . it could be seen as a kindness. It might be – less painful for him to think that circumstances keep them apart. Rather than rejection.'

'Less painful,' Emily says relentlessly, 'but, unfortunately, more dramatic.'

Urgent, vital now, the separation between day and night, land and sea, living and writing. It's writing that makes living tolerable.

Branwell's unhappiness, the ruling passion of the house in the weeks and months that follow, is not really a lack or a negative. It defines him. It is all he has; and it is as if, having made defeated stabs at so many things in life, he means to make a thoroughgoing success of this. A lesser being, a more commonplace person, might be betrayed occasionally into acceptance, into quiet, into momentary pleasure. No such backsliding for Branwell. He is a pedant and perfectionist of misery.

Increasingly, the work at the lamplit table and the reading aloud and the reflective walk round and round becomes – not a diversion, it has never been that – a matter of assertion and will, even faith. Often they are tired – because, say, there has been a great moral battle between Papa and Branwell all day with everyone hurtfully drawn in, or because last night Branwell saluted the small hours by pounding about the house banging on doors and telling everyone between hilarious yelps that he knew their dirty little secrets. But the tiredness is like an unruly dog to be tied up outside the gate. Once done, we can settle.

So, take up your pen and write. Light the lamp. Defy the circumstances. Shape and sense. But don't lose the fire. The process is as demanding as turning a flame into a straight line.

And at last – dare we? Yes, we must – Charlotte can confidently tell Messrs Aylott and Jones that Currer, Ellis and Acton Bell will presently be able to offer three tales, or novels, or works of prose fiction. She feels uncomfortable affixing a label to what is emerging from that nocturnal pool of will. It's as Emily said: doing what they have always done. Creating a world. Anne's is a world very like this one, and you can move about in it with familiarity – but not freedom: it is a place of rigorous consequence, where the weak have to give way to the strong, where her governess heroine Agnes must walk as best she can in the cold shade of money and masculinity. Emily's world fascinates and disturbs: in it you can touch thick Yorkshire speech, and moorland rain slants across your mind with a smell of mossy limestone and yet you are not at home, you might almost be in Gondal or Angria except the towers and the dungeons are of the spirit, the dungeons especially; and sometimes when Emily reads out in her low, almost guttural voice Charlotte wants to run but can't think why or where she would run to.

As for her own written world – well, partly it is here, but it contains Brussels too, and a *pensionnat* with a clever, manipulative proprietress, and she thinks to title it *The Professor* – it's very hard to say anything about one's own work. Anne finds the Brussels part fascinating: just occasionally as she reads out Charlotte catches in Emily's eye a peculiar sceptical look, as if she were hearing a particularly elaborate lie. Which, of course, is what fiction is.

Not that Aylott and Jones will be interested in anything so morally ambivalent as novels, and already Charlotte is copying out the addresses of other publishers. Take up your pen, move on. They have, however, been punctilious in sending on the handful of reviews that *Poems* has received. Some appreciative words, especially for the verses of Ellis Bell. (Move on, don't look back, outdistance time.) Oh, and they have, at Charlotte's request, given a quarterly account of sales.

Poems by Currer, Ellis and Acton Bell has sold two copies.

Two.

(Write, write.)

4

The Blind Hand

'It is customary at this time – that is, the patient often likes at this time to make some spiritual preparation,' said the surgeon. 'But there, of course, Mr Brontë, I touch upon your own preserves, so I will say no more.'

'I am prepared, in all ways, for whatever may follow,' said Papa. And it seemed he was: Papa was at his most comfortable in situations that would have other people clawing the walls.

The surgeon's instruments were not many, nor dramatic: they came in a neat felt-lined box. Not unlike a writing-box, Charlotte thought; and, how very sharp they are; and I must not faint no matter what I see or hear.

Outside, all was sooty, chaotic, rackety. Manchester was the place for eye surgery and here Charlotte and her father had taken lodgings, consulted with the eminent Mr Wilson, and appointed the day for the cataract operation – and here it was. Inside, all was quiet, ordered, ceremonious. Mr Wilson and his two assistant surgeons (to hold him down, they're to hold him down) proceeded into the bedroom with a sort of flourishing decorum: Versailles courtiers attending the removal of the royal wig.

Charlotte sat upright in the little stuffy parlour, staring at a compellingly hideous arrangement of wax flowers under glass. The hired nurse settled her chins and took out her sewing. Mr Wilson called: Papa wanted her in the room. She stood at the foot of the bed. This was the moment when you should think of all the things you wanted to say to him that you had left unsaid, but nothing like that came to her. Instead she kept thinking of the candlestick in Branwell's room: she had reminded Emily to check every night that he had not left a candle burning once he was asleep, and Emily never forgot things anyway, but still her mind kept settling on it like a fly. She fixed her eyes on her folded hands, knotted fingers. Voices murmuring.

How long would it be before they made a start? This endless preparation only made it worse. She had just decided to risk a look when one of the assistant surgeons touched her arm.

'Miss Brontë, shall we go and ask the nurse to come in now?' He smiled at her expression. 'We are all done here.'

Charlotte glanced back as she left the bedroom: Mr Wilson was holding a towel to Papa's white uplifted face. 'What's happening?'

'Well, nothing unexpected arose, and the operation is completed. Now we must await the result after convalescence, but Mr Wilson is sanguine and has the firmest hopes.'

'You mean you've done the operation?'

'Yes, the cataract is removed, by excision of the lens. Mr Brontë is doing very well – really the model patient.'

Charlotte sank down shakily on to a chair. Well: that was Papa. For fifteen minutes they had worked on his eye with sharpened steel, and he had not made a single sound.

'What time is it, Charlotte?'

'Nine o'clock.'

'As late as that? You must go to bed, my dear. I shall sleep soon enough.'

The bedroom had to be kept dark, and Papa had to lie flat with his eyes bandaged, and they had to limit themselves to these little exchanges as too much talk might tire or agitate him. Lie flat, and wait to learn if he was to be a blind man or a seeing one. The required patience seemed to Charlotte to be superhuman.

'Is there much pain, Papa?'

'Some. A certain fiery soreness. It is tolerable. I'm afraid it will be dull for you here, Charlotte: Mr Wilson speaks of a month. I hope you can find a way to occupy yourself.'

There was one way – to brood and chafe. The Branwell way, as she might have said if she had not seen in it her own ominous propensities. The three novels by the Bells had been parcelled up and sent out into the world, and had come back licking their wounds and unwanted. Never mind: move on: re-tie the parcel, write out another publisher's address, back to the post office. Useless to brood and chafe, as she so easily did, imagining the parcel unwrapped in some crammed inky office on the far island of London, untender hands riffling through the pages. Still more useless to brood and chafe on her own contribution, silently urging them to treat *The Professor* gently because – well, why? Something about it of a last, long, hopeless letter to Brussels?

But that was the wrong way. We don't go that way: move on. All too easy to brood and chafe here, with the silence and seclusion and nothing to see from the windows but mill-chimneys rising like black banners above the marching red-brick ranks. Temptation must always be resisted: look at Branwell. Move on: write.

Because, after all, who was Currer Bell? A dilettante who went into a pet when what he wanted wasn't handed to him on a plate – or a writer? And this was what writers did – the paper, the pen, the ink, the troubled look over the milling herd of ideas, most of them sickly and needing culling.

And who was Charlotte Brontë? Only the woman who had gone to Brussels, taking with her one kind of heart and bringing back one quite different, worn, wrung, incapable? Was there only the woman *he* had known (Monsieur Heger, come on, dare to name him once) or was there not more to her, much more?

She had time, she had authority, for now. In the bedroom the masterful man lay bandaged and submissive, humbly waiting for the revelation of sight, waited on by the nurse. All Charlotte had to do was not make a noise. It occurred to her that this had always been the case. At the parsonage, at Cowan Bridge, at Roe Head, at Stonegappe, at the Pensionnat Heger: hush. Hush. It occurred to her that perhaps the time had come to make a noise.

Plain monosyllables, that was what was wanted for this one: that was what she must be like, introduced plain and short into a world ornate and profuse with hypocrisy. Jane. Eyre. The merest scratches of identity on the vast grey wall of experience. But as surely as the grandest title they proclaimed: I exist.

Who was Jane Eyre? The result of everything that had happened before her.

Time to make a noise. But the only thing audible in that little parlour in a Manchester by-street was the scalpel sound of the sharp, moving pen.

'Anne, if you could only help me to a shilling, you would do me a great deal of good.'

'Dear God, Branwell, you made me jump.' Usually nowadays his entrances and exits were thunderous hinge-breaking affairs: it was unnerving to have him appear softly at her side like this.

'What's that you're reading? Oh, Scott. I used to have quite a taste for Scott. Now I look at the words and I – have to fend them off . . . Anyhow, a shilling, if you could manage it, which I'm sure you can.'

'I thought Papa left you some money.'

'Oh, he left me what I can only call a beggar's dole or driblet or pitiful pittance, but that's gone. All gone.'

'Where did it go?'

He sighed. His sallow face was all disgusted angles. 'Love to moralise, don't you, Anne? Sort the saintly sheep from the damnable goats. But, you see, that's easy for you. You've never been tested. Never anything more morally problematic than, oh, should I miss church today because of my sniffling cold?'

Was that how she was? Looking back, she saw no such safe spaciousness: saw herself always teetering forward on a tightrope with a great dark plunge on either side. But perhaps he was right.

'If I give you a shilling, Branwell, I'm afraid of what you'll do with it, that's all.'

'I see.' Another great sigh: she felt like dry dead leaves before the wind of it. 'So, you're not going to help me. It's Thorp Green all over again.'

'What do you mean?'

'Oh, nothing.' He sketched a pantomime of repenting, or saying too much. 'Look, I'm merely remarking that you seem to observe a great deal. And that it would be nice if people who observe would also act. I don't know how much you knew at Thorp Green. Something at least, I suspect. After all, it was you who brought me there in the first place – and so if I were very harsh and comprehensive I could well say that you were to blame for everything. But I won't lay that burden on you.'

Suddenly, and as silently as Branwell had come, Emily was there. 'Here,' she said, 'I've got two shillings for you, Branwell.' She held out the coins on her broad white palm. When he reached for them her other hand shot out and seized his wrist. 'I heard you, blaming Anne. That's small, Branwell. I don't mind if you drink or run up debts, or if you got into someone's bed that you shouldn't have, or even if you want to spend the rest of your life beating your breast and feeling sorry for yourself. That's human enough.' He tugged, but Emily was strong and held him fast. 'But don't be small, Branwell. We were always taught to admire you and look up to you and perhaps that was wrong, perhaps that laid something of a burden on *you*. But please don't make us despise you instead.'

Emily let him go. He didn't say anything, and he didn't look at either of them: just snatched up the coins, pocketed them and walked out.

'Thank you,' Anne murmured to Emily. She hadn't the heart to say it was too late.

Emily took her arm. 'Shall we play Gondal for a while?'

'Oh! Yes. Yes, that would be nice.'

The bandages were off. Healing very well, Mr Wilson pronounced. Continue the treatment: leeches at the temples every other day, complete bed-rest. Those dim shapes that Papa could discern would grow clearer in time. 'The regenerative powers of the human frame are a remarkable study, Miss Brontë.' From darkness, light. Papa told her he passed the long hours by consulting his memory: he found he could summon chapter after chapter, very nearly whole books of the Bible. 'Remarkable what the mind is capable of,' he murmured, 'when put to it.' She had an acute sleep-killing toothache, but she put it somewhere else, drew the lamp nearer, folded back the cover of another notebook, wrote the words *Chapter Ten.*

On the train home Papa remarked: 'The leaves are turning early this year.'

For a moment they both let this sink in.

Charlotte said: 'How much . . . ?'

'Colours, increasingly strong, which is how I remarked the leaves. Light and dark in strong contrast. Shapes in motion still blur a little. But it is coming back. A miracle.' The rigid patriarchal face softened a little. 'As one might say, seeing is believing.'

At the parsonage Emily and Anne were waiting up. Papa relinquished Charlotte's arm in the hall and stepped forward, hand raised in admonition, as the dining-room door opened. 'Don't speak. Don't speak, girls. Let me – let me see. Anne. Emily. Yes, yes. Oh, but you look tired, you look worn. How is this?'

'Just worrying about you, Papa, and that's over now, thank God,' Anne said.

'Hm. Where is he?'

'Halifax,' Emily said. 'At least, that's where he's been a lot lately. Sometimes he stays overnight with his friend Mr Leyland. Come, sit down, Papa, you must be exhausted.'

'It's all right, Emily, you don't have to guide me any more. Where is he getting the money?'

'I furnished him with a little,' Emily said. 'I know I shouldn't. But it prevents a scene, and – well, we have enough of those. Otherwise, I presume he runs up debts.'

'I see.' Papa sat down heavily. His red-rimmed, impersonally weeping eyes drifted to the parcel that stood on the table. 'What's that?'

'Oh, nothing,' Anne said. 'Just some books we were sending to Ellen Nussey.'

Emily gave Charlotte a secret, rueful nod. It was the parcel of their manuscripts: once again the prodigal, come shabbily back from the big city, unwanted.

Papa was so much better in the morning that his mood was, for him, almost festive. When Mr Nicholls came calling early to enquire after his health, he pressed him to have breakfast with the family.

'So preoccupied as I have been, Mr Nicholls, I fear I have neglected to express my gratitude for the readiness with which you have carried the greater part of our parochial burden. You may rest assured that as soon as my sight sharpens enough for me to read – which, with its daily improvement, cannot be long – you shall have the vacation you deserve. You wish to visit your people in Ireland, I understand. Charlotte, some more tea for Mr Nicholls.'

'Yes, sir. That is, all in good time. Let us consider your full recovery the – the chief thing.'

It was unfair, of course, to compare him with William Weightman: perhaps if Charlotte hadn't known him, she wouldn't have found his successor so wooden, so uncomfortable. When she handed him his tea there was a kind of cumbrous, hovering moment to be got over: it made her want to demand, *What – don't you know what tea is – or are you going to drop it on the floor or ask its catechism – what?*

'You are very good, Mr Nicholls. In a man getting on for seventy,' said Papa, 'it is to be doubted whether the bodily powers can ever be what they were, but the will is a different matter, and if I have my will I shall be taking up my duties very soon.'

'Thank you,' said Mr Nicholls. That was for the tea Charlotte had handed him half a minute ago. As if the words needed to be weighed. She tried, too late, not to be irritated.

'What does it feel like, Papa? Under the knife?' asked Emily, and Charlotte seemed to hear the ghostly cluck of Aunt's tongue.

'The sensations hardly suggest the knife at all,' Papa said, with his stringy smile. 'The whole proceeding is mightily interesting to the curious mind. First they administer drops of belladonna to dilate the pupil to its greatest extent – a piercing sensation, but short. Curious, is it not, that the most virulent poison should have a medicinal use, also that it should bear a name meaning "beautiful lady"? . . . What's the matter?'

Charlotte had jumped to her feet. 'Branwell's home, I think.'

Branwell was home, and before she could forestall him was in the dining-room.

'Papa.' He leaned right across the table, knocking over the milk-jug, to seize and pump his father's hand. 'You're better, I can tell you're better, thank heaven, but I knew, I knew you would be.' He lurched up to the vertical. Not drunk, but with the itchy wakefulness and pulsing mind of a long binge ended. His mouth was firm, his eyes all over the place. Once dapper, Branwell looked now like a man who often slept in his clothes. 'Listen, Papa, let me tell you, because a lot of things have become clear. I had a letter from Dr Crosby, he was the surgeon at Thorp Green, surgeon of course to Mr Robinson but a *friend* to my, that is to *our*, cause, and he tells me the reason she cannot communicate with me – *fly* to me as she would wish – is all the matter of her relatives and the way they absolutely hem her in with constrictions and work upon her just when she is at her weakest and lowest. Explains a lot, you see. It's shocking to think of how she must be feeling and must draw tears, I'm sure, from the hardest of hearts.' He ground his sleeve against his eyes. 'Sorry – I haven't been sleeping, and sometimes my feelings get the better of me.'

'Sit down, Branwell, and have some tea,' Anne said. 'There's no porridge, but if you would like some bread and butter—'

'Extraordinary,' Branwell cried, fluty with irritation, 'the way some people suppose that *eating* is the answer to everything. Just keep eating, and all your problems will be solved. When actually the reverse is true. Well, Nicholls, how do you do? Invited to breakfast, eh – high honour, you know, high honour. Not very talkative, are you? Have to make you a match with my sister Emily here, great one for enigmatic silence she is—'

'Branwell,' said Papa, in his roundest pulpit voice. Then, more quietly: 'You are, as you remark, very tired and in need of rest. Go and take it, and later you and I will have a good full talk.'

Branwell sighed. 'Well, Nicholls, you see how it is. Oh, none of your fault, I know, but do note how you are welcome here where I am not. Really does suggest that you're being groomed to marry one of these midnight hags, be the dutiful son he never had and all the rest of it—'

'Branwell! Enough, sir,' barked Papa; but Branwell, faintly giggling, was already gone.

Mr Nicholls applied himself to his tea; but his eyes, oddly electric eyes in that square dark slab of a face, missed nothing, Charlotte thought; and she had to hate him for a moment, for seeing how they lived. For being a witness.

'I'm sorry, Papa,' Anne said. 'While you were away we have had some – some little troubles in this regard.'

'Don't be sorry, my dear, it is no fault of yours. It is a trouble I hope to take from you.' He pointed to the ceiling, where Branwell's stumbling tread could be heard. 'There – there is another one of my duties.'

Which is worse – the indulgence or the deprivation? The effects of drink and laudanum, or the effects of not having them? A question put to empirical testing at the parsonage, that cruel winter and slow spring.

Papa takes to sleeping in the same room as Branwell. To exhort and pray, at first, perhaps, to be the flesh and blood equivalent of a biblical text on the wall. Soon, though, it becomes a simple matter of necessity: of looking after him. When drunk he is a danger to himself, leaves candles burning, vomits prone and half-conscious. When deprived of drink – and this must happen, the family live on very little and the postal subsidies from the Lady, as Branwell will only call her now, are covert and irregular – he has the horrors. Which sounds slightly melodramatic or comic, but isn't.

'If I kill myself,' he is shouting it in a kind of impatient downright tone, as if to a noisy lecture-hall, and even cramming the pillow over your head won't stop it, 'if and when I kill myself, then according to your beautiful cult of blood-lusting Jehovah I go to hell. And if I kill *you* I go to hell likewise, so really we may as well go together, hey, Papa? Hey? In the name of fuck and cunt and all the other true gods, why not?' This is where it becomes unbearable, and you have to steal to the bedroom door and listen with your curled fingers on the handle; but sometimes then there will be sobs, and Papa's voice taking over soothingly and quiet. And just once there is such peace that Charlotte peeps in, and sees Papa on the bed lying flat on his back – sharp nose and chin jutting, limbs still, just as he did for his operation – and Branwell face down across him like a dropped puppet.

Which is worse, hanging on to hope or giving up hope? Daring to feel he is a little better lately – a little more honest and trustworthy at least – they find a cheery bailiff standing on the parsonage doorstep. Immediate repayment of Mr Branwell Brontë's debt, or removal of Mr Branwell Brontë to the debtors' ward at York Gaol to think about it.

Together they find the money. When the man is gone, Branwell comes down laughing nervously and blowing on his fingers. 'Byron's creditors, you know, were so insistent that he actually had the biggest one living in his house – making absolutely sure he couldn't skip off. They would meet at breakfast. Charming thought, isn't it?'

You're not Byron. No one says it. It is as if no one wishes to disturb the last powdery relics of illusion.

And which is worse, at last? To have no offers of publication for their novels, or to have this offer, grudging, lopsided, but at least some sort of undertaking to publish?

'After all,' Anne says, as they walk round the room in the summer night stillness, 'we paid money to Aylott and Jones, and they dealt fairly with us.'

'But not profitably,' says Charlotte. 'Remember those two copies.'

'Yes, but that was poetry, after all. There's much more of a readership for novels.'

'So we hope. And that's why I'm dubious about this Mr Newby. Not just because he's dubious about *The Professor*. Fifty pounds is a lot of money to pay him.'

'He says it's a necessary insurance, the trade being the way it is,' Anne says. 'And once the books have sold enough to cover the sum, then we are refunded and beyond that come the royalties. So it's a sort of advance.'

'But that's what publishers should be offering us, not the other way round.'

'They're not offering, though,' Emily says. 'And how many have we tried now? I can't believe there are even that many publishers in London. I say we close with T. C. Newby, whoever he may be. As long as he takes all three of us.'

'But don't you think he— Well, he writes as if he's doing us a favour. Don't you think *Wuthering Heights* deserves better than that?'

Emily gives her a suspicious look. 'I thought you didn't care for it.'

'I don't know about *caring* for it,' Charlotte says. 'I know that there was never anything written quite like it.'

'Well . . .' Emily listens inwardly a moment. 'It's grown now. I can't mother it any more. Time for it to go out in the world, and either survive or die.'

'Anne?'

'I think the terms are reasonable enough, if not generous. We are quite unknown authors, after all.'

Charlotte nods, gathers their arms close. 'Very well. Will you proceed with Mr Newby without me? I don't think he wants my *Professor*, and I just have this stubborn aversion to parting with any more money, and there are one or two houses still left to try. No doubt I shall be proved wrong, and have to come crawling back when it's too late. I'm prepared for that.'

So, in an awkward dissatisfying way, the thing trundles along: no one is getting off it, for now, but no one is sure that it is going along the right road, or even that it may not end up in the ignominious ditch. Ellis and Acton Bell, part authors of the volume of poems that sold two copies, contract with T. C. Newby, publisher, of Cavendish Square, for the publication of their novels *Wuthering Heights* and *Agnes Grey* partly at their own expense, and hear very little from that quarter once the banker's drafts are made over. Charlotte crosses out the last address on her parcelled *Professor*, manages to squeeze above it the words *Smith, Elder & Co., 65 Cornhill, London*, and despatches it again into the southern yonder, with a sense more of grimly holding out than of hope. Obliging Mr Greenwood has found her a London trade directory, and Smith, Elder & Co. are not a large publishing house, nor much reputed for fiction. Accounts of voyages, mostly. She tries to put that from her mind and concentrate on finishing her new novel, though cold draughts of doubt keep shrilling round her. Jane Eyre goes on no voyages. Jane Eyre is real to her, real as breath and pain, and light striking your eyes from sleep – but perhaps after all she is only like Zamorna, a private fanciful indulgence, of no use to someone trying to negotiate with the world.

And the world is like that bailiff pursuing Branwell, it's like a creditor waiting in the next room arms folded, with a warrant for you in his pocket. Papa can't make it go away: Papa is, for all his vigour and renewed sight, an elderly man, and a clergyman whose title to this house ends with his life. Branwell can't make it go away: that's all you can say about him for now. So the career of the Bells may simply be a colourful little aberration on the way to the true destiny of the Brontë sisters – governessing and teaching, taking up those unloved posts again where you can get them: making do until you are an old maid. Really, it has all been pointing towards that. You can feel yourself swing and lurch and swivel towards your ordained future like a compass needle.

So when the dream begins – well, we are used to dreams, we are accustomed to the reordering of reality. We did this years ago: made a story, made a book. See the little writing, the tiny stitches. But now the world, unbelievably, steps into the cold private room and wants to join in.

It begins with a refusal. Smith, Elder Co. do not want *The Professor*. But instead of a curt declaration, the refusal comes as part of a long, thoughtful letter saying exactly why they do not want it. It is not Currer Bell's writing they are rejecting, but this rather too slight, monotone example of it. They would be very interested in seeing a full-length three-volume novel from Currer Bell's pen.

Currer Bell's pen flies. Give me a month, she asks them. She keeps expecting a reversal, a knock-back: perhaps she won't be able to finish it, perhaps she won't be in the vein. (This is how they call the writing mood, for it's physical, the story branching hotly through the vessels from heart to fingertips.) Within three weeks, with sandy eyes and a feeling that the top of her skull is open, she is writing the last words of *Jane Eyre*. The next day she is at Keighley railway station, entrusting the manuscript to a scrofulous young clerk who seems to know nothing about pre-paid parcels.

Expect the reversal. A fortnight's silence: well, they don't like the book after all. (Once again the wretched anxiety of the post-hour: very revealing.) But then comes the letter. Mr Williams, the firm's reader who was so encouraging, is even more encouraging. Not only does he admire the book enormously, so does Mr Smith, the head of the firm. They want to publish it.

Very well, this must be the reversal – it will be on some such shuffling terms as the silent Mr Newby has offered Emily and Anne. But no, Smith, Elder & Co. are offering her a hundred pounds for *Jane Eyre*.

'How can you hesitate?' cries Emily.

'It seems wrong somehow. The way Mr Newby has treated you . . . Couldn't you get out of his clutches, and apply to Mr Smith? I'm sure—'

'We'd be no better than him if we did that. Besides, we're getting proof-sheets now, it can't be stopped. Go on, go on, Charlotte, we made our choice, you made yours, and yours has turned out better. Can't you see we're glad for you?'

They are, too. Humbling. Still, there must be a reversal.

Well, there is this, though perhaps it hardly counts. Mr Williams, in his grave, thoughtful way, has some suggestions about the early part of the story. The scenes where the youthful heroine is at Lowood School, presided over by the monstrously hypocritical clergyman Mr Brocklehurst: these vivid but very painful scenes of oppression and suffering, culminating in the death of that poor persecuted girl Helen Burns, might they not be better reduced or recast . . . ?

No. Charlotte digs in her heels. Keep them. Keep the truth. Maria and Elizabeth died, but the truth does not. It is more than twenty years since Charlotte stood trembling before the Reverend Carus Wilson, unable to answer him. Now he has his answer.

But even this creates no difficulties. Mr Williams acquiesces, and now there is nothing to do but wait. Judging by Emily and Anne's experience, it will be a long, lackadaisical business.

She has barely put her name, or Currer Bell's name, to the contract before the proofs start arriving. She has actually gone to stay with Ellen at Brookroyd, expecting nothing for weeks yet, when Emily sends them on. So, in the intervals of quiet chat with Ellen, she marks the proofs of her book; and Ellen sews, and looks not incuriously but not inquisitively on, because she would not dream of asking. And she remarks how her brother Henry has got a little at cross with his parishioners over the matter of a Dissenters' burial-plot, but calmer counsels have prevailed; and Charlotte says good, and corrects a little typographical error in the account of Mr Rochester's bed-curtains being set alight by the mad imprisoned wife. 'Oh, Charlotte, I mustn't forget, I have a rather nice cap for you to give to Tabby – and a jar of crab-cheese for Anne, very good for coughs and chills.'

'Yes, he is stone-blind, is Mr Edward.' I had dreaded worse. I had dreaded he was mad.

'Kind of you, Ellen.'

'And how is good Mr Nicholls?'

'Oh, he's been visiting his family in Ireland. I don't know where you get the notion that he's *good*.'

'What, don't tell me he's bad, my dear Charlotte?' *Reader, I married him.* 'No – he isn't anything, really.'

But now the proofs are done, and this, judging by Emily and Anne's experience, is when it all goes flat and nothing happens for ages. Well, nothing happens for a couple of weeks; and then six complimentary copies of *Jane Eyre*, a novel by Currer Bell, arrive at Haworth printed, bound and complete. Last reflex of pessimism: surely, with such speed, it will be a shoddy printing . . . No. No, you have to abandon those thoughts now. From now, the red jacket and clanging bell of the postman herald miraculous absurdities in quickening profusion.

Jane Eyre, Mr Williams writes, is the book of the season. What does it mean exactly? It means it is selling so fast they are already preparing for a second printing. It means these reviews he sends on from all the major papers and journals, which at first she reads silently to herself, lips pursed and cheeks stinging as if at unthinkable intimacies, until Emily and Anne urge her to read them out loud. *A story of surpassing interest . . . This is an extraordinary book . . . All the serious novel writers of the day lose in comparison with Currer Bell* . . . No, this is extravagance. Go on, Charlotte, go on. *A book of decided power . . . A remarkable production . . . It is a book of singular fascination . . . From out the depths of a sorrowing experience here is a voice speaking to the experience of thousands . . .*

It is like some vast clamour on the edge of the horizon, the distant thunder of a liberating army or a revolution. And meanwhile the first ice appears on the inside of the parsonage windows. And Keeper gets a thorn in his forepaw and Emily pulls it out, growling at him as he growls at her. And Branwell gets hold of some money, probably from the usual place, and is gone for days at a time and comes back weak-legged, skin like dough, conducting a muttered running quarrel with himself about what that damned fellow meant by it, what did he MEAN by it. And Papa says to thank Ellen for the thoughtful gift of the fire-screen. And Mr Williams encloses a letter of praise for *Jane Eyre* from Thackeray. Yes, oh, dear God, *the* Thackeray, whose magnificent *Vanity Fair* has been coming out in instalments for the past year, whom Charlotte admires more than any living writer. It is dazzling and bewildering. It is as if Queen Victoria herself has proposed that they swap places.

And it won't do now to think of this as belonging simply to that far-off island called London, where strange things naturally happen. Mr Williams reports letters and notices from Edinburgh and Dublin, from nearby Leeds, from a naval captain at sea.

'He asked if I had not seen the book in anyone's hands,' Charlotte tells her sisters, 'and so I explained how we live so very retired from the world. Well, he tells me that if I were to go a railway journey I should probably see someone reading it. He says it is remarkable how both men and women read it – mamas and their daughters at the circulating-library, gentlemen in their clubs – everyone who takes up

Thackeray or Dickens takes up Currer Bell.' She tries to quell the excitement in her voice. To rejoice too much seems to invite some retribution: you will have to pay for this.

Sometimes when she wakes in the morning she has to remind herself: it is *not* an ordinary day. I have written a book called *Jane Eyre* – or it has written me – and because of it, I am famous. Although nobody knows me. Superb, and not right. Again, strange flarings of guilt on the back wall of her mind, as if she has purloined loot, buried bodies.

'What is your Mr Newby about?' she says fretfully. 'It's getting on for six months now.'

'Not that long,' Emily says. 'Anne's written him again – but I fancy he'll get matters moving now. Now that Currer Bell is the talk of the town.'

'Oh, don't.'

'Why? Don't you like it?'

'It's just – hard to get used to. Hard to imagine, for one thing. This place is a very good corrective to any grand ideas. Look out there. Stone and sleet, and just about as much spirit and warmth in the people. If I go down to the post-office or to Mr Greenwood's, no one will think anything at all about me – or if they do, it will be that parson's daughter wastes too much brass on such stuff. But elsewhere, people are reading what I've written, my words are inside their heads, and the things I saw and imagined – well, if I've succeeded, they are being seen and imagined by them too. They're thinking about them, talking about them: loving or hating them. It's frightening. I feel like the loaves and the fishes – except the miracle may not work.'

'This was always the danger,' Emily says, quite gently. 'From the moment you wanted to be published. Exposure.'

'Oh, but I never thought it would come to this. I *can't* be a famous person, Emily, I—' She drops into a chair, half-laughing, dazed. 'I've only got one pair of shoes.'

Emily is usually right about human nature, and Mr T. C. Newby does indeed get matters moving now that the name of the Bells is so saleable. Before the first December snow on the hills, the finished copies of *Wuthering Heights* and *Agnes Grey*, by Ellis and Acton Bell, arrive at the parsonage. Full of printing mistakes, laments Anne, but that's not going to matter. Not beside the swelling hubbub on that far horizon. The critics, the reading public, society – all the fascination that has been aroused by *Jane Eyre* is tickled to a frenzy by these new productions of the mysterious Bell brothers. If brothers they are: one of the many questions that buzzes around them.

So, for all his slapdash methods, Mr Newby can report no lack of interest or sales. But the appearance of all three Bells in print seems to intensify something that has always been latent in the reaction to *Jane Eyre*: a shiver of distaste as well as admiration. It was the *Spectator* that first complained about its low tone. Now the theme is taken up, especially about the work of Ellis Bell. Where *Agnes Grey* is praised, it is often simply for being less unpleasant than *Wuthering Heights.* Power, singularity, grandeur even – the words are scattered around Emily's work, but usually spiced with revulsion and horror. These brutal passions, these violent excesses: what can the Bells be like? Or are they in fact one and the same man, a kind of Heathcliff of the pen, compelling and monstrous? Or can they be women? Some things in the novels point to that – but others point shockingly away.

'Apparently if we are women, we are horribly denatured from the proper qualities of our sex,' Anne reads out, 'and our work irredeemably disfigured by coarseness.'

'Ah, that strain again,' Charlotte says, trimming the lamp-wick. 'Of course, we're coarse.'

'What *does* coarse mean, though?' Emily says, with real interest. 'In the way they use it? Is it because I write out *damn* and *devil* instead of peppering the page with dashes?'

'I think it's something to do with being a woman, and telling the truth,' Anne suggests mildly.

'Oh, well, that's different.' Emily looks satisfied.

'It's a wilful misunderstanding on their part of what the writer's art consists of,' says Charlotte, impatiently. 'As if we are to be judged by our material. A woman should write about pretty things, just as she should be pretty herself.'

Emily bends down to warm her hands at the fire, then lies down full length on the rug, cat-like and conning the flames. 'It is piquant, though, isn't it? The way our stories have stirred them up. Like rattling a hive with a stick.' She sighs luxuriously, firelight dabbing molten warpaint on her white brow and cheek. 'I don't know how this will end. But it's delicious to watch it happening, and all the time nobody knows that it's you behind it all.'

Characteristic of Emily to think of it ending; but Charlotte can't think of it in that way, and neither it seems can Anne, who is already working on her next novel.

'Mr Newby says he will take it as soon as may be,' she tells Charlotte, 'so strike while the iron's hot and all the rest of it. But besides that, I have to do it. I can't sit still and think about this – what's happening. People reading our things and talking about us. Fame. What you said about the loaves and the fishes – dear God, there would never be enough of me to go round, folk would famish. That doesn't mean I want to go back or change my mind, by the way. No, no. This is what I want to do. Only I find that *Agnes* is a dead letter now – isn't that strange? And I've got to start something new. Otherwise I'll feel a sort of fraud.'

Snow settles, the ice inside the parsonage windows thickens and blooms, Charlotte receives a banker's draft for a sum five times her governess's yearly salary, wonders what to do with it. Ellen writes: what are they up to of late? Oh, nothing much. I've been dedicating the second edition of my vastly successful novel to Mr Thackeray . . . things that can't be written. To Mary Taylor in the safe nowhere of New Zealand, perhaps, but not to sociable, well-connected Ellen. Not without endangering their anonymity – and that, she knows, is dangerous ground. Anne prefers to preserve it because she is shy: fair enough. But with Emily it goes much deeper. She is content enough now, as she says, secretly observing from a distance. (Standing on a hill and watching a house go up in flames, and knowing you did it, it was you who set the fire.) And she reads the reviews carefully, not firing up at the negatives: taking it in.

'Proud?' she says, when Charlotte tentatively presses her on how she feels: being an author, being read and talked about. 'Strange word. Am I proud? I've made something, and the making isn't all I wanted it to be, because of course one strains after perfection – but it stands. If people admire the thing, or look up at it in horror, then that's well. They're responding to what I've made, not to me.' Yet if there should be any betrayal of their secret, Charlotte can imagine what Emily's reaction would be – or, rather, she can't imagine it, except in terms of earthquakes and noontide darkness.

As for Charlotte, how does she feel? The prospect of publicity alarms her, certainly. There is such a difference between appearing before the public as a square block of bound paper and appearing as – well, that thing in the mirror, past thirty, colourless, turtle-mouthed, great naked eyes seeming to fix themselves on a disastrous day after tomorrow. Yet there is a part of her that wants to stand up beside her book and declare herself, especially as the notices begin to murmur of immorality. And Emily, perceiving this, actually suggests a concession.

'You should tell Papa about *Jane Eyre*. No, really. It will have to come. I heard him speak to the postman the other day, and the postman mentioned this Currer Bell who has such a lot of letters, and Papa said, "There's no one of that name hereabouts."'

'I know, but . . . It will agitate him. He told me – once he told me not to indulge in these dreams about writing because nothing would come of it.'

'Well, you've proved him wrong.'

'I suppose. No, no, we all have. If I tell him, it must be about all of us.'

Emily winces. 'Very well, then. If you must. But just tell him about you first. Get him used to the idea.'

Proved him wrong: yes, so they have. Was that one of the forces that drove the pen, Charlotte wonders. And why is it that, taking up a copy of her book and a sheaf of press reviews – making sure to include a bad one – she still experiences a thrill of fear as she knocks on the study door?

Perhaps because the person doing this isn't Branwell.

Afterwards the scene imprints itself on her memory so neatly, as something to be recalled, smiled over, recounted to Mary Taylor – a story to be dined out on, in fact, if she were a diner-out – that it begins to seem like a scene from her own fiction. And yet at the time she really does live it. Papa is reading a devotional work, sharp nose a few inches from the text as if sniffing out false doctrine.

'Papa, I wanted you to know something. I have – I have been writing a book.'

'Have you, my dear?' No movement.

'Yes – and I would be pleased if you would look at it.'

'Now, you know my eyes are unequal to manuscript.'

'No, Papa, it's printed.'

Now the spectacles come flashing round. 'I hope, Charlotte, you have not been involving yourself in silly expense. For a thing like this—'

'No, Papa, quite the reverse, I shall be in profit. Let me read you a couple of reviews. This is from the *Era*: "For power of thought and expression, we do not know its rival among modern productions."' I wrote it, she thinks, while you lay blind and helpless. 'And this is from the *Examiner*. "There can be no question but that *Jane Eyre* is a very clever book. Indeed it is a book of decided power."' Power. Perhaps that was why she was afraid to come in here: afraid of revealing her power. 'This is the book.' She places the first volume of *Jane Eyre* in Papa's unsteady hand.

Silence from the study all afternoon. Then, news. Martha Brown brings it. Mr Brontë invites his daughters to have tea with him. Exchanging glances, they cross the two yards of hall to pay the visit.

And Papa, rising to greet them, still has his finger in the first volume, very near the end. And this is where no fiction could begin to equal the infinitely wry reality.

'Children,' Papa says, with urbane confidentiality, 'Charlotte has been writing a book – and, do you know, it is very much better than I expected.'

Should they tell Branwell? No one actually voices the question, but it is in the air of the parsonage; it pervades and hums like the winter draughts. Though they keep the books and the reviews out of his way – partly because in blackest mood he is prone to hurling things that come to hand on to the floor or into the fire – it is just possible that he knows. If so, he has nothing to say on the matter. In any case his attention slides away, like butter on a griddle, from anything but his own sorrows. Papa rigorously avoids all mention of their books when Branwell is about, so that seems to be the lead to follow. And it would reveal an unseemly bitterness, Charlotte reflects, to point out that where the slightest achievement of Branwell was proclaimed loudly enough to make the rafters ring, the greater achievements of his sisters are kept quiet: so as not to disturb him.

Just lately, though, there have been signs of hope: if not of improvement, then of Branwell not getting noticeably worse. He is quiet and maudlin, rather than noisy and maudlin. Papa lets him sleep alone again. And then comes the memorable night.

They have been gathered around the table as usual, Anne reading out from her novel in progress: Charlotte feeling uncomfortable. It is well done, it is very well done, but this account of a drunkard's decline, so bare, so inescapable – should Anne do it? Somehow it is like watching someone you love grinding away at a task until their hands bleed. But Anne says quietly, firmly, that she is the very one to do it. And then, perennial owls, inhabiters of the late-night spaces, they go up to bed. Something makes Anne, brushing out her hair, go and glance in at Branwell's room. Easy enough, as the horrors or *delirium tremens* leave him unable to bear a closed door. So she hears the subdued crackle, sees the curling ribbons of flame.

Charlotte is preparing for bed when the cry comes: '*Quick, Branwell's set his bedclothes on fire, they're burning, I can't wake him up.*' It is at once terrible and terribly unsurprising. Emily is there before her. The room is full of stinking smoke. Emily finds Branwell's arm, turns about so it is over her shoulder and hauls him out of the burning bed. The offending candle slides off the counterpane innocently, gone out. Emily drops Branwell in the corner, whips off the smouldering bedclothes, beats and treads them down, then runs to fetch water. On the floorboards Branwell, blind and lost, curls round like a dog in a basket. They step around and over him, mopping and tidying. Mopping all over again when he gapes and unleashes a barrage of sick. Then, at last, nudge and persuade and hoist him back into bed, settling him on his side in case of further vomiting. All this in whispering miming near-silence, so as not to disturb Papa, who fears fire so morbidly he will not even have curtains at the windows.

They pause at the bedroom door to look back and make sure, laden with noisome bucket and sheets, hair straggling round their smut-streaked faces, and this is when Anne says, in her quiet solemn way: 'Here we see the celebrated Currer, Ellis and Acton Bell relaxing at home, in enjoyment of their fame.' And the laughter that seizes them all is so wild, so virulent that they have to bite their lips and stuff knuckles into their mouths as they scurry downstairs, where they can finally let it out: with such snorts, shrieks and wails that if anyone were listening, they might think they were inconsolably crying.

Who are the Bells? This, Mr Williams reports, is a question much discussed in society. Again, unthinkable. The year 'forty-eight has brought so much of stirring and alarming moment: the newspapers throb with the march of the Chartists, revolutions on the Continent, kings fleeing, flags and blood. Such an unimportant question to set beside these – yet, it seems, not so. And not so entirely separate from those great overturnings. Something about these mysterious Bells, passionate voices from the north, shares the temper of the times. One popular solution, Mr Williams writes, is that the Bells are three self-educated brothers, weavers in a Yorkshire mill. Others contend that they are women – and not always, as they know from the reviews, with approval. Passionate voices, where there should be decorous cooings . . . And of course neither does Mr Williams nor Mr Smith know who the Bells are – nothing beyond the fact that their letters go to a parsonage in the West Riding.

But at last the mystery is no longer an innocent one. It comes home to Haworth with the morning post, envenomed.

'We've got to stop being the Bells,' Charlotte announces after breakfast; and from the way Emily starts it is as if someone has cracked a whip over her head.

Mr Newby has recently and promptly published Anne's second novel, *The Tenant of Wildfell Hall*, and has been promoting it with diligence. He has even secured its publication in America – as a new novel by Currer Bell, the author of *Jane Eyre*. Who is also probably, Mr Newby's publicity is suggesting, the author of *Wuthering Heights*. A letter has come winging, and stinging, from Smith, Elder & Co., politely demanding to know what the blue blazes is going on. They can hardly imagine that Currer Bell would go behind their back in any such underhand way but if they could have his categorical assurances . . .

'But it's not your fault,' Anne protests. 'It's our Mr Newby being – well, being the way he is. I don't think he means any harm. He's just rather too inventive—'

'He is doing harm, whether he means it or not,' says Charlotte. 'Harm to our reputations. If this goes on, no one will trust us as writers any more. As long as we hide our identities, we run this risk. We will have to come out and say who we are.'

Emily scowls. 'Oh, I know what this is. Look at me, love me, love me, please—'

'This is our livelihood,' Charlotte snaps. 'And it's our life.'

'Speak for yourself.'

'Very well, I do, yes, I speak for myself when I say writing is my life. This is what we fought for. We struggled to be free of governessing or schoolteaching and dependence, to reach out beyond, and this – this prize came in our way, and I for one am not going to let it go. I'm certainly not going to be swindled out of it. I'll shout my real name from the top of St Paul's before I do that.'

Emily gathers Anne's arm. 'Come away, Anne. Don't be afraid – but Charlotte's gone a little mad—'

'No.' Gently but firmly, Anne detaches herself. 'No, Emily, I don't want to be swindled, and surely you don't either. I'm proud of my work. I know it has weaknesses aplenty, but still I'm proud of it, and I want to go on. What do you suppose we should do, Charlotte?'

Charlotte hesitates, watching them. Sensation rather like that when the night wind dies down: the braced stone and timber of the house relaxes, creaking; a palpable alteration of power.

'In order to stop these lies,' she says, 'and make sure all parties involved know where they stand, we need to *prove* that the Bells are separate people.'

'We weren't, once,' Emily says, drifting to the window. An insane Haworth summer day is out there – a battle of sun, raincloud, hail.

'So we must go to London. We will have to introduce ourselves in the flesh to our publishers. I dare say this would – this would have come in time whatever happened. We couldn't remain anonymous for ever.'

'That depends how much you want to,' says Emily, her voice muffled by the glass.

'Well, I don't mind doing it,' Anne says. 'At least, I do, but I'll pretend otherwise. I've never even been to London before – so bearding these lions in their den will just be an added novelty. Or terror.'

'Oh, if it comes to lions, that really should be us, you know,' Charlotte says. 'Literary lions, ready to be lionized and made much of—'

'Stop it,' cries Emily. 'Don't make it worse. Anne, think – think what you're doing.'

'I have thought, Emily,' says Anne. 'Even before this, I've given the matter a lot of thought.' Her face is still and grave as she adds: 'I don't act on impulse, you know.'

'So you're going to go and present yourself like an exhibit – like a calling-card, to be peered at and pawed and tossed aside—'

'I don't see it like that,' Anne says; and this time the shifting seems to vibrate through the earth. 'I'm just going there to be myself. I'm not Acton Bell, after all: I'm Anne Brontë. But I'd be much happier if you came too, Emily. Won't you? It would clear up everything about the Bells then. And it would help me if you did come. You've travelled, after all, as I haven't.'

'Dear God, now I know you've gone mad. You're trying to win me with flattery,' says Emily bleakly, white and stark. 'Do what you want. Let me be.' Like a cat going to hunt she walks out.

'Papa, we must go to London, Anne and I. We have urgent business with the publishers.'

'London? But, my dear, I can't come with you. I'm not equal to such a journey nowadays.'

'No, Papa, there's no need. You forget I have travelled to the Continent on my own before now.'

'To be sure.' Papa looks, for some reason, very faintly sour at that.

'Well, you must be sure and look after little Anne. Do you start early in the morning?'

'No, Papa – we think to go today – after tea. We've sent our box on to Keighley station. We'll take the night train. We would have gone earlier, only – only we had to talk the matter over with Emily.'

'I see.' As so often, one wonders how much Papa does see: whether there is any cataract over that sharp mind. 'Well, this is all very sudden – but I dare say I must get used to you surprising me nowadays. There remains the question of where to stay. You cannot do better, you know, than the Chapter Coffee House again. I know of no better place in London.'

It's the only place in London you know, thinks Charlotte, and for a peculiar moment feels older than her father.

Emily walks with them as far as the White Lion, sharing their wetting, at least. The Haworth summer day is ending in rage and nonsense, managing a gale, a thunderstorm, and even a spatter of sleet all at once – as if to say, *You won't get this in your precious London, will you?*

'Now promise—' Emily begins, then bites her lip. 'Sorry. You have.'

'We won't say anything more about us than is needed to clear the legal position,' Charlotte says, trying to keep the weariness out of her voice. 'I promise.'

'We'll come back as soon as we can,' Anne says, reaching up to kiss Emily's cold, smooth face.

'Once you've done this,' Emily says, with a sort of twitch that could be a smile or a shudder, 'you can never really come back.'

At Leeds they decide to act on their celebrity and buy first-class tickets. They sit, wet skirts steaming, in the intimidating comfort of buttoned leather and varnish. Charlotte expected the night-train to be a long rumble through anonymous darkness, but every town and village seems at least half awake. Lights spill down valley-sides, platforms ring with urgent voices, horses stamp, milk-churns roll and clash apocalyptically. An uplifted lantern reveals a porter's shouting, laughing face in unforgettable detail, every last wrinkle and bristle, a sudden portrait in pen and ink. At last there is a falling away of hills, and the railway proceeds without so much triumphant strenuousness of cuttings and tunnels and bridges: leaving the north. Charlotte and Anne lean against each other, each yawn and dry-blink an admission that sleep is impossible.

'So many people,' Anne says, as they pass another tight melee of roofs and chimneys. 'Of course you know there are many people in the world, but you don't truly think of it – those thousands upon thousands out there . . . Even if you weren't like us – I mean, if you were very gregarious, you could only ever know the most insignificant little number in your life.'

'In person, yes. But it's rather different for us, with our books. Through them we can be known by many more people than we will ever meet. That's a thought, isn't it?'

'Known by,' echoes Anne. 'That's all right. I prefer the passive . . . And, of course, judged by them too. That's harder. But it spurs you on. I hope people won't think my two are all I'm capable of. I feel I'm still half a prentice-worker. I want to go much further, deeper . . .' She squeezes Charlotte's arm tentatively. 'I know you think I've gone wrong with *Wildfell Hall*. But I had to write it.'

'It's just – so painful. So unsparing. The way the man goes downhill . . . *Is* it Branwell?'

'Perhaps. In the sense that it's all of us – when we let go.'

Oh, thinks Charlotte, I won't let go, not I. Travelling towards London revives old prickly memories: of a time when London was only a stop on the way to her real destination, her life's destination – Brussels. Oh, no, she won't let go. She has been fiercely holding on for a long time now, like someone gripping a piece of solid wreckage, tirelessly paddling: only the most unequivocal sighting of dry land will make her let go of it.

In the kitchen Emily feeds Keeper, giving him the best pieces of mutton she saved from her own dinner. When Tabby takes herself off grumbling to bed, Emily stays there, on the flagged floor, with her arm around the dog's thick neck.

'You see why I can't go along with it,' she says, her voice cool and conversational in the summer-dark silence. She watches her fingers playing in his fur. 'Fingers. Sooner or later it would mean people getting their fingers into your head.' She shivers, then puts her face into his warm hide and howls. 'I didn't wave them goodbye. They went, and I let them go without waving goodbye, on purpose.' Finally she wipes the tears from her face, then fills a basin, washes her eyes and cheeks gently but thoroughly, so not a suggestion of a stain can be seen.

She finds Branwell in the dining-room, half dressed. He has been asleep most of the day, after an epic gin-spree.

'Cold in here, I want a fire. Where's Tabby, where's Martha?'

'Gone to bed. You can't have a fire made up at this time.'

'Why not? We pay them, don't we? They eat our food . . .' He wipes his runny nose on his sleeve. There is a continual catarrhal drizzle in his voice now. His eyes have such a peeled, pulsing look that it is as if being open were not natural to them: as if waking were the tearing of a wound. 'Where the devil are Charlotte and Anne, anyhow?'

'Gone to London.'

He gives her a sour look. 'You're not good at jokes, Emily.'

'I could make you a fire if you like. But I think the cold's inside.'

'Old, that's what I feel,' Branwell says, reaching into his open shirt to scratch his white, bony chest. 'Old – and yet like a baby, with all the dragging travail of life still to come. I wish Aunt were here.'

'Do you?'

'She would make me feel ashamed of myself.'

'Is that what you need?'

'I don't know. Papa can't do it. Poor old man, he still loves me too much. The other night, you know, I actually raised my hand to hit him. Didn't do it. Do you hate me, Emily?'

The question surprises her. 'No, I don't,' she says, fully and honestly.

He smiles at the ashes, an awful smile as if an embedded hook is tugging at his lip. 'Charlotte hates me.'

Emily laughs a little, takes up the scuttle. 'No, no, Branwell. Charlotte envies you.'

He stares after her. 'My God, Emily, you really are not good at jokes.'

Stepping out into London's streets, Anne thinks: I couldn't possibly have done this without Charlotte. And then: I've gone backwards.

Because after all what about Thorp Green? She went there alone, very young, and there she held down a demanding job longer and more successfully than any of the others could manage.

Ah, but remember how it all ended. Nothing to crow about there.

Nothing to blame herself for, either. Surely. But deep inside, when she thinks of Thorp Green, a great black mark is scored across a white page, the point digging through and tearing.

Since then she has been remade as Acton Bell, she has reconstructed herself with words, most excitingly and satisfyingly. But that was done at the desk, in remoteness. It is a shock to think that she was ever a person who went out into the world – like these uncountable people, going about their strange errands in these giant, glaring, overused streets: catching her eye and for a moment seeming to fix it and her,

her strangeness, her incapacity to belong to this. And that's why she clings close to Charlotte and almost wants to cry out to them: *It's all right, I'm with her.*

Because this is the thing about Charlotte: she does it. She is as shy as any of them in a way, visibly suffers the same anguish on entering a roomful of strangers, cannot produce any of those graceful nothings that Ellen Nussey manages so comfortably. And she is, besides, terribly conscious of how she looks, in a way Emily never is and that Anne has taught herself to get over. She turns her face about to hide the set of her mouth where she has a protruding tooth, and that makes her look more awkward than she is. And yet she does it: she carries on. She bespoke their rooms at the Chapter Coffee House this morning: she blushingly but firmly insisted that they have hot water for washing in the face of the yawning maid, who claimed they would have to sleep a night there first; she stops someone to ask directions to Cornhill. She would probably deny that she is brave, and indeed probably never feel it. But she acts as if she is. Perhaps that's the secret of courage.

Though it is a Saturday, the premises of Smith, Elder & Co., booksellers and publishers, are open and busy. The shop at the front is full: books being asked for, brought down from high shelves, inspected, wrapped. Anne can't help a feeling that, making no purchase or order, they really have no business there. It is Charlotte who grabs a passing shop-boy's arm and says: 'We wish to see Mr Smith, if you please.'

He frowns at them. 'What name?'

Ah, the crux of the matter. Anne almost smiles to herself, but the shop-boy's stare cows her.

'We would prefer not to give our names as yet,' Charlotte says. 'We wish to see Mr Smith on a private matter.'

The boy grunts. 'Well, I'll see.'

He is gone a long time. They glance over some of the books stacked on the counter.

'None of ours,' Anne whispers.

'All sold out, of course. Why are we whispering?'

The boy is back: with him, a gentleman. A very gentlemanly one too, young, well dressed, whiff of cologne – but he does not look at all encouraging and in sum this is, thinks Anne, a rather dreadful mistake. Again she almost feels like laughing. The Bells, the books, the reviews and letters and banker's drafts, perhaps they dreamed or imagined them all: perhaps they were playing Gondal or Angria all the time.

But no, watch Charlotte, see how she does it.

'Did you wish to see me, ma'am?'

'Is it Mr Smith?'

'It is.' A smooth lustreless civility: there might be anything behind it.

'Thank you for seeing us, Mr Smith. Perhaps if I show you this letter – from you – it will help you to understand our business with you.'

A letter to Currer Bell – opened. Mr Smith looks up from it sharply. 'Yes, I wrote this. Where did you get it?'

'It was addressed to me,' Charlotte says. 'I am the Miss Brontë to whom all your letters have been care of . . . and I am also Currer Bell.' Anne has never seen anyone's scalp lift so clearly, so forcibly, as Mr Smith's of Smith, Elder & Co.: it is like a sigh of recognition made visible. 'This is my sister, Miss Anne Brontë. A.B. You see? We have come to give you ocular proof that there are at least two of us.'

'Currer Bell. Acton Bell. Great merciful heavens, but this is magnificent!'

In Mr Smith's smile – it produces quite beautiful dimples – in his sudden radiance and warmth and the way he reaches to seize their hands, Anne suddenly sees William Weightman again. And for a moment she is afraid: it is as if someone in a far-off locked room is rattling at the door; and she is afraid, too, that following Charlotte will not help her. But then she shakes Mr Smith's hand, and William Weightman and all his works disappear. Mr Smith's hands are square and brisk, they are business. Business, yes, better.

'Well, I was never more agreeably surprised. Currer – of course, certainly, I'll be quiet. Come, come . . .'

Mr Smith conducts them to a little cramped panelled office at the rear of the building, with a sooty skylight above. A clerk finishing a letter squeezes himself out to make room for them.

'A thousand apologies if I was less than forthcoming at first, but I simply could not imagine what the matter was. I never imagined that one of my most valued authors was waiting to see me. My dear Miss Brontë, Miss Anne, you should have written to let me know, I could have prepared a much more suitable reception for you.'

'It was all done in haste,' Charlotte says, 'and in response to your letter. About that shocking villain – no, Anne, he is – Mr Newby, and the lies he is telling about us. As you see, we are not one and the same. Currer, Ellis and Acton Bell are three sisters. Ellis is our sister Emily, who—' Anne presses Charlotte's foot with her own, warningly. 'Well, Ellis wishes to remain anonymous. As do we all . . .' No, thinks Anne, you don't, Charlotte, even if you hardly know it yourself yet. 'But not at the price of being swindled or, worse, appearing to collude in a swindle.'

'I have written Mr Newby,' Anne says, surprising herself with the calm sound of her own voice, 'insisting that he stop these misleading representations when advertising my book – but I get no answer.'

'Ah. Of course, I cannot comment on the professional standards of a fellow-publisher, but I *can* say that your statement does not entirely surprise me,' says Mr Smith, with a dry look. 'But come, let us put that unpleasant topic aside for now, and let me express again my extreme delight in actually meeting you at last. Plainly, yes, you have chosen so far to avoid the eye of publicity – but can I dare to hope that this visit marks a change in your position? At the very least, let me introduce you to Mr Williams – our reader. The one who first alerted me to the existence of *Jane Eyre* . . .'

Mr Williams, whiskered, lank, much older than his employer, is as worn and hesitant as Mr Smith is bright and decisive. But he looks as honoured as he says he is to meet the Messrs Bell, and listens to their halting talk about their books and their lives with a kind of humble eagerness that makes Anne realise— Well, it makes her realise. This is it: true, real, not Gondal; they are famous authors. And now it is as if all those thousands and thousands of people she thought about on the train journey are stepping out of their houses and throwing open their windows and turning in the streets all to gaze, gaze at them in curiosity.

Alarming. Is it unbearable? Probably not. Watch Charlotte, see how she does it.

'But now, let's see, while you are in town you simply must not miss the Royal Academy exhibition. And then there's the Opera—'

'Really, sir, we intended to stay only as long as it took to see you and to see Mr Newby about our business, and then go home again.'

'Oh, but, Miss Brontë, now you are here – at the very least you will allow me to introduce my mother and sisters. They will never forgive me if they hear they missed the opportunity to meet the Bells. And not just them – there are many others, believe me, not least Mr Thackeray who would be transported at the thought of meeting you. Trust me, it could be done with a certain degree of incognito . . .'

You can't have a certain degree of incognito, Anne thinks, it's an absolute. But never mind. Watch Charlotte: perching on the edge of her seat, covering her mouth with her hand, looking up searchingly and doubtfully into Mr George Smith's close-shaved handsome face.

Ironing. Though they are fresh-laundered, everyone's clothes, Emily notices, have a different smell when you iron them. Papa's shirts have a kind of bristling outdoor smell. Branwell's smell, somehow, sad.

She wonders what they are doing now, Charlotte and Anne – then catches herself up. She does not want to wonder. She doesn't want to pay what they have done the tribute of attention. Let it be. It's nothing beside these fascinating ripples of white linen and the flat-iron, boat-like, steaming across them.

Saturday. Papa asks Mr Nicholls to join him for tea and, as Emily is just passing with arms full of laundry, extends the invitation to her. She goes along, though she could well spare it. Mr Nicholls is very well in his way, but she has nothing to say to him. Luckily he and Papa have plenty to talk of. Papa is all twinkling humour.

'You will have your work cut out, sir, for Haworth traditions die hard. Oh, I admire you, you have my full approval, but I would not care to square up to the washerwomen myself.'

'I hope to make them see what they are doing,' says Mr Nicholls, gruffly, frowning. Such black hair, brows, eyes, and then the clerical black he is wearing – it is too much of black, the dose of him is too strong, he needs adulterating. 'Spreading their washing out to dry on the tombs does not, I admit, hurt anyone. But there is disrespect in it. Oh, the dead can't know about it, they reply. But the living do, the living of all ages and classes see it, and must conclude that we don't care about the dead, to let this happen.' There is a dogmatic rhythm to his voice, which he seems to become suddenly aware of; he stirs his tea awkwardly, with a great clatter, looks over at Emily – or rather, glances at her and then either side of her. 'Miss Brontë is from home?'

'She is, sir,' Papa says, still twinkling, 'gone on a – a visit; and Anne likewise. I expect them back in a day or two.'

Mr Nicholls's eyes glide away. And Emily thinks: You didn't ask about Anne. You weren't interested in where she is. Oh. Can it be? She makes a swift review of Mr Nicholls's behaviour when Charlotte is around, his promptness in jumping out of chairs, opening doors . . . Oh. For a moment she almost feels sorry for him – for the magnitude of his mistake. If it were possible for her to talk to him, she would say: No good, Mr Nicholls. You are much too near. We can't love the near, we Brontës. With us, only the unreachable stands a chance.

'It's only the *Barber*, I'm afraid,' Mr Smith says, as they ascend the staircase at the Opera. So wide, Charlotte thinks, you could drive a wagon down it. She has never imagined that a staircase could be this wide. She pictures an architect planning it, and someone looking at the draft and saying, 'How can you have a staircase that wide, or why?' Mr Smith has chivalrously taken Charlotte and Anne's arms. That is the kind of man he is, though they are so undeniably drab and odd in their poky day-dresses: one glittering, jewel-crusted lady has already stopped in her tracks to stare, to take them in from head to foot. On either side of them float the polite Misses Smith, naked powdered shoulders gleaming, as if they are taking a bath in satin.

'I beg your pardon – what barber?'

Mr Smith licks his lips. 'I'm sorry, I didn't explain. The piece tonight is Rossini's *Barber of Seville*, which some people find a little stale now. Ah, good evening, how do you do – let me introduce, Miss Brown, Miss Anne Brown. Thank you, never better.' Their *incognito*: she has insisted on it, partly out of consideration for Emily. 'All these false names, Miss Brontë – I'm afraid you will hardly remember who you really are.'

She looks about her as they enter their box: at the great throng of fashionable people. So many, and you can never know them. She looks at the handsome, attentive man at her side, remembers or reminds herself why he is attentive. She shakes her head. 'Oh, I'm not likely to forget that, Mr Smith.'

Sunday, day for Branwell of opportunity, day of Papa doing what Papa does and the house empty and freedom – a little freedom and space to plan out the means of survival of the next day or two, meaning drink if it is to be got and opium likewise from Betty Hardacre's druggist shop, their proportion or combination to be decided by the response to the request—

'I shouldn't, Branwell,' says John Brown, lurking shadowy and shrinking in his own hall, as if he were an intruder in his house instead of living in it. 'By rights, I shouldn't. You're fearful liverish already by the look of you. I can let you have sixpence, I can't say more. By rights . . .' He keeps clinging virtuously to this phrase, John Brown who has always liked drink and bawdy and subversion; it is sad and absurd to see his lips pursing over it.

'By rights you and I and half the sinners in this parish should be roasting over a slow fire,' Branwell says. 'But nothing goes by rights in this world, John, as you well know, so what do you say to a shilling, a shilling which I can faithfully promise will be repaid you tomorrow or at the latest . . . ?'

Ah, God bless you. Yes, sometimes they give in from the sheer boredom of hearing your excuses. Turning to go, Branwell stumbles a little. Extraordinary thing. Could have sworn there was only one step at John Brown's door.

Emily opens her writing-box, mends a pen, and then interrogates her mind and circumstances. Why won't it come? How did it come before? All she can remember is a stealthy combination, the people of Gondal and their hatred and passions fretting her mind as she walked up on the moors and then slowly she found them slipping through the membrane and changing as they did so: Catherine, Heathcliff, shapes. That membrane is the blessed intervention between you and the rest of life. You only let certain things through it: and only if you have a choice.

But writing, no, it won't come at the moment. Again, it's probably to do with what they are doing, on the distant isle of London. Things are no doubt being determined there. Currer and Acton Bell are being exposed and examined, and soon there will surely be the same requirement of Ellis Bell.

No, that's not what she wants. And, yes, she can imagine Charlotte's urging: why write at all, then, why publish? And all she can think of in reply is an image. It comes from Gondal, from the misty, dripping heights to the north of Regina: where there looms above the treeline a vast slab-like profile carved into the rock, and no one knows who set it there, or how; and no one can even agree on whether the giant features are those of a man or a woman.

'No, really, I don't feel equal to meeting Mr Thackeray,' Charlotte says, as Mr Smith takes her in to dinner. 'You must understand I'm not used to – well, any of this.' This including the dining-room of the Smith home in Westbourne Place, the acre of mahogany, the palisades of silver. Emblem of difference – that these wine-bottles indolently reclining in the ice-bucket can be a normal part of a normal evening. She thinks of Branwell. The thought is both empty and jagged, like a broken egg-shell. 'And as for meeting him after I made that colossal blunder with my dedication – no, I think I would run screaming.'

Admiring Thackeray, flattered that the author of *Vanity Fair* had written admiringly to the author of *Jane Eyre*, Charlotte addressed him in the preface to the second edition and dedicated the book to him. Reward of vanity, perhaps: she soon found out that Thackeray's wife, like Mr Rochester's in her novel, had gone insane and been incarcerated – in a humane asylum rather than an attic, to be sure, but the coincidence was strong enough to set tongues wagging. Perhaps Currer Bell, or Jane Eyre, or both, had been governess to the Thackeray family, and that explained it all . . . Not many people, she gathers, were that credulous. Still, even thinking of it makes her cheeks kindle and her tongue stick to her palate.

'He would be very sorry if you did, for you have my word he was not in the least put out by what was an absolutely innocent mistake. If anything he was more troubled on your behalf.' Mr Smith hands her to her seat. Cutlery multiplies before her: how much will she be expected to eat? She glances over at Anne, reassures herself that she is comfortable with Mr Smith's mother, a bird-neat, unruffled little matriarch who probably has eyes in the front, back, sides and top of her head. 'Thackeray is first and last a gentleman. Between ourselves,' Mr Smith leans in confidingly, 'I could wish him sometimes a little less of the gentleman and more of the writer. Like a graceful amateur, he shrugs off what he can do, as if it's of no account. Luckily serial publication pins him down and makes him produce a *Vanity Fair* whether he likes it or not. How do you feel about serial publication, Miss Brontë? It isn't a prerequisite, but it has worked so well for Thackeray, and of course Dickens . . .'

Charlotte is shaking her head. 'No. I couldn't do it. I couldn't say anything if I knew that people were waiting for me to speak.'

'You prefer to startle them?' Though a manservant hovers, Mr Smith is pouring the wine himself. But all of these things he does with no fuss or flourish: his body performs elegantly while his mind is attentive, fixed. His gaze also. He has rather beautifully heavy-lidded eyes, which reveal the whole shape of the eyeball; and meanwhile the cheek-dimples lurk, ready for amusement.

'Perhaps. I only know that writing that way there would be too much . . .' she thinks of Emily '. . . exposure.' He looks keenly interested: indeed, he looks keenly interested in her all the time. But as an author: I know that. I won't let go for you, thinks Charlotte.

* * *

I must try and remember all this for Emily, thinks Anne. Vermicelli soup, cod in oyster sauce, whitebait, saddle of mutton, stuffed shoulder of veal, sweetbreads, asparagus – remember it, without feeling sick – celery sauce, currant sauce, French salad, jellied fruits, meringue . . .

'You tek the master's tray in,' Tabby says to Martha Brown. The kitchen is awash with greasy steam. 'I'll finish pots. D'you suppose we shall see owt of his lordship?'

'I doubt it,' Emily says. 'I couldn't get a word out of him. No, there's no need to lay the table just for me, Tabby. I'll eat here.'

On Papa's tray, the three thick slices of boiled beef, Tabby's special grey mashed or mushed potatoes, a slice of thinly buttered bread. Emily's is the same, with the addition, forbidden to Papa's delicate digestion, of a batter-pudding, which, as she made it herself without Tabby's intervention, is light and golden rather than having the consistency and hue of an old shoe. Tabby does thunderous things with the pots and the sink: as she gets slower and less capable, she compensates with noise. Keeper and Flossy wait worshipfully for the meat they know they will get. For several minutes the resemblance of this to every other Sunday pleases Emily and she feels everything in its right place and the feeling is happiness like clear cold water. Then the thought of the absentees and what they are doing seeps in like a slow stain.

'You've hardly et owt,' Tabby says, as Emily nudges her aside at the sink.

'Enough. Have yours, Tabby. I'll do this.'

'That pan'll want soaking first.'

No, it won't. Not if you tackle it this way, fierce, scrub till your knuckles bleed, more scalding water from the copper, clean till it hurts.

'I can't see,' Anne remarks. They have run the gamut of the National Gallery and the Royal Academy exhibition, and what she means is that after taking in so much through the eyes her capacity has run out. Torchlight, leopards, seas, pearls, undergrowth, faces: especially the faces, seeming to want to tell her so much. Can't, simply can't see them any more.

'It's tiring,' agrees Charlotte, and her face is indeed stark and chalky. But you know somehow that it's different for her, that she wants to carry on and not lose a single moment's opportunity.

'I keep thinking of Branwell,' Anne says. 'He would have loved all of this.'

Charlotte makes no comment. Sometimes it's as if she doesn't know who Branwell is.

Boarding the train again: London clanging and swarming indifferently about them, unchanged by their brief presence. And yet not so: in spite of themselves they have created a little stir that will ripple outward. Perhaps Emily was right, Charlotte thinks, and after this things can never be the same. The morning light has a splintery, hard look as if designed for a universal headache. Porters hurl their bags like weapons, and the shutting of the carriage doors sounds like a series of explosions. She tries to calculate how many hours' sleep she has had in the past four days: probably adds up to about one full night. Certainly by yesterday her consciousness was curiously thin, as if experience were being transcribed on tissue-paper. Appropriate perhaps for their visit to Mr Newby in Mortimer Street: Anne went in mild but determined, Charlotte armed for a knock-down fight – but somehow, faced with the pale, bland, ever-talking nonentity that was T. C. Newby, nothing much got done. He was so delighted to meet them at last, so ready to agree with them that his conduct in advertising the Bells' novels misleadingly was shocking, not to be tolerated, must stop at once . . . When they left, loaded with courtesies and assurances, Charlotte had a feeling of trying to grasp wet soap. She still doesn't trust him, but Anne is prepared to give him the benefit of the doubt.

'And not everyone,' as she said, 'can be like your Mr Smith.'

Charlotte wants to say: He's not *my* Mr Smith. Though he is much in her mind. A revelation: that compact, spruce intelligence, that pleasant space he makes where business meets art. After dinner he sat by her and told her about his first reading of *Jane Eyre*: how he had gone into his study on a Sunday morning after breakfast expecting to give the manuscript a cursory look-through, and how the shape of Sunday dissolved around him as he read on. 'I missed lunch. I missed my ride. I went in to dinner only to bolt my food without a word and hurry back to the study.' Humorous rays around his eyes. 'My poor mother and my sisters thought I must be offended with them . . .' Very flattering. Very flattering the whole whirling, bemusing, unreal visit. And luckily she was too sensible and too old to be *too* flattered.

She settles herself in the carriage beside Anne, noticing the odour about their clothes, the sooty London smell that will fade as they travel north. And she groans: such a long, long way to go.

⋆ ⋆ ⋆

'How could you? How could you do it when I explicitly told you *not* to – how? Well, deliberately, through malice, of course. The only explanation.' Emily's chair slams backwards, overturns, as she stalks out.

Well, Charlotte tells herself, you should have known you wouldn't get away with it. In London it just slipped out – *we are three sisters* – but she had allowed herself to believe, or hope, that that would be the end of it. And since they got home everything has gone so well. Emily, after a short spell of coolly ignoring their return – exactly like a cat – was at last curious, even eager to know what went on in London. 'Yes, tell,' she said, 'tell properly.' And so, lying on the rug, she listened to it all, eyes mistily fixed as if on an inner stage, lips curling, just as she absorbs Papa's memories of Ireland or Tabby's tales of phantoms and blood. And finally she said: 'You see, I didn't need to go at all. You brought it back for me.'

But now – ill luck. Kindly Mr Williams has sent on some reviews of *The Tenant of Wildfell Hall*, with a thoughtful covering letter asking all three sisters not to be diverted from their artistic path either by praise or blame . . . As she read it out, Charlotte felt the sweat start to her brow: saw Emily's head go up. She tried to hurry on, but it was no good.

'Three sisters. You told them. You told them about me.' Scrape of the chair. Emily would not listen to her. Should have known you wouldn't get away with it. And now Emily is gone, with a bang of the front door.

Charlotte says: 'I'd better go after her. But it really did just slip out, you know that.'

'I don't think there's any need,' Anne says, faintly smiling. 'Emily's like wood: she burns fast and burns clean.'

'All the same, I'd better . . .' She is not unwilling to get out of the house, anyhow. Since her return from London it seems smaller, and not cosily so: more like a soaked garment that has shrunk on your body.

She opens the front door to find Mr Nicholls coming up the steps: quite noiseless for so sturdy a man. He gives her that lifted, piercing look that so annoys her – as if it is a tremendous and inexplicable surprise to see her about Haworth parsonage.

'Miss Brontë. You're seeking your sister? She has just taken the moor path.'

'Thank you, Mr Nicholls.'

He steps aside to let her past with excessive emphasis, as if they are in the narrowest of passages. Then he surprises her by saying: 'Can I be of assistance to you in any way, Miss Brontë?'

She does consider the question, because it is so curious a one: she sets herself to try and imagine any possible situation in which Mr Nicholls could be of assistance. But he seems to take her effort as a snubbing silence, and goes frowning in.

It costs her a lot of breath to catch up with long-legged, furious Emily. Yes, furious still, as is clear from her whipped-round face and whipped-out stinging remark. 'So, who is it you're trying to impress this time?'

Charlotte does not answer. Or, rather, she answers in kind. 'It's all right to be afraid, you know, Emily. Everyone's afraid of something.'

Emily glares, but the glare comes from the bottom of a deep shaft of betrayal and grief: like a faithful dog suddenly beaten and cringing. And when she turns and strides on, Charlotte knows there is no hope of catching her up now.

Anne, left alone, sits with Flossy's elegant head on her knee and reads her reviews.

'Well, Flossy, listen to this. Apparently though I am powerful and even faithful to nature, I am also morbid, coarse-minded, and brutal, and addicted to offensive subjects, like all these Bells. What do you think of that?' She strokes the dog's soft ears, and the haze that covers her eyes and bends the printed words is quickly gone. The trick with disposing of tears is not to blink. She learned it a long time ago.

Emily is gone half the day. Charlotte finally tracks her to her bare little bedroom, where she is sitting hunched up on the bed, rubbing her long, stockinged feet.

'This is for you.' Charlotte holds out her hand. 'Look. A sprig of heather. I picked it for you.'

Emily shows her teeth. 'So a single sentimental gesture makes all well again.'

'It's been known to.' Charlotte sits down on the bed. 'Especially in novels. You must have walked a long way today.'

'All the way to London, where I declared to them all, there *is* no Ellis Bell, and disappeared in a puff of smoke.' Blindly Emily seizes Charlotte's hand and presses it hard against her cheeks and forehead as if it were a cold compress. 'That wasn't right – what I said to you. You're not really like that. I'm only afraid you don't care enough for yourself and you'll throw yourself away one day.'

'So, a sentimental explanation makes all well again,' Charlotte says, smiling, her voice a little shaky.

'And I'm afraid to write – to speak,' Emily says, ignoring this, studying the veins on the back of Charlotte's hand. 'Because now they're all ears. This will get better, though, won't it?'

'Everything will get better. Trust me.'

'Oh, I do. Always have. That's my trouble, perhaps. No, I don't mean that you let me down or anything like that, I mean that I leave things to you. A lot of what people call life I leave to you, Charlotte.' From the passage comes a sudden outbreak of tumbling, scuffling noise. 'Oh, Lord, that'll be him again. He had another of those peculiar little fits while you were away. Made him fall down. The horrors.'

Charlotte follows Emily out to the passage, and finds Branwell at the top of the stairs, holding grimly on to the wall. He looks dreadful: but, then, when someone habitually looks dreadful, you stop noticing it, or remarking degrees of dreadfulness.

'Damned dismal dark old hole. Look. Summer day, and dark as a, dark as . . . Lost my footing for a moment. Nearly went pitching down.' He jerks his head, twitching the great hanks of matted hair out of his eyes: how long must it be since he had that hair cut? 'What's the matter with you two?'

'Nothing, Branwell,' Charlotte says. 'We haven't been quarrelling.' And then wonders why she should say that.

Papa invites them – the three of them – to drink tea in his study. The absence of Aunt throbs like the socket of a drawn tooth.

'I am not sure, my dears, whether you agree, and would be glad to have the fruits of your observation – but I think I must call in Mr Wheelhouse again to attend Branwell. I know he and Branwell have not drawn well together, and to be sure he is not our much-missed Mr Andrew. Nevertheless, a doctor. And I feel the need of a doctor's counsel. But tell me with utmost frankness what you feel.'

'First you'll have to get Branwell to agree to seeing him at all,' Charlotte says. 'That won't be easy. He is so wild and irritable.'

'So he is . . . but lately his constitution seems so much undermined by his – his habits,' says Papa, carefully, 'that I doubt he would be able to put up a fight, as it were. If I insisted.'

'But what do you think the doctor can do, Papa?' Emily says. 'Stop him drinking?'

Her downrightness seems to set the tea-service trembling. Papa winces. 'A good doctor may help him towards a resolution of that problem – perhaps. But my concern is the damage done to his health by these practices. Just lately at night his breathing has alarmed me. It is not, I think, the mere stertorousness of intoxication, nor the accentuated respiration commonly associated with *delirium tremens*.'

Now Charlotte is alarmed: when Papa's polysyllables multiply, it means he is really ill at ease.

'There is the – the weakness for laudanum as well,' suggests Anne, softly. 'That may have its deleterious effect. But by all means, Papa, let us send for the doctor. It might be the thing that gives Branwell a jolt, and helps him alter his ways.'

'Someone must broach the subject.' Papa's spectacles glitter at Charlotte. 'Perhaps you could persuade him, my dear. You have always been closest to him.'

Charlotte's heart thumps. Why does she want to deny that? Why does it sound to her like an accusation?

'I'll try,' she murmurs. 'Is he in his room?'

'I believe he went out,' Papa says – adding hastily, 'He has had no money from me. He knows he may have a shilling on Monday and nothing before. And I have asked John Brown not to give him any likewise. As for the public houses . . .' They let the silence lie. Unlikely Branwell will find any credit there, as it is not long since the threat of a court summons came from a Halifax inn. Papa has paid the debt, and life in its ordinary outlandish way has gone on; only occasionally has Charlotte allowed herself a ghostly smile at the thought of this house once being the proposed Misses Brontë's School for Young Ladies.

She will wait, then. It isn't long before she hears the sound of the front door. She goes out to the hall and finds Branwell clinging to the table as if he were on the deck of a pitching ship. And for a moment anxiety gives way to the dull weary reflex: oh. Oh, he's drunk again.

How, though? And no smell of it.

'Guess what, Charlotte,' he says hoarsely. 'I've been for a walk. An actual walk. Rather taken it out of me. Billy Brown saw me and lent me an arm on the way home.' He smiles, and the effort sends a shudder through him, and his eyes are unbearable. 'Consequence of sedentary habits . . .'

All her carefully rehearsed approaches are abandoned. 'Branwell, you must see the doctor.'

'Really? What for?'

'So – so he can help you.'

'Oh, I want no doctor, Charlotte. They never helped anyone. Two classes of people: doctors and priests –' he lurches away from the table, bangs his fist on the study door, and shouts it '– doctors and bloody canting priests, they never helped anyone.' He sucks greedy, whistling breaths and moves towards the stairs, begins to haul himself up.

Charlotte follows, goes to put herself under his arm. He looks down at her. 'No. No, not now.' He detaches himself from her, and toils up alone.

Papa, after a little while, opens the study door with a look of surprised innocence. 'Well, my dear? Did you speak to Branwell about the matter?'

'He says no, Papa. But he is – he is not himself.'

'You have it exactly,' Papa says, with an eager catch in his voice. 'Not himself. So it must simply be done. I shall send for Dr Wheelhouse in the morning.'

The morning: when it all comes together. After breakfast Charlotte goes upstairs to find Tabby poking her head into Branwell's room.

'What I want to know is, will you be getting out of that bed before noon? Only Martha wants to change the linen.'

Branwell's voice in answer comes faint and peculiarly musical. 'Will I, Tabby – it's not a question of will any more. And Martha wouldn't care for this bed-linen, trust me.'

Turning, catching sight of Charlotte, Tabby growls and shakes her head. 'Eh, he's been sick in his bed again, I'll be bound.'

Charlotte edges past her and goes in. (How do you know that this time it is different? How do you know when a headache is gone?)

Branwell is sitting up in bed. His skin is white – pure, negative white, the white of moths and blind worms that never see the sun. He is looking down with interest at the large bloodstain that covers half his pillow. 'Just like a map, look. Like the map I made of the Glasstown Confederacy – do you remember?'

'Yes. I remember.' Her voice comes out rusty, as if she has not spoken for years. 'Oh, Branwell . . .' There is a rapping at the front door. 'That will be Dr Wheelhouse.'

'Will it now?' He gives her a look full of sad calculation. 'Ah. I'd run away if I could. But my attempt at standing on my feet this morning was discouraging.' He falls back against the blood-mapped pillow. 'To be sure, there's nowhere to run.'

Charlotte waits in the dining-room with the others while Dr

Wheelhouse – brisk, bullish, rather glib – makes his examination. There is a little shouting from the patient, even an obscenity or two. Emily, narrow-eyed, mouths the words 'Good for him.' Anne shakes her head. Papa stares at the fly-leaf of his Bible.

Dr Wheelhouse appears at the door. 'Sir – ladies. I have made a thorough examination—'

Papa leaps in. 'I suspect, my dear sir, my son was not a co-operative patient – but he has not been himself for some time. I will not disguise from you the excesses to which he is prone – you have been made aware of them in the past, of course – and I fear you will have found his constitution much weakened as a result.'

Dr Wheelhouse coughs. He is not as bullish as usual. 'Certainly, Mr Brontë has impaired his health by these – excesses. But his condition now – sir, ladies, I think you would wish me to be frank. The wasting of the patient's frame, and the condition of his lungs, indicate a consumption, far advanced, and increasingly rapid. I am sorry to say that Mr Brontë is dying.'

'Well, there was one clue,' Branwell says. 'Lately I haven't been doing all that ranting about wanting to end it all. Must have realised it was –' his chest rises quivering as he surmounts the word '– superfluous.'

'We didn't know,' says Charlotte, at his bedside. 'We couldn't tell—'

'How far gone I was, eh? Neither could I. Hard to pinpoint it.' He looks down mildly at his white hand on the counterpane, as if it were a small pet sleeping there. 'The moment when you stop living and start dying.'

A last quixotic effort to get up and dress is abandoned. There is more blood. Branwell's voice becomes curiously thick, as if he has fur growing in his throat. They take it in turns to sit with him. He is a model patient. He is – well, he is much more like himself.

Papa prays at the bedside, long and passionately. He prays for an earnest repentance, for the forgiveness of his son's manifold sins, for grace, mercy. Charlotte, coming in to relieve him, sees Branwell looking faintly alarmed yet also embarrassed, as if hearing someone recite their own bad poetry. When Papa is gone he draws Charlotte close to his pillow confidingly and whispers: 'I try to go along with it, you know. But listen – do you know how I think it will really be? I think it goes round in a circle. Consider: days and nights do – waking and sleeping – the earth turning. I think life may be a sort of loop. And you know what that means – I shall be a child again.' He gives a gravelly chuckle. His breath is strangely sweet. 'I shall be little Banny. That won't be so bad at all. I was better then. It's this business of being a man that beats me.' He gives a great sigh, and seems to be dozing for some minutes. Then he says: 'You're very quiet.'

'I didn't want to disturb you.'

'Hm. If only I had been so thoughtful lately, hey? You want to say it, but of course you can't, not to a dying man.'

'You're not dying.' She thrusts the word away, like a low branch coming at your eye.

In reply he holds up his wasted arm. It trembles a few inches above the coverlet. 'There. That's as high as I can lift it. Seems unlikely I'll get better. Charlotte, look under those books – see the packet there – give me. That's it. Letters. Never fear, I'm not about to start reading them at you. Just need to hold them again. Strange the power of these things. Just a little spilling of the self on to a sheet of paper. Light as an autumn leaf, and got the whole world in it . . . She did feel something for me, you know. There was something real.'

'Branwell, don't.'

'Oh, I know I've tired everybody, dwelling on it so. But I truly did love her. I know she could be a capricious woman – vain – silly sometimes. I know she was bored, and at first I – I simply gave her an escape from boredom. But when you love you love through, you see through – as I saw through to the woman she might have been. Oh, the people we might have been! Could there be any more wonderful set of people, if you could only gather them together? No, it was love, for a time: for a time, it was real. And believe me, Charlotte, it is the greatest thing.'

'I believe you.'

He seems glad of that.

Dr Wheelhouse returns, but doesn't stay long: there is nothing he can do and, besides, Branwell doesn't like him. All he wants, as the life goes out of him with a kind of marvellous swift efficiency, is his family.

'I do,' he breathes, as Papa calls on him again to repent of his sins. 'I am truly sorry for the bad things I've done in life. But what hurts me – it's knowing I didn't do anything great or good.'

Anne says: 'You did. You kept the love of all of us.'

Emily nods. 'That's right.'

'Did I . . . ?' The terrible tender eyes, rolling in the bone planes of his face, turn to Charlotte.

'Yes,' she says. This new sensation must be what they call your heart breaking. 'Yes, you did.'

Nine o'clock in the morning: birds busy, full sun, time of things beginning. They are all there, round the bed. Papa's voice is dry and gritty with prayer. The last struggle is grim, and it is a relief when it is over. Afterwards there will be a rumour around the village that Branwell rose to his feet in dying, but this is not so. Simply, his last convulsion pushes him right up off the bed into Papa's arms, as if wanting to be lifted and carried again: little Banny.

'You can't,' Tabby says, taking hold of Charlotte and Anne's hands. They are hovering outside Papa's study, hearing him howl *my son my son*; and they want to try and console him. 'You can't do anything. You'll only remind him . . . Look to yourselves, my dears.'

Emily sits apart, her jaw set: she pronounced no amens. She looks as if she is working out some hard sum in her head, perseveringly, even though she keeps getting a different answer every time.

Mr Nicholls comes, and sits with Papa for a while. Presumably he attempts consolation as well, for when he leaves, Papa goes with him to the door, head low, shoulders slumped, saying: 'I thank you, sir, you are very good. I regret I am not in a way to be comforted just now, and can only hope that you may never live to know such a day. My only son.' As the door opens he braces himself against the unleashed daylight as if it were a fusillade. 'I could have borne any loss better than this.'

It is a cold day with a sharp east wind when Branwell is buried in the church, an east wind come from far icy plains and steppes, scouring and buffeting and chilling to the core: doing what it has to do.

Back at the house after the funeral Emily, normally impervious to cold, keeps stirring the coals and huddling closer to the fire; but somehow she cannot stop shivering.

For a time Charlotte is helpless. She cannot write the letters or hem the mourning; she cannot sit with Papa and listen to his choking groans, his rattled fragments of prayer. She cannot even lie on her back or sit straight: she can only slump or curl. Perhaps in refusing to acknowledge the world that killed Branwell, she is defying it.

And yet she sees that killing as the culmination of a long process. And what thrusts her distorted face harder into the pillow is the knowledge that she cannot truthfully say she has lost him: she who chose to lose him a long time ago, like a dog turned loose in a wood. And only now do you see the dog come limping to your doorstep to pant its last there, submissively.

'I'm sorry,' she says dully to busy Anne. 'I don't know what – what can rouse me.'

What can rouse her?

This. Sudden and peculiar sensation of the absence of colour, as she watches Emily crossing the yard with the feed-bucket. Grey stones, black dress – and Emily's face and hands pure, bloodless white.

Charlotte says: 'Anne, please. Ask her. Just ask her if she won't consider seeing Dr Wheelhouse. She'll take it better from you.'

Anne looks doubtful. 'I don't think she will take it at all. She hates doctors even more than poor Branwell.'

Odd how in just a few weeks Branwell has taken on this new identity. *Poor Branwell* is how everyone refers to him; and somehow it suits. It makes nothing better, but it suits.

'I know . . . Perhaps then if you were to say we are concerned that her cold doesn't seem to be easing, and – no, she won't like that either. I mentioned her cough, and she gave me a look as if I were mad. Oh, dear God, I don't know what to do. Perhaps I'm reading too much into it, after Branwell. But you've noticed it, haven't you? The way she pants and catches her breath when she gets to the top of the stairs?'

'No. I mean, it's not just the top. She's out of breath by the time she reaches the half-landing,' says Anne: observant to the last. 'I will ask her. But I don't want to. You understand, don't you?'

Yes. You get your head bitten off, or else a paralysing silence. But Charlotte understands at another level, where neither she nor Anne dare say it out loud: what they really fear is the straight answer.

Later, when they gather in the dining-room by the lamplight, Charlotte flashes Anne an enquiring look, and Emily deftly intercepts it, and says: 'No, no doctor. Having a cold is nuisance enough, without all this fretting. Charlotte, you said Mr Williams had sent some reviews. Let's hear them.' And she sits down very carefully, breast pumping up and down; and you know she has not breath to speak again for minutes, and you would press her and force her do so, to prove it, to make her admit it – if you were cruel, or loved her less, or were less terrified.

Questions, then: hovering about the silenced house.

The spoken ones – agonisingly planned and prepared. 'Emily, you've been so busy lately – why don't you rest a little, and give that cold a chance to clear up?' There: like completing, with quivering hand, an elegant house of cards.

And down it goes. Emily frowns at her with a sort of weary puzzlement. 'Charlotte, what *is* the matter with you lately?' she says, opening the oven to draw out the bread. 'Your conversation has become quite tedious. I'm sorry – I know, I know you're grieving for Branwell.' The smell of new bread wafts up; and Charlotte thinks how strange it is that that warmest and kindliest of smells should take on such a ghastly association, be tainted with such dread. Lifting the bread-tray sets Emily gasping and wincing: she clatters it down and presses her hands to her side. But she will not meet Charlotte's eyes. And soon Charlotte realises Emily is waiting for her to go: to go, and not to have seen this at all.

Question to Papa: will he not overrule her, send for Dr Wheelhouse anyway as he did with Branwell? (Except, of course, this is different, it must be.) Papa is bearing up: the unearthly cries and poundings of the first nights are gone. Now it is as if the yielding topsoil of self has been stripped off, and a layer of deep, hard endurance revealed. Papa shakes his head.

'I fear it is no use, my dear. I have already spoken to her, in the frankest terms, of my anxiety for her health. And she says that if I send for a doctor, she will refuse to be examined by him.' He sighs. 'As, of course, is her right. Poisoning doctors, she calls them. She is quite in earnest. I am curiously reminded of the attitude evinced by the simple country folk in my youth in Ireland; a kind of superstitious fear that a doctor actually brings illness.'

Or, rather, thinks Charlotte, to send for a doctor is to admit that you are really ill.

No easy answers to the spoken questions. What about the unspoken question – the question that rises overpoweringly as the year limps to its end: an unslayable giant of a question such as you never expected to face – *how do you live in darkness?*

Branwell dying, gone: surely after such a thing there should be, not healing or peace, no, just an absence of great matters, a quiet space in which to wander numbly and think or not think. Instead there is this: the sound, clear and unavoidable wherever you are in the house, of Emily's barking cough. Like most repeated sounds, like the tick of a clock or the swinging of a gate, if the ear follows it for a while it begins to take on odd cross-rhythms and pitches, to suggest words. And there is this: the way each day there is a new prominence to Emily's cheekbones, brow-ridges, jawline, as if each day the artist adds another sharp white highlight to the picture of her sickness.

How do you live in darkness? You hope for a gleam. Branwell's decline was so swift, yes – but Emily is not Branwell: he had already undermined his constitution; Emily is strong. And this freezing weather is bound to make her feel worse. Come a warmer spell . . .

'Let me feed the dogs, Emily,' Anne says. 'It's bitter cold in that passage.'

'Why, don't be absurd, you feel the cold more than me. Anyhow it's my job, always has been,' Emily says, and goes on chopping and filling the bowls. Coming out of the back-kitchen through the knife-draughts of the passage she staggers a moment. Anne and Charlotte rush to help her. She will not look at either of them until they let go of her arms.

Later: 'Mr Williams has sent some more books, Emily. He knows you are – a little low and out of spirits, and thought it might help. Look, Emerson's essays, the ones we were talking about. Shall I read to you?'

Emily, sitting by the fire, just nods. She looks stiffly temporary there; but she cannot lie on the hearthrug any more, not without requiring help to get up again.

Charlotte reads. Anne sews. When there is a pause, Emily says, her eyes on the fire: That was kind of your Mr Williams, when he doesn't even know me.' And then a hint of her old sceptical half-smile creeps across her face. 'Of course, if he did know me, he wouldn't be kind at all. Go on, Charlotte.'

Charlotte reads on. After another page Anne touches her arm. 'She's asleep.'

'Well.' Charlotte closes the book. Her mouth is dry. 'That's good.'

'Yes. She needs the rest.'

So they disguise it, so they tiptoe round the great crack that has opened up: for Emily never drops off to sleep in the evening. Emily can only achieve sleep with patience and difficulty. They look at her. Her skin is blue beneath the eyelids, and wasting has made her teeth prominent through her lips, giving her a downright and contradictory look. Anne strokes her hair back from her forehead, and her glance at Charlotte admits the strangeness of this: the youngest, the one who is always looked after, changing places.

'She ought to be in bed,' Charlotte says, and for a skewed moment she is about to call on Branwell, see if he is sober enough to carry Emily. (How live in this darkness . . . ?) 'Do you suppose we could carry her up between us, safely? Only if we wake her, she won't let us support her, she'll insist on walking, and then she makes herself worse . . .'

They try it. She weighs very little: only the length of her limbs makes for awkwardness. They get as far as the bottom of the stairs before Emily stirs, looks blearily round at them.

'No.' She wriggles out of their arms, sets her feet on the stair. 'No, you've done enough for me.' And she goes up alone, head stiffly high, clinging to the banister. The clock on the half-landing counts off the slow, slow steps.

You hope for a gleam. Or, when that hope is over, you just hope for a suspension, for nothing happening. Instead there is this: Martha Brown coming to Charlotte before breakfast, nose reddened, eyes solemn, to tell her about the comb.

'She made me swear not to say anything, but I don't care, I've got to. She was combing her hair, and it was so slow, like she could hardly pull it through even though her hair's gone so fine and thin, and then she dropped it, and it went into the fire. She couldn't even reach down for it. I had to get it out for her. Oh, won't you get the doctor in?'

'We did the other day. She wouldn't let him near her. He left some medicine, but she won't take it.'

No suspension, no respite. Instead there is this: Emily transporting herself, a taut, creeping bundle of pain, down to the dining-room, and sitting on the couch, and taking up her sewing; and then dropping it and leaning back, able to do nothing but breathe, unable to breathe.

'Papa.' Charlotte flings open the study door. First time she has neglected to knock.

Papa looks up from his blank desktop. 'Surely not.'

Surely not. Sensible words, really, saying it all, the shattering impossibility of comprehending it, of the world's containing such wild fantastications of torment.

Papa kneels by the couch. It is, of course only stiff joints that make him sag down in that way, as if he has been poleaxed.

'Lie down, my dear. You're tired. I think you should lie down easy.'

Emily shakes her head; and then, frowning, lies back on the couch. Papa lifts her feet up. Outdoor shoes still, as if in defiance. Charlotte sees his lips moving: prayer. Silent, for now.

The morning is formless, endless, a horrifying sample of infinity. Emily lies open-mouthed, blinking and rasping: a bright winter sun is at the window, swept by sudden overcloudings, which periodically cast the room into an abrupt darkness as if some vast trap has closed over the house. She looks too insubstantial for such suffering, as if a mule's pack should be clapped on a spindly foal. But that, of course, is just Emily's body.

At last a twitch of her fingers beckons Charlotte to bend low by her side.

'If you want to send for a doctor,' Emily whispers, 'I will see him now.'

And that is when she knows.

Dr Wheelhouse comes, looks, and stays: there will be the matter of a certificate. Keeper scratches at the door, and Anne lets him in: he lies down by the couch, stays there mountainous and patient.

Two o'clock in the afternoon: time of second shift at the mills, of potatoes going into pans, December light not fading but staining. They are all there, gathered round the couch: last kisses, though uncertain whether she can feel them. Emily's departing groan is angry: or is that just the consumptive ulceration of the throat? Another question that cannot be answered, like how can you live in darkness, without a gleam; how can you bear it when it isn't bearable? Dead, Emily looks about fifteen.

Once more the opening of the vault, the tablet neatly incised and revised by John Brown, the black-edged cards and letters; once more the lightly laden procession to the church. It feels not so much like something new as a return to unfinished business. Many people of the village turn out to goggle: the family up at the parsonage have not been so interesting for ages. How old were this one? Thirty. Eh, well, when it runs in the blood . . .

'Charlotte, you must not fail me,' Papa said that morning, not for the first time. 'You must bear up – I shall sink if you fail me.'

She will not fail him – that is, she is continuing to exist, and that in itself seems powerful and exceptional. Keeper follows the coffin down to the church, barely pausing to investigate smells. There has been a little thaw, and the uneven surface of the lane is covered with puddles. The reflections in these, of sky and rooftop and trees, are clear and faithful yet subtly alien: it is like looking through a hole into another, slightly altered world, a world below. Everything, in fact, is brutally clear to Charlotte's eyes. The scene thrusts itself on her vision with insistent detail, acknowledging no hierarchy of significance. She has lately, within the space of two months, watched her brother and her sister die, and here are gateposts and cobblestones and a crow alighting high on a bare branch and horse-dung and wheel-ruts all demanding to be seen by the same eyes.

How do you live in darkness? Darkly, perhaps.

Or perhaps the mistake is in framing the question at all: the assumption that one knows what darkness is, its depths and intensity. Here is a new piece of learning for a new year. They bury Emily on the twenty-second of December, and before the Christmas season is over Charlotte is sitting up in bed and listening to a muffled thumping noise that resolves itself into Anne desperately, privately coughing into her pillow.

Well: they have, after all, ended up here at last – by the sea.

Scarborough is Anne's favourite place, and sea air is recommended for her condition by a broad range of medical opinion; and right from the moment when Papa brought in the eminent consultant, who listened to her lungs and nodded, it has been agreed between Charlotte and Anne that they will do everything they should do. Not Emily's way: the reverse. Perhaps this is a way of answering the question: work against the darkness.

So Anne has submitted to the regimen of blisters applied to her side and reeking doses of cod-liver oil, of rest, and milk and vegetable diet, which the doctors say cautiously may be of use in arresting the progress of her disease. And Charlotte goes along with her willingly, participating – it is even a sort of co-operative project, like a twisted echo of the old times writing round the lamp.

'What did the doctor say?'

'He does not think the inflammation is much advanced. But he cautions against the damp air at night.'

'Yes, I see. We must make sure the shutters are fast early in the evening.' They are obedient to the doctors, humble even, like dutiful schoolchildren with a firm headmaster. It is a sort of bargain. And it keeps your eyes fixed on the minutiae of the moment – doctor tomorrow, remember your dose – so that you don't look up, to the shadowed stretch of the future.

And now, in the cold spring, a move to the seaside. Sensible: but Charlotte suspects that Anne, in her quietly determined way, has another aim in view; and that is, whatever happens, she is not going to make that last journey down to the vault in Haworth church. Instead, as best she can, she is running away to sea.

Here's another way to answer the question: pretend it doesn't exist. Nearly four months they have managed since the consultant put away his stethoscope, so what else might not be possible? So the departure from Haworth, with Ellen Nussey as their companion, was a cheerful one, or at least they pretended it, which comes to the same thing. Anne rubbed Flossy's ears and told him to be a good dog till she returned; she kissed and embraced Papa fondly, gently, as if she were going to see him again soon. Marvellous what you can contrive.

Charlotte spoke a word with him while Anne was being helped into the gig.

'I'll write you directly we arrive, Papa. And after – whenever I possibly can. I don't know how long we shall be gone, of course.'

'We' – defiance, or denial? But Papa made no comment. There was a kind of upright quietude about him – has been, in fact, ever since the diagnosis: Papa braced, earnest, waiting.

But waiting means waiting for something, and that Charlotte will not countenance. Things happen, but they may not happen. On the train from Keighley Ellen entered into the spirit.

'It has been a backward spring – quite wretched down in Northamptonshire, so my brother tells me – but look at all the green now. I think we are entering a proper dry spell. I should think the air at Scarborough will be exceptionally good, Anne.'

And when they changed trains at York, and the porters had to carry Anne from platform to platform, and people stared at her little shrunken dangling legs, Charlotte read what they were thinking, and felt quite indignant. Idiots. Thin, no, she is not thin, that's your perception, we are quite all right.

And so beautiful here, such an invigorating presence of cliff and bay, such generosity of light and space and air – you *know* it must do some good. Anne is eager to point out the beauties to them, even show them.

'I want to take you across the bridge. There is such a magnificent prospect. And then a donkey-cart on the beach. It's so refreshing. Sorry, I'm dictating. But this is my place, you see. Dear me, proprietorial now. But I was so very happy here. To be sure I was with the Robinsons, but that was easily forgotten – easily, with views like that. Did you ever see anything like that bay? It lifts you – right up.' None of Emily's pallor: though she is all bone, there is a glow on Anne's skin and in her eyes as she conducts them, in their new-bought bonnets and gloves, around the sights, holidaymaking.

Except that very soon she cannot walk at all, and must keep to their lodgings on The Cliff. Even here, though, she has a broad window where she can sit and look out at the sea, and that must be something. Though there is the matter of her breathing. Clipped, delicately effortful: Charlotte thinks of sewing up thick hessian with an embroidery needle and silk thread.

Then comes the morning when Anne, ready to go down to breakfast, stops at the top of the stairs and grabs hold of the newel-post.

'Oh dear. I'm sorry – I don't feel as if I can go down. It looks so far. It looks –' she half laughs, with a flash of panicked eye-whites '– well, aptly enough, it – it looks like a cliff.'

'Never mind,' says Ellen. 'We'll carry you, won't we, Charlotte?'

And that's when Charlotte, remembering Emily and the way they had lifted her bird-boned weight in their arms, cannot pretend any more. 'No, no, no – Ellen, don't even think of it, I'll have nothing to do with it . . .'

Ellen only looks mildly surprised, and saying she will manage on her own goes down a step and receives Anne like a child into her arms. She gets to the bottom, just, staggering; and Charlotte following sees that it is indeed like a cliff, and Anne's nodding, lolling head is like something falling, falling out of sight.

Downstairs, in the pretty spidery sitting-room all hung with fancywork and lace, Anne wipes the milk moustache from her lips and lowers herself into the easy chair.

'Well,' she says, faintly smiling, 'at least I shan't have to have boiled milk any more. No, no.' A gentle quelling gesture. 'It's coming. I can feel it. I'm trying to think what's best to do. Should we try and get home first, to see Papa? Would that distress him more than if I stayed here? I want to do what's best.'

Charlotte can only nod, agreeing: yes, keep to the bargain. But inside there is crumbling and toppling. *I want to do what's best.* For others, of course. Oh, God, Anne, she howls inwardly: you should have thought of yourself instead, long ago.

She sends for a doctor – easily come by in this invalids' haunt, prompt and plump and prosperous. But even his professional manner wobbles, becomes lip-licking and faintly furtive when he sees Anne. Charlotte tries to adjust her eyes to his, to see what he is seeing: the truth. But still she can only see her sister – pretty, thin, yes, ill – but never, no, not ever going to be anything other than this: alive.

Anne forestalls the doctor as, after sounding her lungs, he begins to hum and haw and fumble with his bag. She takes hold of his wrist and calmly asks: 'How long?'

He studies her, no longer evasive, for a few moments. He shakes his head. 'Not long.'

Anne looks as if she has received a great kindness. 'Thank you.'

So, moving is out of the question; and Anne settles back to wait. And as for questions – well, now Charlotte's answers are at an end. There are no answers. These last few nights she has been lying awake, listening to the sea, and thinking back – not idly, but with purpose: putting up props of memory. She has thought of Maria and Elizabeth, and how terrible that time was, and yet how you lived through it and surmounted it; and so there is the lesson, there is the foundation on which you can build. But now she knows otherwise. The sturdy positive is a delusion. Instead, think of all your worst anxieties and fears, all the ones you have ever had, from the pot you suspect you left to boil dry, to the clatter that is surely the sound of a housebreaker outside your room, to the vision of there being a hell but no God. And imagine they were all true, all along. This is how Charlotte prepares herself for the final blow.

The sleek doctor returns hourly. He seems fascinated by Anne, the way she lies on the sofa patiently waiting.

'Such fortitude, ma'am,' he says aside to Charlotte. 'Really I – well, I don't think I have ever known anything like it.'

'No,' says Charlotte, from the end of a long tunnel, 'you never have.'

Sea and sunlight sprawl, epic and dazzling, beyond the salt-misted window. Charlotte holds Anne's hand, and watches her go: much more peacefully than Branwell or Emily, a drifting into last sleep. Such hideous expertise this is: this connoisseurship of the deathbed. Soon the irregular pulse ceases, the warm hand becomes an accident of shapes.

At last Ellen bends over Charlotte, timidly touching her shoulder. 'Let go now, Charlotte,' she says. 'Come. Let go.'

And Charlotte does let go: helplessly, embarrassingly, with nine months' worth of stored tears. But why not? Soon enough she will have to look, through dry, sensible eyes, at the unimaginable future.

5

After words, afterwards

They sit at the open drawing-room windows, faces tilted to catch the hay-scented breeze. There is a pool of sunlight around Charlotte's feet and a pool is exactly what it feels like, warm and immersing, so that you stir your toes idly in it. From another room comes the sound of children laughing. The sunlight touches surfaces about the long, spacious room, the piano lid, the Delft plates, the porcelain vases, with the richness of intimacy: light and this room, this whole house, have always been on familiar terms.

'Do you remember,' Charlotte says, stirring, 'when we first met, and I told you something of my life – and you said you had never heard a story like it before?'

'I do, now,' says her companion, 'and it strikes me it was rather pert and forward of me to say it.'

'No, no,' says Charlotte, faintly smiling. 'Because that's how I feel, now that I have seen your life. Your family – Mr Gaskell so kind and attentive, and your girls who really are charming and not just the way we pretend children are – and your home that really feels like a home. And the good work you do in Manchester – *and* you find time for writing as well. Busy and useful and content – but I'm sorry, perhaps you want to protest against my description.'

'No, only that you make me sound better than I am. But I should hope I am content,' says Mrs Gaskell.

'Well, all of that – it seems to me as remote and unreal as the life of a Red Indian in a tepee. And that in turn makes me wonder whether I am not rather a strange being after all.'

'Everyone is a strange being in their way. I think we simply stop noticing it, or train ourselves to do so, as we grow older. When you are a child every person you encounter appears the most fabulous grotesque. Just the other day I had to reprove Julia for staring at the old-clothes man, who has a great toper's nose. But another part of me quite sympathised with her, because it *is* a nose worth staring at – huge, luxuriously fleshed. If it were a bull it would win a prize at a fair. My dear, shall I ring for some cordial or iced water? Or will the effort of drinking it make us hotter, do you think?'

'Hotter. I do very well just sitting here, thank you, luxurious as the old clothes man's nose.'

Charlotte smiles at her friend, who could never even through a child's eye have appeared a grotesque. It is clear that she has been a beauty and, having turned forty, is entering a luminous, rounded handsomeness: to be with Elizabeth Gaskell is to feel physically better, to feel yourself as well aired and bright and comfortable as her house. Once or twice Charlotte has even wondered if she is not too good to be true. But, no, that is the old, crabbed, suspicious side of her, the side that expects no good of life, ever. Perhaps also she is a little astonished at this: being able to think of Mrs Gaskell as *my friend*. Of course she has had them before, there have been Ellen, and Mary Taylor and even – she treads carefully over the thought like a slippery patch – George Smith, but this is the first true friend she has made as a writer.

And also as that strange maimed creature, the survivor, the only – well, only what? No word for it. Not sibling. Sibling, like sister, is in all ways a relative word. And when your brother and your sisters are dead and gone, you are no sibling. She remembers when Maria and Elizabeth died, and how she was torn from the warmth of the middle, exposed. When Branwell and Emily and Anne died, how much greater the exposure: she was thrust into the vastness of space, a speck in nothingness. But, ah, how much pain could be contained in that speck.

And how she could not talk of it. Because either you did so all the time, living on it, battening on it (and she had wanted to do that at first) or you put it away. She watched the breath go out of them, one by one: she breathed on, moved and saw and heard and wept while they hardened into bodies in front of her. And either you stayed there, in those locked, hellish moments, or you forced yourself to live elsewhere. The world, in other words.

(But that place did not disappear, of course. You could step back in at any time, and feel it walling you in with a terrible lovingness: stay here, stay because this is where everything stopped, really, did it not? Stay.)

'You know, I'm glad to hear you say you weren't impressed by the Great Exhibition,' Mrs Gaskell says, waving away a bee – a Manchester bee, big and assertive. 'We all seem to be working ourselves up into a tremendous state of hubris over it.'

'I did not exactly say I wasn't impressed,' says Charlotte. She knows she has this awkward, painstaking, pedantic way, and can't help it. That's where she's fortunate in knowing Mrs Gaskell, who doesn't mind it, who likes to wade deep into a conversation, not paddle in the shallows. 'Rather that it seemed such a vast, noisy celebration of *things* – wonderful ingenious things, many of them, but still things – that it seemed to look to a time when there would be just things and no people. And be quite happy with that.'

Ah, but that isn't the whole of it. In London she has been staying with George Smith and his family, and it was Mr Smith who took her to the Exhibition. As soon as she saw the Crystal Palace rear up glittering above Hyde Park she was terrified. *Great Glasstown*. Branwell and the Twelves and the children's study came beautifully, horribly alive. It needed all George Smith's calm urbanity to prevent her crying out on the spot or running away. Inside it was better – not good. The accumulated goods of the world: too much to see and yet also, you think, is this all there is? The steam-driven cravat-fastener? Ingenuity and invention gone out of control lead to a sort of madness, as well she knows. Was it her fancy, or did that glass roof tower so high it had clouds under it? Meanwhile her giant, dwarfing loneliness: meanwhile the one thing needed, against all this everything.

'London is rather exhausting to the spirit at the best of times, isn't it?' Mrs Gaskell says. 'I find it so, even though I was born there. I feel myself quite an adopted daughter of the north now. I want to prevail on you to stay longer, you know, Charlotte – to recover your spirits and get all that clanging materialism out of your head.'

'You're very kind. But I really must go home, and settle down to some writing. George – Mr Smith, I should say – is very patient, but he has begun to talk of my new novel with a sort of airy smirk, as if it were some dubious product of fairyland. And, besides, Papa will be needing me.'

Without saying anything, Mrs Gaskell reaches out and squeezes Charlotte's hand. It is not the gesture, which is typical of her, that makes Charlotte jump but its corporeality. In the long shadow-chamber that has been her life since the deaths, her friendship with Elizabeth Gaskell has been one of the most substantial things – yet still, like everything, not quite real. You expect your hand to go straight through her.

* * *

Papa will be needing me.

So it had been, in the first months after that cataclysm. She and Papa had clung together in mutual need barbed with anxiety – every sniffle and cough greeted with dread. When that faded, they would stare painfully at each other's faces, seeing the other faces, the resemblances. For longer still it remained natural to turn, expectant, at a creak or a footstep – but it was always, drearily, one or the other of them. They could not surprise each other.

The only other presence was Mr Nicholls. Those desperate times saw him at his best; or, rather, it was a time when imperturbable steadiness was useful, and inexpressive gruffness preferable. (The tender tact of William Weightman, for example, would have been unbearable.) He walked the dogs, dealt with correspondence, and sat with Papa over tea when Papa could only gaze and sigh and then look at him with a sudden frowning shudder: *Why aren't you Branwell?*

The dogs never quite seemed to reconcile themselves to the glaring absences. It had been, in a way, the most painful moment of the return from Scarborough, where Anne had been buried. Papa knew. But Flossy had come bounding and frisking, running behind Charlotte, then looking searchingly up in her face. How could she take Anne away, and not bring her back?

How indeed? On the first night back the emptiness of the house had hit her like a blow. She could not sleep. By the time the next evening came she was in a state of panic at the thought of darkness. Pacing, clutching herself, muttering under her breath, she crossed a continent that night. She had had a revelation that nearly flattened her: that the human capacity for pleasure was finite, while its capacity for suffering was limitless.

When she threw open the shutter at last, and found the hills brimming with light like honey in a comb, she realized that it was the shortest night of the year.

Eventually, tentatively, another presence made itself felt. Her work. Charlotte's new novel went with miserable slowness, but still it was a companion, and a companion who never demanded a social simper from her, was comfortable with her messy and ill-tempered. The book called *Shirley* haltingly emerged. As it went on, Emily began to appear in it. Somehow Charlotte couldn't stop her. She had to live. Emily had not been meant to die: it was an anomaly, an earthquake. Anne had been better equipped for death, as she had for life.

The book was finished, and Mr Smith and Mr Williams were polite rather than enthusiastic. One imagined them thinking, *After this, she'll be better – this one is working the bereavement off.* What she could not explain to them was: this was no phase. She was not going to emerge from this glossy and flourishing. She was having to learn to live permanently in a new, cold, sluggish element: to be a different creature.

Writing itself had to be learned all over again. Before this, it had been a shared act: the lamplight, the reading aloud, the walks round the table. We three. Now it was a dual struggle with art and solitude. Sometimes, when Charlotte sat at her work after Papa had gone to bed, she would suspend her pen and just listen. The silence in the dining-room was so pregnant, you felt you had to attend to it, that something must come of it: the air seemed to retain their scents and voices; the shadows on the wall almost resolved themselves into Emily's leanness, Anne's trim profile. She froze in a kind of sick joy, waiting, knowing: because from that pregnancy, oh, the terrible stillbirth, the confirmation of desolation: the silence going on and on.

Mr James Taylor: she knew of him, as the manager at Smith, Elder & Co., but had never expected him to appear on her doorstep. But as *Shirley* was finished, and Mr James Taylor was just then returning from a holiday in Scotland, he proposed to pick up the manuscript on his way south and take it to London in person.

Charlotte had somehow fixed his image in the middle between Mr Williams, the gentle reader with the hound-dog chops, and spruce, authoritative Mr Smith. No such thing. Both in their different ways knew how to put her at her ease. James Taylor did the opposite. From the moment he stepped into the parsonage hall he crowded his attention on her. Throughout the visit she moved in an oppression of beaky nose and pale, devouring eyes without lashes. Oh, of course, who was she to decry a lack of good looks? But it was the way he thrust them at you, like a beggar exhibiting a sore.

'I will be frank with you. It has been a matter of the greatest moment to me – to meet Currer Bell in the flesh. And not only that.' He stopped. He had a way of leaving these pauses, like explosive charges. 'Of conveying to you my enormous admiration.'

'Thank you. Well, now you have done it – and you need not allude to the inevitable disappointment.'

'Now exactly why do you say that?' His sharp nose twitched, homing in on her. It was just a casual remark that George Smith would have smilingly brushed aside, but you felt that Mr Taylor was ready at any moment to sit down – on the ground, if need be – and thrash it out.

Nothing wrong with that, of course, she liked people to be serious, to have plenty of mind – in fact, if James Taylor's pouncing expression reminded her of anything it was of her own, glimpsed once reflected in the parlour mirror at Pensionnat Heger, when Monsieur Heger was talking . . . Oh, but it was just the ghastly incongruity – if she interpreted aright his clinging handshake on parting, his earnest hints at a future meeting. Here I stand in the wasteland of sorrow, an object of romantic interest. As if someone had tried to climb into your sick-bed.

'You must,' he remarked, turning at the bottom of the steps with a sweeping gesture, 'find great inspiration in this wild and rugged scenery.' He made it sound more like an order than a question.

Charlotte did not quite shake her head. 'Mostly I look at the sky.'

'It is inevitable, I think, that you will become known,' Papa said at breakfast, as Martha brought in the latest heap of letters. 'There must be great curiosity at the post-office, for one; and then the originals of *Shirley* will be locally recognised, I feel sure, just like Cowan Bridge in *Jane Eyre*. The evidence will be collated. You must reconcile yourself to becoming a public person, my dear.'

Charlotte shook her head, opened one of the letters, and found a curious noise escaping her throat.

'What is it, my dear?'

'It – it's a letter of appreciation from a lady. She describes herself as not quite an old maid. And if Currer Bell really were a gentleman, she says, she would fall in love with him.'

Only a little while later did she realise what that noise was. It was laughter. She felt as if she had been betrayed into obscenity.

Mr Nicholls, inevitably, knew she was Currer Bell. When she saw him carrying a copy of *Shirley* away from Papa's study she was just a little perturbed, because she had put in a satirical sketch of the local curates, including him – though he was presented as the best of a bad lot. But presently she heard from John Brown, with whom he lodged, that Mr Nicholls had disturbed the peace of the house by laughing uproariously at the whole chapter.

'Yes, he has been reading it out loud to me,' Papa said later, 'with great approbation. Now he wants to read the other book, as he terms it.'

Charlotte shrugged. She could not imagine Mr Nicholls making much of *Jane Eyre*, any more than you could imagine planting flowers in a stone wall. All the same, it was faintly uncomfortable to think of him reading it: Mr Nicholls of the burly folded arms, the hewn frown, the look of portable solitude, participating in her words and stepping into the embrace of Mr Rochester.

But she need not have worried that he would embarrass her with remarks about her work. Mr Nicholls, though so often about the house, and even glimpsing her in the act of writing, never addressed her as an author. In fact, remarks seemed not to be in his line altogether.

'I'm afraid we shall have snow again,' she said, handing him his tea. 'It has that feeling – not quite so cold, and something heavy and still in the air.'

He listened as if she were speaking a foreign language, badly; then frowned and applied himself to his tea. 'Oh, well, if we have snow, we do,' he said. This odd impatience, as if he wanted to break through the trivial talk to some vital subject, which he never broached. And I was afraid I was socially awkward, Charlotte thought, as far as she thought anything.

Shirley sold, and the reviewers remarked again on the unfeminine coarseness of Currer Bell, and Mr Smith and Mr Williams urged her to come to London and savour her fame a little; and Tabby retailed the peculiar news that one or two people, strangers, had come looking for Haworth parsonage. What for? Just to look at it, seem'ly, on account of the books coming from here. Just to look. Charlotte shook her head. 'Now this,' she said, 'I find impossible to believe.'

It was Mr Greenwood the stationer – whose twisted shoulder seemed to sink lower in abasement now when Charlotte entered his shop – who showed her the notice in the *Bradford Observer*.

It is understood that the only daughter of the Rev. P. Brontë, incumbent of Haworth, is the authoress of Jane Eyre *and* Shirley, *two of the most popular novels of the day, which have appeared under the name of 'Currer Bell'.*

Only daughter. Seeing it in print – oh, how it burned. Print had made them; it was print that confirmed their unmaking, their absolute silence.

That evening, at the lamplit table, she listened to the swelling silence until, at last, she had to break it. She spoke out loud. She had to. Thinking it would not do. Thoughts smudged like chalk: speech was pen and ink and signature.

'I know you're here. But you're not here. And that's why I can't bear it. I can't just – linger. I shall have to go about to other places.' She tilted her head a moment. 'Yes, that's true – I did always want to, in a way. But not like this. I never wanted it like this.'

Her London trips: she could not help thinking of, and comparing them with, that whirling stormy weekend when she and Anne had first braved the forbidding offices of Smith, Elder & Co. Then it had been exciting but gruelling also; a thing to be got through, a sortie from a bolt-hole. Now there was no bolt-hole left. The burrow had been broken open and ploughed up, and all was level. In a way, it meant courage was the only option. ('Courage, Charlotte. Have courage.' Anne's last words to her.)

William Makepeace Thackeray, the great lion, was to be seen feeding at a distance on her first visit – a dinner at the Smiths', with later a brief introduction, a shake of his paw: too much company, too much shyness on her part for more. Second time round, he made a morning call, and she was a little more prepared.

'This should be the moment, Miss Brontë, when I reveal that I knew all along that Currer Bell was a woman – a Yorkshirewoman – and of clerical family; in short show myself a proper fairground fortune-teller. No such thing, alas. All I *did* think, when our friend here gave me *Jane Eyre*, was that here was someone who was a master, or mistress if you will, of our poor mishandled English language. So many authors nowadays overdrive it – or else they let the old nag wander at will on the verges.'

He was a huge, heavy, booming man, his snub-nosed spectacled face always drawn up in an incipient sniff. Sometimes the sniff seemed at the ironic expense of the world; occasionally, at himself.

'You embarrass me with this praise, sir,' she faltered. She wasn't being coy. She was in the presence of – for her – a deity. 'You who write with such – such elegance, ease, airiness, qualities I cannot command—'

'Airy, aye. That's because when I sit down to write I seldom have a thought in my head, except how to pay the wine-merchant's bills.'

'Oh, the material world is, I know, a sad distraction for the artist – especially when he must support a family.'

'On the contrary, Miss Brontë, the material world is my great spur. When I sit and sigh and scratch and call on the muses, neglectful jades that they are, for inspiration, why, I only have to consult my bank-book, and then I feel as inspired as anything.' Thackeray gave his great laugh – rather a steely laugh that seemed faintly to threaten you if you did not join in.

'You spoke of English authors. What do you think of the new French novels? Is there not the same insipidity – the want of force?'

'Oh, your Frenchman is a jaded, cynical creature,' Thackeray said, taking up a position on the hearth like a guardsman and flexing his thick legs. 'Put a pen in his hand and he is either sensual or frivolous. Do you know France at all, Miss Brontë?'

'No. I have been on the Continent, but at Brussels.'

'Ah, I know Brussels – enchanting little toy-town capital, is it not? The Belgians are so proud of their little chequerboard kingdom, one cannot help but smile. Paris, now, there is the true flavour of the Continent, garlicky and gamey though it be . . .'

His bear-like arms seemed to sweep away all that was most important in her experience: his talk was all skittering hurry, as if one should never linger on anything – lest you saw too deeply into it? Yet there was such thought in his work – though, certainly, he had a weakness for easy sentiment.

'London, mind, take it all in all, is the prince among cities. All the world looks to it, even if in bitterness and envy. You wouldn't live anywhere else, would you, Smith?'

'As a publisher, I have no choice.'

'That is what I like about it,' Charlotte said, 'not the society, but the place given to art and literature.'

'Dear me, literature, eh? We must be careful of talking shop, Miss Brontë,' Thackeray rumbled. 'Our publisher friend here will look on in alarm in case we gang up and organise against him – like your striking weavers up in the north setting fire to the mill, or the mill-owner, whichever blazes up the best, hey?'

The clouds of worshipful incense parted, and she gazed at him levelly, curiously. Was it nerves that made him talk like this? Yet he seemed vastly at ease. Here was a man who had known great sorrow – his poor insane wife – but who seemed to saunter in the world as in a great pleasure-garden. Perhaps that was the secret. Bear-like you swept sorrow away, you trampled on it with those shining boots, you dismissed it with that hard, ringing laugh. Better than hugging it to you, perhaps. After all, Papa had once called her a self-tormentor.

'It's possible you alarmed him, Miss Brontë,' George Smith said later, when Thackeray had gone, 'and that was why he talked in that rather flippant vein.'

'Alarmed him? How? I stood quite in awe of him.'

'Well, that's partly it. And then you did go on to tackle him about the tendency – what was it—'

'The weakness for easy sentiment that mars his work when inspiration flags, yes,' she said.

'Quite.' Mr Smith smiled and sat down by her. Few men looked so well smiling. 'And, by the by, I do agree with you there. Heaven knows, I'd like to have him on our list – but if I did, I would insist that he cease the habit of ending a chapter with a verbal shrug, as if the tale he is telling really doesn't matter. Because it does matter: the writer and the reader have entered into a solemn contract, not to be broken.'

'I'm glad someone else feels so,' she said, a little breathless.

Mr Smith sat back. 'And then your telling him to his face that he is the foremost moralist of his age, and how he must feel his responsibility in approaching his next work.' He chuckled. 'My dear Miss Brontë, no wonder he was alarmed.'

She looked away. This was how it was with George Smith: you thought you were plunging into the depths, and then you found yourself standing ankle-deep in the shallows. She took disappointed refuge in prickliness. 'I'm sorry, Mr Smith, this is very dull of me, but I cannot like being laughed at. The dour Cromwellian strain in me, no doubt.'

'Laughter can express admiration, you know,' he said, not at all put out. 'Besides, as Thackeray would be the first to admit – *if* one could ever get him to make a serious admission about writing – the author of *Jane Eyre* scarcely needs to sit in a lower place than the author of *Vanity Fair*. There are many, you know, who would put the precedence the other way round.' He let that settle for a moment, then consulted his watch. 'Time for my ride.'

From the drawing-room window Charlotte and Mrs Smith watched him go, upright and easy in the saddle.

'George has a fancy he will grow fat unless he takes exercise, that it's in the blood,' Mrs Smith said. 'His father did put on a little weight later in life, but I see nothing of that in George. However, I encourage him, because it gets him out in the fresh air and away from his desk. He works, as you well know, Miss Brontë, dreadfully hard. He feels his responsibility. He was scarce twenty, you know, when he had to assume the headship of the family; so much depended on him, and still does. He must always make the right choices. There is very little leeway for mistakes.'

Shrewd, thoughtful, sturdy Mrs Smith: who welcomed Charlotte to their household unaffectedly, covered her shy silences, divined when her shattering headaches came on her, acted as an unpretentious and sensible guide to the sights of London – seldom, in fact, had Charlotte ever known another woman so sympathetic. Curious that now and then, behind that bright, bony English face, she seemed to glimpse the dreamy, killing gaze of Madame Heger.

Thackeray, nothing offended, invited her to dinner at his gracious bow-windowed house in Kensington. A stable of well-bred and well-dressed literary ladies had been assembled: Charlotte knew at once, from their covert glances, neck-strokings and instant smiles that she would have nothing in common with them. The test came after dinner, when they left the gentlemen to the port. One of the ladies roused herself dutifully to bring her out. 'And so, do you like London, Miss Brontë?'

After thinking about it, Charlotte said: 'Yes and no.'

Hen-like fluffing, a sigh, a turn away. Why? Surely the question ought to be properly considered. Fortunately, Thackeray's daughters' governess was there. Someone she could talk to.

Thackeray, mottled with port, joined them only for a short while, then, grimacing, made some excuse and disappeared. George Smith told her later that he had gone off to his gentlemen's club.

Charlotte was not surprised. In a sense, she thought, he never left it.

'You have never sat for your portrait before?' Mr Smith said in the carriage.

'No – well, yes, I have.' She had to dredge up the words. 'To my brother. He trained as a painter. He painted us once as a group, with himself in the middle. Well, of course, with four you can't really have a middle . . .' Remarkable, the pain across the years: the freshness. 'But that was different. He knew me as a person. This Mr Richmond – all he will have is my appearance. God help him.'

'Ah, but that's his trade – and his genius. He studies the face – reads – translates. I fancy I have seen you doing the same, Miss Brontë.'

'I didn't know I was so transparent.'

He seemed to stifle an answer. 'Well, I assure you the sitting will not be long. And it would make me happy to be able to send it to your esteemed father. Visible evidence, Miss Brontë, of your fame.'

Charlotte shrank back into the corner of the carriage. When it came to herself, visible evidence was the kind she could do without.

* * *

'Nay,' Tabby said, peering at the portrait above the mantelpiece, stepping back, shuffling closer, shaking her jowls, 'nay, it's not really like. He's made you look too old.'

Too old? thought Charlotte. How could that possibly be? And then she shivered with the boredom of her own misery, her inescapable self.

Visible evidence of her fame: it came also in the shape of a man like a handsome, talkative horse; a great doer and thinker, doctor, educational reformer and whatnot; great hunter and seizer of the famous, among whom Charlotte now had to count herself. A tremendous refuser of no for an answer: Sir James Kay-Shuttleworth. Even his name, she thought, had too much in it. Mentally she renamed him the Shuttlecock; though she was the one he was soon batting about. A visit to his estate at Gawthorpe, where he bored her charmingly, was not enough: he harried her with courtesies and hounded her with invitations. But Papa was all for him, especially with his roots in the north. The set around Smith, Elder & Co. in London were all very well in their way, he seemed to suggest, but she ought to cultivate society closer to home . . . . What *was* he suggesting, in fact? Something of danger in George Smith's society?

Well, there, though she said nothing, she could have amply reassured Papa. It was absurd. George Smith was handsome, for one thing (beautiful even – yes, allow it), and younger than her and socially successful – in short, he was just made to marry a golden dolly. For another, her heart was quite dead to all such influences. She had tested it. How? By experiment. She had allowed herself to suppose – as a sort of theorem – that the gap between his attractions and her plainness could be bridged: that his social and financial expectations didn't matter; that the watchfulness of his mother could be evaded; that through his admiration of her as a writer George Smith was led to a different kind of admiration. There: set up all these imaginary conditions – and now, hark to the heart.

Nothing. Or at least – not so much agitation as need worry her. Right from the beginning of their association, she had known he would not be the one for whom she would let go. In fact, she very much doubted that she would ever let go now: just carry on clinging to the wreckage, treading water, watching inevitable night come.

One good thing came from the benevolent persecutions of the Shuttlecock. When she could no longer refuse his invitations, she went to stay at his summer house by Lake Windermere – and there her fellow-guest was Elizabeth Gaskell.

Charlotte knew of her – her novel *Mary Barton* had contested the bookshelves with the works of the Bells, and there had been an exchange of letters, which had convinced her they would get on. Leaving aside, of course, the terror of getting to know someone. And on being first introduced to Mrs Gaskell – handsome, easeful, sure of the world and its existence – Charlotte had cringed and shrunk. She had, as she phrased it to herself, turned Brontë. But Mrs Gaskell's warm, steady gaze expressed interest without hurry. They leaped from wary liking to full confidences within a day.

'I always felt that Lowood School must have had a true original,' Mrs Gaskell said. 'But from what you tell me, you rather softened it than exaggerated it when you put it in *Jane Eyre*.'

'Well, there are certain things one cannot do in fiction, as you know. One cannot disgust the reader – as life too often disgusts us. The reader wants to be gently handled. In life two of my sisters died as a result of their treatment at that school – but put that in a book, and people would soon complain that you were straining for effect.'

'Did it help you? Getting Lowood down, and Mr Brocklehurst – yes, I can tell he was real too – getting it all on paper?'

'I don't know. I know with the real Mr Brocklehurst I felt silenced, horribly silenced – all the girls were – and my elder sisters were silenced by that school for ever. And so the pen allowed me, at last, to speak out. But I don't think writing truly helps or hinders: it's just a thing one must do. Isn't it so for you?'

'It has become so,' Mrs Gaskell said, after a moment. The parlour window overlooked the lake, and the sun on the water sent little rosy patterns shadowing across her face. 'I first turned my hand to *Mary Barton* because my husband urged me to it, because if I had not done something I would have gone mad. My little boy died. William. He was not quite a year old. I wanted to die too. I still had three little girls and my dear husband and yet you know, Miss Brontë, I didn't care about them, not a bit: which was very wicked of me. I only wanted William. The effort and distraction of writing was meant to save my mind; and it did.' She suddenly turned on Charlotte a penetrating, stripped smile. 'But I have never stopped wanting William. Wanting him back.'

And after that, there was no question of their not understanding each other.

If only her relations with Mr James Taylor could have found some comfortable base. But it was not to be. On her London visits she managed, shamefully, to avoid him or else dilute his concentrated attention by always having other people about her. (Not that that made her any less aware of him: knowing Mr James Taylor was in the room was like knowing there was a loaded pistol hanging on the wall.) At Haworth she received and struggled to answer his letters, which folded were about as thick as prayer-books. It was a relief at last when he was assigned to go to India, where Smith, Elder & Co. had a Bombay house – because now, with the prospect of being away for years, he had either to come out and say it or let the matter drop.

He came out and said it: again breaking a southward journey from Scotland to call at Haworth. Charlotte listened, fixed her eyes on the brown moles that dotted the backs of his doughy-pale hands, and said the only thing she could say. Relief again; yet she was sorry for his sake that that was all she could say, and that the sum of his perseverance and sincerity would not work out. He accepted it, hollow-cheeked, apparently cool; and went away. Probably not to be seen again for five years, if ever. And Charlotte sat with her writing-box open and the page unspotted once again and thought: What is wrong with me?

And so, when the invitation from the Smiths came once more, she seized it: especially as it was the time of the Great Exhibition, which was Papa's fascination. She could observe it and absorb it and then bring it home to him, as she used to bring such things home to Emily. Thus her tale comes full circle: thus Charlotte is brought to stay at the Gaskell house in Plymouth Grove to sit by the open windows, talk with her friend, smell the hay-scented breeze, on her way back to Haworth.

Expecting nothing. And when something does come, it is not out of the blue. Rather, it is reminiscent of a painting she saw at the Royal Academy exhibition, a vivid, crowded canvas of a musical party. As she gazed, one figure slowly stood out in bolder and brighter relief, a figure that the artist seemed to have invested with extra life: the complexion glowed, the eyes shone, and at last the figure seemed almost on the point of stepping out of the picture to join her. Such is the process, at last, at Haworth, where a figure melts out of the background and changes everything. This is the greatest surprise of all: the transformation of the familiar.

★ ★ ★

First, life as a pattern. There's comfort in it. Supporting Papa: writing – she does get the old nag moving at last; letters from London, keeping a little window open on that world; friendship, which means, above all, Ellen.

Oh, she is glad of Ellen: always there, always herself, when so much of the world has turned itself inside out. And yet Charlotte begins to see being consistent as a sort of hardening: only cold stone never changes. Since her sisters died, Ellen has been somehow easier: as if someone has left the room and now we can talk.

'Thank heaven neither of us has been foolish enough to marry,' Ellen says once, as they walk arm in arm; and though Charlotte likes the feel of it, the familiar dawdling tenderness, she seems to hear doors slamming. Here we are and here we stay. Yes, comfort of the pattern. But just occasionally you see how the pattern is more like the grille of a dungeon, clamped over your life.

For her new novel she has gone back to the experience of Brussels – but coolly, coolly. She has found a way to do that, and still keep the fire inside.

'Miss Brontë. I was wondering – how your new book was progressing.'

It is Mr Nicholls, stepping into the dining-room after walking the dogs, and asking his slightly unusual question.

'Pretty well, I thank you, Mr Nicholls.'

He coughs, looks around the room as if seeking some small item he has mislaid, or perhaps – given his habitual dark frown – that someone has taken from him. 'It must be – writing a book must be . . .' She waits wonderingly, prepared for anything '. . . very tiring.'

'Oh! Yes. Yes, in a way. But of course it is not to be compared with labouring in the mill or the quarry.'

'Well, no, of course not,' he says, in a faintly aggrieved tone, as if she suggested it was; and is gone. Charlotte finds herself hoping that Mr Nicholls is not turning into a literature-fancier. There has been a comfort, when so much has changed and vanished, in his remaining ruggedly and cussedly himself: you don't want a tree to turn into a pergola.

'I don't know what's wrong with our friend Mr Nicholls,' Papa says abruptly, one morning. 'There is lately a sort of mooning manner about him not at all to my taste.'

Charlotte raises her eyes from her letters. Tradesmen's invoices: with her earnings from her books she is making some improvements to the house. At last, at last curtains – though Papa makes a face about them, as if at some wildly Oriental and effeminate luxury.

'I've noticed he is a little low-spirited,' she says, and then thinks: Have I?

'More like a green-sick girl. Is he unhappy here? "Not exactly so," he sighs. Then sometimes he talks of moving back to Ireland. "Well, if that is your wish," say I, "pursue it: form your decision." "I don't know what I want," says he.' Papa snorts. There is something of Emily's contempt for weakness about him – but sharpened, made lethal. 'I should have made a poor fist at life if I had not been able to make a clear-cut decision.' And he takes up the paper-knife and rips into his letters, like an unflinching surgeon.

The book is finished, and despatched, and as before there is that feeling of emptiness and dissatisfaction. Perhaps worst of all this time. Cool the handling, yes, but of necessity – the thick gloves of technique protecting her from the kiln heat of the material. Much of that time in Brussels has come vividly back to her in the writing of *Villette* – things even she had forgotten, or made herself forget. And the creative amputation has throbbed again. She named her heroine Lucy Frost, then changed it to Lucy Snowe. Something to be said for both of them – and she did say it, out loud, lifting her head from her work as if they were still there: 'Frost, or Snowe, which do you think?'

And again the dizzying clifftop revelation, that she must decide for herself.

Decide for yourself.

She has hardly stirred from Haworth during the writing, and the experience has left her feeling wrung and strung and, yes, almost as if she needs someone with infinite patience and dexterity to untangle the knots inside.

Also, the sending away of the parcelled manuscript requires her to lift her head, clear her eyes, acknowledge the future again. Papa, ever relying on her; sometimes now when he talks to her adopting a hectoring tone, as if she were in the habit of contradicting him. The days, the years. The loss of Branwell and Emily and Anne is still like a physical pain. One you learn to live with, perhaps, like a weakened muscle, a gammy knee: you learn to favour it, put no weight on it – yet sometimes for all your care you half collapse as the jabbing pain of it goes through you. That, presumably, will go on, moderating by tiny degrees, as the hour hand of a clock moves. There's an image for you and your future, if you like: the inching of the hour hand, barely discernible, relentless.

And then one quiet Monday evening after tea Mr Nicholls asks her to marry him, and nothing can be the same.

'It is a piece of impudence which I cannot countenance, and you may be sure I shall tell him so,' says Papa, 'and I refer to the mere *asking*, not the even greater impudence of the supposition that such an approach could ever be anything but a repugnant absurdity.' The long-windedness is a sign of danger, just like the veins standing out on his forehead. 'And I devoutly hope there has been nothing in your conduct towards him, Charlotte, that could have encouraged him to take this unwarrantable liberty.'

'No, Papa, I cannot think there has. It was a very great surprise to me also.'

Yes: so it was when Mr Nicholls, instead of leaving the house after spending the evening with Papa, had tapped on the dining-room door and walked into Charlotte's lamplit world. And yet even as she looked up in surprise, part of her said, *Ah, it's this*, and riffled through a little sheaf of recent memories – Mr Nicholls attentive to her, Mr Nicholls strangely silent around her, Mr Nicholls happening to encounter her on her moorland walks. And what's this one? Herself finding Mr Nicholls quite conversable, feeling not displeased when he joined her . . . ?

'Miss Brontë, I can't bear it any more, I've suffered it for months now and if I don't – speak – put an end, I think I shall go mad.' Mr Nicholls smelled of outdoors. He was shaking all over – really. She has never seen a man shake with emotion like that – not even Branwell. It is faintly alarming, like seeing some impressive engine overheating.

Yes, a great but not a complete surprise. 'I know,' he said, 'I am not generally a man to be communicative – to betray his feelings. But you must have suspected something, Miss Brontë. Because it would not be hid – what I feel—' His voice cracked.

'I – I noticed some alteration in the way you have spoken to me lately, Mr Nicholls, but I had no notion that—'

'Well – never mind – it's out now. I must tell you how much I admire you – how desperately I love you. I must ask if you could ever consent to be my wife. If you can't say yes then – well, I ask you not to say no. Nothing final. Let me hope.'

All, she supposes, conventional enough for a proposal. Except not conventional at all, coming from Mr Nicholls, from whose deep chest every word seemed to be ripped, catching like a fish-hook. And all she wanted to do for the moment was stop it.

'I dare say you are surprised,' he went on. 'I have done everything I can to suppress what I feel. Not because I'm ashamed of it – because of my fear that you could not reciprocate. But now my love has beaten the fear. It's been so long – I don't know how long. Perhaps at first I would not allow myself to think of it. But it was there even before your terrible losses – and all through that dreadful time I longed to give you comfort, to help you though it was not my place, and you were surely beyond comfort . . . Still I wished it could be in my power to lift you up – to carry your burden. And now – now if it could be in my power to do so, I would ask for nothing else from life. I beg you, Miss Brontë, to consider – please consider.'

'Mr Nicholls, I can't—' She saw him blanch at those words. 'I can't think what to say, you must let me – let me alone for now, and perhaps tomorrow I can give you an answer. But really, I . . . Have you spoken about this to my father?'

He lowered his eyes. 'No. I tried to bring myself to it, but in the end I didn't dare. I thought – I was afraid of being dismissed out of hand.'

'Well. You know, of course, that I will have to speak to him about this.'

'Yes. I'm sorry,' he said huskily; and in all the chaos of bewilderment and agitation a little firm grain of understanding passed between them.

'Never mind. Go now, please.' There was such a wound in his look that she added: 'I'm not – sending you or ordering you away, it isn't like that, but really – let me be for now.'

So she has managed to get him out of the house, and has reported, as she must, to Papa; and here is his furious, crimson reaction.

'I should hope it *was* a great surprise to you,' he growls, 'though I would say shock, disagreeable and unpleasant shock before surprise, Charlotte. To have that skulking fellow dare to address you – oh, I shall make short work of him. He will regret trading on his place here. When a mongrel dog comes sniffing about, there is only one thing to do. It must be kicked and kicked hard.'

'Papa, this is too strong. Mr Nicholls was perfectly respectful. It was simply a proposal that—'

'A proposal that is a damnable insult. The man is my curate. Where are his connections, that he should aim at you? His fortune? You would be throwing yourself away. He has presumed, Charlotte, presumed shamefully on his position here. I hope you made him know it.' He glares at her with bloodshot eyes; and from nowhere, and before she can block it off, comes the thought, *Ugly old man*. 'You did return him an absolute negative, did you not?'

'No, Papa. I said I would give him an answer tomorrow, I would consider—'

'Consider?' He roars it out. 'There is nothing to consider, except what is to be done with such damnable, sneaking impertinence. And if you do not see it . . .'

'I do, Papa, I do.' It has been a good while since she has been scared like this; and it is hard to say exactly where the fear lies, whether it is fear of Papa, or of his making himself ill. 'Don't agitate yourself, Papa. I shall – I shall say no to him tomorrow.'

And it is true she doesn't want to marry Arthur Nicholls, and doesn't think of him in that way, or at least she never has before. But she can't stop thinking of the way he trembled, the way he seemed almost on the point of being sick: the way he loved, most surprisingly, as she knows love, with misery and anguish.

'I have written him,' says Papa at breakfast, 'requiring his promise that he will never again mention this obnoxious subject, if he is to continue as my curate.'

So Charlotte writes to Mr Nicholls also, to say that it is better if he doesn't ever bring it up again, but that she doesn't share in her father's harsh sentiments. It seems the least she can do. In the village she hears Mr Nicholls's name spoken with a snigger. Once she sees him coming towards her from the other end of the street, and their slow, mutual approach would almost be absurd if it were not so excruciating. What to do? Dart into an alley? Turn tail? Ignore him or speak to him? Whatever one does there will be something definitive in it. And there is simply nothing definitive in her feelings about him or their situation. If anything, one wants to unpick it and start again. But as they draw level, and she sees how he passes her with flaming averted face and almost tottering steps, one emotion does take shape. She feels sorry for him. Falling in love with her, it would seem, is a disastrous thing to do.

Falling in love with her – with her real self, Charlotte Brontë, not

Currer Bell. The thought of it leaves her a little stirred and more baffled. She feels the need to run. Luckily she has a standing invitation from the Smiths in London. A pleasant stay: but even as she talks with George Smith and warms herself at his easy rationality the square, dogged, tortured face of Mr Nicholls keeps interposing itself between them.

'He has applied to a missionary society, to go abroad,' says Papa at breakfast, just after her return. It is always just *he* now. There is something remarkably degrading about it. 'He will not stay here. I had to give him a reference. Well, you may be sure I did.' He smiles, not pleasantly.

'Papa, may I ask you something?'

'Certainly, my dear.' His look is stony.

'Is it just the fact of its being Mr Nicholls – or is it the notion of my marrying anybody at all?'

'I have observed before, my child, that when you come back from London you have this pert, chop-logic way with you. I'd be obliged if you would give me some more tea.'

She does so. He waits until she has placed his cup and saucer at the exact time-honoured distance from his plate before taking a sip.

'Now, tell me what the publishers are saying about *Villette*. Have they hit upon what I consider the book's only deficiency – the lack of a clear, happy ending?'

'It was mentioned . . .' He is becoming quite the jealous guardian of her fame. Shifting foundations: her money is visible in the furnishings of this house, this house which is now above all the house where Currer Bell lives – as well as, incidentally, Currer Bell's father. Yet he uses that expression *my child* more frequently now. Is that how he wants her? Half celebrity, half child? And not a woman: which is, she thinks with fearful fascination, what Mr Nicholls wants and what he sees when he looks at her. 'But I don't believe there are any happy endings, Papa. Only happy beginnings.'

Villette is out, and so are the reviews; and for once, Currer Bell is not reproved for coarseness.

Other things, though. Emotional unhealthiness. A painful and sickly preoccupation with love, surely unbecoming in what is now generally known to be an authoress.

'I'm afraid it's as you discovered with *Jane Eyre*, my dear friend. We are not supposed to feel it, or at least not of our own volition.' Charlotte is staying again with Mrs Gaskell: not so happily this time, because there is more company and all her old shyness seems to have descended on her; but anything to escape the atmosphere of home. 'Only when the gentleman presses his suit are we allowed to look into our hearts and see there – great heavens, I love him, and I didn't know it.'

'And then the love is meant to have about as much effect as putting a daisy-chain round your neck . . .' She wonders whether to speak to Mrs Gaskell about Mr Nicholls, but something holds her back. Perhaps the knowledge that though Mrs Gaskell is her true friend, their friendship has been a thing of the open light: she knows nothing of the dark, twisted roots beneath her. Charlotte might have spoken to Emily and Anne, perhaps, but there is everlasting silence; and Ellen wants no one to be closer to her than herself. No: for the first time, this question is for me alone. 'Well – you will come and see me some time soon, won't you? I'm afraid Haworth is – well, it's everything I've described to you, but I hope you'll come in spite of that.'

Mrs Gaskell laughs. 'I am all the more eager.' It is hard to imagine her being really put out: like a cat that can curl up on a fence-post, she seems to have the knack of making herself comfortable wherever she goes. I must have the opposite of that, thinks Charlotte; and once again, her own gloom bores her, and she vaguely wonders what it must be like to have someone think so well of you that this never happens.

'He has abandoned, I think, the missionary plan,' Papa says, when she returns from Manchester. 'Instead he is simply looking for a curacy elsewhere. His writ here has not long to run. A pity; there used to be a better side to him. But now he has revealed himself so drivelling – so unmanly . . . It will be a great relief to everyone when he goes.'

How we like to say 'everyone' when we really mean 'me', thinks Charlotte. And yet, in a way, she would share that relief. Because how can they live like this? There are no more tea-drinkings or dog-walkings, but still she sees Mr Nicholls about, and he sees her. And when he sees her, he is still more visibly stricken. He looks as if someone has slapped him across the face, but someone with whom he could never dream of retaliating. It is chastening to know you are walking about in the world and making a man feel like this.

Imprudently, she attends the church when he is administering communion. He looks gaunt and hard: there is something at once lost and fierce in the look he gives the communicants appearing before him, as if he is as likely to turn on them as tender the wafer. This is a mistake, she thinks, just before she approaches him.

The whole congregation sees it: the way he trembles, fumbles, and at last has to turn away. Paralysed, she watches his high, hunched shoulders shaking – and knows this cannot go on.

Yes, this is right, thinks Charlotte, when the day of his departure from Haworth comes: high time, all for the best. The deeds of the school in Church Lane are to be handed over, so he will have to call at the parsonage: Charlotte listens out for his knock and keeps resolutely out of the way. She hears his and Papa's voices, very clipped. Soon the noise of the front door again. She peeps out. Mr Nicholls is lingering about the gate, not wanting to go.

Because of her. Terrible responsibility. Come on, this can be got over: go out to him, say some sensible brisk things. When she gets to the gate, she finds him slumped sideways against it, stiffly hugging himself, crying like a whipped child.

'Oh, don't – please, Mr Nicholls, this is dreadful.' Sobs, with a large male chest cavity behind them, are amazingly loud. 'Please – you mustn't give way so.'

'Why not?' he groans, wiping his eyes. 'It's how I feel.'

'Yes, but—' She stops, because she cannot follow the *but* to anywhere useful. 'The feeling will go, believe me, and everything will soon be better.' And then she thinks: How hugely untrue that is, from my experience.

'I'm sorry. I know I must embarrass you with these demonstrations.'

'No, no, it isn't that. I don't want you to think that I – well, that I think in the same way my father does. I can't give you the hope you want, but I'm not happy with that and I wish I could.'

'Do you?' He raises his square, stormy face. 'What needs to change, then, before you can?'

Charlotte shrinks a little in spite of herself: close to, you see how big he is. 'Oh – look, Mr Nicholls, we never exchanged pleasantries. All you did was *present* me with this – this—' Love, that's the word, she knows it and his expression says it: love. 'This attention. I am not unflattered by any means, but . . .' Not unflattered, she thinks: new heights of mealy-mouthed nonsense. 'I didn't know how you felt. How you feel. And how was I supposed to know? You hide these feelings, they are not to be seen on the surface.'

'That means they are all the stronger. Surely you of all people understand that.' Suddenly he has the look of a man about to take a leap.

'After all, wasn't that the case with Jane Eyre? Didn't she hide the strongest and truest feelings beneath the surface? – the little governess, overlooked, yet inside . . . inside—'

'Jane Eyre wasn't real.'

'But of course she was. Is.'

Charlotte feels utterly stuck for an answer – for any answer: as if the power of speech has permanently ended, here at the garden gate. But she can't walk away from him in silence. No, not that. She knows the cruel power of silence. Waiting for a word. She finds his hand. 'Goodbye, Mr Nicholls. I wish you well.' It's not being loved, she thinks: it's having love thrust upon you as an achieved fact. 'You know there must be no communication between us.'

He has plied his handkerchief, is in command of himself now. 'Yes, of course.' They regard each other levelly for half a minute, then go their separate ways.

Waiting for a word . . . She thought *Villette* might have purged that old pain – and in a way it has; but instead of feeling it now she remembers it, very precisely, all its long refinements of torment. Letters, what did Branwell call them? Something about containing the whole world. A world of sadness too, potentially. She thinks of this when the first letter from Mr Nicholls arrives at the parsonage.

She recognises the handwriting on the cover, and is prompt to hustle it out of Papa's sight, which is sharp enough for things you do not want him to see. For a long time she hesitates before opening it. But what does this mean? Is she going to send it back unread? Too cruel. Imagine it . . . imagine it.

So she opens and reads the letter. There is no dash or brio in Mr Nicholls's way of writing, nothing to dazzle or beguile. He writes to tell her of his continued love for her, to apologise for the distress he may have caused her, to apologise too for being unable to forget her and unable still to abandon all hope even though he has removed himself from her . . . He writes a good many things, forceful, earnest, not wild. He knows, as he says, he should not be doing this, but he cannot help himself. He will stop if she forbids him. Another letter, and another. He hopes she will understand, he cannot help himself, there is some relief in writing even without a reply . . .

Understand? How can she not understand that? Is there anyone else on earth, she wonders, who could understand it better?

After the sixth letter, she replies, temperately telling him there had better be no more letters. And so comes another, so full of joy at being answered that really she cannot – humanly, she cannot do anything but write again.

Another thing Branwell said: that being loved was the greatest thing, and there was nothing like it. Of course poor Branwell was wrong about a lot of things, but not everything.

One deceit is no worse than another. Mr Nicholls has moved back to the district, is staying at Oxenhope.

Will you meet me?

To write as they have written and not to meet makes, after all, no sense. And she is determined to show sense in this matter. After all, Papa has shown so little of it.

In stark frozen snow she makes her way to the field-path that runs down to Oxenhope. She wonders what she will feel on seeing him again; half-trusts to some clinching revelation.

Instead, when she first catches sight of the dark stocky figure, she finds something absolutely simple and absolutely surprising: she is glad.

He is standing beneath a tree. Tall, straight trees like this are a rarity in these parts, and against the whiteness the potency of its bare shape is all the more striking. Natural that people in the old times should worship them, seeing a giant, a transformed mortal, a god.

His expression is so desperately anxious that she asks: 'Did you think I wasn't coming?'

He shakes his head. 'I was thinking I shouldn't have arranged it so. You must be dreadfully cold.'

A strange moment: it occurs to her that her father has never said that to her in her life.

'Have you been waiting long?'

'Years,' he says.

For a moment she has a suffocating sensation. 'Mr Nicholls, I've agreed to meet you—'

'Thank God for it, and thank you.'

'I was going to say I've agreed to meet you only on condition – well, that we do not conceal our association from my father any more.'

'Certainly,' he says at once. She realises he is ready for anything. There is a frost-like crispness and keenness in his air: that clean outdoor smell about him. She looks back at her own footprints along the lane; and sees how far she has come. For a moment she considers the question: do I want to run away? And the answer comes, not much less prompt than his own: no, I don't.

'When I say that I think he has been cruelly unfair, I – I still don't want you to think badly of him. He's old, set in his ways – and perhaps, I think, a little afraid.'

'I understand. I don't resent anything, anything at all in Mr Brontë's behaviour.'

She studies him. 'Don't you really?'

'No. I regret it, where it has been the means of – of keeping me from you. But if I were to resent and be angry, then – well, that would be pointless, a waste of feeling. All my feeling, Miss Brontë, is for you. That's all.'

She looks away: not displeased – but her palate shrinks a little from such a concentrated essence of decision. 'I'm not as good as you, Mr Nicholls. I have many resentments. I'm afraid all my feelings are impure – mixed up with hate, with shame and shadows.'

'To hear you talk!' he says, standing back to look at her. 'Don't you know you are wholly admirable?'

She frowns. 'Oh, Mr Nicholls, you can't think that . . .'

'Why not? I do, because I love you. Don't you see?' There is an air of surprised explanation about him, as if all her life she has been committing some basic grammatical error that he is pointing out to her.

'It's not that simple,' she says. She stares at the low tree-branches before her chilled face – gnarled and iron-black and knotted with age: incredible to think that from this would come, in its season, the feathery freshness of a sapling. 'You don't know me.'

'I don't know the person you've described,' he says, in his downright, contradictory way. 'But, then, perhaps you don't know yourself, Miss Brontë.'

'Oh, I do.' She faces him. 'We must make that clear from the beginning.'

'Well, as you say.' He inclines his head: face lit, waiting. She sees that nothing is going to put off or alter his love – except her refusing it. Curious thing: he wants to marry me, and he does not want to change me.

She ought to be used to this, from her writing: the way a character, quite limited and one-dimensional at first, begins to stand out more boldly to you, to reveal unexpected facets, to seize more of your attention. Arthur Nicholls has played a minor role in her narrative – but now she finds herself eager to fill him out and bring him forward. The family in Ireland of which he has never made any boast, but who seem to be well-respected and cultivated (and, Papa, have you found that out, and is that part of it, Papa?). The kindness, even indulgence, to children, who unerringly spot him as a joiner of games and dispenser of halfpennies. The moods of muddy depression that occasionally visit him, sapping his energy, blocking his way.

'I know now there is nothing to be done with them: they're just some flaw of the temperament, and I must simply wait for them to go.'

'Don't you ever fear that –' her voice is not quite steady '– that this one is different, this one won't go, this one will be – me, for ever?'

He considers; and then, consideringly, takes her hand. 'No,' he says, 'not now.'

'You shouldn't do that,' she says, looking at his hand encasing hers. 'That's as if I've said yes.'

He loosens his grip. 'Take it away, then,' he says.

And she leaves it there.

'How long, really?' she asks him.

'Years,' he says, and his dark, slightly truculent eyes seem to glance reminiscently down the length of them. 'I can't calculate. Long before your brother and sisters died. After that, of course, I could only look on. Try to imagine what you were feeling. And then there was your writing. I could see you were living through that. Living on it. I didn't want to interrupt it.'

'Years,' she echoes: marvelling, yet with recognition. The way suffering bends time. Again they are walking the field path to Oxenhope. The snow is melting. Her arm is in his. Where else would it be, after all? Each step leads to another step. Even a casual walk must end in a destination. 'It's true – about the writing. But that doesn't mean it's a – a thing I no longer need. Arthur, I must still write.'

'Well, of course,' he says reasonably. 'You are one of the leading authors of the day.'

And at that she wants to laugh – not with irony or bitterness: a warm laugh, if such a thing is possible. And then she thinks: Of course it is. Just never, till now.

'And then, you know – we must think about Papa. How to address the question. He has accepted this – our improving our acquaintance, as he puts it – grudgingly. He's never quite easy. But the next step . . .'

'I'm prepared for that,' he says, 'if you are.'

Yes: the question turns on her.

In London, Mr Williams wryly told her about a play based loosely on *Jane Eyre* that had been staged at one of the minor theatres. 'Loosely' and 'minor' being the important words. A very heated piece, apparently, with virtue threatened and hero staunch, and villainy hissable and unequivocal. It comes to mind now, as Charlotte finds herself living in exactly such a play.

'Never,' Papa storms, and stands glaring and flushed in the study doorway, ready to slam. Practicality has forced him to rethink his position, to a certain extent. Mr Nicholls's replacement as his curate has not proved satisfactory. Papa is missing Mr Nicholls's efficiency. So, the return of Mr Nicholls is to be considered. But as for the next step—

'Papa, think of the sacrifice he will be making. He could get a much richer living elsewhere; but what he proposes is to remain your curate, on the same stipend, and to continue to perform the majority of the parish duties. And living here in the house as – as my husband, he will be able to assist you further in so many ways—'

'Never. I will never have another man in this house.' Papa slams the door.

The moment for a chorus of boos, perhaps, and curtain. But this is real life, where each small step leads to another step: where revelation is slow and undramatic. My husband – yes, she has agreed to consider Arthur Nicholls in this light. She does not quite love him, but something sufficiently like love bulks near at hand, a headland beyond the fog. The adoration he offers her is so single-minded, so complete, that to turn it down altogether would seem a disgraceful waste. And she has always deplored waste, knowing as she does that in this world there is only so much good to go round.

Yes, Papa: I'm going to marry a poor Irish curate. And it is a beginning, and I can see how that must sting, when you are past all beginnings. But I believe I am allowed it. I came to think I was one of those people who are doomed never to be happy. Now I want to explore – I have to explore the tantalising alternative.

'I'm afraid I'm not like one of the heroes in your books,' he says, the first time they kiss. And then: 'Except, of course, that I'm marrying a heroine.'

'Good heavens, I'm not one of those.'

'No?' The frown, the abruptness she is coming to understand: it represents a sudden surfacing from thought. 'Well, Charlotte, I don't know what else to call you.'

'I'm not leaving you, you see, Papa.'

They have had a long, wounding session of it; but at last Papa is sitting beside her, and allowing his hand to rest in hers. It is the quietness, perhaps, that makes Tabby put her head round the door. 'So, are you seeing sense?' she grunts.

'You speak as if that were an easy matter, Tabby,' Papa says, with a kind of dark glitter in his eyes, giving Charlotte's hand the faintest of squeezes.

The wedding is at Haworth; and at the last moment, the night before the ceremony, Papa says he feels too unwell to give Charlotte away as planned. Well, Charlotte thinks, he must be allowed that. He has had to watch so much being taken from him: natural the refusal to hand over, even symbolically, the last you possess.

Instead one of the guests, Miss Wooler, her old employer at Roe Head, will perform the role. Being given away in marriage by a woman, and a learned and independent woman, there ought to be some significance in this for Currer Bell, the creator of Jane Eyre and other women who will not know their place. Aptness – or perhaps irony: for, after all, she has not ended up like Miss Wooler but instead is doing the conventional thing. Even showing herself desperate to do so: she is sure that is the conclusion drawn in some quarters. Well, my dear, it will be her last chance, so she has snatched at her father's curate. And certainly she is not marrying like Jane Eyre, in passionate union with the mate of her soul.

A whole tantalising bundle of significance, then. But Charlotte, entering the church porch, finds herself unable to grasp any significance or weigh any question or draw any conclusion at all. Charlotte – who has often found the strenuous activity of her mind actually exhausting her, whose very sleep seldom refreshes her because her dreams are all complex arguments and narrative. Even this white muslin dress and veil with ivy-leaf embroidery – she recognises it as something very foreign to her, something that ought to call forth a wry comment or reflection. But instead everything has become strangely basic and unconnected. It is a wedding-dress. It is quite pretty. I am in it.

Perhaps the mind is stepping back to allow room for the feelings. Not just those she is experiencing now, but those she expects to undergo in becoming a married woman. Oh, yes, they need a wide arena. She has already allotted spaces for everything from fear and pain to disappointment and regret to joy and transformation. How those spaces will be filled she has no idea. On her last visit to Manchester she tried subtly to sound Mrs Gaskell out about how she had felt when she married: what little anxieties she had had, and how they were resolved; whether your feelings for the man, and his feelings for you, somehow got the pair of you over what must be – well, she could only think of it as some complex and demanding obstacle. Every other important thing in your life you approached with *some* knowledge, some preparation.

But nothing much could be got from Mrs Gaskell, not without actually asking questions Charlotte was too shy to ask – even assuming, in fact, that she could frame them. When all she really had, and has now still, is a vast apprehension of strangeness. How did I come to this, or this come to me? The majority of women come to this, yes – but that doesn't make it any more approachable.

She has things to take into account, small counters of credit. Mr James Taylor, for example, whose intellect was attuned to hers in a way Arthur's could never be, was unthinkable as a husband because she found him physically repulsive, would actually have to step back from him even when he was saying something interesting. She likes being near Arthur, finds his touch pleasant and even reassuring, likes to study the way his thick black hair curls at the root. Very well so far. And then there is the way he obviously feels about her, the strength of his embrace, the way he looks at her as if he sees something different from that angular plainness she finds in the mirror. It is known – widely, surely – that beautiful women are what men desire and wish to go to bed with, but perhaps that, too, can be got over.

Still as she walks to the altar she moves in a great empty space, with only moving currents in its unknown air – a touch of apprehension, of wonder, of disbelief. How does it go? Where does your self go?

The sight of Arthur at the altar does a little to reassure her – adds a solid floor to that nebulous space, at least. It is wrong to say Arthur looks happy to be marrying her, as that suggests something clear and serene. Rather, he looks as if some calamitous bad news has proven to be false, and he can hardly adjust himself to the dazzling reversal.

* * *

For the honeymoon, they are to go to Ireland to see his family, by way of Wales. The wedding takes place early in the morning: they reach Conway by evening, there to stay overnight – the wedding night – at an inn.

It is thoroughly pleasant travelling with Arthur – with her husband. This, she thinks, this is good. Previously on journeys she has only been transported to her destination like the mail. Novel sensation to have someone wanting her to enjoy the journey, concerned about the comfort of her seat and whether she is warm enough; as if these things are important. And someone to talk to about the places they pass through, and the knowledge that he likes nothing better than to talk to her; and the way he doesn't try to say clever things, though he is very observant. Yes, she could happily go on travelling with him for ever.

But that great space awaits. And as they arrive in wind and rain at the inn, all thick stone and ponderous beam-ends, a sneeze confirms that that stuffiness in her head this morning is what she feared: she is starting a cold. She thinks: I shall give myself to my husband sniffing. And then she realises that her thoughts, at least, sound more like her own.

Mr and Mrs Nicholls. Hearing those words as the maid calls them to supper – perhaps it is the Welsh lilt – dizzies her, and nearly undoes her, with its unreality. No, we're not, it's all a fraud, part of her wants to cry – the last unruly rally of her misgivings, perhaps, even though they have already tamely surrendered the flag.

He is very quiet after supper, as they retire to their bedroom: stirring the fire, winding his watch, shifting about. Swiftly Charlotte thinks: This is terrible, what's the matter with him, what have I done, is this where he reveals himself to be a surly beast? And then she reminds herself – or someone or something reminds her – that he isn't a stranger; she has come to know him quite well, and what she should know above all is that when he is silent Arthur is feeling most deeply. Often, indeed, in perturbation, uncertainty – or sheer nervousness.

She says: 'Arthur, should we get ready for bed?'

'Ah – yes, we should, to be sure,' he says, as if this were a neat and ingenious idea.

So this unexpected business, performed in opposite corners of the room, of taking things off and wondering where to put them, of struggling into nightgowns and smoothing hair. Unexpected – not that there is anything she does expect, except perhaps a vague image of tigerish pouncing and despatch.

Then there is this awkward hiatus in which she cannot leave the fireside and go to the bed. Can't tell why, she isn't afraid or even reluctant, and when he comes and kneels down with her there to kiss and embrace her she doesn't mind that at all; it's simply that she has turned stiff and stupid and unable to proceed. And this is when he says, looking down at her hand in his: 'You must understand – my dear Charlotte, you must understand I know nothing at all of this. I'm afraid you'll have to be patient with me.'

'Dear, dear,' she says. She never expected to laugh: never expected that laughter would open her to him like this. 'Oh, my dear, we are a pair.'

In the end he picks her up – or she puts herself into his arms – and he carries her to the bed. 'You're as light as a feather,' he says. Which is certainly not original, as a simile. However, he means it.

She winds her arms around his neck. 'I feel it,' she says.

Crossing to Ireland, she moves in strange landscapes, but has no consciousness of herself as a stranger. There are people waiting for Arthur and for her, with uncomplicated welcome: or if complicated at all, by admiration. Arthur's bride is the famous authoress. When the house in which he was raised by his uncle and aunt appears at the crest of a wooded rise, she is taken aback. 'You – you never made any boast of this.'

'Well – after all, you know, I didn't build it. I was simply fortunate that this was my home.'

Ah: because of Papa, she thinks; and realises that protection takes many forms.

She loves this: the way he lies against her in bed as they drift into sleep – or, rather, as he drifts first, for she always stays blinking and gazing and defying the darkness a while, no matter how tired. She loves the way he enfolds her whole back, arms around her, his instep against her heel. She is still herself, free to look outward – but she needn't worry about what is behind her: that's dealt with, there are guards there. Absurd perhaps to conclude that she has always felt her narrow back to be broad, exposed, and awaiting a blade. But no more absurd than the fit of weeping that overtakes her one night in the big hollow bedroom in his aunt's house, with the turf fire winking itself into shadow, and the echoes alarming him out of sleep.

'Nothing – it's nothing, Arthur, really. Lie back, please.'

He does, though with a look of reservation, as if he means to fathom this when the time is right. Charlotte wishes he could – or, rather, she hopes he does not, because it will surely dishearten him. She cried because she had no reason to cry. Because she is experiencing content – not those abstract fancies, happiness and fulfilment – and to find herself joining that large club of people who feel that life treats them on the whole pretty well is a jolt. A profound, earthquake jolt. It shouldn't be happening.

'Because,' she explains quietly, sitting up in the bed and hugging her knees, 'I feel I'm getting their share. We all should have had this. Emily, Anne, Branwell. But I came in for the whole inheritance. So I love it but I think I shouldn't have it. And it isn't that I don't want it. I just – I just wish I could hear their voices once more. That's all.'

Sea.

This is the place to see her, finally. At Kilkee, she meets her sea. Her sea: the sea she has longed to see all throughout the Irish honeymoon. The true sea, the ocean: the Atlantic monopolising the horizon and crashing and foaming on rocks below the cliff. This was her mother's sea. And – she hopes Arthur understands – now that she is here, now that she has come to it, she just wants to see: not to talk. To see; to listen.

And he does understand. He makes sure the rug is comfortably round her, and cautions her not to go too near the edge, and then keeps at a little, loving distance of silence.

Charlotte lets the sea take her thoughts. It is everything she hoped it might be, her sea – and more. Most unexpected, and beautiful: yes, there they are, listen; she cocks her head and above the shriek of the wind and the thunder of the surf she can hear them, at last, the lost voices coming through.

Author's note

Charlotte Brontë died at Haworth Parsonage in March 1855, less than a year after her marriage to Arthur Bell Nicholls, of an illness possibly related to pregnancy. She was thirty-eight years old.

The Rev. Patrick Brontë lived until 1861.

1. The novel opens with the death of Maria Branwell Brontë, Charlotte and Emily's mother. How does this scene influence your interpretation of the rest of the story? Why do you believe the author chose to begin the book with this event?

2. At the end of the first chapter, upon their mother's death, the Brontë children "...draw together in a peculiarly precise huddle, as if they stand on a rock, just big enough for them, above an encircling sea." Water is used as a metaphor throughout the novel, but its presence is particularly felt in the first and final chapters. Considering the Brontës lived on the English moors, far from the ocean, why do you think this metaphor is so pervasive?

3. At the beginning of the story, although Branwell's "arithmetic" proves otherwise, Charlotte feels the safety of being the middle child, surrounded on all sides by the love of her sisters and brother. When her eldest sisters die, Charlotte is suddenly thrust into "a world where there was no longer any middle to inhabit, only edge, brunt, naked extremity." How does this shift transform Charlotte? How are Emily and Anne similarly shaped by their positions in the family?

4. Discuss the Brontë family dynamics. What was Patrick Brontë's legacy to his children, all of whom he outlived? Describe Charlotte's relationship with her sisters Maria and Elizabeth, as well as her relationship with Emily and Anne. How did Charlotte, Emily, and Anne's relationship with Branwell evolve over the years, and what influence did he have on their life and work?

5. Discuss the lesson the Brontë girls learn from the nature of Tabby's stories: "So the flow never ends, no conditions can ever dry it up or freeze it solid: there is always another story."

6. The sisters and Branwell first began writing about their imaginary world of Angria. What do you believe this world meant to each of the siblings? As a child, did you have your own imaginary world or imaginary friend?

7. If their lives had been easier, if they had not faced so much hardship, do you think the sisters would have still written their literary masterpieces, albeit in varying forms?

8. *"Could there truly be any choice between chaos and order?"* wonders Patrick Brontë. In *Charlotte and Emily,* Jude Morgan seems to suggest that chaos and order, art and desire, nightmares and daydreams are all intertwined in genius. How does he make this suggestion? Do you agree?

9. The Brontë sisters wrote under the male pseudonyms of Currer, Ellis, and Acton Bell. Why? How is the choice of these names significant? How is their decision to write under pseudonyms indicative of the era and the biases that the sisters struggled against?

10. Each of the sisters has a different understanding of the function of art, and Charlotte and Emily wrote two very different tales with two diametrically opposed heroines, Jane Eyre and Catherine Earnshaw. If you've read both *Jane Eyre* and *Wuthering Heights*, discuss these differences and any similarities among the sisters, their novels, and their heroines.

11. How are secret desires important in Charlotte and Emily's literary worlds?

12. What does the novel have to say about the glories of spirituality and the degradations of religion?

13. How do you feel about Charlotte's marriage to Arthur Nicholls? What do you think attracts her to and repels her from the institution of marriage?

14. Why do you think the novel closes with Charlotte at the sea, with only a mention of her death in the author's note?

15. A critic once claimed that Jane Eyre was "soul speaking to soul"— if you've read Charlotte Brontë's masterpiece, did you find this to be true? In reading *Charlotte and Emily,* did Charlotte, Emily, or Anne's lives connect with your own in any particular way?

For more reading group suggestions, visit
www.readinggroupgold.com.

Timeless historical novels from JUDE MORGAN

"This lustrous historical romance... captures the spirit of early nineteenth-century Britain through the extraordinary lives of the wives and lovers of its greatest poets." —*Entertainment Weekly* (Editor's Choice, Grade A) on *Passion*

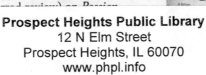

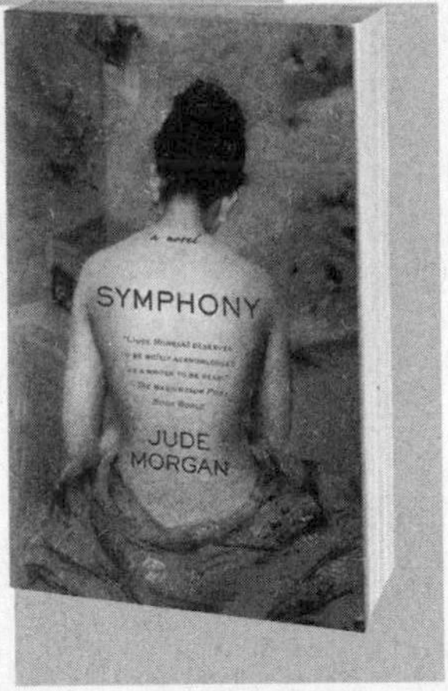

"Deeply imagined and gorgeously written... brings a fascinating past to brilliant light."
—*Publishers Weekly* (starred review) on *Passion*

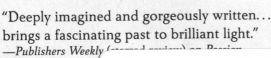